THE WORLD OF THE GATEWAY

The Gateway Trilogy (Series 1)

The Gateway Trackers (Series 2)

WHISPERS OF THE WALKER

WHISPERS OF THE WALKER

The Gateway Trackers Book 1

E.E. HOLMES

Lily Faire Publishing

Lily Faire Publishing
Townsend, MA

www.lilyfairepublishing.com

ISBN 978-0-9984762-0-9 (Print edition)

ISBN 978-0-9895080-9-4 (Digital edition)

Cover design by James T. Egan of Bookfly Design LLC
Editing services by Erika DeSimone of Erika's Editing
Author photography by Cydney Scott Photography

For Joseph, my music maker, my dreamer of dreams, and my partner on this most wonderful adventure.

"The quality of mercy is not strained.
It droppeth as the gentle rain from heaven
Upon the place beneath. It is twice blest:
It blesseth him that gives and him that takes.
'Tis mightiest in the mightiest; it becomes
The thronèd monarch better than his crown.
His scepter shows the force of temporal power,
The attribute to awe and majesty
Wherein doth sit the dread and fear of kings;
But mercy is above this sceptered sway.
It is enthronèd in the hearts of kings;
It is an attribute to God Himself;
And earthly power doth then show likest God's
When mercy seasons justice."

—William Shakespeare

"The Merchant of Venice"

CONTENTS

HOME SWEET HOME

I KNEW SHE WAS WATCHING ME BEFORE I GLANCED UP. I could feel the waves of animosity—sheer negative energy—radiating down toward me from the window two stories above. My fingers twitched inside the pocket of my jacket, itching to draw a face I had not yet seen. I balled my fingers into a fist and calmed them with my familiar mantra:

"Patience, now. Art will follow."

I bounced on the balls of my feet, trying in vain to keep warm, as I stood outside on the sidewalk. On general principle, I'd refused to break out my winter coat in early October—I was still mourning the warmth of summer. As a result, I was now freezing my ass off. I yanked the collar of my sweater up to my chin, and watched my breath turn to damp swirling clouds around my head.

A smart, two-door sports car rolled up beside me and slipped deftly into a very narrow parking space. A short, harried looking woman jumped out; I watched as she shut the car door with her foot while hastily twisting her hair into a messy bun.

"Are you Jessica?" she asked.

"Yes. Tanya? Nice to meet you," I said, holding out a hand.

Tanya was so preoccupied with trying to extract a set of keys from her pocket that she didn't notice my offer of a handshake. After a few awkward seconds, I lowered my hand and thrust it back into my pocket—where it could at least stay warm.

"So, um, this is it, obviously," said Tanya, gesturing vaguely over her shoulder at the house. It was one of the boxy old Colonials which crowded the historic district of Salem; the houses stood shoulder-to-shoulder along the block as if they were all vying for position. A tiny, grassless strip of a yard stood before each, adding even more uniformity. The house looked stately from across the street, but up close I could see that its yellow paint was starting to peel, and its windows looked warped in their black-shuttered frames. A tarnished plaque next to the front door read: "The Samuel Harner House, 1704."

"It looks really cool," I said truthfully. "I'm a sucker for historic houses."

"Yeah, me too," Tanya replied, although she sounded rueful rather than enthusiastic. "That's why I bought it in the first place." She thrust a sheaf of papers at me. "These are all the details about the apartment, which you might've seen online. Is that how you found it?"

"Yes," I said, but I didn't look at the papers. A movement had caught my eye; a lacy white curtain was fluttering in a window high above.

"It's the third-floor unit... Although," and she laughed a little hysterically, "I can now offer you the first or second floor as well, if either would suit you better."

"No, no, the third floor is fine," I said, smiling at her. "I'd rather not have the noise of upstairs neighbors."

"Although neighbors might not be the trouble," I added in a whisper to myself. The curtain above us twitched again.

We stood staring at each other for a moment. The keys jingled agitatedly in Tanya's hand as she gnawed on a fingernail; it was already bitten to the quick.

"So... can I see it?" I asked finally.

Tanya opened her mouth as though to tell me something, but shut it again and nodded. Then she turned without another word and marched to the door. I stood quietly beside her while she fumbled with the keys, then attempted to jam one of them into the lock with her shaking fingers.

"What site did you find the listing on?" she asked me, to break the awkward silence as she struggled with the keys. "I like to ask, so I know which of my advertising methods works the best."

"Oh, uh... Craigslist, I think?"

"Mmm-hmm. Okay, great." Her response was perfunctory; she wasn't listening to me at all.

And that was good, because I hadn't found the apartment on Craigslist. In fact, I didn't even know if the apartment had been posted on Craigslist, although it seemed a pretty safe bet. No, I'd learned of the apartment while I was working at a nearby coffee shop.

2

Two students, both girls, had been swept into the Juniper Breeze Café by a biting, bitter wind two days earlier. Their faces were pink and raw; their scarves were yanked up around their ears. They had stumbled over to the counter, hopping up and down to warm themselves, and ordered skinny lattes before sliding into an empty table in front of the pastry display.

I had half-listened as they debated between ordering a Danish over a scone, but then perked up my ears as one checked her phone with a groan.

"Oh, God. That other place isn't going to be available until next Thursday."

"The one on Halifax?"

"Yeah."

"Shit. I really liked that one."

"What are we going to do now? I'm not spending another night in that apartment."

"Neither am I. I'll text Katie and let her know we'll be crashing for the next week."

"Yeah, but what about all our stuff? And our security deposit?"

"I don't know. At this point, I just want to say, 'Screw it.' Oh my God, this is such a mess."

I set the two lattes carefully down on the table in front of them. "Sorry, but I couldn't help overhearing. You're moving out of your apartment? Is it local? I'm looking for a new place, and I'm sort of in a hurry."

The girls exchanged an uncomfortable look before one of them shook her long, wavy blonde bangs out of her eyes and said, "Uh, yeah, it's only a couple of blocks from here on Brimfield Street, but... well, trust me, you don't want to live there."

"Oh, really? Why's that?" I asked.

They looked at each other again, clearly unsure of how they should answer.

"Loud neighbors?" I suggested.

The second girl, who had short, dark hair, gave a harsh laugh; it was just possible to detect a note of hysteria in it.

"You could say that," the other answered. Her face was turning the same shade of red as her scarf.

"Well, I don't mind a little noise. What's the address?" I asked, pulling a pen from my apron.

The blonde girl sized me up, then said, "112 Brimfield Street. Unit C."

All trace of laughter fled from the brunette's face. She whacked her friend on the arm before hissing, "You can't just tell her that!"

"Why not?" the blonde murmured back. "If we find a new tenant, we might have a prayer of getting our deposit back."

"But you can't let her... that's not right!"

"You heard her, she said she doesn't mind some noise," the blonde said, glancing at me again. Her eyes lingered in a familiar way on my hair, my clothes, and my elaborate, recently acquired tattoo. I repressed a sardonic grin and tried to look politely puzzled.

The brunette threw a disgusted look at her friend before turning back to me. "Look, just take our word for it, okay? You really don't want to live in that apartment."

"Why?" I pressed. "I really need a place."

Then, ignoring a glare from her roommate, the brunette unleashed the entire story—not a solitary detail of which deterred me in the least.

§

"Come out, come out, wherever you are," I sang under my breath.

Tanya looked up from her struggle with her keys. "What did you say?"

"Oh, nothing. Just humming to myself," I replied, watching her hand tremble violently as she tried another key. "Is everything okay?"

"It's fine. It's just... it's been a hell of a week, if you'll pardon my language," Tanya said, and the laugh that bubbled out of her could have been a precursor to tears. Just as she finally managed to fit the key into the lock, it shot out from between her fingers and landed noisily on the front step.

We both stared at the key for a moment. Then I bent down, picked it up, and offered it back to her. "We all have weeks like that. It'll get better," I said.

Tanya forced a smile that clearly said, "You don't know what you're talking about." She didn't take the key from me.

"I'll get it," I said, and thrust the key into the lock. It turned easily, and I pushed the door open.

4

"Thanks," muttered Tanya, as she pulled the key from the lock and stepped over the threshold. Her expression looked as though she were expecting an imminent lightning bolt to the head. When nothing happened, she exhaled a long-held breath and began trudging up the stairs, cocking her head for me to follow.

"The house is old, obviously," she said as she climbed, "but the heating system was replaced five years ago, and the whole house has been deleaded. I redid all the kitchens when I bought it, so the appliances are less than three years old."

"Great," I replied, since she seemed to expect a response. I was barely listening, though. New heating system or not, there was a definite chill in the air that deepened as we ascended the stairs. Every cell in my body tingled with a familiar sensation, a latent sensitivity to the presence of someone who belonged in another world entirely. By the time we reached the top of the staircase, my breath was visible and chugging out of me like puffs from a tiny locomotive.

"So... I'm guessing that new heating system isn't actually on right now?"

Tanya turned to look at me. "Yeah, uh... I didn't expect it to be so cold so soon," she said with yet another slightly wild laugh. I knew she was lying. She was a New Englander; the area was notorious for its unpredictable—and often freezing—weather. The poor woman was in panic mode, however desperately she was trying to hide it. I nearly took pity on her and told her the truth about why I was here, but since I didn't know exactly what I was dealing with yet, I decided to keep my mouth shut.

Tanya pushed open the door to the third-floor apartment and flicked on the light. We stepped inside the entry hall. The hostile presence I felt was so powerful that I could taste the sour acidity of it on my tongue. Tanya could feel it too, I realized, although how she perceived it—apart from the cold—I couldn't tell. But her body language told me all I needed to know; she knit her brow ferociously and seemed to withdraw into herself. Perhaps the cold was causing her to anticipate the manifestation of something she couldn't understand, something that had perhaps appeared to her before.

"So... um, this is it," she said so weakly that I almost couldn't hear her. Her whispers hung in the air, like little hovering cumulus clouds of fear.

"Nice!" I replied brightly as I began walking briskly around the apartment; the unit contained a huge brick fireplace and several large built-in bookcases.

I stepped into the kitchen, which was a fair size. "Oh, yeah, I can see the appliances are newer," I said encouragingly.

A blast of cold pulsed from the living room and into the kitchen, causing Tanya to gasp and my hair to blow back from my face.

"These old places are pretty drafty, huh?" I said, trying to keep my tone light. "You should think about replacement windows, eventually." I couldn't hide a small shiver.

Tanya blinked and forced a smile. "Uh, yeah. It's on the wish list."

I opened the nearest cabinet, then ran my hand over the counter near the sink. "It seems really clean. Can't say that about many of the places I've seen."

"Yes, I had a service come in after... uh, before I started showing it," came Tanya's shaky response.

"So this is the half bath?" I asked cheerfully, pretending I had missed the hesitation in her answer. I poked my head into a small bathroom off of the kitchen. As I glanced inside, the antique mirror over the sink fogged over as though someone were breathing all over it. Then two slender-fingered handprints appeared on the mirror's cloudy surface. The tiniest of whimpers escaped Tanya. I turned quickly to face the kitchen, as though I'd seen nothing unusual.

"I could totally see us living here," I said. "Can I check out the bedrooms?"

"Of—of course," replied Tanya, with the faintest trace of hopefulness in her voice. She took a deep breath and followed me.

The apartment's three bedrooms were directly off of the living room. I poked my head into the first bedroom. It was small but cozy, with a wall of exposed brick and lots of shelf space for books; I could almost see Hannah curled up in a chair in the corner, lost in her latest library loot.

Almost. It was kind of hard to picture Hannah sitting there, while also staring into a very angry set of eyes.

"Ah, so there you are," I said quietly.

The spirit looked young, maybe twenty-five. Her jet-black hair was braided back from her face, and she had a goth look that made my own penchant for black look tame. She was wearing a decorative lace corset cinched over a long, trailing dress; a pentagram and other mystical charms hung from silver chains around her neck. As I stared at her, she extended her arm towards the nearest item—a vase of fake flowers on the windowsill—and, with a sweeping gesture, caused it to fall to the floor.

Tanya screamed, dropping her last vestiges of pretense. I turned to her.

"It's okay!" I said with a gentle nudge. "It was just a vase. You're jumpy, huh?"

"I... I just... what?" Tanya stammered.

"This vase fell over," I said, trotting over to it and picking it up. "Might have been the draft when we came in. These old houses can have crazy cross-breezes sometimes." I was really putting on a show; this was some first-class improv.

If Tanya looked confused, it was nothing compared to how the spirit now looked. She gazed around for something else to scare me off with. Then, with a smirk, she reached toward the lamp in the corner. As she opened and closed her hand, the lightbulb began to flash on and off.

I looked at the lamp and chuckled. "Old wiring, huh? I'll be sure to bring some surge protectors," I said, speaking half to Tanya, half to the spirit.

Tanya had reached her limit: She dropped her face into her hands and started to cry. I took advantage of her momentary distraction and looked the spirit straight in the eye. She stared back at me, wide-eyed, and dropped her hand to her side.

"What the hell?" I heard her mutter.

"I can see you," I whispered. "And your little poltergeist tricks won't work on me, honey—You can chill with the antics."

The spirit's expression turned into a mix of shock and fear. She vanished. I walked back over to Tanya and placed an arm around her shaking shoulders.

"Hey. It's alright."

"No it's not," she sobbed. "It's not alright. It will never be alright!"

"Why not? It's okay, I've already decided that I'll take it."

"You'll...what?"

"I'll take it. I want the apartment."

Tanya shook her head violently. "No. No, I can't let you. It's... it's haunted, okay? I'm sorry I didn't tell you, but I haven't been able to rent this place out for longer than a month or so before the tenants leave. I sank all of my savings into this house, and now..."

"It's okay. Tanya, look at me." I grabbed her gently by the shoulders, shaking them slightly so that she raised her head and looked me in the eyes. "I know it's haunted. I knew it before I walked in the door."

Tanya blinked at me. "You did? How could you possibly have known that?"

"I can just tell. It's one of my most interesting and annoying traits. And you don't need to worry about renting this place to me. I'm telling you I can handle it. In fact, if I have some time here, I can probably get the spirit to leave."

"Oh my God, do you really think so? I've tried everything! Three different priests, a psychic, and I even had a neo-pagan grad student teach me about cleansing and sage-burning. I was actually walking around with this smoking bunch of herbs, coughing my head off! But nothing worked. I'm completely at the end of my rope! You have no idea!"

"I do. I really do. Give me a month in this house. You'll be ghost-free in no time."

"This is so bizarre. I don't even believe in ghosts. At least, I never have," Tanya whispered, shaking her head.

"I know that most of the time when people say this, it's bullshit—but I *do* know exactly how you feel," I replied gently. "So what do you say? Do I get the apartment? Can we move in next week?"

Tanya still looked torn. "I guess so, but I just don't understand why you'd want to live with a ghost!"

I smiled grimly as my new roommate shimmered into view in the corner, with her arms crossed and her eyes looking daggers at me.

"I know Tanya, it must seem strange to you. But actually, I'm not sure I know how to live *without* ghosts anymore."

2

MOVING DAY

As I heaved a box of books onto my bed, I came to an unassailable conclusion: My obsession with book hoarding was reason enough to never move ever again.

"I've never been so happy that I can't participate in heavy lifting," said a trilling voice. I turned just in time to see a slender male spirit, eternally seventeen years old, drift through my bedroom wall and float to rest on my bed like a feather. He caught my eye as he shook the specter of his stylishly shaggy black hair out of his face, and winked. "Being dead has to have some benefits."

"Hey, Milo. I thought you were going to Hannah's seminar."

"I did, but she kicked me out. It was presentation day. Too boring. I was trying to liven things up a bit while Hannah was waiting for her turn, but she said she couldn't 'concentrate.'" Milo gave the last word air quotes, as though he had never heard of concentration before and remained unconvinced that Hannah hadn't simply made it up.

"So what, I'm stuck with you now? I thought I'd at least be spared until I started unpacking my clothes. I know how you love a good fashion intervention."

"Alas, your wardrobe has become far less fun to criticize since you got that big-girl job," Milo said with a theatrical sigh. "Seriously, you've taken all the fun out of it!"

I threw a battered paperback copy of *Sense and Sensibility* at him, but of course it flew right through him and landed with a dull thud on the bed beneath him. "It's taken all the fun out of it for me, too," I said.

Adulthood had lost no time slapping me in the face upon graduation. I could've taken the more typical route of moving back home again, but I could hardly call my aunt Karen's Boston brownstone "home," since Hannah and I had only lived there for a couple of summers. Karen was my late mother's twin sister, and she would gladly have welcomed us back; in fact, now that she was divorced from Noah, I think she'd actually been looking forward to having us knocking around the house for a while. But, "adult" or not, I was just as stubbornly independent as I had always been: I didn't want to freeload. Plus, staying with Karen would've meant living with the Durupinen connection as well.

Moving into Karen's would essentially have amounted to living in the heart of our family legacy—a legacy that had taken me years to come to terms with, and which I only grudgingly now accepted. Until I was eighteen years old, I'd been kept completely in the dark about our family's secret: Karen and my mother were Durupinen—they formed two halves of a Gateway that allowed spirits trapped in the living world to Cross to the spirit realm.

When my mother died a few years ago, I began—inexplicably—seeing ghosts. As these ghosts tore my freshman year to shreds, I learned about our family's Durupinen heritage, which dated back countless centuries. I also learned that I had a twin sister; unbeknownst to Karen—or anybody else—my mother had split us up at birth to protect us. Hannah, who we later learned was the most powerful Durupinen in centuries, had spent her life in foster homes and mental health facilities; she had experienced spirit Visitations from an early age. When Karen and I discovered Hannah's existence, we'd rescued her from a psychiatric home. Only then did we learn that my mother had passed her gift—if you wanted to call it that—on to both of us. This meant that Hannah and I either had to take on the role of becoming our clan's new Gateway, or risk destabilizing the entire spirit world. No pressure, of course.

That surely would've been enough for anyone to deal with, but shit only got stranger and more dangerous from there. Hannah and I then had to move to Fairhaven Hall in England, the seat of the Durupinen's Northern Clans, to learn how to manage our abilities. It was there, under a cloud of mistrust created by my mother's having fled the Durupinen life—she had run away the moment she knew she was pregnant—that Hannah and I found out why my mother had split us up. We were the subjects of the Prophecy, a thousand-year-old presage that portended our causing the fall of the Durupinen and the rise of their enemies, the Necromancers. The Necromancers were essentially a rival sect almost as old as the Durupinen; they were hell-bent on reversing the Gateways and taking control of the spirit world for themselves.

In other words, we showed up to our first day of ghost school wearing name tags that said, "Hello, my name is Harbinger of the Apocalypse." Again, no pressure, right?

Things went downhill fast from there—like betrayals and kidnapping and monsters downhill. I eventually took refuge with the Travelers, an obscure forest-dwelling Durupinen clan, where I learned the Prophecy had been misinterpreted by the Northern Clans for centuries. The Travelers taught me how to Walk—to straddle between the worlds of the living and the dead—and my Walking ultimately saved the Durupinen, and possibly the entire world, from the Necromancers. Then Hannah had saved *me* from being trapped forever in the world beyond the Gateway. But it was a close, close call on all fronts.

Even though Hannah and I had now gotten as far from the Durupinen mother ship as we reasonably could, we knew our lives would always, on some fundamental level, be controlled by our connection to the spirit world. And no matter what we wanted to do with our lives, our calling would always be there, keeping part of us planted firmly in the world of the dead.

And so, we faced the challenges of post-college life, but we did so while constantly looking over our shoulders for spirits. Not a day went by when we didn't stop to investigate whether the woman waiting for the bus or the man keeping pace just a few feet behind us was, in fact, alive—or if they were manifesting spirits. Fun.

We moved to Salem so Hannah could start her master's degree in social work at the local university. I subsisted on a collection of coffee shop and restaurant jobs while I waited to see if my art history degree was worth the paper it was printed on. Finally though, my resume-blanketing panned out, and after a grueling interview process I landed a part-time job at the Peabody Essex Museum, where I led tours, made arrangements for visiting classes, and shadowed the curator. The pay was terrible, but I adored being surrounded by art. Although, as Milo pointed out, my new work wardrobe left quite a bit to be desired: I now had to trade in my signature look for pleated pants and blazers.

"At least I've mostly stuck to black," I said, gesturing to the row of work-approved attire now hanging neatly in my new closet.

"Yes, well, a leopard can't change her fishnets..." Milo sang.

I laughed. Milo could be a consummate pain in the ass sometimes, but he was very funny. He was also our Spirit Guide—we likely wouldn't even be alive now without him. When he died, he had somewhat-accidently Bound himself to Hannah; he had later pledged at our Initiation to serve as Spirit Guide to us and our Gateway.

"No, she can't," I replied, as I arranged my books carefully on the built-in shelves near my window. "Any word from our spectral roommate?"

"No, she still won't materialize. I think you scared her off when you confronted her."

"Maybe, but I'm sure she's just regrouping. I felt fear, but she was angry, too. I don't think it will be that easy to get rid of her."

"Did you draw her?" Milo asked. "So I'll know who I'm looking for?"

"Yeah," I said, pulling my newest sketch pad off of the desk. I flipped it open to the right page before chucking it onto the bed for him to examine. "That's her."

"Oh, she looks delightful. Real Queen of the Dead," Milo quipped, clearly amused by his own irony.

I had barely said good-bye to Tanya and shut the door to my car before the urge to draw the girl had overwhelmed me. That's how it was these days; my lifelong love of sketching was morphing into a spirit-recording compulsion. Fiona had told me during one of our long phone conversations that this "compulsion" was a sign of my gift coming into sharper, more powerful focus.

"That'll be the Muse coming out in you," she had said, with definite satisfaction crackling in her voice. "When they refuse to show themselves, that'll be when the urge will overpower you most. If your gift develops at all like mine, you may start waking up to some surprises in the morning."

"Surprises?"

"Yeah, that's right. As in, 'Surprise! I built a fecking spirit sculpture out of paperclips and twine in my sleep.'"

Fiona wasn't exactly exaggerating. I hadn't sculpted anything out of office supplies yet, but sculpture was her preferred medium, not mine. But twice during my senior year I'd had to repaint the wall in my dorm room at St. Matthew's after a nighttime Visitation turned into sleep-drawing, and once Tia had had to reprint a paper after I'd covered every page of it with portraits of a man who had a bullet hole in his forehead. Nowadays I often slept with a pen tied to my wrist and blank paper taped up on the walls around my bed. It was easier—and cheaper—than continually buying paint.

I looked over Milo's shoulder and down at the drawing. The sketch had poured unbidden out of me the moment I'd put a trembling hand to the blank page. As I drew, with my hand moving at a supernatural speed, each new detail had become instantly familiar, despite my having only glimpsed at the girl for a few moments.

The girl's livid face now glared back up at me from the sketchpad. Her eyes and lips were ringed with dark makeup, and the corner of her mouth was pulled up in a defiant sneer—like an entitled, rebellious teenager in her first mug shot. If I'd continued to draw beyond her shoulders, she surely would've been flipping me off.

"And Tanya has no idea who she is?" Milo asked.

"Nope," I said. "She didn't even know the spirit was a 'she' until I told her. Tanya has never seen her before, except as a shadow, or out of the corner of her eye."

"Yes, we spirits do like to do things like that. Preserving our mystique is way up there on our list of priorities, for some reason," Milo replied. "I still don't know why you don't just Ward the place and be done with it."

I shook my head. Warding, which involved drawing runes around specified areas to keep spirits out, was effective, but wouldn't really solve anything in the long run. "I'm waiting to see how hostile she is when the tenants here are onto her. I'd like to avoid Warding if I can. It will keep her out, sure, but we'll never find out who she is or why she's still hanging around if we just kick her out onto the street."

"And we care who she is because...?" Milo's voice trailed away. I threw him a dirty look and he put up his hands in surrender. "I'm kidding, I'm kidding. I just don't like to share my spectral space. It bums me out."

"Well, you can suck it up until we find out why she's here and convince her to Cross," I said firmly. I stepped back to admire my newly stocked shelves. "There. Done!"

"Only fifty thousand more boxes to go!" Milo said brightly.

I ignored this comment and continued. "We'll be able to get rid of the spirit more quickly if we do our homework. I've already knocked on a few doors on the block and asked the neighbors if they recognized the sketch. Not a single person has seen her before. But now half of them *do* think I'm crazy. As usual." I sighed. "What about you? Any luck with the dead neighbors?"

"Like an obedient Spirit Guide, I've been asking around. The old woman who haunts the brick house on the corner says she thinks our spirit moved in around ten years ago. At least, that's the first time she noticed her. Our girl keeps to herself, doesn't play well with others. She's scared off the previous owner and at least a dozen tenants."

"Okay. Well, it's a start," I said, shrugging.

"Hello? Jess?" A tentative voice called from the stairs. I felt my face split into a wide smile I could barely contain.

"Yeah, I'm up here!" I called back. I trotted out of the bedroom just in time to see Tia Vezga, breathless from climbing, stagger into the entry hall. She had two suitcases in one hand and a fishbowl tucked under her other arm.

Tia was my very best friend from college. Without her, I surely would've lost my mind when the spirits began revealing themselves to me my freshman year. She had never doubted me when I began talking about ghosts and hauntings, and—no matter how crazy I might've sounded—she had always treated me with her unique mix of intelligence, sweetness, and respect. She'd been quick to lend me her impressive investigative skills many a time, even when I had her researching some pretty far-fetched stuff, and it was she who had encouraged me to take David Pierce's parapsychology course—a course which changed my life in more ways than one.

"Tia! You made it!" I slammed into her with a hug that perhaps more closely resembled a tackle, causing her bags to tumble to the floor.

"Ouch! Be careful of Sequins!" she gasped, handing me the fishbowl and returning my hug.

"Aww, Sequins! Behold! The world's most tenacious betta fish!" I cried, tapping on the glass. Sequins was a carnival prize who had survived four years of college, four dorm rooms, and once, an exciting trip onto the bathroom floor while we cleaned his bowl. I couldn't believe he was making yet another move with us; he was obviously magical, maybe even immortal.

"More tenacious than me," Tia panted. I barely made it up the stairs! This is what I get for letting you pick the apartment, I guess.

It's bad enough that it's haunted, but a third-floor walk-up? Really?"

"Yeah, but just look at it!" I said. "The fireplace, the wide pine floors, the exposed brick!"

"You sound like an HGTV special," Tia laughed. "But you're right, it's beautiful."

"You'll love it, I promise," I said, and flung my arm around her neck. "I'm so glad we're roomies again!"

"Me too," Tia said. "Where's Hannah?"

"She's got class, but she'll be back soon. She can't wait to see you. Let me show you your room!"

I half dragged her through the living room. Tia tried to comment on the built-ins, but I pulled her into the corner bedroom, which overlooked the tiny back yard. "This is it. This is the one I picked for you."

The room was almost perfectly square, with a tiny fireplace in the wall that it shared with the living room. A large wooden beam divided the room's two high eaves into shadowy triangles overhead. A desk had been built into a small alcove, tucked away like a library carrel; several tall open shelves were built into the space above it, perfect for books and rows of labeled, neatly organized, binders—the very things that formed the basis of Tia's happy, ordered existence.

"You were absolutely right," she exclaimed gleefully. "This is perfect. I'm going to get so much work done in here!" In her excitement, she adopted the same tone that someone else might've used when talking about a dream vacation.

"Tia, I might be the one who sees spirits, but you are definitely the weird one," I said affectionately.

She ignored the dig. She immediately sat herself at the desk and began examining its drawers and built-in cubbies. "Speaking of spirits, is this new one going to be a huge distraction? It's going to be more important than ever to be able to study. If someone is going to be, I don't know, knocking my books off the shelves all the time..."

I put up a hand to silence her. "I won't let that happen. We'll Ward your room if we have to. I would never jeopardize your medical career. I'm counting on you to save me when my body breaks down from insomnia and excessive caffeine consumption."

"And how about Milo? Is he here?" Tia asked.

"Yes, and he's excited to see you, so how about we Meld already!" Milo shouted from the doorway, even though he knew full well that Tia couldn't hear him yet.

"Okay, okay," I said, and turned to Tia. "Give me your wrist. Milo's longing to be the center of attention again."

Melding was a handy little trick we'd learned after a few months of us all living together in our on-campus suite during my first year back at St. Matt's. After weeks of having to repeat everything Milo said to Tia, Hannah decided it was time to research options for facilitating communication before we all lost our minds. The Book of Téigh Anonn—the Durupinen bible—was full of Castings, many of which were too complicated or too terrifying to attempt, but the page devoted to Melding was simple and straightforward. After a little practice, Melding became very easy to do. In fact, the hardest part of the entire process was convincing Tia to go through with it.

As we discovered from our research, not all Meldings were equal. In fact, if I took two random strangers off the street, one living and one dead, and tried to Meld them, the living person would most likely have only the faintest sense of the spirit's presence. On the other hand, Melding was especially effective when the spirit and the living person were both closely tied to the Durupinen who performed the Casting; a Melding between my best friend and my Spirit Guide created a powerful connection.

Tia held out her hand, as she had done countless times before, and I untucked the pen I'd stashed in my hair and sketched three simple runes onto her palm, while muttering the Gaelic Casting as I did so.

"There we go. Spider-sense activated," I told her as I finished. "Try not to wash it off."

Tia lifted her head, shook her hair out of her eyes, and caught sight of Milo. She laughed.

"Hey there, stranger! Long time, no see!"

"Feast your eyes, girl!" Milo cried, and performed a catwalk strut for her benefit.

The Melding would only last until the runes wore off, and then we'd have to do it again. And it only worked on Milo. If our goth spirit turned up, Tia wouldn't be able to see her—although, if I had to bet, I'd guess our girl would make her presence known in other ways, ways that didn't require a Durupinen temporary tattoo.

"This place is so great. I know it's haunted, but I can't believe the deal you got on rent," Tia said, once she and Milo had ceased gushing over each other.

I nodded. "I felt guilty taking it. I know Tanya only dropped the price that low because she couldn't find anyone to rent it to, what with the preexisting roommate. But at least I'm providing her a service. I'll take care the spirit, and she'll be able to rent out the other two apartments. It's a win-win, really."

"Was it hard to get Finn's stamp of approval on the place? I know how picky he is," Tia asked, glancing quickly at me.

Part of me inwardly cringed at the idea of Finn's "approval." When I'd first found out about the Caomhnóir—the soldier-like units who protected the Durupinen and their Gateways—I'd rebelled against the idea with everything I had. Having a Guardian assigned to us made me miserable—and Finn was especially miserable, although not for the reasons I had thought. Long story short, he'd proclaimed his love to me—in poetry, no less—and for a while it had seemed like we could have a future together. "Seemed like" being the operative words.

"Well, he might start sleeping on the living room floor until he gets a better sense of how hostile this spirit is, but other than that, he approves."

"So, does he have a place to stay yet, or..."

"Oh yeah, he's all set up in a cushy apartment, fully furnished. Caomhnóir benefits. He just got a new car, too."

"Really?"

"Yeah. An Escalade, I think. You know the type—shiny and black with tinted windows and a carbon footprint the size of a dinosaur's. Every time we ride in it, Milo asks Finn how long he's been driving for Uber."

Tia laughed. "Wow. Must be nice."

"Right? Where's my sweet ride and my free apartment? I call bullshit," I said.

"No, *I* call bullshit," Milo chimed in. "Are you telling me that if the Durupinen offered you that stuff you'd take it?"

Being the civilized young adult that I was, I stuck my tongue out at him. Of course I wasn't going to take Durupinen handouts—not that they'd been offering much lately. I'd made it pretty clear how little I'd wanted to do with the Durupinen since walking out of Fairhaven Hall nearly three years ago. Hannah and I were supposed to stay and complete our training, but after thwarting a near spirit-apocalypse, we'd both decided we'd had enough of the Durupinen—and the Durupinen, for once, didn't argue. I think we'd offended them when we refused a seat on their Council, which was fine by me. Karen had helped us complete our training at home in Boston, which was basically unheard of. But, then again, I think the Council was too terrified of Hannah's raw power to say no.

Usually, the Durupinen would find ways to ease the transition into life as a full-time Crosser of the dead, but we'd slammed that door pretty forcefully behind us; opening it for perks meant letting in a world of trouble we had no desire to revisit. So, yes, despite my grumbling and complaining, Milo was right. But naturally I wasn't going to give him the satisfaction of saying so out loud; he was insufferable enough as it was.

"So you guys are okay? You and Finn, I mean?" Tia asked, with a delicate hesitation in her voice.

"We're fine," I said firmly. "We're always fine."

"Wow, you really should stop using the word *fine*," said Milo. "It's pretty obvious you have no idea what it means."

A knock on the door interrupted what would surely have been a brilliant and crushing reply. I held my tongue, and jumped up to answer the door.

Karen stood on our threshold with two large brown paper bags and an ear-to-ear grin.

"Happy housewarming!" she cried.

"Hey Karen! I didn't know you were coming today!" I said, stepping forward to take one of the bags; they looked heavy and precariously balanced in her arms.

"Oh Jess, funny story!" Milo called brightly from the living room. "Your Aunt Karen called and left a message saying she was going to stop by this morning! Call her back if you want her to reschedule!"

"It's so hard to find good help these days," I said to Karen, who laughed, but then hesitated in the doorway.

"Is it a bad time? I don't have to stay long. I just wanted to drop these things off for you girls. And I thought I could lend a hand getting you set up."

"No, it's fine! We're just unpacking, but I could use a break," I replied. "Come in, come in! I'm excited for you to see it!"

"Hi Karen!" Tia came bounding into the entryway, and greeted Karen with a warm hug.

"Tia, it's lovely to see you! I didn't realize you were moving in today!" Karen said, returning Tia's squeeze.

Tia shrugged. "I only had one morning class today, so I thought I might as well get started. I'm so glad Jess found this place! Grad housing wasn't working out at all—living with my suite mates was a nightmare."

"Hey K-K!" Milo said, materializing beside me and peeking into Karen's bags.

"Ugh, no one likes that nickname!" I groaned, as we crossed through the living room and into the kitchen. But Karen just laughed.

"Hello Milo," she replied. "Settling in alright?"

"Home sweet haunt!" he chirped.

"Oh Karen, thank you so much, this is great!" I said, pulling a tub of cleaning supplies and a potted succulent out of the first bag.

"You're welcome! I was going for a combination of practical and decorative," she replied. "And I promise, even you can't kill that houseplant, Jess."

"Famous last words," I muttered.

"And I got you some kitchen staples. A set of spices, a colander, and, of course..."

I opened the other bag. It contained a fancy new coffee maker, and about fifteen boxes of macaroni and cheese, the orange-powder kind that gives you the delightful feeling that you're five years old again every time you eat it.

"Woo-hoo! My dinner of champions!" I cried. "Aw, and the macaroni is even shaped like SpongeBob. You know me so well."

"Naturally," Karen replied. She was, by this time, well aware of my utter lack of cooking skills—a talent she also conspicuously lacked. Not cooking hadn't caused her too much inconvenience when she'd had Noah to do some occasional meal prep, but now Karen lived off of takeout more frequently than ever.

"So? Who's going to give me the grand tour?" Karen asked. I had a wildly strong moment of déjà vu, remembering Karen use that very same phrase years ago. The memory flashed across my mind—me, having just lost my mom, wandering awestruck through Karen's immaculate brownstone for the first time, knowing that I would have to live there yet too scared to touch anything. In that moment, when all I had wanted to do was sprint for the front door, I could never have imagined that Karen would become—in just a few years—someone who not only knew all of my favorite vices, but enabled them. We had come a very long way; I think my mom would've been happy about that.

Our "grand tour" only took a minute or two, but Karen pronounced every room "perfect!" in her quintessentially supportive way.

"There's... um, just one thing I noticed that you might want to take care of," said Karen quietly as we all congregated in the kitchen again.

"What's that?"

"Well," she began, throwing a cautious look over her shoulder to make sure that Tia couldn't hear her. "I'm pretty sure I felt something in one of the bedrooms, and it's possible that..."

"Oh yeah, don't worry, we know all about that," I said. "Tia does, too."

Karen glanced a bit sheepishly over at Tia. "Oh. Did you know there was a spirit attached to this apartment when you decided to move here?"

It was my turn to look sheepish now. "We, uh... might've used that knowledge to take advantage of a greatly reduced rent."

Karen raised an eyebrow. I held up my hands defensively.

"I also agreed to help get rid of the spirit so the landlord can rent the other two units," I explained. "I'd say that is a very fair trade, wouldn't you?"

"Okay then. Just make sure you aren't turning into one of those people you keep trying to bust," Karen replied firmly.

"What's that supposed to mean?" I asked, truly stung. "We're not scamming anyone! And Tanya's finally going to start making money on the other units again! We're offering a public service here, for the greater good. You can't say that about any of the people we go after!"

"No, you're right. I can't," Karen said almost apologetically, before taking on a firmer tone. "But it's a fine line sometimes, Jess, and I just want to make sure that you're always squarely on the right side of it, okay? And speaking of your projects, don't you think it would be a good idea to—"

I could think of any number of things it would've been a good idea for me to do in that moment. However, the most pressing of those things was ducking for cover as a chair flew at my head.

20

3

MADAME RABINSKI'S MYSTICAL ODDITIES

WE DROPPED TO THE FLOOR, COVERING OUR FACES. The chair hit the wall with such force that one of its front legs splintered off and spun across the room, coming to rest only inches from my face. The temperature in the kitchen had dropped about twenty degrees in a matter of seconds, and Tia's scream still hung like a speech bubble in the space above us.

"What the hell was that?" Karen gasped from somewhere behind the kitchen island.

I pulled my arms off of my head and looked around. The spirit had never even shown herself, and she was already gone from the room. And so, I realized, was Milo.

"Did you see where Milo went?" I asked the room at large.

"N-no, I had my eyes shut," Tia muttered, still curled up on the floor. "They're still shut. Probably not going to open them until sometime next week."

"It's okay, she's gone I think," I said. I sat up straight, closed my eyes, and reached into the depths of my mental space, where my connection to Milo waited, pulsing in its eagerness to bring us together.

"Milo? Are you okay? Did you see her?" I thought-spoke to him.

"I'm on her tail now," Milo said faintly. If Milo were alive he would have been out of breath from the chase, but instead his fatigue manifested itself by making his voice weak and muffled. "She's trying to shake me, but I've got a lead on her energy. Bitch is going down."

"See what you can find out, but be careful, obviously," I said.

"Obviously."

I pulled away from our connection and placed a gentle hand on Tia's shoulder. She flinched as if I'd slapped her.

"It's okay Tia. She's really gone. Milo is tailing her."

"I knew you had a spirit here, but you didn't mention she wanted to kill you!" Karen cried, as she pulled herself to her feet and straightened her glasses.

Tia sat up and drew a shaky breath. "Remind me why I decide time and again to live with you?"

"Because you love me?"

"Do I, though?" she asked; although Tia's voice was still audibly shaking, she smiled as she said it.

"Unconditionally," I said, and returned the smile guiltily. "We'll have that spirit out of here really soon. I promise."

"This kind of thing is a Durupinen occupational hazard. As Jess' best friend, I'm afraid this is collateral damage." Karen said, reaching a hand out to help Tia to her feet. "I was the least popular girl in my sorority, I'm sure you can imagine. Too many strange things happened when I was around. You really ought to Ward the place, Jess, if the spirit is that hostile."

"We haven't had a chance to put the Wards up yet because Hannah's had that huge project for class," I explained. "I was also kind of hoping we might find out a little more about the spirit before we kick her out, maybe even get her to Cross. But if she's throwing furniture, she's got to go." I turned back to Tia. "Soon this place will be as ghost-free as our dorm was, I promise. Well, at least as ghost-free as after I got back from Fairhaven, anyway." Unfortunately, Tia and I had had more than our fair share of Visitations during our freshman year, before I'd started my paranormal education.

Tia stood up, dusted off her jeans, and assumed a businesslike air. "Well, you can make it up to me by helping me haul my med school textbooks up here."

I stood up too, flexing my non-existent muscles. "You got it, boss.

"I'll help, too," Karen said. She was smiling brightly for Tia's benefit, but I caught her eyeing the door to the living room warily as we followed Tia into the hallway and down the stairs.

"So where's Sam this afternoon?" Karen asked. "How did he get out of moving his girlfriend into her new apartment?"

"He's working," said Tia. "He had to trade shifts at the nursing home to get time off for his internship next week."

"A likely excuse. Maybe he's protesting—you *could* have moved into his apartment instead." I kept my tone intentionally—painstakingly—casual.

Tia refused to even look at me, and instead raised her chin in a dignified manner as she popped open her trunk. "Sam is well aware that his apartment is much too far from the Commuter Rail for me to live there. Besides, living with him would be one thing, but living with his two roommates? Absolutely not." She wrinkled her nose, as though she could smell the socks and unwashed dishes from here.

This was Tia's go-to defense. She and Sam had been together since I set them up in our freshman year, but he was much more eager to take big life steps together than she was. There was also, of course, Tia's strict religious upbringing, which would never allow "living in sin." But most of all, it was Tia's laser-focus on her education and career that kept her from taking the next step in her relationship. Ambitious, bright, and dedicated to her goals—that was our girl.

I opened my mouth to tease her just a bit more, but all I could get out was a grunt. With a wide, innocent, smile on her face, Tia had just thrust the biggest, heaviest box from her trunk into my arms. Knowing full well I deserved it for joking about such a touchy subject, I turned without complaint to lug the box up the stairs.

§

"We'd better get rid of this spirit soon, because I'm never moving ever again," I said to myself as I panted. I had just heaved a huge stack of broken-down boxes onto the curb. After three hours of unpacking, I was finally beginning to understand the trend toward minimalist living. I mean, who actually needs three boxes of black boots?

"Sorry. I failed you," Milo said dejectedly. His voice preceded him as he popped into view.

"I thought you said the bitch was going down? What happened?"

"Traffic jam."

"A what now?" I asked, genuinely stumped. I'd heard of many

23

things in my time as a Durupinen, but a spirit traffic jam was a new one.

"I underestimated the spirit population here. It's like trying to track a single drop of moisture in a heavy fog," Milo said, shaking his head. "I'm not sure if it's because local spirits choose to stay here, or if spirits from other places are drawn here, but I've never existed in a place so crowded with my kind."

"Your kind? You mean flamboyant pains in the ass?"

Milo stuck his tongue out at me, but otherwise ignored my dig. "There's just way more of them than anywhere else I've ever been, except for Fairhaven. I haven't been here long enough to investigate exactly why yet. Maybe Salem has a fierce deadside club scene?" Milo mused, with a faint longing in his voice. "But whatever the reason, our roommate used it to her advantage and got lost in the crowd. I just couldn't keep a good hold on her energy."

"Well, Salem *is* supposed to be one of the most haunted cities in the country. The witch trials and all that. I always thought the ghost stuff was just a rumor to attract tourists, but maybe there's more to it?"

"Oh, there's definitely more to it. Although I guess that could be what brought a lot of the spirits here."

"What, you mean like... spirit tourists?"

Milo shrugged. "Sure, why not? When you're dead, travel expenses aren't really a thing anymore. If you're strong and sentient enough to find your way, why not see what all the fuss is about?"

I laughed. "I never really thought of that before, but it makes a weird kind of sense."

"Most of what I say does, if you think about it long enough. I'm like your fairy godspirit, doling out pearls of wisdom." said Milo, winking at me. He winked a lot; I think he picked the habit up from our friend Savvy. Some days Milo winked so often that he reminded me of an undead emoji.

"I think Karen was right," I said. "We're going to have to call the town and see if they will take this cardboard and everything. Or see if there's a recycling place we can bring it to." Karen had only just left, but not before ordering us a pizza.

My phone chose that moment to vibrate so loudly that I jumped.

24

I glance down to see a familiar face looking back up at me from the phone's screen. "Sorry Milo, I have to take this."

"Whatever, I'm out of sage advice for the moment. I'm heading back to Hannah's class. It's finally her turn to present—they went reverse alphabetical order—and I don't want to miss it," he said.

Milo faded from view as I answered the call. "Don't you have a fortune-telling scam you should be running right now?"

"No, my fortune-telling scam was yesterday," snorted the feisty voice on the other end. I could almost hear the hair toss that accompanied her response. "Today is spooky rigged séances, but I took a break for lunch."

I threw my head back and laughed. "What's up, Annabelle?"

"What's always up when I call you? Get over here. I've got another one, and you're not going to believe it."

"The list of things I wouldn't believe is so tiny it would probably fit on a Post-it note," I quipped. "But I need a break from all this unpacking, so I'll be right over."

These sorts of calls came frequently from Annabelle these days, and I looked forward to each and every one of them. Not because we were best friends or anything—although we were much closer now than I had ever imagined possible—but because we both had the same passion for our "projects." These projects took nearly every free moment of our time; we pursued them with an excitement bordering on obsession.

Our "obsession" began when we arrived back in the States after Fairhaven, with all of us reeling from our long and arduous ordeal. We each tried to pick up the pieces and move on; we each attempted to salvage what we could from our former lives and reconcile those pieces with what was left of ourselves. For Annabelle, that meant starting all over again without her shop—which she'd "accidently" set on fire in an effort to throw the Necromancers off her trail.

But starting over without her store was nothing compared to the loss of our friend Pierce, who the Necromancers had murdered in their cross-continental search for me and Hannah. For years, Annabelle had been an integral part of Pierce's ghost hunting team, using her own gifts to help collect evidence of paranormal activity. When my Visitations first started, it was Pierce and his team who helped me understand what was happening to me, and it was

Annabelle who—in a way—introduced me to the Durupinen and got me the help I needed.

With Pierce gone, Annabelle couldn't bear to rejoin the paranormal team. Pierce had been the team's leader, and although the rest of the guys—minus, of course, head-Necromancer-in-disguise Neil Caddigan—had tried to carry on without him, they took fewer and fewer cases as the years passed.

One night, after the team had all but disbanded, Annabelle had called me.

§

"I need your help," she told me in her "urgent" voice.

"Oh God, what? What is it?" I said at once, as my mind leapt into overdrive with visions of returning Necromancers.

"Some sadistic fraud has Oscar convinced that the old team is being haunted," Annabelle replied.

"The old... you mean Pierce's team?"

"Yeah. I haven't seen them in a while. I just couldn't... it was too hard."

Annabelle's voice was curt, almost dismissive, but I knew enough about compartmentalizing pain to know why she sounded the way she did.

"I get it. So what's happening?" I matched my tone to Annabelle's; I figured it would make things easier on her.

"When I told them I couldn't come back, they started looking for another medium to join the team. They weren't having much luck, but then a few weeks ago Oscar said he'd met a possible replacement. The woman claims not only to be a powerful medium, but says that she has a message for the whole team."

"A message? You mean, from a spirit?"

"Yes," Annabelle replied, in a muffled voice that told me she was clenching her teeth. "But not just from any spirit. From David."

My heart leapt into my throat, choking me. For the tiniest moment I forgot what I knew, forgot the very thing that had torn through every last fiber of me: Pierce wasn't just dead, but he'd Crossed over, beyond the Aether, to the realm on the other side. I knew this because Pierce's spirit had passed right through me during his Crossing. I knew this because I'd *met* Pierce on the other

26

side when I was Walking. If anyone knew that David Pierce was gone, it was me.

"That's not possible," I said stiffly.

"Oh, I know that, believe me," said Annabelle. "But Oscar and Iggy and the others don't, and we need to do something. You need to help me take this woman down—or I might just lose my shit and take her *out*."

I couldn't have been happier to oblige. We got together and did some research. Natasha Blake—real name Esther Smith—spent years trying to make it as a stage actress before reinventing herself. Her new identity was a medium who was constantly bombarded with communication requests from tormented souls.

Hers was an old enough con, but well executed. The key to her scams was that she never waited for a victim to come to her. Once "Natasha" identified her mark—usually someone who'd recently lost a loved one, preferably by sudden or violent death—she would then carefully research everything about her victim's life before setting up a "chance" encounter. Once she had gained her victim's trust—usually by mysteriously providing information no stranger could possibly know—she began charging exorbitant amounts of money for further spirit contact.

It wasn't terribly hard, I'd thought, to suspect Natasha of fraud, but grieving people do desperate things—and Natasha lost no opportunity to take advantage of this. It didn't take much digging into her past to uncover a veritable heap of victims; why no one on the team had looked into Natasha's history thoroughly, I didn't know. But when we were sure we had enough proof, Annabelle and I went to the team with our news.

We broke it to them as gently as possible: Pierce wasn't reaching out from beyond the grave. That conversation was awful—utterly wrenching for all of us—but since we had qualitative evidence of Natasha's scam, the team believed us in the end. The news was particularly hard on Oscar, who had introduced Pierce to paranormal investigation and had been a "ghost-hunting" mentor to Pierce for years.

A few nights later, Annabelle, Hannah, and I had had a satisfying chat with Natasha. We explained that she was now being watched: Unless she wanted us to haunt her forever like the spirits she pretended to see, she would go back to being Esther Smith. Then, for good measure, we brought out the big guns; we convinced

Hannah to use her ability as a Caller to conjure a horde of spirits to scare the shit out of Natasha. Natasha, sobbing and begging in terror, agreed to leave New England. Last we'd checked, she was living in Florida and working as an amusement park performer.

The experience could have torn the vestiges of Pierce's team to shreds, but instead it banded us all together. Suddenly, we had a new mission: We would work together, with all of our various talents, to unmask and destroy every paranormal con artist we could find. We were self-styled ghost-justice vigilantes—and it was awesome. And I knew that no one would approve more of how we chose to carry on his legacy than Pierce himself.

§

Annabelle's new shop was only a few minutes' walk from our new apartment; it was nestled into the smallest of a long row of storefronts just a few blocks from the harbor. The sign above the door had a faded, weathered look, as though Madame Rabinski's Mystical Oddities had been there for a hundred years, even though Annabelle had only opened her doors eighteen months ago. Annabelle had only been able to reopen her shop here in Salem thanks to a hefty insurance payout after the "accidental" fire at her first shop. Normally insurance fraud would've pissed me off something fierce, but I suppose if the Necromancers and Durupinen were going to destroy your life, there had to be some compensation; this kitschy, bizarre little shop was one of them.

The reason Annabelle had chosen Salem was abundantly obviously on this brisk October afternoon, when the streets were packed with the most bizarre and obnoxious crowds of tourists you could ever find anywhere. Salem was "Witch City," the home of the notorious Salem witch trials; every year the lead-up to Halloween brought hordes of costumed people eager for a taste of the paranormal. As I shoved myself unceremoniously through the throngs, I cursed under my breath—it would be a couple more weeks until the city once again became tolerable. But I knew these tourist weeks were important to the local economy; Annabelle would most likely make the majority of her profit for the entire year from October's earnings.

Even though Halloween was still over two weeks away, Annabelle's shop was packed to fire-code capacity with plastic vampire fangs and bad wigs, the wearers of which were staring in fascinated horror at Annabelle's collection of merchandise. Annabelle dealt in magic and mysticism of every variety—voodoo dolls, Santeria candles, Wiccan spell books, and antique vampire hunting kits lined her shelves; if Annabelle judged that the average suburban tourist would find an object to have the right creepy or fascinating "otherness," she stocked it in multiple colors.

I squeezed past a group of girls dressed as the characters from Sailor Moon; they were giggling at a collection of Victorian post-mortem photographs. I found Annabelle behind the counter. She was putting a Ouija board into a brown paper shopping bag for a customer.

"And you're sure this thing isn't going to, I don't know, open a demon portal in my kitchen?" asked a middle-aged Wonder Woman as she took the bag and her receipt. "I mean, I just want to do this for fun."

"One can never tell what will happen when we tamper with the spirits," Annabelle answered, with the shadow of a wink in my direction. "We must always exercise caution. Read the instructions carefully and all will most likely be well."

Wonder Woman turned and barreled past me, as though she were trying to leave as quickly as she could before changing her mind. Annabelle keyed something into her register before looking up at me.

"And what brings you to Madame Rabinski's Mystical Oddities today, my child?" she cooed.

"Oh shut up and tell me what's happening, would you?"

"Of course! I would never withhold information pertaining to someone's future," she said, and then called over her shoulder, "Sarah! I need you on the register please!"

Sarah, smiling broadly, appeared so suddenly she might have teleported. "No problem, I'm on it!" she said, straightening her name tag.

I ducked under the counter and followed Annabelle into a back room stacked high with boxes.

"What's all this?" I asked, gesturing to the nearest teetering pile.

"The trappings of All Hallows' Eve, my dear," she replied. She perched a pair of reading glasses on her nose as she started digging around on her desk.

"This is all for Halloween?" I asked, awed.

29

"Yes. Sidewalk sale. I could retire on the profits from pentagram jewelry alone. Idiots."

I couldn't help but laugh. If these tourists knew even half the stuff that I, as a Durupinen, knew about the spirit world, they'd run screaming in the other direction. Annabelle, too, had a Durupinen connection; her family's Gateway had closed generations ago, but she was still spirit Sensitive. The Travelers—some of whom were in fact distantly related to Annabelle—had called her a Dormant, a term which she loathed.

"Ah-ha! There you are, you sneak!" cried Annabelle, as she pulled out a manila file folder with a dramatic flourish.

"Is this what was so urgent?" I asked, reaching my hand out for it.

"Not 'what,' but 'who.' After your Poughkeepsie project this weekend, I think we'll want to start focusing on this guy for our next case—although I'll have to take a back seat on this one, too, until the Halloween rush is over. His name is Jeremiah Campbell, and he's quickly becoming the most influential paranormal personality in the country," Annabelle said, handing me the file folder; it was crammed so full of papers that I had to grab it with both hands.

I flipped the folder open and stared down at a photo. A handsome, chiseled face with a wide, pearly grin looked back up at me. The man's hair was dark and thick, graying at the temples in a way that, somehow, made him even more attractive. Why was it that men could get away with graying, while women were unequivocally expected to dye every strand at the first hint of gray? I found myself getting angrier about it than the moment warranted.

"Are you alright?" Annabelle asked. I looked up to see her staring at me in concern.

"Yeah," I said, half-laughing as I snapped myself out of it. "I'm just having an internal struggle about hair care and patriarchy. Never mind me, keep talking."

Annabelle blinked at me. "Right. Anyway, Campbell started making a name for himself about two years ago as a medium in New Orleans. It's kind of odd. One day he was a successful real estate broker in North Carolina, and the next he quit his job, filed for divorce, and moved onto a former plantation on the edge of the Louisiana bayou."

"Midlife crisis?" I suggested. "Did he also acquire a sports car and a much younger girlfriend with even younger boobs?"

"No, just the opposite. He gave up everything, holed himself up on the plantation, then started restoring it to its pre-Civil War glory. Of course he had plenty of money, even in spite of the nasty divorce, to get himself set up. But he severed ties with everyone—business partners, friends, and family.

"So... he sounds like a bit of a nut. But why should that bother us?"

"I'm getting to that," Annabelle said. She picked up a paperweight—a shrunken head encased in a glass—and extracted a magazine from under it. She tossed the magazine across the desk to me. A statuesque woman stared intensely up at me; her flawlessly gorgeous face was tilted thoughtfully on a swanlike neck that emerged from a yellow ball gown.

"I assume you've heard of Talia Simms?" Annabelle asked.

I snorted. "Well I don't live under a rock, so yeah, I've heard of her." Everyone who'd seen a decent movie in the last five years knew who Talia Simms was. She was only twenty-seven, but she'd been nominated for three Oscars in as many years, and had won two of them. And in between blockbusters, she found the time to do indie films with strong female leading roles. On merits of her talent, brains, and beauty, Talia had become a media sensation almost overnight. But ever since her boyfriend died the previous spring in a motorcycle accident, her face had become ubiquitous. The tabloids had latched onto her ill-fated storybook romance, and simply wouldn't let go. Talia was talented. She was gorgeous. She was...

"Living with Jeremiah Campbell?" I gasped.

"Not exactly," said Annabelle. "That headline is a bit overdramatic. She's not living *with* Campbell—they're not a couple—but she *is* staying at his plantation retreat. She's completely dropped out of public life."

"Wow. Okay, explain."

"Campbell claims that he has a constant companion, an angel, who allows him to communicate with the dead."

"An angel? Is he for real?"

"He certainly seems to think he is. And he's gained an incredibly enthusiastic—and wealthy—following. He has at least two dozen different clients—well, devotees might be a better word—who've followed him to Louisiana. These people have given him extravagant amounts to communicate with the dead; he's used that money to turn his plantation into a sort of retreat where they can commune with the spirit world."

"And Talia Simms is one of them?"

"It would appear so. She's been photographed coming and going from Whispering Seraph."

"Whispering Seraph?"

"That's what Campbell calls his property."

Annabelle and I shared a long and enthusiastic roll of the eyes. Who the hell did this guy think he was?

"The press hasn't really gotten wind of what Campbell really does; so far, they've treated his plantation like a high-end rehab, or an overpriced spiritual center."

"Yeah, I get it. For five grand a night you're treated to hot yoga, a steady diet of organic smoothies, new-age Buddhist-inspired chanting, and a heaping helping of plastic surgery, right?"

Annabelle laughed. "Something like that. But more likely, we think Campbell's extorting her. Talia would probably do anything to talk to her boyfriend again."

I shook my head before looking down at Talia's photograph again. She was one of those celebrities who always looked a bit uncomfortable in her own skin, as if she couldn't quite fathom why everyone kept looking at her but she was too polite to ask. She almost never smiled, at least not on the red carpet—and whatever smiling she did do disappeared completely when the tabloids started splashing Grayson Allard's death across their covers.

Sarah clattered her way through the doorway's curtain of wooden beads. "A gentleman would like to know if you'd consider taking a hundred dollars for the catacomb skull?"

"He can't be serious! A hundred? This isn't a flea market." Annabelle paused, then adjusted her bangles and composed her face into a serene mask before sweeping out through the beaded curtain. Sarah followed her.

While I waited for her to return, I thumbed scanned the article on Talia Simms. The paparazzi had managed to snap a few photos of her in a wide-brimmed black hat and oversized sunglasses as she walked through the wrought iron gates of Campbell's classic Southern plantation house. Even with her face half obscured, her misery was obvious. My first feeling was overwhelming empathy;

I knew what it was like to lose the person closest to me, and I understood the near-crippling need for answers that followed such a loss. But right on the heels of that empathy came a surge of anger so powerful that it nearly choked me. The thought that anyone could take advantage of such pain, that someone would twist it and mold it for profit, made me see red. I chucked the magazine onto the desk in disgust.

"I'll be so happy when Halloween is over and this parade of loons marches back where it came from," Annabelle grumbled as she flounced back into the office.

"Yeah, but in the meantime, you'll take their money with a wink and a smile," I said.

"A wink and a grin, more like," she said, and flashed me a perfect shit-eating grin in demonstration and for good measure. Turning grave once more, she gestured to the file still on the desk in front of me. "So? What do you think?"

I picked up the photograph of Jeremiah Campbell. "I think this guy is going down. Hard."

Annabelle smiled again. "That's my girl."

"We're going to have to really think about this one, though," I said. "It's not going to be as simple as buying a ticket to an event, like this weekend in Poughkeepsie. Campbell sounds like he's really exclusive. How would we even get a foot in the door?"

"I haven't worked that out yet," Annabelle admitted, "but it definitely merits further research, don't you think?"

"Absolutely. Let's get to work on this one. Can I take this?" I pointed to the file.

"Yes, that's your copy. I've got my own," she said.

"I'll get Tia to work on it, too. You should call the team and tell them to start packing for Bourbon Street."

"You'll see them before I will. *Ghost Oracle Live* is tomorrow, right?"

"Yeah, that's right. I wish you could come."

Annabelle laughed. "Me too, but did you see it out there? It's a madhouse. If I left, Sarah would get eaten alive by vampires and slutty Disney princesses."

"I know, I know. You need to be here. We'll kick ass in your honor, I promise." I said, giving her a little military salute. "I'll get Hannah to make copies of this file at school, and I'll give them to the guys when I see them. Good luck with the costumed masses."

I tucked the file under my arm, ducked out of the office, and began to battle my way across the shop to the front door. The cast of Sailor Moon was still there; they were now ogling an occult-themed jewelry display.

"Excuse me," I said as I edged behind them.

The nearest girl turned to give me more room, caught sight of me, and gasped. "Oh my God," she squealed, rummaging in her bag for her phone, which she extracted with fumbling hands, "You're a real witch, aren't you? Can we get a picture with you?"

Keeping my face as solemn as possible, I shook my head. "I'm sorry. I can't. I don't appear in pictures. It's part of my witchy magic. Now if you'll excuse me, I have to get back to my coven. Tonight we're sacrificing children in the woods with our familiars, and they do so hate it when I'm late."

Annabelle was right—idiots, all of them. I walked away, leaving a stunned silence in my wake.

4

PARANORMAL VIGILANTES

"THAT'S TOTALLY MEDIEVAL," Milo said with a cringe. "I mean, that's not even creative—we're not in the Dark Ages. Where do they get these people, anyway?"

"Catholic school?" I suggested. "Anyway, why should I be offended? It's the actual Wiccans who I feel sorry for. Imagine trying to peacefully practice your religion while being constantly accosted like that?"

It was early Saturday morning. Tia was already up, dressed, and out for a run along Salem Harbor. Hannah had gone out after her seminar with some friends to celebrate finishing their first major presentations, so I figured she was sleeping in. As for me, I'd been so wiped out from unpacking that I'd fallen asleep with my face in the Campbell file before Hannah had gotten home.

I now had the entire contents of the file spread across the living room rug. I should've been working on preparations for Poughkeepsie, but once I'd started reading about Campbell, I couldn't stop. I was borderline obsessed; Campbell was definitely one of the strangest situations we'd investigated so far.

"Hey," came a wisp of a voice that I now knew as well as my own. "What are you doing up so early?"

Hannah shuffled into the room, looking even tinier than usual in her oversized striped pajamas and her very fluffy slippers. Her slender fingers were cupped around a steaming coffee mug with the words "Morning People Suck" on it. She must've slipped into the kitchen while I was too buried in the file to notice.

"I just can't stop looking at this new case," I said, stifling a yawn and reaching for my own coffee, which was now room temperature. I took a swig anyway. That was the thing about me and coffee—hot, iced, burned, lukewarm, day-old, I didn't care as long as it packed a caffeinated punch.

"A new one? Already?" she asked. "We haven't even finished with the Freeman case yet."

"Yeah, Annabelle gave it to me yesterday. I'll let you study the folder on the drive to Poughkeepsie. It's pretty intriguing."

"Great," said Hannah. She was never one to turn her nose up at new reading material, even a case file.

"Enough about this stuff," I said, gathering up the papers into a stack and placing them into the file folder. "I got your text but I need details. How did your presentation go?"

Hannah shrugged, biting her lip. "It was okay, I guess. I got that embedded video clip to work, thank goodness."

"Were you happy with how it went?" I pressed. When I first met Hannah on the day we'd rescued her, she had drawn a protective shell around herself so intense that she could barely interact with anyone, with the exception of Milo. She'd improved a lot—hanging out with new classmates wouldn't have even been possible for her a year or two ago—but she still wasn't one to volunteer details, even to me.

"I guess so," she said with a non-committal shrug.

"Oh please," Milo sighed, slipping into the room. "She was brilliant!"

"So she actually let you back into the class yesterday?" I asked.

"I was on my absolute best behavior, halo intact," Milo said, rolling his eyes. "Our girl needed some moral support and a friendly face in the audience."

"A face I had to force myself not to look at the whole time, in case everyone thought I was crazy, staring off into space like that," Hannah said pointedly. She raised her eyebrows defensively at Milo. "I told you not to come. I could've managed everything just fine by myself."

"Of course you could've," Milo said. "But I'm a proud Spirit Guide, okay?"

"But really, how'd it go?" I asked.

Milo raised his hand in the air like a fifth grader who wanted desperately to be called on. "Can I tell her? Can I tell her?" he pleaded.

Hannah's stern expression softened into a grin. "Fine, go ahead." She folded herself into a snuggly little knot next to Milo on the sofa. How she made cuddling next to a freezing cold spirit look cozy, I still couldn't figure out, but I didn't question it anymore.

Hannah may have been my sister, but Milo was her soul mate. Pun intended.

"She absolutely killed it! The professor kept nodding and smiling, and checking things off his list. Everyone clapped at the end—and not just politely, but like they knew they just got their asses handed to them!"

Hannah giggled. "It's a class, Milo, not a competition."

By way of a reply, Milo shouted grandly to an invisible audience. "Everything's a competition. And you won! My baby is a star!"

"Alright, take it easy there, Milo. You sound as hard-core as Mama Rose," I said. "Seriously though Hannah, I'm proud of you. I know you were worried, even though we all had no doubt you'd do great."

"Thanks. First major grad school project done!" she said happily.

"Just in time for our first major paranormal-vigilante take down! Are you excited?" I asked.

"Nervous," she replied, with her smile sliding off of her face as if it had just dripped down into her mug. "Look I've been thinking about it a lot since we bought the tickets...

"Here we go," I muttered.

"Are you sure this is really a good idea? It's so... public."

"That's *why* it's such a good idea!" I said, shoving the Campbell file into my bag. I pulled out a second, much bigger file. "Lionel Freeman will never give up this gig unless he's forced to... it's too lucrative."

Lionel Freeman was a celebrity psychic, which in my opinion made him the absolute lowest of the low. He didn't just profit marginally from his "gift:" He built an empire on its crooked back. He was the star of his own reality TV show called the *Ghost Oracle*, where he went around and met with clients while the cameras were rolling; he always had a conveniently timed and comforting message from the deceased ready for each meeting. Freeman had this habit of closing his eyes and holding two fingers to his temple when he "received a message," as though he could hear the spirit better by pressing a button on the side of his head. It was all so staged, so incredibly insulting—I almost couldn't believe that people fell for it. The first time I watched the *Ghost Oracle*, Tia had to take the Dustbuster to the carpet for a half an hour afterward because I'd thrown so much popcorn at the television.

Of course, it was obvious to us that Lionel Freeman was a master at digging into his guests' backgrounds. But what Freeman's research didn't tell him was that Annabelle and I were masters at digging around too. We began reaching out to people who had been featured on past episodes; it was shockingly easy to see a pattern emerge.

People wrote to Freeman with their sob stories, begging to appear on his show. The irony was that those letters probably contained every detail Freeman needed to craft a really convincing lie. Some people even made specific requests—they'd beg Freeman to reach out to their dead father and ask if it was okay to sell the family home. Things like that. And so, of course, these poor people—these vulnerable and confused victims—would turn up for a session with Freeman and get exactly what they'd asked for. Hell, they ate that shit up.

The show had become so popular that Freeman started hosting live events all over the country. Thousands of people showed up; they shelled out absurd amounts of money for tickets, just for the chance that Freeman might invite them onstage with a message from the other side. He held his events in theaters and even small stadiums, most of which were packed to the rafters with the desperate and grieving. This weekend, we would be among the desperate and grieving, too—and we'd put a stop to Freeman's scam. For tonight's event, we'd had to buy our outrageously marked-up tickets from price-gouging resellers, but we'd finally managed to get a foot in the door. And a foot was all it would take for us to show the world exactly how much of a money-grubbing charlatan Lionel Freeman really was.

§

A sharp knock echoed from our door, interrupting my thoughts; I jumped up and flung it open.

"Hey—oh! Hi," I said, rather breathlessly, especially considering that I'd only walked about two dozen steps to the door.

Finn stood in the hallway, kicking at the threshold absently with one foot. "Morning."

I could feel my pulse quicken in my neck. I fumbled around with my hands, suddenly and inexplicably unsure of what to do with them.

"What are you doing here?" I asked.

He shrugged. "I thought I'd better come for the meeting, so I know what the plan is for today."

"How did you know there was a meeting?" I asked, frowning. I certainly hadn't told him about our plans for the morning, and I was almost positive Hannah hadn't either.

"Jess, it's my job to know when these things are happening—even if you choose not to inform me," replied Finn gruffly, crossing his arms.

Finn wasn't getting away with that, not on my watch. "That wasn't really an answer to my question," I said flatly.

"I must admit I was hoping you'd not notice that," he replied as his expression turned even more truculent.

I felt my blood starting to boil. Part of me wanted to take Finn by the collar and shout, "What time warp do you live in? It's the 21st century! I don't need a big strong man to protect me!" But of course—as much as I hated to admit it—it just wasn't true, at least not totally. The Durupinen did need protection, and only trained Caomhnóir could provide it. The challenges of our calling meant that we sometimes found ourselves in situations that we couldn't handle on our own—and it seemed I was particularly good at landing myself in these. But we didn't need the Caomhnóir because they were men; we needed them because they were trained in military-grade defense, and experts in the Castings that kept us safe. If Finn hadn't been there to do his job, I would've been dead several times over by now.

But I swallowed my tirade. Finn and I had had the "invasion of privacy" and "surveillance and spying are illegal" talk one too many times. Nothing I could say would make the slightest bit of difference to how he went about his Caomhnóir duties.

Resigning myself once again to his job as my friendly neighborhood stalker, I waved Finn through the door. I was almost polite about it, too.

"You're early," I said, following him through to the living room. "The team won't be here until..."

"I know that. I wanted to speak to you before the others turn up," Finn said, pulling off his leather jacket and draping it carefully over the back of the nearest chair.

"Good morning Finn," said Hannah quietly. She wiggled up from the sofa and went into her bedroom, with Milo in tow. Finn nodded to her as she left. These days, Hannah liked to give me and Finn plenty of space.

"Well then, fire away," I replied, plunking myself back down on the floor and reaching for my coffee.

He sighed, as though he already knew I wouldn't like whatever he was about to say. I perked up a bit, putting myself on guard.

Finn began carefully. "I recognize that I have no authority over where you decide to go and what you decide to do..."

"Correct," I interjected. "But I have a feeling that whatever you're going to say flies right in the face of that assessment, doesn't it?"

Finn didn't answer my question, but instead dropped into the chair closest to me and said, "It does, yes. I've come to persuade you not to go through with this trip."

"Seriously, Finn? You're going to start that right now, four hours before we're supposed to leave?"

"Yes. Now's the perfect time," Finn insisted. "I've been looking into this event. I think it's much too large and much too public for you to tackle, even with the team backing you up. I appreciate your mission, Jess, but there's got to be a better, more private, way to take this Freeman fellow out."

I felt my hackles rise, as they so often did whenever someone made the merest suggestion that I couldn't do something. "We're prepared, Finn. We've researched Lionel Freeman for months, and we know exactly how he operates. This is going to be a piece of cake."

"And what if you get caught?" he asked. "What if you get arrested?"

I laughed. "Arrested? For what? We're not doing anything illegal! We're not breaking in—we purchased tickets, just like everyone else."

"And what about the surveillance Iggy and his lot will be doing? Is that also one hundred percent on the up and up?" Finn asked.

I squirmed a little. "Probably?"

Finn scowled. "Getting the police involved—potentially or otherwise—is too risky. Have you considered how this might jeopardize our security? Did you ever stop to think about that?"

"Oh, Finn, get a grip on yourself," I groaned. "I'm not going to go charging in there with a 'Durupinen Vigilante' T-shirt! We're just going to surreptitiously upset Freeman's usual bag of tricks so that he can't take advantage of anyone else."

"Really? Surreptitiously? Are you capable of doing anything surreptitiously?" Finn asked.

"Yes, surreptitiously. I've been doing this stuff for over a year, and none of the Durupinen have even noticed. This isn't our first rodeo, Finn, it just happens to be our biggest. Look, if you're so worried about it, stay here. Stay out of it. That way you won't get in trouble with the Durupinen overlords!"

Finn's face turned red at my words, and his features twisted into a furious, knotted expression. "There's no question of your going without me, so I suppose I'll just have to be prepared to tidy up your mess. I don't know why I bothered bringing it up. You've never listened to a word I've said in my life! Why did I think you'd start now?"

"I did listen to a few of them," I said quietly. "But they didn't mean much, in the end."

Finn opened his mouth with every intention of arguing with me, but I met his eye, challenging him. He somehow turned even redder, snapped his mouth shut, and stalked off into the kitchen. I sat and watched his retreat, hoping my words had hurt him. I wanted—needed—Finn to feel a tiny portion of the hurt that ached and ached inside every time he looked at me.

I tore my gaze away from him and found Hannah and Milo peeking out of the bedroom at me; of course they'd heard everything. The pity in their faces was unbearable.

"Jess—" Hannah began.

"Let's have some breakfast, then get everything in the Freeman file organized for a final review," I said, refusing to look at either of them. "The team will be here soon, and we have a lot of prep to do."

§

By five o'clock that afternoon, Hannah, Finn and I were buried in the masses of a near-hysterical audience; we were now lined up outside the Bardavon 1869 Opera House in the heart of downtown Poughkeepsie. The building was the oldest continuously operating theater in New York. Its massive flashing gold marquee proclaimed the imminent arrival of "Lionel Freeman, Ghost Oracle." Seriously, how freaking full of himself did this guy need to be to proclaim himself a "ghost oracle?"

Up and down the line, audience members were chattering

excitedly; some were even crying with anticipation. Each and every one of these people was hoping to get a message from a spirit. Yet as far as I could see, not a single one of them was actually haunted.

"I pulled out my phone and texted Iggy. *You in position?*

Thankfully, before I could even stop to wonder how long it would take for him to respond, my phone buzzed with Iggy's reply. *Yep. Good to go.*

I was relieved. Parking was always tricky in a downtown area; it was crucial to our plan that the team set themselves up on the corner nearest to the theater's emergency exits. They'd disguised their van just for the occasion; today they were "local plumbers."

"The team's in position," I announced.

"Right. Good then. But they should've reported to us, not the other way 'round," scoffed Finn, terribly unhelpfully. Did he think the whole world worked with the Caomhnóir's military precision?

I ignored him and turned to Hannah. "I'm not getting anything, are you?" I murmured.

She shook her head. "There are spirits around, obviously, but not in line. The theater actually has a few resident spirits. Does this place have a reputation for being haunted?"

"If it does, I'm sure Freeman will capitalize on it. That might even be why he picked it for a venue," I said. "How about you, Milo? Anything else?"

"Nope. I'm a lonely floater. There's the ghost of a homeless woman, but she's attached to the area, not the crowd. If Freeman is going to connect with a real spirit tonight, I am his one and only option at the moment."

I nodded in satisfaction. Milo had just given me further confirmation—not that I needed any—of Freeman being a complete and utter phony.

My phone, which was clutched in my hand, began to vibrate. I looked down at the screen. It was Tia.

"Hey roomie! Miss me already?" I answered brightly.

"Yes, and I need you to come back right now. Please?" came Tia's almost-hysterical reply.

"Wait, are you serious? What's the matter?" I asked.

"Did you forget to do something before you left?" she asked shrilly.

I racked my brain. I'd packed everything we needed. I'd locked the door. I'd emptied the trash. I'd even left Skittles on Tia's desk for study fuel. "No, I don't think so," I finally answered.

"Think harder, Jess," she pressed. "Think really, really hard."

"Tia, I have no idea what you're tal—"

"I'm sending a picture to refresh your memory," Tia said. She was so upset that her breaths were coming in gasps.

Bewildered, I looked down at my phone as her message appeared. I opened it and let the picture download. The image that appeared was of our living room, where every single item—from our sofa to the lamps to the pictures on the walls—had been overturned. The room looked as if it had been ransacked by robbers.

"Oh my God." I gasped, as I looked up at Hannah and Finn in absolute horror. "We forgot to Ward the apartment before we left!"

"That's correct!" Tia squealed. She was now so loud and tense that Hannah and Finn both heard her voice coming from the phone. I held the picture up for them; Hannah clapped her hand over her mouth.

"You said you'd tend to that after meeting with the team!" Finn said, in what I thought was an unfairly accusatory tone.

"I was going to—but we had a lot to review! Then we were rushing to get out the door, and... I forgot!" I put the phone back to my ear. "Ti, is there anywhere else you can stay tonight, until I can get back there and fix it? What about at Sam's place?"

"At Sam's? Overnight?" she cried, as though I had suggested she stay in a mausoleum in an abandoned graveyard instead of at her own boyfriend's apartment. "I... I guess I could do that. Oh, but my mother will know, Jess, she'll *know*!"

For the sake of her feelings, I held back my laugh. Tia was close with her parents, but their stringently Catholic views did cause some tension in her relationship with them. Her parents' particular brand of overprotective love was one thing when Tia had first moved away to college, but c'mon, she was now an adult, and a med student at a prestigious Boston university. Plus, Tia was easily the most inherently responsible person I'd ever met. Apron strings, meet scissors.

"How, Tia? How will you mother know if you don't tell her?"

"She just will! I can't lie to her, Jess. She always knows! She'll take one look at me and fly off the handle!"

"But that spirit will take one look at you and send all your stuff flying out the window! I think you just have to go for it and hope for the best," I said.

Tia groaned. "Alright, alright! I'll be at Sam's until you get back. But don't even think about asking me to come home until the Wards are up and there's not a spirit within a mile of that apartment! Well, except for Milo, obviously," she corrected herself.

"I promise. We'll evict our spectral roommate as soon as we get in the door," I said. "I'm so sorry, Tia. Seriously, I am. I'll make it up to you."

"There aren't enough Skittles in the world, Jess!" Tia grumbled. She hung up without saying good-bye.

"I feel really bad," I said, looking up at Finn and Hannah. "She's really angry. I hope she'll be okay."

"She'll be fine, she's tougher than she looks," Finn grumbled, bouncing up and down to keep warm. "What are we doing here now anyway? The show doesn't start for two more hours. We had plenty of time to get the Wards up before leaving. Why did we have to come so early?"

"Because this is the most important part of the night!" I said, a bit too loudly. I lowered my voice before continuing. "This is when Freeman sends his spies out to get stories and details. They plant themselves in the line, acting like ticketholders, and start casually chatting with the audience members, or else just listen in on their conversations. Then they feed the info to Freeman through an earpiece during his show."

Finn raised his eyebrows. "Really?"

"Oh, yeah, and that's just the beginning!" I said, fighting to keep my anger from increasing my volume. "He uses his social media network to gather information, too. See over there?"

I pointed toward the front of the line, where a woman had just appeared wearing VIP access badges over a bright pink "Reconnecting with Lionel Freeman" T-shirt; she had a stack of at least ten more shirts in a big mesh tote bag. A man with a video camera followed her, filming everything.

"Share your reconnection story on Lionel's fan page! Free T-shirts!" she called out to the crowd; instantly, people began practically falling over each other with eagerness. "And don't forget to share your selfies on Twitter and Facebook. Hashtag, 'ghostoracle!'"

Finn's mouth fell open. "They let themselves be recorded? Voluntarily? For the Internet?"

"Yup. Then Freeman's team pulls information from the videos and feeds that stuff to him too. It's right out in the open for everyone to see, but no one realizes it."

"Or if they do, they ignore it. It's really easy to ignore hard evidence when you desperately need to believe in something," Hannah said empathetically.

"Here, see for yourself." I pulled my phone out of my pocket, opened up the *Ghost Oracle* Facebook page, and started scrolling through the posts. Photo after photo showed smiling fans at live events; each picture had a short but detailed caption describing why they were there and who they hoped to connect with. "God bless the Internet, right?"

I watched the storm clouds gather on Finn's brow. "Absolutely vile," he pronounced. For once, his churlish tone was actually appropriate.

"I know it is. That's why we're here early," I said. "Identifying his shills may be key to disrupting the scam. Starting now." And with that, I pulled Hannah and Finn in close, cheek-to-cheek. "Smile like you mean it!" I said.

I held my phone up as if we were taking a selfie, but actually kept the camera's focus pointed outward so that I could take several shots of the woman with the VIP badge. She was now listening with an eager, yet somehow empathetic, expression to a sobbing woman who was pouring her heart out for the videographer. While clutching her new pink T-shirt, of course.

"Got it!" I said happily, releasing my grip on Hannah and Finn. I immediately texted the picture to Iggy.

"And now one more for real!" I said, pulling them in close again. Milo floated into the frame too, as if the camera could actually pick him up, and mugged his fiercest, super-sexy pose.

"Geez, Finn, look a little more excited, would you? This is to cover our tails!"

"Right. Sorry," Finn said, while making a pathetic attempt at an excited face that made me snort with laughter. Hannah giggled too.

"Oh my God, stop Finn. You're making it worse," I said as I snapped the picture.

I quickly uploaded the photo to the *Ghost Oracle* Facebook page, and read aloud as I typed the caption.

Can't believe we got Ghost Oracle tix! Need Nana Mamie's advice. Take the internship 1,000 miles from home? Miss you every day, Mamie! Xoxo #ghostoracle #cancersucks.

I held up my phone to show Finn, Hannah, and Milo the post. "Now we look like we're here for the same reason as everyone else. If it's on the Internet, it must be true!"

Finn looked horrified at being included in a social media post. "Sharing" was against his Caomhnóir instincts. He shook his head ruefully and said, "Okay, then. What's next?" For someone who had grumbled the whole way down here, he certainly seemed very interested in participating now that all this was really happening.

"Now we find Freeman's plants," I said, tucking the phone away.

"How are we supposed to do that? They're blending in. That's the whole point, isn't it?" Finn asked.

"Are you a Caomhnóir or not? Use your eyes, Finn. They're wearing earpieces," I said. "They might be really small ones, so they won't be easy to spot. We need to split up. Look for anyone who seems to be eavesdropping on conversations, and for anyone wearing anything that looks like a Bluetooth."

"And after we've finished peering into strangers' ears what do we do? If we find a plant, then what?" Finn asked.

"Find a way to get a better look at that earpiece. If we can figure out exactly what kind of devices they're using, Dan should be able to find a way to mess with them. We'll meet up at the back of the line in fifteen minutes to check in."

"Okay Jess, sounds like a plan," said Hannah.

"And I'll do my deadside thing!" added Milo.

"But how do we—" began Finn, but I was already pushing back through the crowd.

"Figure it out!" I called back to him. "You'll think of something!"

I eased my way through the group, politely smiling and mumbling, "Excuse me. Sorry!" over and over again while watching for any signs of surveillance. At first, I only saw rabid Freeman fans. A group of women was taking a selfie with a life-size cutout of the grinning "oracle" himself. In the cutout, Freeman was dressed in his trademark black, Nerhu-collared suit. His face was almost elfin, with round cheeks, bright blue eyes, and ears that stuck out from his greasy slicked hair like satellite dishes searching for a signal from the afterlife. The Nerhu collar particularly enraged me—it was a transparent attempt to associate himself with mysticism and religious authority without actually being ordained in, or endorsed by, any religion at all. I had never been a religious person, but I did consider myself a moral one—and this guy was absolutely devoid of a moral compass.

I searched for several more frustrating minutes; the longer I investigated, the more my doubts got the better of my nerve. What if we couldn't find the plants? What if our theory about how they communicated was wrong? Even if we did manage to find a spy, what if we couldn't get enough information about their methods? Or, worse still, what if someone figured out what we were trying to do and we got caught? We'd never attempted anything this elaborate before, and I had to admit the size of the task was starting to intimidate me. Freeman was a machine, a powerhouse of publicity. He obviously had this all down to a science, while we were just amateurs winging it.

I had just about talked myself into giving up when I spotted her—a youngish woman with downcast eyes and her long dark hair pulled down around her face. She was leaning just a bit too casually against the wall, right next to a pair of middle-aged women who were gabbing loudly about their house being haunted by their older sister.

"She always hated anyone we brought home, right Kathy?" one of them said.

"Always," Kathy agreed, nodding vigorously. "Always rolled her eyes at the dinner table when we talked about a boyfriend. She wouldn't even come outside for a family picture when Gail here went to her prom."

Gail sighed. "Maybe it was because she couldn't get a date herself. Not that she wasn't pretty, you understand, but she just didn't know how to flirt, you know? So, last year, when I brought Tony to the house for the first time..."

I joined the group, gently nudging my way in until I was next to Freeman's plant. I kept my eyes on Gail and Kathy, and nodded along with the rest of their audience while hoping that my face was convincingly awash with curiosity. The plant shifted closer in and, as she did so, I heard her quietly mutter, "Are you picking up all of that? She'd be great."

"...and we were watching *Wheel of Fortune* when this light in the living room started flickering on and off, and I just *knew*. I knew she was trying to spoil my date—just like she did when she was alive.

Because that light never acts up, does it, Kath? Only when Tony comes over..."

The plant looked up and pretended to be interested in the story. As she lifted her head, just before her hair swung forward, I saw it for a fleeting instant—a tiny flash of silver tucked inside her ear.

As carefully as I could, without attracting notice, I lowered my bag on its long strap until it rested on the ground, then tucked it against my feet. I felt around with my foot, found the strap, and wound it around my ankle. I listened for a few more seconds to Gail and Kathy's story, steeling myself. I felt a surge of adrenaline as I prepared to make my move.

I took a deep breath and fell, as awkwardly as I possibly could, right into the unsuspecting plant. It marked one of the few moments in my life where I was awkward intentionally.

"Whoa! Shit!" I cried. I reached out as I lurched forward, grabbing the plant's hair and taking her down with me.

She screamed. I yelled. Several other people were knocked off balance and almost fell with us. As we both tumbled to the ground, I heard something small and hard hit the pavement.

Bingo.

"Oh my Lord, I am so, so sorry! I just tripped over my bag!" I said. "Are you okay?" I asked, reaching down to tug the strap off of my foot.

"Yeah," the woman said distractedly. Then, with her eyes widening, her hand flew to her now-empty ear.

"I'm such an idiot," I babbled on. "Oh, no! What's wrong? Did you lose an earring?"

"No, I... I was just... I had this..." the woman stammered, as she searched the ground frantically. Then she began fumbling through her hair, feeling down her shirt—searching anywhere that the earpiece might have fallen.

Everyone around us was offering to help us up, asking if we were okay. Even Kathy and Gail had stopped yammering on long enough to find out what all the commotion was about. I spotted the earpiece lying in the shadow of my bag. Under the cover of the flurry, I picked up the earpiece and examined it. I had just spotted a tiny "Fuji TZ-90," written on its side when the earpiece began emitting a piercing feedback squeal.

"Is this what you're looking for?" I asked, holding it out to the plant.

"Give me that!" She reached out and snatched the earpiece from my hand, closing her fingers tightly around it to deaden the noise. Everyone was staring at her now, curious about the sound.

"I'm so sorry," I said again. "I know those hearing aids are expensive. My uncle used to have them. It's not broken, is it?"

Some of the blind panic left the woman's eyes as I handed her the perfect cover story for what she now held in her hand. Taking a deep breath to steady herself, she managed to smile at me. "No. No, it's fine. It does that sometimes. Excuse me."

She ducked out of the crowd and walked quickly to the head of the line, before popping around the corner of the theater and out of sight. After assuring a few more concerned bystanders that I wasn't hurt, I too slipped out of line and jogged along until I found Hannah and Finn at the very back of the crowd.

"Milo is still looking, but I couldn't find anyone," Hannah said anxiously as we huddled together.

"I'm fairly certain I did, but he left before I could get close to enough to spot his earpiece. I took a picture of him with my mobile, but it came out rather blurry," Finn said, pulling the phone from his jacket pocket. "I can show you, if you..." He narrowed his eyes at me. "You look disheveled. What's happened?"

I quickly told them the whole story as I pulled my phone out and began dialing Iggy.

"You did what, sorry?" Finn asked, gaping at me. I shushed him as Iggy picked up his phone.

"What's shakin' ghost girl?" he said as he picked up. Iggy had tried to stick me with that nickname the first time we'd met, but only Pierce ever got away with calling me that.

"Still not answering to that," I said. Iggy laughed raucously. I could hear Oscar shushing him in the background.

"Alright, I got your picture of the T-shirt hawker, so we'll be keeping an eye out for her. Any luck with the com system?" I heard a click; Iggy had switched me to speakerphone.

"Yes. I found one of the plants!" I cried excitedly, before remembering to lower my voice. "She was wearing a small silver earpiece that said 'Fuji TZ-90" on it."

Dan whooped loudly with excitement. "How the hell did you manage to find that out?" Iggy asked incredulously.

"Who cares!" I said. "Does that help you or not?"

"Hell yeah, that helps!" Dan shouted. "Those earpieces work on a radio frequency. If we can find it on the scanner, we can hijack it—or at the very least record it."

"How do you hijack it?" I asked.

"You just use another device on the same frequency. It'll disrupt their signal and send whatever we're broadcasting through to Freeman's devices."

"Yeah! Instead of hearing info from his staff, he'll be jamming out to my favorite playlist!" Iggy said with a laugh.

I fought down the urge to literally jump with joy. "This is incredible! Just imagine Freeman standing up there in front of the audience with no idea who any of them are or why they're here! He'll be screwed! He's going down in flames!"

"Don't get ahead of yourself, Jess," Iggy cautioned me. "There's still some major hurdles to overcome. We'll get back to work here. If we find that frequency, we'll let you know! In the meantime, text any more pictures you get of Freeman's team."

I made an attempt to calm myself, but the smell of victory was already strong in my nostrils.

5

THE GHOST ORACLE

OUR SEATS AT THE BARDAVON THEATER had been carefully chosen. Hannah and I sat in the house right dress circle box closest to the stage, where we had an excellent view of the entire audience in both the orchestra and the balcony. Our seats gave us a very unique perspective of the stage; we would be watching Freeman from the side, almost at a ninety-degree angle to the rest of the audience, but with the added bonus that we could see deep into the stage right wing. Watching the crew members in the wing would add an entirely new element—and source of information—to the show. Finn was seated in the dress circle box directly across from us on house left, where he could see deep into the stage left wing. If we craned our necks, we could even see a section of the catwalk above the curtain line. For "obstructed view" seats, we had a fairly unobstructed view of pretty much everything.

And of course, we had an added weapon: Any nook or cranny we couldn't see from our seats could be handled by Milo's special brand of ghostly reconnaissance. The last we'd checked, Milo was hovering near the dressing rooms, hoping to catch a glimpse of any special tricks Freeman might be employing.

"Only about five minutes now," Hannah whispered to me.

"I know," I said, looking up from my phone, which I was checking obsessively every few seconds. "I can't believe Iggy hasn't updated us yet. How are we supposed to know if they've found that frequency?"

Hannah just shrugged. One of her knees began bouncing, venting some of her nervous energy, as she reached out to Milo. "Milo? How's it going? Did you find Freeman?"

"No, he's not here yet." Milo's voice filled our heads simultaneously; we'd learned recently that he could connect to both of us at the same time, like a spirit version of speakerphone. "I overheard two of the crew members waiting by the door, and they said Freeman never arrives at one of his shows until just before it starts. They're actually going to broadcast him driving up and walking into the theater in real time! I bet he does it to boost his own cred—he can't possibly know anything about his audience if he's only just arrived, right? I'm outside now near the stage door, waiting for his car to show up."

This information only ratcheted my tension even higher. This guy couldn't be allowed to continue getting rich off of other people's grief. It had to end tonight, or we might not get another chance. Plus, if we didn't take Freeman down now, I'd have to see his smug, sanctimonious face on television every week. In the long run, I suppose this last part was the least of our concerns, but it added fuel to my resolve.

"Wait, something's happening out here," Milo said suddenly, quite literally breaking into my thoughts. "Security just opened the door, and now there are three camera guys. He must be about to pull up."

But we didn't need Milo to tell us things were starting. Even as he spoke, the lights in the theater dimmed. The curtain rose, revealing a large screen. An eerie, synthesizer-heavy soundtrack began to blast from the speakers; a booming baritone voice worthy of movie trailer voiceovers began speaking.

"Ladies and gentlemen, welcome to the one place in the world tonight where the veil between the living and the dead can be lifted, where the mysteries of the beyond can be penetrated. Welcome to the one place where true peace can find each and every one of you. Welcome to the *GHOST ORACLE LIVE!*"

The crowd leapt to their feet, shrieking wildly, throwing their arms in the air. Some of them were already sobbing in the hope of being called to the stage to experience Freeman's "talents" for themselves. The screen lit up with the familiar opening of Freeman's show—a montage featuring Freeman with various families as his words made them break down over and over again. Sickening.

A picture-in-picture image appeared in the top corner of the screen, showing a black stretch limousine rolling up in front of the theater. As the theme song came to a close, the picture-in-picture took over the whole screen. The live feed showed Freeman exiting his limo and striding confidently through the stage door; his own crew members, all of whom were wearing headsets, applauded wildly as he made his way through the backstage area. Freeman's face was so smug I wanted to slap the smile right off it.

I looked down at my phone again, panic setting in. "Damn it Iggy, we're running out of time! Give me some good news!" I muttered.

Then the door to the backstage area opened and a cameraman backed into the wing. He was followed by Freeman, who we could now see was a full head shorter than almost everyone he passed—although this was minimized on-screen by the camera's low-angle shot. As if on cue, Freeman paused for just a moment, closing his eyes and performing his signature fingers-to-his-temple gesture. The crowd went wild.

"These poor saps," I thought to myself, as I waited for the slightest hint of what I really wanted to see: A second later Freeman obliged. Using his signature gesture as cover, he subtly slid his thumb up and touched it, ever so briefly, to the opening of his ear.

Hannah didn't need the sharp jab to her ribs I gave her. "I saw it, I saw it!" she hissed, as we both continued applauding along with the crowd. "He's got the earpiece in, Jess!"

"Which won't matter at all if we can't screw with it!" I whispered back. I looked out across the theater and found Finn's gaze. He nodded grimly while bringing a finger up to his ear. He hadn't missed it either.

"Well, this is it," I said to Hannah. "I'm giving Iggy ten minutes and then we're moving on to Plan B."

Hannah whimpered, "Come on Iggy! I really don't like Plan B!"

A deafening roar exploded through the theater as the "oracle" himself finally walked out onto the stage, grinning from ear to ear and waving manically to his adoring masses.

"Good evening my friends!" he called in his melodic voice—a voice honed, as I knew from my research, during his three years at an acting school in Los Angeles. "Welcome! I want to welcome all of you to the *Ghost Oracle Live*! Thank you for tuning into the show, and thank you for being here tonight! I know you've all seen what I can do—but what you really want is to experience the miracle for yourselves, am I right?"

More thunderous applause, more shouting and screaming. Still no text from Iggy. My mouth was starting to go dry.

"Milo? What are you doing?" I asked through our connection.

"I'm checking out all these crew members. One of them has got to be the person who's going to feed him the info," Milo answered. "Tons of them are wearing headsets, but it seems like they're talking with each other, not with Freeman."

"Yeah, stagehands have to communicate so they can coordinate the lights and stage effects; Iggy warned us about that. He said if the headsets have cords, we don't have to worry about them—they're on a closed circuit. It won't be what Freeman is using."

"You could've told me that ten minutes ago!" cried Milo. "I wouldn't have wasted all that time!"

"Sorry, sorry, I forgot," I said. "If you don't have any luck there, more crew members are in the tech booth way up in the back of the theater."

Milo sighed dramatically by way of a reply.

Freeman, meanwhile, was still buttering up his crowd. "...the only way I know how, and that's to help people. To help you. That's how the *Ghost Oracle* first began. And that's how we're going to begin right now. But please, I need complete silence while I connect with the spirit world." I wondered if anyone else noticed that Freeman never quite allowed his right ear to face the audience; he always kept his head, or his body, carefully angled away from the crowd.

Freeman may as well have pulled out a remote control and muted the crowd. The silence that fell was absolute. I could feel the tension in the crowd's stillness, as though every person in the room was channeling their hope of being chosen into the intensity of their silence. On stage, Freeman stood with one hand raised up in the air and his other pressed against his temple in his trademark position. His lips were moving as if he were actually talking to visitors unseen.

My phone vibrated loudly in my lap. I glanced down at it and saw a text from Iggy lighting up the screen. *No luck with the frequency. Will keep trying, but time for Plan B.*

I turned to show Hannah, but then Freeman's head shot up and he called out over the crowd.

"I have a message for Jess."

I froze. "He doesn't mean me," I told myself. "He can't mean me. There's probably a dozen other 'Jesses' in this theater right now."

"This message is for Jess... I'm getting a 'B' last name... a 'B'..."

My mouth turned from dry to parched. My palms began to sweat as I thought, "Please, no. This wasn't part of the plan. Please, say any name other than..."

"Ballard! I'm getting Ballard. Is there a Jess Ballard in the audience here tonight?"

Hannah actually screamed, then clapped her hand over her mouth when she realized her mistake. The audience began applauding again as a spotlight followed Hannah's scream and dazzled us with its hot, relentless beam.

"Oh my God," I said. "Oh my God. How?"

"The selfie!" Hannah squeaked. "You posted that selfie online!"

"There she is! That's her right up there! Come on down here, Jess, someone's got a message for you... and we're all going to hear it tonight!" Freeman called, extending his arms out to me as though he expected me to leap into them from the balcony.

I put up a hand to shade my eyes from the blinding spotlight; I waved my other hand in the air, just to acknowledge the crowd. Then I turned to Hannah and pulled her into a hug so I could whisper into her ear, "Plan B! There's no time to wait for Iggy! Plan B!"

I pulled away from her and kissed her on the head, meeting her horrified eyes for just an instant. "You can do it," I told her.

I stumbled out of our box, with my legs shaking like mad, and started descending the narrow staircase leading to the orchestra level. As I did, I tuned into my connection and heard Milo cussing his head off.

"Girl, you have *got* to be kidding me! How many damn selfies were on that Facebook page? How many interviews did they do in that line? And they picked *you*? Sweetness, you'd better start playing the freaking lottery!" he shouted.

"Yeah yeah, there's no time for your sass, Milo!" I thought-spoke to him. "Plan B, go!"

Milo groaned. "Why can't we ever do things the easy way? Okay, so I might be a bit of a drama queen, but this is *not* my thing!"

"Stop whining and get ready! Go to Hannah, she's freaking out already," I replied.

"Shit, okay, I'm on it. Hannah, I'm coming, sweetness," Milo said, and I took a deep calming breath. Hannah would be able to carry out her part in the plan as long as she had Milo with her—hell, this wasn't even nearly the most dangerous thing we'd ever faced. All she needed was Milo at her side, like a spirit security blanket, and Hannah could do anything.

One of Freeman's crew members stood at the bottom of the stairs; he reached out a hand to assist me down the last few steps.

"Congratulations! Very exciting for you. Right this way, please, miss—and do watch your step," the man said, grabbing my arm and forcefully steering me into the aisle.

Faces were grinning at me maniacally from every direction, accompanied by unrestrained applause and shouting. It was nothing short of disturbing to see the fervor of Freeman's audience; some people were actually reaching out as I passed them, as though something magical was going to rub off on them if they touched me. The man escorting me actually had to fend a woman off with his forearm; only then did I realize that he wasn't just here escort me to the stage, he was here for my protection as well.

Instinctively, my eyes searched for Finn up in his seat, but it was empty—meaning that Finn must now be in full Caomhnóir mode. In the next second, a commotion on the floor caught my eye: Finn was in a heated altercation with a security guard stationed by the stage. Finn kept pointing to me, and I could tell that—if he didn't calm down—he was going to be thrown out before we could even get Plan B underway.

"Milo!" I called through our connection. "For *Christ's sake*, pop over to Finn and tell him tone it down before he gets himself kicked out of here! We need him to be able to expel the spirits if things go south!"

"Ugh, that boy!" Milo said. "When's he going to learn?"

I was so focused on Milo and Finn that I hadn't noticed that my escort was now trying to wrangle me up a set of stairs that led onto the stage. Willing myself not to flip out, I refocused on my own situation and put one foot in front of the other.

I talked myself down from my panic. Worst case scenario was that Freeman would deliver a bullshit message from a grandmother who I'd completely made up. All I had to do was nod along and smile, and maybe squeeze out a few tears if I could manage it. No big deal, right?

This was just a minor alteration to Plan B. Either the plan would work, or we'd just have to come up with a new plan and try again another day, at another event. But as I reached the top of the stage stairs and turned to the audience, I felt a surge of fierce emotion I couldn't even identify. All I knew was that our plan was going to work—and it was going to work tonight.

"Jess! Welcome to the stage!" Freeman announced. He strode toward me with his arms extended as if he fully intended to hug me. I took a step back involuntarily, but then planted myself firmly in place. I had to play along.

"Thank you," I said. Almost instantly, a crew member trotted onto the stage and thrust a handheld microphone at me. "Thank you," I said again, taking care to speak into the microphone this time.

"Jess, I know you're here today because—like so many of our audience members—you're hoping to hear from someone who's no longer with us, is that right?" Freeman asked.

"Uh, yeah, that's right," I answered.

Up close, I could see that Freeman was wearing thick pancake makeup. Pearls of sweat were already beading up along his hairline from the heat of the stage lights. A tiny microphone was clipped his lapel. His damn *Nehru* collar mocked me.

"And who have you brought with you today to share in this miraculous experience?" Freeman went on. He was grinning at me in a way that made him look like an insane Cabbage Patch doll.

"My twin sister, Hannah," I said, pointing unnecessarily to the dress circle box. The spotlight found Hannah again, but she didn't wave or smile. She was sitting very still with her eyes closed, and—although no one else in the theater could see him—Milo was right beside her. Anyone in the audience would have thought Hannah was praying, but I knew better. An energy was beginning to stir, a subtle shifting of the air.

My panic gave way to a thrill of excitement. Hannah was Calling. "You want to make contact with spirits, Freeman? Fasten your freaking seatbelt." I thought to myself.

"Now, Jess, I'm going to establish contact, and see just who it is that's trying to get in touch with you," Freeman said, with a rehearsed gentleness in his voice. He had traded his grin for a look of intense concentration.

"Okay," I replied, in a tense voice that played right into Freeman's theatrics.

Freeman put one hand on my shoulder and the other to his temple, and then squeezed his eyes shut. We stood that way for several tense moments of utter silence.

And then it started.

A chill began to creep beneath my skin and into my bones. The stage lights above our heads began to flicker rapidly, as though a surge of electricity was running through them. Gasps rose up in the audience.

Freeman opened his eyes and looked up, clearly startled, but he recovered almost at once. "Either we're having some technical difficulties or someone is very impatient to speak with you," he said with a slightly tense laugh. A few audience chuckles met his words.

He closed his eyes again, "Jess, I'm getting a maternal figure, someone elderly. Did you lose your grandmother in the last few years?"

"Yes," I said, giving Freeman an "aw shucks" smile. "Gee, I was hoping it might be her."

"Well, you were right!" Freeman said as a violent shiver rocked his frame; the coldness from Hannah's Called spirits was starting to penetrate the heat of the stage lights. His smile slipped. "And... uh... did you have a special nickname for your grandmother?"

"Why, yes, I did!" I said, adding what I hoped was a note of astonishment to my voice. "How did you know that?"

"Because she's telling it to me, Jess! Is it... I'm getting an 'M' here..." He closed his eyes again.

All at once, three stage lights blew out with gunfire-like pops. As I looked upward, I saw at least a dozen spirits hovering around the edges of the stage, all staring with a singular intent at Freeman. I chanced a glance at Hannah, whose mouth was now moving rapidly.

Under cover of Freeman's nervous jokes about my grandmother being "a bit of a firecracker," I tuned into the connection. "How's she doing, Milo?"

"She's okay. She's keeping it reigned in, but we both know that's a relative term," he answered. "Forget firecrackers, here come the fireworks, sweetness. Steer clear of the electronics!"

Even as he said it, a deafening feedback squeal blared out of the microphone in my hand; I dropped it in alarm. Freeman's lapel microphone began squealing as well, and he started batting at it like a wasp that had landed on his shirt. As I watched him swatting and swearing at it, three spirits streaked like lightning into the left wing; two more spirits vanished into the tech booth at the back.

"What the hell is going on here?" he blurted out, before quickly recovering himself. "So sorry everyone, the uh... spiritual vibrations are very strong tonight. Jess's grandmother must have quite the story to tell. She's trying to hijack my microphone!" He laughed again, but the sound was forced—and no answering laughs came from the crowd. The sweat from Freeman's brow was starting to trickle down his face, creating streaks in his foundation.

The still image on the screen behind us began to flicker, and then the video of Freeman's entrance began to play in reverse. Freeman tried his best to ignore it.

"While our tech crew gets their act together, let's see if we can't connect to your grandmother, Jess. Now you said you had a special name for her. I'm getting an 'M' now. Is it... Mammie... no, Mamie!"

"Yes, that's right!" I said, pressing my hands to my cheeks in a clichéd gesture of surprise as the audience, now refocused on me, gasped collectively.

Freeman flashed his used-car-salesman smile again, apparently convinced that he'd been able to maneuver his way out of this rocky start to the show. "Your Mamie's here in this room with us now, Jess, and she has a special message just for you! She's say—"

"Turn it off! How do you just turn it off!"

"I don't know! Just unplug it!"

"It *is* unplugged!"

Panicked voices from backstage cut Freeman off. The crew's equipment was going absolutely haywire—and apparently, some of them were now on-mike. Headsets were literally flying off of people's heads. As I watched, an iPad propelled itself out of a stage manager's hands and smashed against the wall. She shrieked and bolted toward the exit, pushing another crew member out of her way as she ran. In the aisles, the camera operators were tugging fruitlessly at every knob, lever, and switch, as the cameras' "now recording" lights blinked on and off. One of the camera lenses even popped out and rolled across the carpet.

The audience, meanwhile, was slipping into hysteria. People

were whipping out their cell phones and taking pictures of the chaos. Others were screaming, some were crying; a few were even fleeing down the aisles toward the exits.

I locked eyes with Freeman. I didn't hide whatever was showing on my face—excitement, glee—fast enough. He leaned into me, careful to keep his grin plastered to his own face. His whispering through that grin made him look utterly deranged.

"What's happening here? Do you have something to do with this?"

I merely shrugged. "You're the ghost expert, Mr. Freeman. You tell me."

But then, even as I watched the havoc, a terrible thought occurred to me: If Hannah's Calling couldn't prove—right here in front of audience—that Freeman was a fraud, this chaos would only further solidify Freeman's association with ghosts. It was a glaring flaw in our plan; how had I missed that?

"Milo, she's got to do more than just scare the shit out of everyone!" I urged through our connection, even as I stared Freeman down.

"My girl's just building the drama," Milo answered. "Wait for it, now."

Freeman tightened his grip on my shoulder and projected his voice out over the commotion. "Stay with me, everyone! Let's stay calm, please! It's merely a bit of spiritual interference! Let's hear what Jess' Mamie has got to say! If we listen to her message, maybe everything will calm down," he cried, with a note of badly repressed hysteria in his voice. He wiped away a trickle of sweat and placed two shaking fingers to his temple again. "Ah, yes! Yes, I can hear Mamie! What's that she's saying?"

"Come on, Hannah!" I thought, almost like a prayer. At that moment, everything stopped. The screen behind us went blank. The lights ceased flickering. Freeman stood there, fingers on his temple, pretending to concentrate. The audience held its breath. All was utter stillness.

Invisible to every eye but mine, a spirit shot down from the theater's ceiling; flying as straight and swift as an arrow, the spirit collided with Freeman's body. Freeman fell to his knees, shrieking in pain as a piercing whistling rent through the air. Freeman clawed in desperation at his right ear until the source of the whistling, a tiny silver earpiece, fell to the stage floor.

The show only got better from there, at least from my perspective. As though someone had scripted it, the tiny earpiece began transmitting a voice; the voice was so loud it seemed as if someone were holding an invisible megaphone next to the earpiece.

"Did you get that, Lionel? She wants Mamie's advice about an internship. An internship far from home. Got that?" The voice echoed through the theater for all to hear.

At that moment, the screen behind us lit up again, but this time it didn't show a video of Freeman. Instead, a screenshot of his Facebook feed was projected for all to see: There, right in the center of the screenshot, was the picture we'd taken before the show... complete with my caption below it.

The audience gasped. Freeman turned and stared with unmitigated horror at my smiling face.

The earpiece betrayed Freeman again. "Her photo has a 'cancer sucks' hashtag, so ask her about a cancer connection." Every word, clear as crystal, reverberated through the space. It was all I could do not to burst out laughing.

As realization spread like a wildfire through the audience, the spirits Hannah had Called flew into formation at the edge of the stage; they floated there with their arms at their sides, awaiting their next instructions like obedient soldiers. From the corner of my eye, I watched as Hannah raised both clenched fists a few inches into the air and, with a deep, cleansing breath, unfurled her fingers.

"That's right, sweetness," I heard Milo's gentle, calming encouragement to Hannah through our connection. "Say thank you, and let them go now. Just let them fly on home."

The spirits drifted up and away from the stage, before vanishing into the shadows above. It would've been an almost-peaceful moment if it weren't for the absolute riot breaking out in the audience.

People were booing and shouting obscenities at Freeman, who had dove to the floor and snatched up the earpiece; he was now trying desperately to muffle the voices still coming from it. Crew members sprinted out from the wings and began pulling Freeman and myself clear of the curtain, which was now rapidly swinging closed.

As we stumbled back, half-caught in the heavy, dusty folds of fabric, I seized my chance. I yanked my arm out of the crew member's grasp and bolted for the stage right wing. No one tried to stop me as I sprinted toward the glowing red exit sign at the end of a long brick hallway.

"What was that? What the hell just happened here?" I could hear Freeman shrieking behind me. "Is my car waiting? Get my fucking car ready, now! I need my lawyers on the phone, get me my goddamn phone, now! And where's that girl? Someone find that girl and get her back here!"

But no one was going to find "that girl." That girl was already jogging down the block to join her frantically waving co-conspirators, and she was laughing the whole way.

6

BUSTED

O SCAR FLUNG OPEN THE BACK DOOR OF THE VAN. I tumbled inside just as the first of the angry ticketholders began streaming out of the theater doors. Oscar slammed the door shut behind me and I lay, panting and laughing, on the van's floor. I looked up; Hannah, Milo, and Finn were all looking down at me. I reached up, grabbed Hannah by her shirt, and pulled her down on top of me into a bear hug.

"You are incredible! My sister is such a badass!" I shouted, kissing her repeatedly all over her head and face.

"Thank you very much, but can you let go of me now!" she giggled.

"You guys should have seen it, she was amazing!" I said to the team. "Freeman is done! He'll never work again! I bet they're on the phone right now, canceling the next season of the *Ghost Oracle!*"

"What happened?" asked Dan. "It was a disaster from out here! We couldn't tap into their frequency at all!" Dan had a nervous habit of running his hands through his hair; it was now standing up like a mad scientist's. "And just when I thought we'd finally found the frequency, every piece of equipment in here went haywire!"

"Yeah, it was pretty damn awesome!" added Iggy.

"The EMF detectors were off the charts, then every single battery drained and died in a matter of seconds!" Oscar said, grinning from ear to ear. His smile revealed a gold tooth and several missing teeth. "The computers, the cameras, the radio scanner, everything just went black. I knew you must've taken matters into your own hands!"

The team was tickled all but pink. Haywire equipment, instantly-draining batteries, and through-the-roof electromagnetic readings were a sure sign that spirits were afoot. And for these three maniacs, otherworldly detection was always cause for celebration.

"Luckily for us, the theater had some resident spirits, so when the show started and we hadn't heard from you, Hannah was able to reach out to them and convince them to do the dirty work for us," I explained. I then gave the team a carefully worded breakdown of the events in the theater. Even though we worked closely with the team, we had to avoid using any Durupinen terms. We also had to make sure to downplay the extent of Hannah's abilities: As far as they knew, she was just a slightly more talented version of Annabelle or myself.

By the time I had finished, Iggy was laughing so hard tears were rolling down into his beard and Oscar was cackling like a mad old crow. Even Hannah was looking pretty pleased with herself. The only person unmoved by the hilarity of it all was Finn. Surprise, surprise.

"Finn, you could crack a smile you know," I said to him. "We won. Victory is ours." Then I looked at him a little more closely. "Wait, are you bleeding?"

"I may have gotten into a slight row with a security guard on my side of the theater," he said, grabbing a handful of shirt and touching it to his eyebrow, which was thick with congealed blood.

"Yeah, I think I caught a glimpse of that. Why, exactly?"

"I wasn't comfortable with you on stage alone without protection, especially once the spirits started interfering. You weren't supposed to be on stage at all! That wasn't part of the plan," Finn said, a bit defensively.

I managed a great feat of self-restraint and refrained from rolling my eyes at him. "I know. I wasn't thrilled either. But it all turned out fine, so I—"

"Look, Freeman is leaving the theater!" Iggy shouted, and we all scrambled to the nearest window to watch as Freeman's limo rolled up to the stage door, where a crowd of angry audience members had congregated. A dozen security guards formed a human wall to protect Freeman from the hostile crowd, but, even so, many patrons hurled their programs and T-shirts at him while shouting things like, "Fraud!" and "I want my money back!" and "Shame on you!" The crowning moment, at least for me, was when Gail, immediately identifiable in her bright blue homemade *Ghost Oracle* T-shirt, pulled a bottle from her purse and chucked it at Freeman. The bottle hit Freeman on the head, covering him in what looked like a chocolate diet shake. It was the perfect indignity for a man who had stripped so much from others for his own personal gain.

§

Iggy had offered to drive home with us instead of in the van since Hannah still hadn't worked up the courage to take her driver's test, but I'd refused his offer. I knew I wouldn't fall asleep at the wheel after a victory like that. Plus, there was no danger of my getting even the slightest bit drowsy with Finn in the backseat watching me like a hawk.

I wiled away the hours on the drive home by talking through every detail of the evening and reliving every triumphant moment, until Finn disappeared behind one of his little black books and Hannah dozed off. My sister was so wiped out from Calling that she had fallen asleep mid-sentence while trying to respond to me. Even Milo, tired of my chatter, blinked out in order to conserve his energy.

When we finally pulled up to the house almost four and a half hours later, I still hadn't calmed down. I found myself hoping our resident spirit would make a fresh attempt at scaring us off—I could've gladly gone ten rounds with her in that moment. I killed the engine and leaned across the seat to nudge Hannah awake. Finn, ever on high alert even in the most mundane moments, had jumped from the car before I'd finished parking and was already waiting impatiently by the door. Christ, was he going to make us some warm milk and tuck us in before he considered his duty done and went home?

Hannah, disorientated, blinked confusedly as she awoke. "Wow, are we back already? Did you drive the whole way without stopping?"

"Not quite," I said, flinging off my seatbelt and bouncing out of my seat. "I stopped to pee and get a slushie in Connecticut, but you slept right through it."

Hannah yawned and rolled awkwardly out of the car, landing heavily on her right foot, which seemed to have fallen asleep as deeply as she had. "What time is it?" she asked as she straightened herself up.

"About 12:30 AM," I said.

"I feel so bad that you're still up!" she replied.

"Don't sweat it," I told her. "I know how much Calling drains you. It's not like you could've driven anyway."

"I know, but I could've at least kept you company. How do you feel?"

"How do you think I feel? I'm on a high!" I had my keys in my hand and intended to unlock the door, but Finn—who'd mysteriously procured his own set of keys—had grown tired of waiting; I reached the door just as he flung it open. I pushed past him and marched up the stairs, with Hannah limping along behind me on her still-tingling foot. Finn brought up the rear, stomping unnecessarily loudly.

"An asshole like that crippled in front of hundreds! And we're the ones who made it happen? As soon as I regain the feeling in my ass after all that driving, I'm going to break into my happy dance!" I was practically singing as we climbed the stairs.

I froze when I entered the living room. Two men stood in front of the fireplace with their hulking, muscular arms folded across their chests. I'd never seen one of the men before; the other was, most unfortunately, familiar.

"I'd hold off on the dancing if I were you," Finn said quietly.

"Hello Seamus," I said, trying to sound calm and unconcerned. "Long time no see."

Seamus barely looked at me except to nod in my direction. His words were for Finn; a Caomhnóir wouldn't deign to speak to a Durupinen if he could avoid it, even if he had just broken into her home.

"Apologies for the intrusion, Caomhnóir Carey. We don't mean to overstep into your territory, but we have been ordered here by the High Priestess of the Northern Clans."

Finn merely nodded; his lips formed the very thinnest of thin lines as he pressed them together against whatever tirade he was withholding.

"No need to apologize to Finn, Seamus. It's not his apartment you've broken into. But hey, don't worry about us—the ones who actually *live here*," I said loudly. "But enough with the pleasantries. To what do we owe this totally unwelcome pleasure?"

Seamus turned reluctant eyes on me, as though it were an inconvenience to have to adjust the angle of his neck in order to address me directly. Swimming deep in the dark of his eyes was the same suspicion and disdain that had plagued so many Durupinen-

Caomhnóir relationships. "You've been summoned to Fairhaven Hall to stand before the Council of the Northern Clans," he said bluntly.

Hannah and I looked at each other. "Me?" we said simultaneously.

"Both of you," Seamus clarified.

"We've been *summoned*?" I asked, trying not to let my fear override my indignation.

"As I've just said, yes."

"What gives anyone the right to summon us anywhere?" I asked.

"The High Priestess and the Council have every right to summon you," Seamus began. "They are responsible for all members of the Northern Clans, and you are answerable to their laws and dictates. You are required to attend a disciplinary hearing."

I exchanged a startled look, first with Hannah and then with Finn. "What the hell for?" I asked. "We haven't done anything wrong."

Even as I said it, I racked my brains. *Had* we done something wrong? Had we broken some rule or messed up a Crossing? We'd just seen Karen yesterday; she was still serving as our mentor, guiding us through the early stages of being our clan's Gateway. As far as I could tell, she seemed to think we were doing just fine.

"That's for the Council to decide," Seamus said, interrupting my silent, panicked assessment. "We have merely been instructed to escort you."

His companion swaggered purposefully forward. Instantly, Finn was in front of us; he assumed a combative stance as he pushed both me and Hannah backward protectively.

"We're not going anywhere until you tell me what the hell this is about!" I practically shouted my words, but before I could say anything else Finn held his hand in front of my face to silence me. It was such a condescending gesture that I actually had to repress an impulse to bite his finger.

"Seamus, this is highly irregular. What is this disciplinary hearing for?" Finn asked, struggling to maintain a respectful tone toward Seamus, who was, after all, one of his former teachers. I knew that wouldn't prevent Finn from beating the hell out of him, though, if it came right down to it.

"I've not been authorized to reveal that information," Seamus said curtly.

I opened my mouth to argue, but Finn beat me to it. "Oh, come on, Seamus. Put yourself in my shoes. Would you allow Celeste or Catherine to walk blindly into a situation of this sort? I need a good bit more than that if you want my cooperation."

Seamus considered this; a muscle twitched in his jaw as he looked from Finn, to me, to Hannah, and then back at Finn again. "Very well, but I'm only showing this to you because it's public," he said, backing off and pulling a cell phone out of his back pocket. "Any of you could've stumbled across this on the Internet. If anyone asks, that's where you saw it, without any prompting from me. Understood?"

"Understood. Thank you," Finn replied.

My heart began to hammer as I waited for Seamus to find whatever it was he was going to show us. He stared at the screen for a moment, evidently waiting for the site to load, then turned the phone so that the screen faced us. We all crowded in to watch.

He'd pulled up a YouTube video. Despite the timestamp indicating that the video had been uploaded less than four hours ago, it already had thousands of hits and hundreds of comments and shares. I squinted against the bright light of the screen. The title of the video was "TV Psychic Unmasked as Fraud... BY GHOSTS!"

The camera, most likely a cell phone, was panning shakily across a sea of upturned faces. Onstage was Lionel Freeman, accompanied by a young woman holding a microphone who looked all too familiar.

"Shit," I muttered.

Some asshole, giving not a damn about the rules against recording in theaters, had begun filming me the moment I walked on the stage, and had recorded—with increasingly loud and frantic breathing—our entire take down of Freeman. To my horror, he had even panned up to the dress circle box and recorded Hannah Calling; I watched the footage as Hannah, with her eyes closed, muttered to herself and twitched her hands as if she were the puppet master of the chaos below—which, I suppose, she was.

"Did you see that?" came the excited voice from behind the camera. "Did you see it? That girl up there in the box is controlling it! It's the sister, right? Didn't she say that was her sister? It's the two of them!"

The man started toward the edge of the stage, but tripped or stumbled as he fought across a row of seats. He dropped the phone to the ground and the video cut out.

We stared at the screen for a few more moments. The video had now gone dark, but the page stats told us that the number of views had jumped up by nearly fifty while the video had been playing.

"This has gone viral in the last few hours," said Seamus. "Or rather, it has the potential to go viral if we don't stop it. We're already treating it as a matter of clan security. The Trackers will have it down within the hour, I don't doubt."

"This happened only a few hours ago," I said. "You live in England. How the hell did you get here so fast?"

"We were in the States already," Seamus said, looking at Finn again. Finn's face flushed, as he clenched his fists at his side. "And so the Council requested that we take charge of the situation. It's quite fortunate that we were already in New England, because the damage has been extensive—even in this very short amount of time."

"Fine, I admit that wasn't the smartest thing we've ever done," I said flatly. "But if the Trackers are going to take it off the Internet, what's the big deal? The media has the attention span of a goldfish. By tomorrow, everyone will be freaking out about some cat meme. Our video will already be ancient history."

"That's hardly the point," Seamus said gruffly, slipping his phone back into his pocket. "You've ripped back the curtain and shone a spotlight on our inner workings, workings that must remain secret. The Council no longer trusts your judgment in matters of security. They require your presence at a disciplinary hearing. You will attend."

"What if we just... promise not to do it again?" I asked weakly.

Seamus shook his head. "Not good enough. A face-to-face meeting is required. This is not a request."

I looked at Finn for assistance, but he didn't meet my eye. Instead, he continued to glower at Seamus, almost as though he knew there was no argument to be made.

Hannah piped up at last, her voice small but fierce. "We can't just pick up and leave without notice. We have jobs. I'm in the middle of a semester! Jess has a great job at the museum! The Durupinen aren't allowed to recklessly jeopardize our educations and careers—it's part of the agreement we made when we left Fairhaven."

"Nor are you allowed to recklessly jeopardize our code of secrecy," Seamus countered. "Nonetheless, the High Council has put nothing at risk for you. All of the necessary arrangements have been made with your professors and at your places of employment."

I groaned as I thought of my boss at the Juniper Breeze Café, where I was still working part-time. My boss would've expected an employee to work her shift even if she'd come down with the bubonic plague; I didn't see how I could be anything but fired for taking unscheduled time off. I knew the Peabody Essex Museum would be a little more forgiving, but not by much.

"How long are we going to be gone?" I asked.

"Until matters are settled to the satisfaction of the High Priestess," Seamus replied.

"And what about the hours we're going to miss while we're gone? How are we supposed to make our rent if we aren't getting paid?" I shot back.

"You will be compensated at twice your hourly rate," Seamus said.

I blinked. "Right, well... that's... okay, then."

Seamus evidently took this to mean we had now agreed to come, because he nodded curtly and marched toward the door.

"Wait a second! We can't just leave right now! We need to..." I stared around wildly, trying to find the most persuasive reason for staying. My gaze fell on a single picture still upside-down on the fireplace mantle. "We have to Ward the apartment! Our roommate will be back in the morning and we have a hostile spirit here!"

"You *had* a hostile spirit here," Seamus corrected me. "She was in the apartment when we arrived. We have expelled her and Warded the premises. We also took the liberty of tidying up her mess. Your roommate is quite free to return."

I swallowed back my panic. "We have to pack."

"Everything you will require has already been prepared for you," Seamus said, gesturing to a pair of small black suitcases sitting beside the entryway door. I had never seen them before.

"You went through our things?" I growled through clenched teeth.

"Clothing, passports, shoes, toiletries, and Casting bags," Seamus went on as though I hadn't spoken. He looked not the least bit abashed. I shouldn't have been surprised. He'd already broken into our apartment and basically announced we were being kidnapped. What did he care about rifling through a few drawers?

I stood rooted to the spot a moment more, casting desperately around for another reason to stay, but I couldn't find one. I could only think of my own near-crippling outrage at being treated this way. I looked at Finn, who grimaced but cocked his head toward the door.

"We haven't a choice," he said quietly.

Hannah took my hand and I felt Milo pop into the mental space between us.

"What do my girls want me to do?" he asked. Milo's energy was tense, pulled taut like a bow.

"Just come along, I guess," Hannah's voice joined in. "I don't think there's anything else to be done just yet."

Together, we followed Seamus out the door and down the stairs. A sleek black Lexus sat waiting for us across the street; I was certain the car hadn't been there when we'd arrived home—there's no way Finn would've missed it.

"We need to call Karen. She's going to lose her shit when she finds out about this!" I said to Hannah as the car door slammed shut behind us.

"Good idea. I bet she'll be on the next plane. Let's call her now." Hannah's voice was shaking.

I pulled out my phone and, seeing Seamus glaring at me in the rearview mirror, I said, "I suppose we're allowed a phone call? Aren't all prisoners allowed one phone call?"

He narrowed his eyes at me. "The High Priestess has not expressly forbidden it, so yes, I suppose you are."

I kept my eyes on the phone's screen. I couldn't bear to look at Hannah, who had harbored so many doubts about publically going after Freeman—doubts that I had talked her out of again and again. Yet as hard as it was to look at Hannah, looking at Finn was worse—he had tried to talk us out of the plan less than twenty-four hours ago, for this very reason. The acrid scent of "I told you so!" was pungent in the air, but I refused to acknowledge it.

The car screeched away from our house, whisking us once again out of our own lives and into the sticky snare of the Durupinen web.

How foolish of us to think we'd escaped it.

7

RETURN TO FAIRHAVEN HALL

WHEN IT CAME TO TRAVEL, THE CONVENIENCE of the Durupinen network was a blessing, and I appreciated this one and only perk. Thanks to the speed of a Durupinen private jet, and a mysterious power to avoid things like security lines and customs officers, it was a mere matter of hours before a Caomhnóir drove us through a pair of familiar wrought iron gates. Before I even had a chance to fully process what it would feel like to be back at Fairhaven Hall, I was staring up at the hulking, foreboding outline of the castle, and shivering in the chill of its shadow—a shadow which now seemed to be pressing upon me with an actual physical force. Fairhaven was beautiful and ancient and practically tingling with teeming spirit energy, but damn it, I had never wanted to come back here again.

Why, *why* was I back here again?

Hannah took my hand and squeezed it, as though she could hear exactly what I was thinking. I leaned into the reassuring warmth of her beside me. Our joined hands buzzed with the intensity of our Gateway connection, a feeling I had come to associate with comfort rather than fear.

"It's way too early for this," Milo announced, as if he were still on a human-body schedule. "I bet they won't even offer you some coffee, Jess. Charlatans!"

As anxious as I was, I chuckled, and found myself wondering if Milo actually missed caffeine.

Hannah leaned over and snapped me back into the moment. "Ready?" she murmured.

I laughed, although there was nothing particularly funny about the situation. "Not even remotely. But let's get this over with." Now that Milo had mentioned it, I *did* really want a cup of coffee.

The entrance hall of Fairhaven looked just as I remembered it from my first arrival nearly five years ago, but the events that had soon followed haunted the hall as surely as the many spirits that roamed the grounds. I could no longer appreciate the beautiful woodwork, the grand marble staircase, the gothic arches curving gracefully toward the ceiling, or the magnificent chandelier as I once had. All I could see now were the horrific details of my sprawling Prophecy mural, which I had sketched—while in a Psychic Trance—in ash across the walls with ravaged, burned fingertips. Every trace of my mural had long since been scrubbed from the entrance hall, but never again would I be able to see this room without also seeing my mural. I knew Hannah felt it too.

Finn had followed us into the castle, but he had taken up guard just past the doorway. What he was on guard against, I wasn't sure—did he think the Elemental was going to rush the castle doors again?

Three figures stood at the far end of the vast entrance hall, on the grand staircase; their hands were folded in front of them as they silently awaited our arrival. Although we walked steadily toward them, it seemed to take an unnaturally long time for us to reach them, like a creepy optical illusion. As our echoing footsteps drew us closer, two of the faces became immediately familiar as two of the women stepped down to greet us.

"Welcome back!" Celeste cried.

I let the irony of her greeting pass as Celeste enfolded me in a hug that ought to have been unfamiliar, but instead felt unexpectedly comforting. She stepped back from me, then clasped her hand warmly on Hannah's shoulder, giving it a quick squeeze—Celeste knew Hannah well enough to forgo any hugging.

"And Milo!" Celeste cried. "Still keeping an eye on these two?"

Celeste had said it warmly enough, but Milo turned somber nonetheless. "Of course!" he replied. "I didn't take that Spirit Guide oath lightly."

Perhaps determined to keep the moment light, Celeste ignored Milo's angst; she turned back to us and looked me over with a satisfied smile. "You look well! Karen's been keeping me up to date on all of your news, of course. You've both done so well for yourselves—the Peabody Essex is quite the respected institution, Jess. And from what I gather, Hannah, your graduate program is keeping you on the hop."

"Thank you," we both replied simultaneously. Neither of us really knew what else to say—our lives were now so far removed from Fairhaven.

"And about your aunt, tell me, how is she?" asked Celeste, ever cheery.

"She's pissed, actually." I replied, "She texted me just before we pulled up. She couldn't get a direct flight, but she is on her way—she's changing planes now. We're under strict orders not to go into that Council Room without her here to back us up."

Celeste sighed. "Yes, I thought she might come. I'll be glad to see her, even if the circumstances are less than ideal. And how have the two of you been keeping?"

"We're just peachy," I said. "At least, we were, until we got hauled across the ocean to the principal's office."

"That's right," said Hannah in her quiet—but nonetheless formidable—tone. "But now, I'll miss classes."

Celeste's smile faltered, but she hoisted it back into place almost at once. "Don't worry. It will all be just fine."

I raised my eyebrows. "Really? Because I have to be honest with you, none of this has felt very 'fine' so far. Shouldn't we be worried?"

"I wouldn't be too worried, no," said Celeste. "A lot of this is pomp and circumstance. Sometimes the Council likes to exert its authority purely to prove that it can. It helps keep people in line." She pursed her lips together in a thin line that left us with no doubt of what she thought of such shows of power.

Milo buzzed into our heads through our connection. "Geez! Whatever happened to 'forgive and forget?'" he asked theatrically. I felt Hannah repress a small smile.

"Yeah, they're just flexing their muscles. But they haven't forgotten how you once brought us all to the brink of destruction and then saved us from it," said Fiona, who stepped down and extended a hand, which I shook. It was rough, callused, and splattered with white, chalky plaster. When I touched her hand I felt her familiar energy coursing through it, a strange mélange of art and death. Surely no one else's hand could feel like that.

"It's good to see you, Fiona," I said, and I meant it.

"Glad you aren't burning the fecking place to the ground this time," she replied, with just enough of a smile to allow Hannah to look her in the eye.

"We just got here," I said pleasantly. "Give a girl a chance. I'm surprised to see you waiting here. How did they tempt you down from your tower?"

"I didn't have any choice, much like the two of you," she grumbled. "If the Council is called, all members must come running—all else be damned. They couldn't give a good goddamn about what I was working on up there!"

"Are you working on anything good?" I asked innocently.

Fiona's face went scarlet in reply. I'd almost forgotten how easy it was to work her into an absolute tizzy.

"Might ask you the same thing," she growled. "I don't suppose you brought anything for me to look at while you're here?" she asked, crossing her arms. "I'm not much of a mentor if I can't see your work in person the one time we're on the same continent."

I'd been mailing my artwork to Fiona for the last three years, on an almost-weekly basis. I'd spent a small fortune on postage, but she'd practically had an aneurysm when I suggested scanning and emailing, so I'd just sucked it up. Half the time, Fiona would refuse to send my work back to me, claiming that it wasn't worth the cardboard mailer it came in. I never saw these sketches again; from the way she talked, I assumed she recycled them as toilet paper. But other times, I'd receive my drawings back in the mail and they'd be covered in crowded, nearly illegible Post-it Notes; her comments always contained the most insightful, illuminating advice I could ever hope to receive from a fellow artist. Sometimes the notes were harsh, sometimes they were constructive, but, above all, they were always utterly true. Once I'd learned to stop getting offended—which wasn't easy at first—I'd learned more from Fiona than anyone else. I just had to keep reminding myself that if Fiona didn't think I had promise—real talent—she wouldn't have wasted her time. And, as a correspondence student, she couldn't fall back on her old standby technique of throwing furniture at my head when she didn't like something.

"Seamus didn't exactly give us a chance to leisurely pack for the trip," I said, and both Fiona and Celeste grimaced knowingly. "But luckily I brought my sketchbook with me yesterday to kill time on the ride to New York—it's still in my bag. Don't worry, I've got plenty for you to criticize."

A throat-clearing cough drew my eyes up to the staircase. The third figure had stayed firmly planted on the landing during this friendly exchange of greetings. She now had her arms crossed so tightly that they appeared to be knotted, and a strained expression filled her face. It was a sharp contrast to the first time I'd seen Catriona, when she'd been lounging casually in my darkened bedroom as though she'd owned the place, utterly unconcerned about the havoc her presence was about to wreak upon my life. Little did she know then how much havoc I would soon wreak in her life—although I could not, and would never, blame myself for it.

Catriona was almost as tightly tied to her cousin Lucida as I was to Hannah; like us, they were bonded together for life as the two halves of the same Gateway. But that bond was torn asunder when Lucida turned traitor and joined the Necromancers. Now Lucida was rotting away in some Durupinen prison, stripped of her birthright—and rightly so, after everything she put us all through. But Catriona was the fallout, the forgotten casualty of Lucida's crimes. As long as Lucida was locked away, Catriona was cut off from her own calling, unable to help spirits to Cross without her other half.

"Catriona," I said uneasily, nodding to her.

"Jessica," she acknowledged me with a curt nod. Her eyes blazed as she looked at me; standing in the reflected heat of that gaze I knew that she blamed me for all of it—from Lucida's imprisonment, to the hollow emptiness deep in her eyes. Why the hell was she waiting out here? Surely she didn't want to be a part of our welcoming committee.

I turned back to Celeste and Fiona, finding it much easier to look at them than to subject myself to Catriona's glare. "So what are we facing here? Have they already sentenced us without a trial?"

Celeste smiled, but it was a halfhearted little thing. "I know what it must feel like, and I don't blame you for being upset, but you're not being sentenced and you're not on trial."

I snorted. Catriona had now trained her smoldering, wordless gaze on Hannah; I stepped between the two of them—casually, I hoped—before Catriona could say a word to her. I felt Milo's approval through our connection; I couldn't tell if Hannah felt it too, but I hoped not.

"What would you call it, then? We're not stupid, Celeste. We realize we screwed up. Please, can you just give us a better idea of what to expect when we walk through those doors?"

Celeste heaved a sigh and dropped the nostalgic-teacher routine just a bit. "The whole Council will be in there. They've already met to discuss the issue, but the response was... mixed."

"Meaning some of them actually want to cut us some slack?" I asked hopefully.

"Meaning some of them are still terrified you'll open a portal to hell and drag them all through it if they mess with you," Fiona said. "Anyone else who pulled a stunt like this would've been met with swift, decisive action, but with you two they're dragging their feet."

Hannah and I looked at each other, eyebrows raised. "This qualifies as dragging their feet?" I asked incredulously. "That video was barely a few hours old when Seamus and his henchman pounced."

"Well, the truth is, your activities with the paranormal team have been on their radar for a while now," Celeste said.

My shock was fleeting, and replaced immediately by a certainty that was as heavy and uncomfortable as a stone dropped into my stomach. Of course the Council knew what we were doing; they had the most highly skilled Trackers in the world. Naturally, I knew they kept tabs on all Northern Durupinen, but perhaps it was foolish of me not to expect them to put a priority on those who were considered rebellious—and we might as well have had *rebel* tattooed across each of our foreheads.

"If anyone but the two of you had taken up that sort of work, the Council would've put a stop to it immediately," Fiona said. "But, to be frank, half of them are bloody terrified of you. Well, really, just of you," she added, cocking her head at Hannah. Hannah turned bright red; her pallor changed so fast that Fiona might have pulled a can of red paint from her overalls and doused Hannah in it. "They'll never admit it, but they've given the two of you much more breathing room than they've ever given any fledgling Durupinen before, and that's the truth."

Knowing Fiona's penchant for overdramatizing, I turned to Celeste for confirmation. She nodded her head grimly.

"It's quite true," she said, almost as though she were apologizing. "If any other Apprentices had walked out of these halls without finishing their training... Well, they wouldn't have done, let's just leave it at that. Allowing Karen to oversee the remainder of your training was an unprecedented accommodation. If I hadn't been part of the voting, I would never have believed it."

"And how did you vote?" I asked her, little expecting her to actually tell me.

"I thought you should have the chance to go home. You'd been through enough here."

I turned to Fiona. "And you?"

"You think I like waiting for your work to arrive in the mail?" Fiona asked, picking at the hardened plaster beneath her fingernails. "This arrangement is shite. I said they should make you stick it out here like everyone else. Not that anyone listened to me. Like I said, they're terrified."

"Anyway, the point is," Celeste began, throwing a sharp look at Fiona, who merely grinned in reply, "they've let things go a good bit longer than they typically would. But they couldn't ignore it any longer, not with that video splashed all over the Internet."

"You couldn't just take the video down?" Hannah asked.

"We did," Celeste said. "But there's no point if we don't do anything to properly ensure there won't be another."

A strapping young Caomhnóir I'd never seen before appeared near the base of the stairs. "They are ready for you," he said firmly; without even waiting for a reply, he turned and marched toward the Council Room doors, confident in his assumption that we would follow without hesitation.

"Does it matter whether *you're* ready for *them*?" Milo muttered aloud, with a true hint of protectiveness in his voice. I reached back and grabbed Hannah—she was frozen like a deer in headlights, incapable of propelling herself forward.

"Karen said to wait for her to get here," Hannah whispered, as we followed the nameless Caomhnóir.

"Yes, well, it doesn't look like we're being given that choice," I said. "That's their mistake, though. They're the ones bringing the wrath of Karen down upon themselves. I wouldn't want to be on the receiving end of that firestorm."

"But we need her. We're going to be in so much trouble, Jess!"

"Deep breaths sweetness, deep breaths. You heard Celeste—this is all for show," Milo cooed, as the first hints of nervous tears began glistening in Hannah's eyes.

"Don't worry, Hannah," I said robustly, clapping her on the shoulder. "It's just a little bit of trouble. Everyone gets into trouble once in a while. It's healthy. You don't want to be one of those people who leads a boring, trouble-free life, do you?"

"Yes! I want to be the most boring person I know!" she hissed. "I don't like trouble, but sometimes... I don't know, Jess. Sometimes I think you do."

We looked at each other. Her eyes bore into mine, and I dropped the bravado.

"I know. Sometimes I think I do too."

8

CONSEQUENCES

THE GRAND COUNCIL ROOM HAD BEEN FULLY REBUILT in the time that we'd been away from it. The restoration was very, very good: If we hadn't been the reason that the Council Room had nearly burned to the ground, I would never have doubted that I was looking at anything but the original stonework, tapestries, and stained glass. The morning sunlight streamed through the stained glass windows, throwing a patchwork quilt of jewel-toned colors across the floor.

The Council, enthroned on their benches, rose intimidatingly before us like a choir about to sing a dirge of our doom in a minor key. My feet suddenly seemed to be made of lead, although, feigning bravery, I willfully held my head high as I shuffled myself forward. I had no desire to catch the eye of any of the Council members until I absolutely had to; I cast my gaze into the far corner of the room. There, my eyes locked with those of my father, Carrick.

I defy anyone to say they have a more complicated relationship with their father than Hannah and I had with ours. In the first place, Carrick had had a forbidden, illicit relationship with our mother shortly after she completed her training at Fairhaven. At that time, Carrick was Caomhnóir to the High Priestess, as well as my mother's former teacher. Since he had held a position of power, their relationship, I felt, was inherently unequal. Then Carrick had abandoned my mother at an incredibly vulnerable moment, following the death of my grandfather. When my mother had discovered she was pregnant, she went into hiding: Carrick knew of my existence but had never managed to find me, and my mother had hidden Hannah so well that Carrick never knew she'd been born.

Some eighteen years later, when Hannah and I had arrived at Fairhaven as Apprentices, Carrick had chosen not to reveal his relationship to us until months after we'd met—and even then he'd only done so in a moment of extreme duress. Nevertheless, Carrick had been kind to us in those intervening months; he'd kept watch over us from afar, and had even saved our lives at least twice. And, as if all this weren't complicated enough, there was one more minor detail: Carrick was a spirit, having been killed in a car crash while my mother was still pregnant—he'd died before we were born.

As I stared into Carrick's eyes, or rather, into the spirit-incarnation of his eyes—I'd never actually seen in his living face—I didn't know what to feel besides a strange, almost hollow longing. I couldn't exactly tell what the longing was for: Did I want to run to him? Scream at him? Have a deep and meaningful talk with him? Punch him good and hard in the face? I couldn't be sure; maybe I wanted all of them. Or maybe the hollowness had nothing to do with my feelings toward Carrick as he was now, and everything to do with the fact that I'd never be able to do any of those things with my living, breathing father.

Carrick nodded to me, attempting to reassure me. I nodded back. There was little reassurance to be had at that moment, and he was hardly the place I'd go to look for it, but I appreciated the gesture, I think. He tried to catch Hannah's eye as well, but she was so anxious and focused on the Council that she wouldn't so much as look in his direction.

Beside him, Finvarra, the High Priestess of the Northern Clans, rose from her throne-like chair. As she stood, all thought of my father was wiped away by my shock.

Finvarra, once so luminous and beautiful, looked pale, drawn, even haggard. Although I'd known she was around seventy years old, I would never have used the word *old* to describe her until this moment. Her neck looked almost too thin to support her head, which wobbled ever so slightly as she stepped forward. Her eyes were sunken and their fierce sparkle had dulled; her silver hair, once so lustrous and full, hung like a lank, dry shroud down her back. The arm she raised to summon us forward was skeletally thin.

Beside me, I heard Hannah gasp quietly. "What's wrong with her?" she murmured, as we continued our long trek toward the benches. "Did you know something was wrong with her?"

"No," I whispered back. "I have no idea. She looks really sick. Did you hear she was sick?" I asked Finn, who marched in lockstep on my other side.

Finn shook his head, and although he was trying to maintain his stoic exterior, I could see that concern for Finvarra had crept into his eyes.

I, too, tried to keep my poker face in place. This wasn't the moment for me to focus on Finvarra's health; I had enough to worry about.

We came to a halt about ten feet before the benches, on the floor's large Triskele inlay. As though they had been waiting for us to make contact with that very spot, spirits began drifting casually in through the walls, like a crowd drawn to a public spectacle. Their faces—at least of those I could see—were staring at us hungrily, completely transfixed. The faces of the Council, however, were growing confused, even frightened. It seemed the spirits, whoever they were, had been neither invited nor expected. Bertie, the Council Reporter and Savvy's former Caomhnóir, began typing frantically on his steno machine.

"Easy, sweetness," Milo muttered, leaning into Hannah with a familiar, calming tone. Hannah took a deep breath and released it, and with that, many of the spirits started to look around as though surprised at their surroundings. Several faded out of view; others remained, but hovered on the outskirts of the room, unsure of what to do.

"Sorry," she whispered, with her voice shaking. "I didn't even realize I was doing it."

I realized that Hannah, in the midst of her fear, had unwittingly Called the spirits to her. As a child constantly experiencing Visitations—and throughout her years of doctors and social workers assuming her to be mentally ill—Hannah had learned to transform her gift into a coping mechanism; she'd use the spirits to comfort her when no one else could or would. And now, without even realizing it, she had reverted back—Calling was her SOS.

I could certainly understand the skittishness of the Council members as they kept a wary eye both on Hannah and the newly materialized spirits; the last time she'd Called spirits into this room, everyone at Fairhaven had nearly been killed. It hadn't been Hannah's fault—she'd given the Council the chance to let us go peacefully. When they'd refused, Hannah had Called the spirits; an unintended fire ensued.

Finvarra flashed a warning look at Hannah, who blushed and mouthed, "Sorry," before gesturing to the remaining spirits, encouraging them to leave. Then Finvarra raised her arms even higher than before; the whispering rows of Council members muttered themselves into silence and resumed their judgmental air.

Finvarra cleared her throat and spoke. "Welcome back to Fairhaven, Clan Sassanaigh. I trust your journey was pleasant. Thank you for coming." Her voice, for all its commanding tone, betrayed a tiny but audible tremor that had surely not been present the last time we'd spoken. Nonetheless, her words brought my anger and indignation flooding back. Pleasant journey? She was kidding, right?

"You didn't really give us much of a choice, did you, High Priestess?" I asked, trying to keep as much of that anger and indignation out of my tone as possible. I don't think I managed it very well, because Hannah nudged me lightly with her elbow. The meaning of the gesture was as clear as if she'd shouted in my ear: "Calm down Jess. Don't blow this before the conversation has even started."

"It was you, Jessica, who didn't give us much choice," Finvarra said. "As you seem to have no patience for pleasantries, shall we get right down to business?"

"Absolutely. I've never been one for small talk," I said a bit stiffly.

"I will cut right to the chase then, Jessica. You both made it quite clear when we last said good-bye," Finvarra began, "that you had no desire to come back here. Given your great service to this order, we have done our level best to honor that wish. We have provided accommodations rarely granted to any other Apprentices throughout history. We have offered the space you required, far from these halls. I little thought you would squander that opportunity by endangering our secrecy. I assume you know why you're here?"

"Yes," I said curtly.

"Do you remember the oath you made, to do all within your power to protect our secrets and preserve the sanctity of the Gateways?"

"Yes," I said again, getting even more agitated. I hated answering to anyone in general, but stupid questions *really* weren't my thing.

"I wonder then, how you could have chosen to do something so foolish."

I waited, but Finvarra didn't continue. "Was there a question in there that we're supposed to answer?" I asked.

Rather than infuriating Finvarra, my attitude evidently exhausted her. She sighed in a resigned sort of way and sank back into her seat, waving a weary hand in Siobhán's direction as though to say, "You deal with this."

Milo used the pause to whisper to me "Rein it in Jess. Rein it in." I suppose he had a point; the last time we stood in judgment before the Council we *were* almost thrown into the dungeons.

Rising to her feet and clearing her throat importantly, Siobhán said, "Yes, there are several questions we would like you to answer. To begin with, what were you thinking—going after someone so high-profile? In front of all of those people? With cameras everywhere?"

"I was thinking that Freeman makes all of his money by scamming grieving people, and that he's a pretty big asshole," I said, with my anger starting to burn through some of the intimidation. "Do you know how much he's worth?"

Siobhán glanced at the others on her bench. They all looked bewildered by the question. Hannah tensed up even further—if that was possible—and Milo gasped audibly.

"I can't see how the man's wealth has any bearing here," Siobhán replied, sounding a bit flustered.

"Well then maybe you should've done a little more research. We certainly did ours. Between his television show and his touring gigs, Freeman's worth over twelve million dollars. And he made every penny of that preying on people who were desperate to talk to the dead!"

"We are well aware of what he does," Finvarra said, chiming in from her throne.

"Oh, I see. And you're cool with that?"

"I do not concern myself with it, if that's what you're inferring with the word *cool*," Finvarra said impatiently. And indeed, the only cool thing about her was her tone, which was growing icier by the minute.

"Oh, I see. So we should devote our entire lives to helping the spirits to Cross, but not spare a single thought for the people they leave behind? That makes sense," I shot back.

"The people they leave behind," Finvarra replied, as a few people shifted uncomfortably in their seats, "have many others who can help them. They have families and friends and counselors. They have therapists and doctors and many others who can help them to move on. Being left behind is part of the human experience—we have been dealing with it since the dawn of time. The spirits only have us. They are our primary responsibility."

"Okay, I get that," I said, trying to be reasonable. "And we haven't shirked that responsibility. We perform lunar cycle Crossings monthly, and we've dropped everything, many times, to help a spirit Cross. Hannah walked out of a final at St. Matt's to help a spirit who just couldn't wait another minute. She nearly failed the class!"

I looked at Hannah for support. She nodded solemnly, but was still unable to find her voice in front of the Council. She looked even smaller than usual, collapsing in on herself as if she were trying to will herself into vanishing.

I reached over and squeezed her hand quickly before continuing. "We've kept our word, and committed ourselves to our Gateway—but that doesn't mean we have to stand by and watch people being exploited. Because you're right: People have been grieving for as long as we've existed. Yet in all that time, we've never found a way to make loss any easier—not really. Even with all those things you talked about—doctors and therapists and all of that—losing someone we love is still the most painful thing we experience as human beings, and everyone knows it.

"But then these scumbags come along, and they use other people's pain for their own profit. They hone in on the gaping hole left behind by the dead, and they fill it with lies and false promises! They bleed desperate people dry. There were people at that show who'd emptied their bank accounts to be there! They sold valuable possessions and God knows what else, just for the chance that Freeman might give them a message from the other side."

"I understand all of that," Finvarra said, taking the opportunity to interject while I calmed myself with a long deep breath through my nostrils. "This is not a foreign concept to us, Jessica, the concept of loss. In fact, I would argue that we are much more intimately acquainted with it than others in this world."

"Yes, but that's what protects us from the worst of it," Hannah said, finally finding the courage to speak. Her voice, as quiet as it was, landed with the force of an explosion. The atmosphere in the

Council room changed dramatically; all eyes were now on Hannah, and many of them were wary.

After a moment, Hannah went on. "We know there's something more, don't we? We *know* the spirit goes on after the body dies, but the rest of the world doesn't have that knowledge—not for sure. All that they have is faith. That's it. Faith is powerful, but it's not the same as knowledge. When *we* lose someone, we may be sad—maybe even devastated—but we have a *knowledge* that sees us through."

"Exactly," I said, and, having drawn strength from Hannah, my voice was calmer and surer now. "People like Freeman can't be allowed to exploit that! They need to be exposed for what they are, and who better to do it than us?

"That is enough!" Finvarra said, with a shadow of her old authority and strength in her voice. "Your concern is admirable, but you have allowed it to cloud your judgment. You have risked exposing our order. We cannot permit this to continue."

Finn's hackles rose reflexively at Finvarra's pronouncement. Whether I liked it or not, Finn would protect us from anyone, even the High Priestess. Hell, he'd done it before, and in this very room.

I swallowed hard. Beside me, Hannah had clammed up again. In the tense silence of that moment, I began wondering what the Council could do to us. What could the consequences be? I mean, we were stuck being Durupinen, weren't we? They couldn't somehow... take that away?

In the moment those questions formed in my head, I was gripped with a fear so powerful that it took my breath away. It clamped around my chest, squeezing the air from my lungs. I felt faint. Never would I have thought that I'd feel anything but relief at the idea of being free from the Durupinen gift—a gift I still frequently referred to as a curse. Any sane person would choose a spirit-free life, wouldn't they? Who would want spirits interfering with her life on a daily basis? And what did it say about me, being so suddenly terrified of losing my gift? I thrust my hands into my pockets to hide them; they were now trembling violently.

After a calculated pause, Finvarra continued. "We have decided we will give you a choice," she declared. "The first option is probation. We will lay out the stipulations under which you will be allowed to return to your life in America, the first of which is that you will be accompanied by two Caomhnóir, in addition to Mr. Carey. Regrettably, it seems Mr. Carey cannot persuade you away from these risky activities—despite performing his duties admirably. The additional Caomhnóir will police your activities and determine if you are following the terms of our arrangement. They will report only to me."

My mouth dropped open in horror. It almost didn't matter what the second choice was: I would never agree to live my life like this. I looked at Hannah. She looked almost equally horrified, but her horror was tempered with resignation—between foster care and mental health facilities, she'd spent most of her life trapped "in the system;" I knew she didn't have a lot of fight left in her against this sort of thing.

Why the hell hadn't I listened to my sister when she told me we had to be more careful? Because I never listened to anyone, that's why. Wasn't that what Finn had said? I chanced a glance at him, too. He was still at attention, and although I could tell he was trying to maintain an impassive expression, I also knew that he'd begun silently grinding his teeth.

"Your second option," Finvarra said, and I snapped my gaze back to her, "is to work for the Northern Clans as a Tracker."

§

My jaw dropped. "Work... for you? As a Tracker?" We'd spent the last three years rallying against Fairhaven and all it stood for. We'd all but told off the Council. We'd just exposed the Durupinen's secrets. And now Finvarra was welcoming us back into her fold?

Unsure of what to do next, I turned to Hannah for help; her mouth, too, was hanging open in shock.

"Oh, snap," gasped Milo under his breath. While his quip was perhaps not the most original reaction, Milo had summed up our feelings perfectly.

I struggled to find my own voice; it sounded a bit strangled as I squeaked out, "What do you mean?"

"We want you both to work as members of our elite squad of Trackers," Finvarra repeated. "Your activities, while reckless at times, have proven effective. They have also presented an intriguing possibility that—I must admit—we had not previously considered."

"How so?" I asked.

"We do not generally associate with paranormal scientists and so-called ghost hunters. In light of our own abilities, we have no need for their gadgets and theories and séances. However, for the average person, there's no denying this spirit exploration can be both convincing and comforting. And ghost hunters can be transparent in their attempts, whereas we must always operate in secrecy for our own protection."

I blinked. This didn't add up. We'd been basically kidnapped in the middle of the night, hauled across the ocean, then chastised for doing the very same thing that Finvarra was now telling us that she wanted us to do. When would my life start making sense?

"I guess I don't understand exactly what you're asking us to do," I replied, after a long, stunned moment. "I thought you wanted us to stop."

"We want you to stop being reckless," said Finvarra. "However, your agenda—and your team in America—could potentially be more helpful to our cause than you, or indeed we, might have realized."

Apparently, my expression was still broadcasting my confusion, for Finvarra again looked to Siobhán for assistance. Siobhán nodded and stood up.

"We've often enough had to deal with the kinds of people you've targeted in your work," she began. "Although we don't want people exploiting the spirit world and its mysteries, we can't step in every time it happens, for our own safety. You're both well aware, I'm sure, of the danger we'd be in if the rest of the world discovered us."

I nodded. On this point, at least, I could agree with everything being said. I'd seen firsthand the desperate lengths people would go to just to connect with a deceased loved one. There'd be no rest, no peace, for the Durupinen if we were known to the world. We'd be exploited and used, perhaps even experimented on in the name of science and knowledge. As devastating as our conflict with the Necromancers had been, it somehow nearly paled in comparison to what surely awaited us if the general population knew of our abilities.

"Most of the time," Siobhán continued, "these people are simply frauds like this Freeman fellow. This is regrettable, yes, but not our responsibility to police. Once in a while, however, one of these scam artists manages to stumble upon something related to our world, and is able to pull their abilities from that."

"Something related to our world?" I asked, frowning. "Like what?"

"Any number of things. A rune left on a wall somewhere; a spirit we tried but failed to Cross, a gemstone or candle used in one of our Castings. We are generally very careful to leave no trace of ourselves, although some of us," and here Siobhán arched her eyebrow at me, "are more careful than others. Our abilities, and the tools we use, ripple out through the spirit world. They leave traces when they're used. It's almost always possible for our Trackers, with the use of certain Castings, to identify when Durupinen are involved in a spirit event. We keep an eye out for these ripples—and we follow up on them to ensure our secrecy."

Passing over the nearly ungraspable idea of "magical" ripples, I asked, "But if the Trackers are already doing that, what would you need us for?"

"The victims involved in these events, desperate as they are, often need empirical evidence to convince them of fraud. Often, we cannot provide this without revealing ourselves. But you could take a different approach. You would have the dual resources of modern technology as well as your Durupinen gifts. Taken together, these could make you valuable members of the Tracker team, uniquely suited for certain assignments."

The Council was staring at us—and, in turn, Hannah, Finn, and Milo were staring at me. I had no idea what to say. I was still reeling at the idea of being offered a Durupinen job—never mind all this ripples-and-technology stuff.

Hannah spoke up, giving me an opportunity to recover. "If we do decide to become Trackers—and I'm not promising we will—what would that mean for our lives back at home? What about my classes?"

Siobhán glanced quickly at Finvarra, who roused herself from a half-torpor and sat up a bit straighter in her seat. When Finvarra spoke again, her tone was brighter, her words spilled out a bit faster.

"You may stay where you are, and maintain your jobs and other activities, if you so desire. We will not dispatch further Caomhnóir assistance unless you deem it necessary for one of your assignments. You would be given cases that require your particular set of skills and resources."

"What about the paranormal investigation team we work with?"

I asked. "Annabelle has been here at Fairhaven, but what about the rest of the guys? Can they really assist on these cases while remaining in the dark?"

"If the proper care is taken, there will be no need for them to know who they will be working for. I understand they undertake this work on a volunteer basis?"

"Yes," I said. "We all do." In truth, working with the team was the part of my life that made the rest of the Durupinen bullshit feel worth it, the one perk to a damned difficult job I could never quit.

"Very well, then. They will be volunteering for the Durupinen cause. Given their passion, I am sure they will not disapprove, even if you are unable to reveal how you find your cases."

"And what if one of them stumbles across the truth—or part of it—like Pierce did?" I asked, endeavoring to keep my voice steady even as the thought of Pierce flooded my chest with sadness. "I won't stand by and watch their lives be ruined while you use them for your own purposes."

Siobhán looked at Finvarra in concern, but Finvarra waved her away for the moment and continued. "We can make allowances, if need be. We will not knowingly endanger or take advantage of the team—you have our word. If any them find out more than they should, we will make the same allowances as we would for other Durupinen friends and family... as long as they comply with our codes of secrecy, of course. However, you must try to avoid that, if at all possible. We will consider it a last resort."

"What about my job? I'm just getting settled. Am I going to be expected to drop everything and be at your beck and call?" I asked.

Siobhán answered, giving Finvarra a chance to recover—even a few words had caused her to begin fading again. "You can keep your job if you want, but your employer will need to be flexible, as will Hannah's professors. Being a Tracker will likely involve travel, perhaps for weeks at a time."

I snorted. "Do the Durupinen know how things work in the real world? I can't just go to my boss and say, 'Hey I know I'm just a peon, but can I have three weeks off?' I'd be fired on the spot! And how am I supposed to afford my rent and, y'know, food if I can't even..."

"You will be compensated for your expenses and your time," Siobhán said flatly. "Generously."

"Oh. Right." My mind was swimming. I looked over at Hannah,

who still looked as dazed as I felt. "And... you don't expect us to answer right now, do you? I... we... need a little time to think about it."

Finvarra stood up again; it looked like more work than it ought to have been. Carrick hovered a bit closer to her, his face pinched with concern. "We will adjourn the Council for now. Will meet again once you have made your decision—you have until tomorrow night to make your choice. Siobhán will be on hand to answer any questions you may have."

I nodded, and we turned to leave.

"Wait," she said. "There is one last essential detail."

We turned back to face Finvarra. "You should know that you will not be working entirely on your own. You will need a mentor, someone who understands the methods and rules of Tracking, and who can guide you while you find your footing."

Awesome. Another Durupinen babysitter. Maybe this wouldn't be a better option than probation after all.

"Okay. Who is it?"

A slim blonde figure toward the back of the benches stood up. Her expression was grim, and her voice sour. "Me," she answered. That one word contained more distain than I'd ever heard in a single syllable.

But that shouldn't have surprised me, considering that the speaker was Catriona.

9

TABOOS AND TATTOOS

T HE GROUNDS WERE ENVELOPED IN A RAW MIST. It was the kind of damp that seemed to somehow come up through your pores and chill you from the inside. Yet somehow, the sight of the mist blanketing the trees and hills was comforting—the green looked contented, nestled in its cool, dewy blanket. I breathed deeply; being out here felt like freedom in my lungs after the oppressive atmosphere of the Council Room.

"They can't be serious," I said after I'd taken my first cleansing breath.

"About which part? It all seems pretty unbelievable to me," said Hannah as she walked along beside me.

"I mean the part where they expect us to work with Catriona," I replied.

Hannah looked surprised. "Really? Why not?"

I stopped walking and stared at her. "Why not? Do I need to refresh your memory about a certain mentor of yours who faked her own death, aided and abetted in your kidnapping, and nearly caused us to destroy the entire Gateway system as we know it?"

Hannah scowled at me. "No, you don't."

Her face was so fierce that I instantly felt ashamed of myself. "Sorry. That was a stupid thing to say. I'm just... this is all really stressful."

"Yes, it is. For everyone, myself included. Do you think I like being back here, seeing all these people?"

"No, of course not. Sorry," I said again.

Hannah nodded. "That's okay. So what's your point about Catriona? She wasn't working with the Necromancers."

"Maybe not," I conceded. "But if her bond with Lucida is anything like my bond with you, I can't imagine she'd be very happy to even see us, let alone work with us."

Hannah didn't respond. She couldn't seem to parry my reply—which I took as less of a sign of my own debating ability, and more of an indicator that the circumstances spoke for themselves.

"What do you think we should do, then?" she asked. "It might not be so bad, undertaking these missions with permission, instead of being constantly afraid of the Council. Plus, I don't want more Caomhnóir following us around wherever we go."

"Neither do I," I agreed. "It's bad enough having one overprotective watchdog."

We both looked over at Finn, who had followed us outside but had stopped to speak to a Caomhnóir stationed by the castle's door. Now Finn was striding toward us, with his face in its usual stoic mask of determination. He put a hand up as though he were about to call out to us to stop, but the voice that reached our ears was most decidedly not his.

"What the hell kind of trouble have you gotten into now, eh?"

I turned away from Finn's advancing form to see Savannah Todd grinning at us from the shadows of the cloisters, holding a cigarette halfway between the crumpled packet in her other hand and her always-smart mouth.

Tia was my best friend, but Savvy undoubtedly was my best mate. She and her cousin Phoebe were the only other "outsider" Apprentices when Hannah and I had first arrived at Fairhaven, but our bond was much stronger than that. Savvy had helped me and Hannah to Uncage the Silent Child; she had ensured our escape from the Council on the night of the fire; and she'd even followed me into hiding in the Traveler camp before helping to free Hannah from the Necromancers. On top of all that, she'd taken all this in stride—as if risking her life on a near-daily basis was a perfectly normal and reasonable part of friendship.

"Savvy!" I cried. "I didn't think we were going to see you!" I sprinted over to her and nearly knocked her flat with a hug. Never one to be outdone, Savvy grabbed me by the waist, dipped me nearly to the ground, and kissed me full on the mouth before releasing me.

"And how about you, wee one? You fancy a snog?" Savvy asked, as Hannah walked toward us.

Hannah grinned. "Well, I don't want to be left out!"

Savvy threw back her head and roared with laughter, then pulled

Hannah into a rib-cracking hug and planted a kiss on her, too, just as Finn appeared beside me.

"Oi, get in line there, mate!" Savvy said, puckering her lips at him. "There's plenty of Sav to go around."

"I don't doubt that," Finn said bluntly.

"Easy there. I can hold my own in a row, I'm a ginger, remember?" Savvy said, throwing a friendly punch at his arm, which Finn deftly dodged. Then she turned back to us, let out another laugh, and began wiping smudges of red lipstick first from Hannah's face and then from mine.

"Miss me?" she asked, as she rubbed vigorously at my bottom lip.

"Desperately. Best kiss I've had in years," I said with a laugh.

"Really? Well that's a bloody crime, isn't it?" said Savvy, with a pointed look at Finn.

I blushed deeply, but if Finn realized that the comment was directed at him, he didn't acknowledge it in the least. His eyes were trained on a line of Novitiates who were marching in military formation in front of their barracks. "I've got to report to Braxton while I'm here. I'll see you when I've finished," Finn said. "Where will you be?"

I shrugged my shoulders. "Around."

He scowled so fiercely that I put my hands up in surrender. "Okay, okay. We'll be by the small fountain in the gardens, the one on the way to the Memorial Garth. Is that okay with you, Savvy?"

"Just peachy," Savvy said.

"Good enough, I'll meet you there," Finn said. Don't go back into the Council Room without me. We need to discuss this Tracker proposal before we make any decisions."

I raised my eyebrows at him in a long, burning stare. "Rather, before *you* make any decisions," he corrected himself grudgingly. Then he turned on his heel and stomped off toward the barracks.

Savvy called after him, teasing. "Sure you don't want a snog good-bye, Finn? You're much more my cup of tea! Aw, go on, then!"

Finn kept walking, but flung up two fingers over his shoulder in reply. I'd spent enough time in England to know his gesture was the equivalent of an American flipping the middle finger.

Savvy let loose a low, slow whistle as she watched him go. Then she turned back to us. "Off to the Garth, then?"

Hannah looked down at her feet, where she was digging into the dirt with the toe of one of her shoes. "I kind of thought I might...

head to the central courtyard, actually." She kept her tone casual, but the tremble in her voice betrayed her.

"Do you want me to come with you?" I asked quietly.

"No," she answered, shaking her head vigorously. "No, I... it's okay. I just wanted to see it, and maybe... maybe be alone for a little while."

Savvy looked at Hannah, with a deep understanding in her face. "Sure. We can manage without you for a bit. But don't go too far! We need a proper catch-up—I want to hear all your news, yeah?"

"Go ahead," I added, reaching out and squeezing her hand. "We can talk about the Tracker thing when you get back, okay?"

"Yeah, okay. I'll... I'll catch up with you in a little while," Hannah replied. She turned and headed through the cloisters toward the central courtyard.

Savvy and I turned past the cloisters and out into the main grounds. I watched over my shoulder as Hannah slipped into the shadowy central corridor of the cloisters and out of sight.

"You think she'll be alright by herself, mate?" Savvy asked. She, too, had been watching Hannah's retreat.

"I think so. We haven't been back to the Geatgrima, or what's left of it, since... well, since everything that happened. Sometimes you've got to go back to the scene of the crime, even if it's just to let it all go, you know? She's tougher than she looks."

"That's for bloody sure," Savvy agreed. "Still, hadn't we best follow her?"

"No, I've got a better idea. Wait a second." I closed my eyes and felt around inside my own head. "Milo?"

"Reporting for duty," came his singsong voice.

"Hannah is going to the central courtyard, where the Geatgrima was. She said she wanted to be alone, but..."

"Ugh, I knew she shook me off for a reason!" Milo replied. "I'm on it, sweetness."

"Thanks," I said. I felt him drift out of my head.

"Done. Milo's on it," I told Savvy.

"Ah, good old Milo. She'll be alright then."

"Yeah. So how are you? What are you doing here?" Savvy, who had the wildest wild streak of anyone I'd ever met, was possibly the only person who'd been more eager to get away from Fairhaven's oppressive rules, cliques, and incessant reverence of all things Durupinen than I had been.

"I'm mentoring," she said, in a tone that suggested she was embarrassed.

"Mentoring? You're joking!"

She looked affronted. "Oi! I might be a right troublemaker, but I've learned a thing or two."

"I know, I know. I guess I'm just surprised."

"Surprised they asked me, or surprised I agreed to it?"

I laughed. "Both."

"Yeah, me too. If you told me a year or two ago that I'd be working here, I'd have said you were off your nut," Savvy agreed. "But it was a special circumstance. They had to open another new Gateway, and since I'd just gone through the same thing, they thought I might want to help out, you know."

"Another new one? Really? I thought that was a rare thing when it happened to you," I said.

"So did I, but turned out they needed to do it again. I was still working in that shop—you remember the one, where you came to visit me last year?"

"Yeah, I think I might remember a little bit about it," I said. When I'd come to see Savvy, she had asked me to meet her at her shop; she'd given me the address, and had told me that I needed to ask for "Foxy Red" when I arrived. She'd failed to mention, however, that the shop in question was a purveyor of sex toys and bondage gear. When I'd sent her scantily clad coworker into the employees only area to ask if "Foxy" were available, Savvy's response had been unforgettable; while standing next to the display of that month's top-selling dildos, I had heard her snorting and choking with laughter in the back room. The story remained an endless fountain of mirth for her ever since.

Savvy giggled, but her tone was bitter as she spoke. "They gave me the sack last month. They said I wasn't friendly enough to the customers. Pricks." She paused for a moment, then her tone turned brighter. "But before that, Celeste turned up, cool as you please, while I was stocking whips. Said there was a new girl who needed a bit of help adjusting. At first, I only agreed to meet her and have a little chat, but then she took a shine to me. I felt sorry for her, so now I pop in two days a week to meet with her and her sister. It's not a bad gig, really. Pays a damn sight better than that den of iniquity, I can tell you that."

"Wow, that's... really great Sav. Unexpected, but great. And hey, if it means I get to see you while I'm here, even better."

"Well, strictly speaking, I wasn't supposed to be here today, but a little birdie let slip you were coming, so here I am! Your welcoming committee!" She grinned broadly and flung an arm around me as we rounded a corner in the path. "So, sounds like my old chum has been up to all kinds of shenanigans, yeah? What else have you got up to, besides blowing up the Internet?"

"Oh, you know me. Starving artist with an attitude problem, serving fancy coffee drinks and sketching my way through the world," I replied. "My job at the museum is pretty cool, though. I like that a lot, even if I'm doing mostly grunt work right now."

It was a long walk, but we finally reached the fountain. Despite the day's chill, the walk had overheated me; I slipped off my jacket as I sat down on the fountain's lip.

"Oi! Is that new ink?" asked Savvy, her tone delighted. "Come on then, give us a proper look."

"What? Oh, yeah," I said, pushing my sleeve up so she could see the whole piece. "It's only a few months old."

"Blimey," Savvy murmured. "That's elaborate, mate! Looks like your style, too. That's your own design, yeah?"

"Yeah," I said, although I felt a little strange taking credit for it. It didn't feel like I had anything to do with the design, honestly. The image had sprung fully formed from my mind one night when I woke out of a dead sleep, seized with a violent urge to draw. "It was a Muse thing," I added, to make me feel as if I were at least sharing the credit.

"It looks like it could tell a story all its own, mate," Savvy replied. "What's it all mean?"

I ran my finger along the intricate black-and-gray artwork. "The open book at the base is the *Book of Téigh Anonn*. The big, gnarled tree growing out of it is a symbol of my family, and of my clan roots.

"Is that trunk made out of runes?" Savvy asked in an awed whisper. "That's wicked!"

"Yeah, and the Triskele and a Geatgrima are in there somewhere too," I said. "And then the leaves blowing off the top of the tree turn into ravens flying away." With my finger, I followed their trail up my shoulder, where the last of the ravens met my collarbone.

"Ravens? Why ravens?"

"Remember that raven Ileana kept as a pet?" I asked. "The

Travelers believe ravens are bad luck, but Anca told me that Ileana had tamed her raven as a way of facing her bad luck head-on, of taking some control over it. I like to think I've done the same thing with the whole Durupinen legacy. It's just bad luck that I'm stuck with it, so I'm trying to take ownership of it. You know, turning lemons into lemonade."

"Ghostly lemonade," Savvy snorted. "Yeah, alright, I get that. And what's this?" She pointed to an oversized Spirit Catcher dangling from one of the tree's branches.

"That's to remind me of Irina," I said. "I don't remember if you ever saw her when we were in the Traveler camp, but you must know how much I owe her... how much we all owe her, really."

Many years before I met Irina, the Traveler Council had taught her to Walk, despite the known dangers of becoming a Walker. Soon Irina had fallen victim to these dangers; leaving her still-living body behind and existing in spirit form proved too pleasurable and addictive for her to resist. Eventually, returning to her own body and living inside it became pure torture. The Traveler Council, afraid they would totally lose control of her and the clan secrets she possessed, had imprisoned Irina in a disused wagon and trapped her, with experimental Castings, inside her own body; by the time I'd met her, the years of captivity had driven Irina to insanity. Yet despite her madness, Irina had managed to teach me to Walk; she'd given me the knowledge and skills I needed to save Hannah, Walk through the Gateway, and thwart the Necromancers' dark ambitions.

Irina had finally escaped her prison, thank God, when the Necromancers had attacked the Traveler's Camp and had fatally wounded her body. When last I saw her, her spirit—in Walker form—was drifting euphorically towards the starry sky as she stretched her metaphorical wings toward freedom.

"No, mate, I never saw her materialize—but I did feel her presence when she was teaching you. Couldn't miss something that strong, now could I?" replied Savvy.

"So when I look at the Spirit Catcher I remember that even though I'm one of the Durupinen, I'm not captive to them. I have a power that no one else on Earth possesses, and I will make my own life."

"That's deep, mate," Savvy said. "I've got a winking budgie inked on my arse, but that's just because I lost a bet when I was pissed."

"I'm sure the winking budgie is full of deep, hidden meaning—even if you were too drunk to remember it," I assured her, patting her on the back. "And before you ask, no, I don't want to see it."

Savvy shrugged. "Your loss, mate."

As so often happened with me and Sav, what started as a small giggle built itself into unabashed, uncontrollable laughter. We laughed until our sides hurt and tears rolled down our cheeks. When we had laughed ourselves out—a process that took several tries and at least five full minutes—we sat in silence, catching our breath.

"So no, uh... romantic developments?" Savvy finally asked, winking salaciously.

"Are you kidding? Men are following me around constantly. Just not any living ones."

"Oh, come on now," Savvy cried, throwing her hands up in frustration. "I kept mum about it the last time you were here, but... do I really have to spell it out for you?"

"Apparently, because I don't know what you're—"

"Finn! You! Why haven't you two shagged already?"

"Savvy! That's not... we're not..." I stuttered; I was pretty sure my face was now as fiery as her hair.

"Oh come off it, Jess!" Savvy cried, rolling her eyes so hard she just might have pulled a muscle. "What do you think I am, a blooming idiot? You two were on the verge of something when you left here, I felt it. I read the poetry, for fuck's sake! That book was one long love letter to you! If a bloke wrote something like that about me, I'd be shagging his brains out!"

"You're such a romantic, Sav."

"Come on now, mate, what the hell happened?"

I shrugged, meaning to brush her question off, but as I moved my shoulders, I felt the pain knot up inside me as that familiar, made-small-by-rejection, sensation washed over me. I suppose if I had to tell this story to anyone, Savvy was the right person.

"I don't know. I thought something might come out of it. I really did. I think he did, too. But then we got back home and we started talking, and he just... closed himself off."

"How do you mean?" she pressed.

"You know how he is," I said. "It's all work and duty and responsibility first. When we were fighting the Necromancers, I think he was able to forget all of that for a minute. When you think the world as you know it is about to end, it can make you do some crazy things. For Finn, crazy meant allowing himself to have feelings."

"And then when the world didn't end?" Savvy prompted quietly.

"He closed back up," I said, shrugging again—a shrug that dug deep into me and scraped against something raw and painful. "Not right away. I think it took some time to sink in, you know? He *did* start to let me in. Well, actually, we started to let each other in... I don't know if you've noticed, but I'm not exactly a champion when it comes to opening up and trusting other people."

Savvy smiled encouragingly. "It's alright, mate, neither am I. You're doing a bang-up job right now, though. Go on, if you like. I'm listening."

I smiled back, took a deep breath, and went on, "One night, a few weeks after we got home, Finn brought one of his oldest black notebooks over to the dorm. It was full of poems he'd written before we met. He said he'd never shared them with anyone before, but he wanted me to read them. So I did. I read all of them, the whole book, while he sat there nervously, just watching me. And they were incredible, every single one of them."

I paused for a moment, collecting myself before the tears welling in my eyes had a chance to begin flowing. "Then we talked about his poems, about what it feels like to write them. It's this release for him, this... catharsis, just like it is for me when I draw. We talked and talked, and I felt like we really connected for the first time. It was two in the morning before he got up to leave."

"Daft prick," Savvy said with a slight laugh, shaking her head. "And you actually let him go?"

"I asked him to stay. And I meant it. But he said he couldn't. And then he kissed me." I smiled in spite of myself at the memory, even though the moment was so fleeting. "Or maybe I kissed him. I'm not really sure, but we were kissing. I asked again if he would stay, and..."

I trailed off, not sure I wanted to share the rest of the memory. This wasn't just some guy long buried in my past, it was Finn. Finn, who I had to see all the time. Finn, who was pledged to my Gateway. Finn, who was just around the bend in the barracks this very minute.

"Aw, you mustn't leave it there, mate—what happened?" Savvy urged, practically salivating with interest.

"He said he couldn't and he left," I answered.

That wasn't strictly true. What Finn had actually said, while cupping my face between his hands, was, "Not tonight. But some day, if you'll have me, I'll stay and never leave." But those words, whispered in a darkened doorway with his lips a mere breath away from mine, were just for me; I wasn't going to share them. I hadn't even told Hannah, although she knew something had happened between us—probably because I'd floated around like a lovestruck ingénue from a Rodgers and Hammerstein musical for the next day and a half.

"So what went wrong?" Savvy asked breathlessly.

I yanked myself ruthlessly out of my reverie and into the harshness of the present. "I have no idea. He wouldn't tell me. He just showed up two days later, acting like he'd never had the slightest interest in me. When I asked him, he merely said, 'It wasn't what you thought it was.' And he's barely looked me in the eye since! So here we are now... our relationship consists of his overprotective Caomhnóir hovering and our snarky comments about each other's flaws."

Savvy reached out and patted me on the shoulder. "I'm sorry, mate."

"What are you sorry for? You didn't do anything."

"I know that. But I also know you. I know you don't let many people in there," and she landed a gentle punch just above my chest.

"Whatever, it's not a big deal," I said, in a voice that sounded for a moment as if it had come out of a stranger's mouth. "Finn had feelings for me, but they obviously changed. It happens."

"Bollocks. It doesn't 'happen.' He got scared, plain and simple. The milksop."

"What are you talking about? What would Finn have to be afraid of? He already told me how he felt. Isn't that supposed to be the scary part?"

Savvy snorted as her cigarette dangled precariously from the corner of her mouth. "Naw, that's just the first scary thing. It's a never-ending parade of scary from there, I hate to tell you. There's all those 'firsts' to contend with—first date, first shag, first fight. But forget all that for a moment, because that's only the shit *normal* people have to deal with—and we don't exactly hang out on the right side of normal, you get me?"

I nodded. The spirit of a gardener had just trudged by, silently pushing a wheelbarrow over grass that his living feet had never trod upon. I didn't need the reminder—our lives were far from normal.

Savvy went on, "Think about how he grew up! He was born a Caomhnóir. Think about what the lot of 'em drilled into his head from the time he could toddle! That women are evil, and Durupinen are temptresses! They'll distract you from your duties with their Castings and magical tits! That's a lot to get over, isn't it?"

I giggled. "Magical tits? Really Sav?"

"Oh, sod off, you know what I mean," Savvy said impatiently. "All that feminine mystique rubbish."

"That was definitely a hurdle at first," I said, shaking my head, "but I think he got past that even before the Geatgrima opened. Once he got to know me, he got over all the evil temptress stuff. I mean, God knows I wasn't trying to tempt him—I could barely tolerate him! No, I think he got spooked because he's afraid of breaking the rules."

"What rules?"

"The rules that say a relationship between a Durupinen and a Caomhnóir is forbidden," I replied.

Savvy sent two streams of smoke shooting out of her nostrils. "Ah, no way! That's a load of tosh! That rule was put into place because they were trying to stop the Prophecy. But the Prophecy's happened. It's over and done with. So there's no reason for that rubbish rule to exist anymore."

"I know Sav, I know," I sighed. I had made this point in my own head a million times, night after sleepless night, agonizing over why Finn and I weren't together. I never actually said any of it out loud to Finn; I didn't need to. I knew every single argument he'd make: He'd insist it would be too dangerous to mix love with duty; he'd claim that our relationship would distract him, impede him from making logical and rational decisions; he'd say that he couldn't protect Hannah and me equally if he were only in love with one of us.

"Have you thought about... saying something to the Council?"

I snapped back into the conversation. "Have I what?"

"Why don't you tell the Council?" Savvy asked.

I snorted. "Tell the Council of the Northern Clans that I have a crush on a boy? So they can rewrite their centuries-old laws? I can't imagine how that might go wrong," I said, before affecting a high-pitched preteen whine. "But Finvarra, I don't just like him, I *like like* him!"

"But the Prophecy..."

"Forget the damn Prophecy, Savvy. They've got a list of petty reasons to forbid Durupinen-Caomhnóir relationships, and none of those have gone away." I stood up. "And besides, the last thing I need is to draw attention to another rule I broke. I'm in enough trouble as it is."

"Fair enough," said Savvy. "I just thought... It can be brutal out there. With blokes, I mean. I haven't been on a second date in two years, mostly because I don't want to go through the trouble of covering all of this up." She gestured broadly at the spirit-filled microcosm we were forced to inhabit. "Finding someone who isn't an absolute wanker is hard enough, but knowing that someone is properly in love with you and not being able to do shit about it? That just sucks."

"Yes," I said, nodding slowly. "Yes, it does, indeed, suck. In fact, it sucks so much that I'd rather not talk about it anymore. Let's talk about something else... Like what's wrong with Finvarra, for instance?"

Savannah snorted. "Well, she'd probably be a right bit happier if you'd stop broadcasting our ancient secrets over the Internet."

"No, not that," I said. "I mean why does she look so terrible?"

Savannah gawped at me. "You're joking! You mean you don't know? Blimey, I thought everyone knew about her," she said, shaking her head and looking uncharacteristically serious. "She's dying."

My jaw dropped. "What? Seriously?"

"Right serious, mate. Cancer, sorry to say. I guess she's had it a long time, but it hadn't progressed in ages."

"Why not?"

"Leeching, mate," Savvy said flatly. "She was using it to keep the illness at bay, so she could keep running things. Can't do that anymore, of course, now that the Joint Councils have cracked down on it."

My shock gave way to a squirming sense of guilt: I hated Leeching, but even after everything we'd been through with Finvarra, I didn't want her to be ill. Hannah and I were a big part of the reason that Leeching was now strictly prohibited. Many members of the Northern Clans had been using Leeching—the siphoning energy from spirits who were Crossing through the Gateway—as a sort of paranormal anti-aging and full-service beauty regimen. Spirit energy could be used for any number of things, but the Northern Clans had mostly used it to enhance their looks—many Leeched so often that eventually they looked more like flawless Barbie dolls than real women.

Leeching—technically called using an Aura Flow—was only supposed to be employed in the most dire situations, like if a Durupinen were injured during a Crossing, because Leeching had a potentially devastating effect on the spirits. If a Durupinen sapped too much energy from a spirit, that spirit could become trapped in the Aether—the realm immediately beyond the Gateway—lacking the energy needed to complete its journey to the far side. This was a horrible fate for any spirit, but it also left that spirit vulnerable to being brought back to our realm if a Gateway were ever breached by dark Castings. When a spirit was brought back from the Aether, it lost all of its humanity and became a mindless Wraith. If the Prophecy had come to pass, the Necromancers would've used these Wraiths—controlling them with even more dark Castings—as their personal army. The Northern Clan's abuse of Leeching meant there were thousands, perhaps millions, of Wraiths who could be turned against them. Their "beauty regimens" had nearly cost us everything.

"That's... is she getting any other sort of treatment or anything?" I asked. "It's not like Leeching is the only thing that has an effect on cancer."

Savannah shrugged. "Dunno, but if she is, I don't think it's working properly at all. I mean, look at her."

I said nothing, choosing instead to push the unpleasantness away. I didn't need to add crippling guilt to the list of torturous emotions I was currently grappling with.

"So have you decided what you're going to do?" Savvy asked.

I looked up at Savvy, startled by the question. "What can I do? It's not my fault she's sick."

Savvy shook her head. "Of course it isn't! That's not what I'm talking about. I mean, have you decided yet what you're going to do about the Council's ultimatum?"

"They haven't given me much of a choice, have they?" I said, turning to look over my shoulder at the castle in the distance. It seemed to bear down on me, leaning in to catch my answer. "Hannah and I will have to talk about it, but I think it's safe to say you're looking at the newest Trackers."

10

TARGET ACQUIRED

I CLOSED THE DOOR BEHIND ME and heaved a huge sigh of relief. It was done. I'd informed the Council that Hannah and I had accepted their offer. I'd never seen so many of them look so relieved by something that came out of my mouth. Hannah hadn't wanted to come in the Council Room with me; she'd been waiting on a bench in the entrance hall. When she saw the relief on my own face, she broke into a smile.

"Well, at least that part's done," she said, allowing me to put my arm around her as I sat down.

"Yeah, for the moment," I replied. "Karen just texted me. She'll be here in about twenty minutes. Her connection got delayed, so she'll be in an extra fierce mood for the Council—she's going to speak to them as soon as she arrives. After that, we'll see what's next." I looked around. "Hey, where's Milo?" I asked.

"He's off somewhere. There are so many new spirits here now, he said he wanted to get a feel for things 'afterlife style.'" Hannah put these last two words in air quotes, adopting Milo's voice as she did so. "But really, I think he felt guilty—I know he was spying on me in the central courtyard, even though I asked him for some alone time."

I swallowed. I should've known Hannah would've felt Milo nearby. "Naw, that was my fault. I sent him to check on you. Because... well... you know."

Hannah looked at me sternly for a moment before her expression softened. "Yeah, I guess I do know." Then she drew herself up a bit and said more brightly, "Come on, let's go to the dining hall. I need a snack."

A snack sounded like the best idea I'd heard all day. I didn't relish the possibility of having to mingle with anyone, but Hannah and

I were pretty good at keeping to ourselves. Hell, half the time we didn't have a choice in the matter.

As we turned the last corner to the dining hall, I jumped back with a yelp of fright—I backed right into Hannah and nearly knocked her over. Carrick had appeared so suddenly in front of us that I had nearly walked straight through him.

"Terribly sorry, I didn't mean to startle you!" he said, floating backward a few feet so there was a more comfortable distance between us. "I merely... I was hoping to speak with you both while you are visiting us."

"Were you hoping to scare the crap out of us, too?" I cried, my heart still pounding. "Because mission accomplished."

"I'm sorry," he repeated, looking almost sheepish. The expression looked strange on his face, as if he'd rarely worn it before.

"It's fine, it's fine," I said, recovering. I'd been too harsh—now I felt a bit sheepish myself.

"I wanted to... say hello." said Carrick. His words hung in the air for a moment, before he added, somewhat formally, "And welcome you back to Fairhaven."

"Oh, okay. Hi," I replied. The words that came out of my mouth were stilted, far more so than was polite. I couldn't help it.

The awkwardness was so thick you could've cut it with a chainsaw. What the hell were you supposed to say to the ghost of the father you'd never known? There was no social protocol for this.

I raised my eyebrows and looked at Hannah, hoping she'd rescue me. She cleared her throat and said, "Hello, Carrick."

Carrick seemed to be at a similar loss. Now that he was actually in front of us, all of his eagerness to speak seemed to have shriveled up, along with everything he'd wanted to say.

"It... has been a long time," he said, a bit curtly in his nervousness. "I'm sorry I haven't... I didn't think you'd want to hear from me. Finvarra has kept me up to date on your news."

I wasn't sure what to say. As far as I knew there was no Durupinen etiquette booklet on how to talk to your dead father. Plus, we hadn't kept in any kind of contact with Carrick since we'd last seen him—spirits weren't exactly able to keep up via typical forms of correspondence, and neither of us had made any effort to connect with him using our abilities. Our relationship with our father had been less of a relationship and more of an uncomfortable awareness of the other's existence, interspersed occasionally with bouts of wondering what the other might be up to. It was strange to think that Carrick had been keeping tabs on us without our knowing it. I also felt a little guilty about his assuming we wouldn't want to hear from him... and even more guilty as I realized that he was probably right in his assumption.

"Right. Well, yeah, then you know that we've been... fine," I said at last, to break the silence. It was the most generic of statements, but it was all I could muster.

Hannah jumped in, trying to salvage the conversation. "How have you been, Carrick?"

"Well enough, I suppose," he replied, although a frown creased his brow as he said it. "It's been a trying time, these last few months."

"Uh, yeah, we were sorry to hear that Finvarra is sick. But, I'm sure she'll be alright. She's tough," I said.

Carrick gave a tiny nod, pressing his mouth into a thin line. "Yes, well. Let us hope so."

A few more moments of silence crept by.

"Well, we should probably go," Hannah said. "We need a bite to eat before we see Karen. She's probably in with the Council by now."

Karen's name seemed to shake Carrick out of his inarticulate state. "Yes, of course. But before you go, I... that is to say... I wanted to congratulate you on taking the Tracker positions."

I raised my eyebrows. "Congratulations? Really?"

"Yes," Carrick said. "You ought to know that the Council didn't offer the positions lightly. They must have a very high opinion of your skills—and your courage—to extend such an offer. I realize they gave you quite another impression all together in Council Room, but it's true nonetheless."

I looked at Hannah, who looked as surprised as I felt.

"Thanks," she said to Carrick.

"Also, please permit me to say that I know you will perform your new duties admirably," he said stiffly, keeping his eyes trained carefully on the ground. There was the faintest trace of something paternal etched in his voice. Was Carrick trying to say he was proud of us? Did he even have the right to be proud of us after being absent from our lives for two decades?

I knew Hannah was asking the same questions, and I also knew that she—like me—had decided to push those questions deep down for the moment.

"Thank you," Hannah and I both mumbled in unison. Hannah, ever more polite than I, added, "Nice of you to check in."

Carrick cleared his throat. "Right. Well, you must be getting along, and so must I. Do give my best to your aunt. Good luck with your Tracking, and... and in the future."

We mumbled our thanks again, and parted ways. I heard him pop out behind us; whether it was right or not, I felt nothing but sheer relief at his absence.

§

"And I marched right in there while they were in closed session!" Karen cried. "Braxton tried to block me, but I looked right at him and said, 'Do you really want to find out what'll happen to you if you so much as lay a hand on me?'"

"Alright Karen!" I laughed, extending a fist-bump to her. She didn't notice it, though; she was too busy pacing at breakneck speed around the room, with her arms crossed in an angry knot across her chest.

The office we were now waiting in had once belonged to Marion, Finn's aunt, the Council member who had attempted to throw Hannah and me in the dungeons while engineering a coup to place herself on the High Priestess' throne. For her crimes, the Joint Councils had stripped Marion of her Council position at Fairhaven, and had exiled her from the British Isles. When last I asked about her, she was living with her family somewhere in Paris; Marion would be allowed to return to Fairhaven for clan business only by special dispensation from the High Priestess. If you asked me, I'd say Marion had gotten off far too lightly, but she had powerful political ties within the Durupinen system—the punishment the Joint Councils meted out was never intended to fit the crime.

This office—which we'd been waiting in for at least thirty minutes—now belonged to Catriona; we were waiting for our first meeting with her as official Trackers. Knowing Catriona, I could only assume she was keeping us waiting on purpose, flaunting whatever little power she had.

Karen was still raving. "I threatened them with everything I could think of. I told them they were in violation of the Clan Codes. I invoked my rights as your elder, which require that I be present for any meeting that alters your status within the Durupinen system. And I made sure they knew that I'd be appealing to the Joint Councils to report this atrocious breach."

Yep, that was Karen. There was a reason she was a damn good lawyer. She'd be up for partner at her firm soon—and if the shriveled old men who ran that office didn't promote her, they were surely going to lose her to the headhunters who were constantly scouting her.

"Do you think that'll change anything?" I asked.

"Probably not, but it made me feel a little better," Karen said, throwing her hands up dejectedly. "They couldn't have actually enforced that probation, you know. They used it to scare you. There's no official probation, per say, in Durupinen law. They could've sent additional Caomhnóir to follow you around, sure, but they would've been nothing but a pain in the ass. They would've watched you like a hawk, but they wouldn't have authority over any of your actions, just as Finn has no authority over your actions now."

Finn, who was hovering in the corner, snorted loudly and contracted his eyebrows into a 'V'—a sure sign that he was teeming with anger. I ignored him.

"Right, but the thought of being tailed everywhere we go?" I began. "Even if they couldn't enforce anything, the mere idea of extra Guardian presence is intolerable—and the Council knows it. Because when it comes down to it, we're Durupinen no matter what rules we break—the Council's stuck with us, so they'll wield as much power as they can to grind us into submission!"

"Yes, that's true," Karen said. "But I just want to make sure, before you commit, that you both understand there might be other options. I know you already told them you'd do it, but no one can hold you to that. You've signed nothing. And there's a chance we could get this ultimatum thrown out if we take it high enough."

I looked over at Hannah. "What do you think?" I asked her. "Does that change anything for you?"

Hannah didn't answer right away. She was sitting cross-legged in her chair, with Milo squished in beside her; he was slightly luminous, like the opposite of a shadow.

"I don't want to fight it," she said very slowly. "And it's not just because I don't want to cause more problems."

I raised an eyebrow at her; she hastened to defend herself.

"No, I mean it! Just think about it for a minute. This paranormal-vigilante thing has become really important to us. We're always looking for new projects, even when we have a million other things going on. We even went after Freeman when we knew we might get in trouble—and not just from the Durupinen. But now we have a chance to do it for real, without worrying if we're breaking any rules. We'll get to work on cases that really matter, big ones. And we'll have the resources of the Trackers behind us; I'm sure we can learn something from them. Plus there's the money—having the Council fund us will be a huge relief for our finances. I love what we do, Jess, but let's be honest—that *Ghost Oracle* trip was really expensive. Imagine not having to consider if we could afford to take a case!"

I couldn't argue with Hannah on that point. I'd been thinking about the money, too. It took us nearly six months to plan the Poughkeepsie trip, largely because we had to scrimp and save every extra penny to afford the travel expenses and Freeman's overpriced tickets. There was a reason we'd driven four hours each way inside of one day: It saved us from having to shell out money for a hotel room.

Even in the hour since we had informed the Council that we would join the ranks of the Trackers, I had allowed my imagination to run away with me just a tiny bit. What kinds of places might we be able to travel to? What injustices might we be able to stop? As much as I hated to admit it, the Durupinen were likely giving us the chance of a lifetime. It was growing harder and harder to see this as a punishment.

In fact, there was only one factor in this situation giving me true pause, and she had just walked into the room.

Catriona took care to slam the door loudly behind her to announce her presence. It wasn't until she'd strutted behind the desk, dropped into her chair, pulled an apple from her top drawer, shined it on her shirt, and enthusiastically bit into it, that she even bothered to look at any of us. It was quite a show.

"Well, then. Here we are. Isn't this right lovely?" she said in a bored voice.

Karen clenched and unclenched her fists but said nothing.

Catriona took another bite of her apple; she didn't bother to swallow before continuing, and gross little chewed flecks spit from her mouth as she spoke. "Before we get started, I want to make a few things perfectly clear. To begin with, I did *not* volunteer for this job. I didn't want it, and neither did anyone else, for that matter. But as you all bloody well know, the Council doesn't give a damn what any of us want. They have their agenda—our value lies only in how we can serve it, and nowhere else."

Well, she had that part of it right, anyway.

"There's another thing I have to make very clear straight off if we are to work together: I had nothing to do with Lucida's betrayal. I didn't know she was working with the Necromancers—if I had, I would've done my damnedest to stop her. She's my cousin and I love her still, but her mistake was *not* my mistake. I shan't tolerate any confusion on that point," Catriona declared, before taking one last bite of her apple and tossing the core into a trash can halfway across the room.

"Now despite the fact that the Council stuck their noses into every titchy corner of my life, they found not a shred of evidence against me. Because there's none to find. Yet regardless of my own loyalty, the Council seems to be of the opinion that I, too, should be punished for Lucida's crimes. They can't sanction me properly, of course, but they're throwing me those tasks that no one else wants. So here we are, and we all must carry on," Catriona said.

"And has the Council bothered to take into account your obvious animosity toward these girls?" Karen asked. I could see her nostrils flaring from the effort of keeping herself under control. Finn too tensed up; I could tell he didn't trust Catriona with us.

"I don't have any animosity toward them," Catriona replied, using a tone that made it clear she meant exactly the opposite.

I laughed incredulously. "You don't think anyone actually believes that, do you?"

"I'm not bothered whether you believe it or not," Catriona replied, tracing her finger over the suggestion of a wrinkle near the corner of her eye. Perhaps I was imagining it, but I thought Catriona's formerly flawless beauty seemed strained and faded now, like it had been left in bright sunlight for too long. Actually, on second thought, I probably wasn't imagining it; Catriona had been a Leecher, like so many others.

"Oh, you don't care? Big surprise there sweetheart," came Milo's caustic voice through our connection. I wasn't sure if he'd meant for us to hear him or not—every once in a while, especially when he was angry, something like that could slip through. Hannah ignored him, so I took my cue from her and stayed focused on Catriona.

I sat up straighter as Catriona continued. "But for clarity's sake, here's a summary of my feelings toward you both, as they stand at the moment. Jessica, I think you've got a proper attitude. I think your gifts as a Muse and Walker have given you a fully exaggerated view of your own importance. Your actions were rash, stupid, and careless. If the Council had any bottle, they would've thrown the book at you." She looked at Hannah. "And you. I'm not sure what to make of you—nor does anyone else. You're a properly dangerous and unpredictable little match, aren't you? And I wasn't at all put off by your stunt in the Council Room—Lucida's been Calling the spirits since she was fifteen!"

Hannah flushed and retreated deeper into Milo's space. I could feel his anger running through our connection like scalding water through a frozen pipe; he might burst at any minute. "Take it easy, Milo," I thought-spoke to him. "You're not doing us any favors if you lose it with her."

"*You're* warning me to keep my cool? Oh, that's rich!" he replied, but I felt his attempt at reigning himself in.

Catriona continued her diatribe. "As for what's happened to Lucida... well, those were her choices, but the two of you were mixed up in it. I won't pretend I'm not upset about the Council's letting you walk out of here without so much as a slap on the wrists. But I've no intention of having a heart-to-heart with you about it. In fact, consider this the last time I mention Lucida to you. She's not relevant to Tracking. And if you lot want any help from me, you won't speak her name to me again."

Catriona's truculent expression left no doubt that the subject was closed for discussion. I saw no point in beating my head against the brick wall of her determination—and neither, it seemed, did Karen.

"Fine, then. But how will this mentoring arrangement work?" Karen asked bluntly. "What will your role be in their day-to-day activities?"

"I'm not a nanny," Catriona said, addressing me and Hannah. She dropped some of her irritation, and instead took up a more businesslike tone. "On the whole, you two will be on your own. I'll be in touch when there's a case for you, and will give you instructions on handling those cases. You will follow those instructions and report back to me on your progress as needed.

I will oversee the distribution of any resources you need, and organize your travel and other arrangements. If you cock it up, I'll likely be the one to do damage control. But if you follow my instructions and don't make a proper mess of things, we will hopefully see little of each other."

"So that's it, we just... start?" I asked, a bit incredulously. "There's no training or anything?"

"Some Tracker positions require strict training, and heaps of it. But we're not expecting you to forge documents, burgle, or perform any other specialized duties. We are asking you to do is what you have, in essence, already been doing on your own. As you move up in the Tracker scheme, your skill sets may expand. We will train you as appropriate."

"Burgle?" Hannah squeaked, looking petrified. "You mean breaking and entering?"

"No one is going to ask you to do that, Hannah," Karen said soothingly. "And even if they did, you could certainly refuse. You're not required to do anything you aren't comfortable with."

Catriona smiled lazily. "You'd be surprised what you can get comfortable with after a time."

"Yes, a flexible moral compass works wonders," Karen said, as her expression turned disdainful.

"So what now?" I asked, jumping in. "Do we just go home and wait for your phone call?"

"There's no waiting required this time around. The Council already has an assignment for you," Catriona said, reaching into her desk again and pulling out a bulging file folder. "We've been following this one for several months now. Based on what we know so far, it seems a perfect fit for you. Have a look."

She tossed the folder across the desk. It skidded across the surface; I had to jump out of my seat to catch it before it slid onto the floor. I opened the folder and saw a ruggedly handsome face staring back at me—a face I already knew.

"Jeremiah Campbell?" I cried.

A shard of surprise finally pierced Catriona's perpetually bored expression. "You know Jeremiah Campbell?"

"Not personally, but we already have a huge file on him. He was going to be our next major case, once we'd finished with Freeman."

"Out with it then. Tell me what you know," Catriona demanded.

I explained all the information Annabelle had gathered on

Campbell, including all we knew about Whispering Seraph. I went into detail about the rich and famous guests—including Talia Simms—who were flocking there. Hannah had read the Campbell file on our drive to New York; she added in her own always-keen insights as I explained.

"To be honest, though, I'm surprised the Durupinen are interested in him," I said. "He's just another con artist, as far as I can tell; he's not much different than Freeman, except for the wealth of his clientele."

As I rifled through the file, one particular picture caught my attention; Campbell, with an utterly enraptured expression, was standing by the wrought iron gates of his new property; his head was cocked gently to one side as though listening to something no one else could hear. I kept staring at the photo; there was something about it that left me cocking my own head to the side and listening, it seemed, for echoes trapped in the paper itself.

"There's more to the Campbell situation than meets the eye," Catriona said. She held her hand out for the file, which I passed to her. She flipped through it for a moment, then handed a single sheet of paper back to me. It was a photocopy of an old, hand-drawn map. "His property is situated on a site once owned by the Durupinen."

Karen, Finn, and Hannah all peered over my shoulder at the map. The words were in ancient Gaelic, but someone had used a yellow highlighter to show the location in question. One word in particular caught my eye: *Príosún*.

"Was there a *príosún* on this site?" I asked, as my heartbeat sped up. A *príosún* wasn't just a Durupinen jail, it was a prison reinforced by many Castings, where Elementals—horrifying creatures which inspired in their victims the very terror they fed off of—were sometimes Bound for use in Durupinen interrogation and trials. My own experience in the Fairhaven *Príosún* had been one of the most harrowing of my life; I still had nightmares about the Elemental Bound there.

"Yes, indeed," Catriona said, oblivious to my silent panic. Campbell's so-called miracles caught our attention. When we began researching him, we found that his mansion, Whispering Seraph, was built on land which belonged to the Durupinen at one time. It's been abandoned by our clans for centuries, but the one record we could locate documents the existence of a *priosún* on the site."

"And now this man who can *ostensibly* talk to spirits just happened to purchase the property? And he's using it as the hub of his paranormal enterprise?" I asked.

"Quite the little coincidence, isn't it?" Catriona said. "One day, he's a successful real estate magnate, the next he's the spirits' best friend."

"Coincidence doesn't even begin to cover it," Karen murmured, intrigued in spite of herself.

"So you think this guy actually can see spirits now?" I asked.

"We don't know. There's certainly no blood relation to any Durupinen, Caomhnóir, or Dormant—at least not one that we've discovered. But his purchasing this property and using it in this way means there must be a connection we've missed."

"So what are we supposed to do?" Hannah asked. "If we were doing this on our own, we'd be trying to expose him as a fraud. But if you don't think he's a fraud... what then?"

"Simple. We send you undercover to Whispering Seraph. We'll pay Campbell's outrageous fee. You'll pose as wealthy young heiresses who recently lost their best friend—terribly tragically, of course." Catriona nodded her head at Milo. "That's your ticket in, Spirit Guide.

"Wait, I'm a Tracker too?" cried Milo in genuine surprise. "Did I miss that part?"

Catriona rolled her eyes. "No, you're a Spirit Guide, pledged to these girls. If they're on a mission, you are too. Now pipe down."

Hannah looked at Milo. "Is that alright with you?"

Milo didn't answer verbally, but his form grew momentarily brighter in assent. The words that came through our connection, however, didn't match his brightness at all. "Except for that piping down part, you hag!"

Hannah and I suppressed a giggle as Catriona continued. "Once at Whispering Seraph, you'll be a part of his 'Sanctuary,' which is his posh name for his spirit-related services. You are to observe Campbell—we'll need you to work out if he's truly communicating with the spirits. If he's properly Sensitive, we'll need to know how his connection works. We'll also want you to learn what you can about the property. We haven't any way, at this point, of discovering the Durupinen link unless we have someone on the inside."

"And you think we're the best choice for this assignment?" I asked skeptically. "Surely you've got other Trackers who go undercover all the time. Why us?"

"For one thing, you're Americans. Less likely to raise suspicion. You also have the added benefit of understanding how these supposed mediums operate. You'll be able to spot his tricks, if there are any. And of course, Hannah is a Caller, isn't she?" Catriona said, smiling coldly at my twin. "She can command the spirits on the property to help you. And I suppose, in a pinch, you could Walk, Jessica, if you needed to."

"I only Call in emergencies," Hannah said sharply. "I don't use it unless I have to."

"Nor should you, pet," Catriona replied. "But if the emergency arises, you've got an ability that none of our other Trackers have. At least, not anymore."

"Same goes for me and Walking," I declared. "Let's be clear about that."

"And what about me?" Finn asked firmly, stepping forward suddenly. "They're not going into that place unprotected."

"Oh no, we wouldn't dream of it," said Catriona, throwing Finn a contemptuous look. "Many of the wealthy have bodyguards. You'll be undercover as well, Caomhnóir Carey, as a typical guerrilla for hire. That ought to suit you, wouldn't you say?"

Finn's hands clenched into tightly balled fists at his sides, but he didn't respond.

Catriona smiled at him with a false sweetness, as though she could hear every rude thing Finn was being forced to leave unsaid. "Once you've determined what's happening there, we'll be able to formulate a plan to put Campbell out of business. I do realize that you and the Council mightn't be feeling very chummy at the moment, but at least we can all agree that this man needs to be stopped. Exploitation of Durupinen gifts cannot and will not be tolerated."

"Yeah, except for hundreds of years of Leeching," Milo quipped through our connection, causing me very nearly to choke on my next words.

"So, when would we start?" I asked.

"It will take a few days to make the needed preparations. And you'll need to study up on your new identities and properly commit to your backstory. Once we've organized a meeting with Campbell, we'll fly you to New Orleans and... off to the races we go!" Catriona said, leaning back in her chair with a broad smile on her face.

I looked back down at the map in my hands and felt the stirring of something other than fear. We were Trackers. We were going undercover to take down Jeremiah Campbell and his multi-million dollar operation. It was insane. It was dangerous. And I was really freaking excited about it.

§

"I can't believe you're this excited," Hannah said, as we made our way back to our room after dinner.

"I think you were more right than we realized, Hannah. I think I do need trouble in my life." I sighed. "I'm sorry... I know that's hard for you... but we're both committed to stopping these frauds, right?"

Hannah stopped short and looked me in the eye. Thank God we were twins: Her look clearly expressed, "In some ways, we're two very different people, but I love you and wouldn't have it any other way." Neither of us, though, would've ever said anything so stupidly sappy out loud. Milo, who was nearby but hadn't materialized, made an exaggerated puking sound through our connection. We both giggled, relieved that Milo's comic relief gave us a legitimate, unsentimental out.

A movement on the staircase caught my eye. It was Finn. Seriously, did he really need to follow us back to our room?

I pushed my resentment aside, at least for the moment. I owed Finn a conversation, and now was a good a time as any. "Hannah, I'll meet you in our room in a little while," I said, and began trotting toward the staircase before she could object.

"Finn?" I called. "Can I talk to you for a minute?"

At my voice, he clicked his heels together stiffly and stood at attention. Maybe it was the psychological effect of being back in the place where he'd been drilled so relentlessly during his training, but it seemed like Finn had reverted back to the strictest of Caomhnóir behaviors—he'd been at attention more often than not since we'd arrived.

He looked at me, perhaps surprised by my tone, and relaxed his posture. "Yes, of course."

"I just... I want you to know that I considered you," I began.

He scowled. "What do you mean?"

"I considered you when we made this decision. I didn't just make it for myself and Hannah."

"You didn't feel the need have a proper talk with me beforehand, though," he pointed out.

I sighed. It was a very fine line I was walking, between my need for independence and the need to accept that our lives were inextricably linked together—even though "together" didn't come to mean at all what I'd hoped.

"You're right Finn, I didn't. Because it still needed to be our decision—mine and Hannah's. We're the ones who'll be taking on an entirely new role here, the ones whose lives will be upended. You'll still be doing what you've always done—protecting us in our day-to-day lives. That part doesn't change."

"That never changes," Finn said brusquely, and I thought I heard some resentment there. I tried not to let it derail me before I said what I needed to say.

"But I was thinking about you too. I'm not that selfish... I realize that this will impact you. It will probably make your job harder some of the time."

"I never said you were selfish," he grumbled.

"I know, I know. Look, I'm not trying to pick a fight with you, I just want... wanted you to know that," I said, dropping my eyes from his face." I took a deep breath and blew it out slowly. "I thought about it, and felt it would be worse for you if other Caomhnóir were following us around. I thought that would feel like an insult to you."

Finn's eyes widened just a little. "Jess, I—" he began, but then he stopped himself with a violent shake of his head.

"What?" I asked.

"I... appreciate the consideration," he finally said stiffly.

I wasn't convinced that that was what he'd intended to say, but I let it go—let it go like so many unsaid and unexplained things between us.

"Alright," I said. "I'll see you in the morning." I turned quickly and began walking back to my room. I couldn't start torturing myself over Finn, not now. Tomorrow was my first full day as a

Tracker: We had our target, and I was starting to feel like I'd been born for this.

II

THE LAFAYETTE BOARDING
HOUSE

A LOT CAN HAPPEN IN THREE DAYS. Take me, for example. Three days before, I'd been a part-time museum tour guide, part-time barista in Salem. Now, after only a few days at Fairhaven, I was a full-time Council-sanctioned Tracker about to go undercover as a wealthy heiress at a psychic retreat in New Orleans. I couldn't even keep track of how many levels of weird this was.

The Lafayette Boarding House, where we would be staying during our first night in New Orleans, was located in the historic Garden District. The Lafayette Boarding House stood on a street lined with other pristine, elaborate houses—like gingerbread confections brought magically to life. Each Victorian was painted in bright colors, surrounded by a small but meticulously kept garden, and enclosed by a shiny, black wrought-iron fence. I would've been instantly enchanted by the history and Southern charm of it all if I hadn't been so horribly jet-lagged and motion sick. Even with Durupinen "travel perks," our trip took nearly eighteen hours—an ordeal that left me exhausted and longing for unconsciousness.

"Bennett, stop the car for a moment, please," said Catriona.

"But the house is further up the street. This is number twenty-five. The Lafayette Boarding House is—"

"Is that how those little numbers on houses work? My, that is confusing, isn't it?" Catriona said scathingly, tapping a finger to her chin. "Stop the bloody car."

Bennett pulled the car to the curb, muttering resentfully under his breath. Catriona, with a serious expression on her face, turned to us.

"There are a few things you ought to know about your hosts," Catriona announced.

I sat up straighter and tried to look awake. "That sounds serious. What is it?"

"As you know, a fair few Durupinen assimilate into normal society. They get married, have families, hold down normal jobs, the lot. But for some... well, the gift can be isolating, and some of us take that isolation rather to the extreme."

She paused as though she were stringing her words together and testing them out in her mind before letting them fly. "The Lafayette Boarding House is owned by Loretta and Lu-Ann Lafayette. They come from a very old clan—one that's been rooted in this city since the French arrived in the early 1700's. They were never what you'd properly call a political clan—they kept to themselves for generations. By the time Lu-Ann and Loretta came along, the clan was entirely reclusive. In fact, I'm not sure that Lu-Ann and Loretta have so much as set foot off their property since they were Apprentices."

"Okay, so they're hermits. That's what you needed to tell us?" Hannah asked.

"It's rather more extreme than that. Like you, they're twins. But even beyond that, their bond is... particularly close. It's simply... a bit tricky to put into words. You'll see what I mean—they can be a bit off-putting. And the house—"

"My whole life is off-putting," I said, cutting her off. "Thanks for the heads up, but we can deal."

Catriona smirked at me. "Very well. I'll let you 'deal,' as you say. Drive on, Bennett. The Ballard twins are quite ready to meet the Lafayette twins."

A minute later we came to a stop in front of a beautiful two-story house painted in bright red, with a mustard-and-white gingerbread trim. From the outside, the second floor looked almost exactly like the first; identical bay windows and columned porches were stacked one on top of the other, with creeping vines winding up the railings. The vines seemed to be tying the whole house together like laces on a huge shoe. The boarding house sat perched daintily in the center of a spectacular garden, which was bursting with lush plantings and semi-tropical blooms.

The Lafayette Boarding House was as picturesque and inviting as any other house in the district, with one glaring exception—a faded sign, peeling from years in the sweltering heat, hung on the low, wrought iron fence. It read: "The Lafayette Boarding House:

124

No vacancies." Then, just to drive the point home, the unapologetic next line announced: "Trespassers will be shot on sight."

Okay, that got my attention: I was awake now.

"Shot on sight?" Milo read out loud. "Is that even legal?"

"Having the sign is, I guess, as long as you don't actually follow through with it," I replied. Then I turned to Catriona, narrowing my eyes. "They're expecting us, right?"

Catriona smiled. "Yes, of course. It took a good bit of persuading, but they agreed to help."

"How much persuading?" Hannah asked nervously, but Catriona had already opened her door and was sliding out onto the sidewalk.

"How much persuading?" Hannah repeated in a tiny voice, apparently just to herself. My sister was in many ways the strongest person I knew, but the many tribulations that had called upon her strength had marked her with a good deal of nervous energy.

By the time we'd all clambered out of the car, Catriona was already pulling the chain of the house's antique doorbell. I could hear the bell pealing through the enormous house; its echoes overlapped so that it sounded as if each new clang was multiplied.

Finn took a half step in front of me as the sound of locks being undone came from the other side of the heavy oak door, signaling its imminent opening. His arm swung out protectively and instinctively—like my mom's used to do when our car would stop short. However fleeting his touch, his hand against my collarbone left me momentarily breathless. The touch triggered something in him too, because he turned to look at me; a familiar something blazed in his eyes. But the moment was quickly forgotten as we turned and saw what was standing in the doorway.

The opened door revealed a bizarre time warp into which the last ninety years hadn't ever managed to intrude. But even creepier than the museum-home itself were the two diminutive women framed in the doorway. They stood there holding hands, and looked so identical to each other that, at first, I thought a mirror was playing tricks on my eyes. Their faces were pale and chalky; each was plastered with a thick layer of makeup that had settled into their wrinkles in a way that made them look as if they needed to be dusted. Each head of mousy gray hair was parted down the middle and slicked mercilessly into a tight bun. They were dressed in outfits nearly a century out of style—boxy, flapper era, navy blue dresses with square sailor collars.

"There are no vacancies," she said. No. No, *they* said. Both of their mouths were moving, like two red-ringed eyes on a single face, but their voices were so in sync that they were almost indistinguishable.

"Um, yes, we saw the sign out front," Catriona said, gesturing over her shoulder back toward the street.

"No vacancies. No room for a living soul, I'm afraid," they said, shaking their heads regretfully and in perfect unison. "No, not a one."

My mouth hung open as I stared unabashedly. I knew I was being incredibly rude, but I simply couldn't stop myself. Beside me, Hannah was mouthing wordlessly; her face was twisted into an expression reflecting equal parts shock and anxiety.

Milo managed to speak, but he muttered his words so quietly that I felt them through our connection more than I heard them out loud. "Oh, this is some sideshow shit right here."

"Good evening, Miss Lu-Ann. Miss Loretta," Catriona began. "We spoke on the phone. I'm Catriona Harrington, and these are the Ballard girls, their Spirit Guide, Milo Chang, and their Caomhnóir, Finn Carey. They need some Durupinen hospitality while visiting New Orleans, and you very kindly agreed to put them up."

Lu-Ann and Loretta leaned in toward each other so that their cheeks were pressed together, and began whispering to each other in a language I didn't recognize. They stared at us during their rapid, hissed exchange. At last, they drew apart again and their faces broke into duplicate toothy smiles; I noticed that their unnaturally wide eyes didn't reflect those smiles.

"Oh yes, of course. Please do come in out of the heat," they said. They unclasped their hands, slowly turned their backs on us, re-clasped their hands, and walked, with identical clicking steps, down their shadowed hallway.

I looked over at Catriona. She was watching us, choking back a silent bout of laughter. "How are you 'dealing,' then?" she asked, before following the Lafayette twins down the hall. She whistled as she followed them.

Finn cleared his throat. "After you," he said, gesturing to the door.

"Oh, thanks so much," I said acidly, pushing past him.

Hannah followed me inside, then drew her step level with mine. We were walking so close together that our shoulders touched.

Milo followed behind us, although he too stayed unnatural close. Shuffling down the hallway as though conjoined, we probably looked just as strange as our hostesses.

"Are they... what's wrong with them?" Hannah whispered.

"I guess they're just... close?" I suggested.

"Close to what? Insanity?" Milo cried.

We followed Catriona through the dust and the gloom. The house was as frozen in time as the women who lived in it. Heavy drapes were pulled across all of the windows. The only light in the house came from the old-fashioned gas lamps lining the walls; thankfully they'd been refurbished for electricity. The furniture was old and uninviting, and it seemed every piece was draped with a doily or faded afghan. Somber portraits, probably painted by long dead artists, adorned the walls; the people depicted in those portraits glowered down at us. A few paintings, though, were covered in white sheets—they looked like cartoon ghosts hanging in midair.

Lu-Ann and Loretta led us into a formal parlor. Above the fireplace, a portrait of a confederate officer hung as if he were presiding over the room.

"Won't you sit down?" they asked, with two pasty hands extended toward a moth-eaten sofa. Hannah and I dropped onto it at once. Catriona perched herself on the arm of a wing chair. Finn took up a quintessentially Caomhnóir position in the doorway; his eyes darted around the room, perhaps on the lookout for the appearance of further creepy doppelgangers.

"I want to thank you both again. The Council appreciates your cooperation." Catriona said. "We may need to be in the city for some time, and having a local base to work from will be invaluable."

"It's no trouble," Lu-Ann and Loretta said. "Happy to oblige."

"We're hoping that Hannah and Jessica will both be staying elsewhere very shortly, but there are no guarantees. Having alternate accommodation at the ready is necessary. Can I assume you've made the arrangements we requested?"

"Oh yes," Lu-Ann and Loretta said. "We've prepared the rooms as you directed. They will be yours for as long as you need them. Our usual guests have made other arrangements until you've finished your work here."

"Your other guests?" I asked before I could stop myself. "You... um, usually have other visitors staying here?" I looked around at the dust-covered surfaces and the cobwebs hanging from the chandelier.

"Yes indeed, we are always quite crowded," Lu-Ann and Loretta said, with simultaneous sweeping gestures. "We always have been. The Lafayette Boarding House has a wonderful reputation for Southern hospitality."

It was one thing when the Lafayette twins had been giving short answers in unison. Now they were speaking in whole paragraphs, yet never once did their voices diverge. They were starting to remind me of the "twin" form the Fairhaven Elemental had taken when I demanded to speak with it—and if I didn't get control over myself, I was going to completely freak out any moment.

"I don't doubt that," Catriona said, cutting off Milo, who was giving every indication that he was about to let loose a snarky comment. "Well, I don't want to draw things out, as I'm sure you're terribly busy. I've just got some documents from the Council for you to look over regarding your compensation, and then we can get the girls settled in."

"We keep our register and our guest records in the library. Won't you follow us, please?" the Lafayette twins said, leading Catriona through a set of pocket doors into the adjoining room. We got just a glimpse of the library before they slid the doors shut again; surely not a single one of those books lining the walls had been touched or read in years.

"If I knew we'd be staying in the Bates Motel, I wouldn't have agreed to come down here!" Milo hissed. "What in the name of Versace is wrong with them?"

"I'm sure they're just... I mean, I'm sure they're not..." Hannah began weakly.

"They're not what? Functioning with two separate brains?" Milo gave a dramatic shiver. "Why can't we just find a freaking Holiday Inn?"

"The Durupinen always use their networks when they travel. It helps eliminate paper trails and minimizes the risk of outside interference," Finn said. "But still... I'll not deny that they're... unnerving."

"That's the understatement of the century," I said. "And no one in their right mind would stay here unless they lost a bet! Who are these guests they mentioned?"

Finn shrugged. "I suppose they could be lying to protect their pride."

"Or they're so crazy that they don't realize the house is empty. They probably haven't spoken to anyone else in years," Hannah said. "Is it just the two of them left in their family?"

"Who cares? I vote for driving straight to Whispering Seraph and begging for asylum," Milo said.

"Let's not panic," I said, trying to be mature and reasonable. "They're a little weird, but they're not serial killers."

Milo snorted, as though he highly doubted my assessment. "Prove it," he said flatly.

"Whispering Seraph isn't an option yet," Finn said. "We have to wait until Iggy gets here in the morning with the equipment, and we need time tonight to review our cover story. And besides, our appointment isn't until tomorrow—Campbell doesn't reschedule for anyone. We're here for the night. No arguing."

Milo whimpered. Hannah sighed resignedly. I said nothing; there was too much sense in what Finn had said to argue with him. We were stuck here, so we might as well make the best of it.

The pocket doors slid open again, and Catriona and the Lafayette sisters came back into the parlor. Catriona tucked a few papers into a folder, which she then slipped into her bag.

"Right. Well, if that's all, I'll be off. I've got my own... case to work on. For the Trackers. But I'll be available to assist, if need be."

"You're leaving? Right now?" Hannah asked, with her voice sliding up a whole octave in her panic. "Aren't you going to... Why can't you stay?"

Catriona shook her head. "I'm not a babysitter, pet. I've got my own job to see to. I agreed to get you started, and I'll be in touch. Finn will be giving me daily updates on your progress and will keep me informed of any additional resources you may need."

"So that's it?" I asked. I tried to sound unconcerned, but my undercurrent of anger rippled ever so slightly to the surface. "You're just going to leave us here?"

"We believe in trial by fire, love, remember? And you Ballard girls, you're quite old hat when it comes to fire, aren't you now?" Catriona said. There was nothing friendly in the smile she flashed at us now, and every doubt I'd had about her being our Tracker mentor was confirmed by that a single baring of her teeth. "Your abilities are legendary already. I don't expect you'll need any help from little old me."

With that, Catriona sauntered from the room, tossing a sardonic laugh into the air as she went.

§

"You must be plumb worn out," the Lafayette twins said, still talking in unison as they led us up the creaky staircase.

I forced my reluctant voice up out of my throat. "Yes we are, thank you."

"Not at all. You should find your quarters comfortable, we've given you the best rooms. You can rest yourselves."

The second floor consisted of one long hallway lined with polished doors on either side. At first glance, the hall's dust and cobwebs covered everything so thoroughly that the second floor appeared to exist on the other side of a thin, draped veil. Each room had a large brass number affixed to the door, as well as a plaque bearing the name of each room—"The Peony Suite;" "The Rose Suite;" "The Snapdragon Suite;" "The Camellia Suite." I thought the room names were probably a tribute to the house's magnificent gardens.

"Mrs. Biddeford retires very early, so do keep the noise down after dark," Lu-Ann and Loretta said, both gesturing to the Snapdragon Suite. "And Mr. Hughes can't abide the cussing and cursing from young people nowadays, so we must ask you to watch your language in the halls." They pointed to the Peony Suite.

I glanced at Finn, who shrugged. It seemed these unseen guests were just as strange as their hostesses.

"If you do hear a ruckus coming from this room," Lu-Ann and Loretta went on, gesturing toward the Rose Suite, "don't trouble yourself. Dr. and Mrs. Miller fight like cats and dogs, but they really are awfully fond of each other at heart."

Even as they said it, two angry voices permeated the hall from behind the door.

"...can't fathom why you'd think that I—"

"—My dear, I the number of things *you* can't fathom would fill a book!"

Lu-Ann and Loretta chuckled. The silvery sound raised goose bumps on my arms.

We stopped in front of the Lilac Suite and waited while Lu-Ann opened the door with an antique skeleton key; it was one of many keys she kept on the kind of ring a jailer would carry around in an old Western movie. At least the room had been cleaned, unlike all the rest of the spaces we'd seen in the house so far. Everything, from the blankets to the carpet to the curtains, was in various shades of purple, and the room still smelled like mothballs and mildew. The beds had been turned down, and a vase full of the room's namesake lilacs adorned the desk under the window. The flowers added a sticky sweet scent to the air; their aroma mixed with the mothball smell in the worst possible way. The dark velvet curtains had been pulled back so that late afternoon sunlight streamed in through the open windows; when the curtains were pulled shut again, I knew the room would be as dark as a tomb in the dead of night. The shelf over the fireplace held half a dozen porcelain dolls wearing a rainbow of sherbet-colored dresses. Like everything else in this place, the dolls were spooky as hell; I was seized with an immediate desire to stuff them all into the fireplace, stack them up like cherub-faced logs, and set a match to them.

"We do hope you find everything to your liking," said Lu-Ann and Loretta. "There's a bathroom at the end of the hall, and fresh towels in the closet. Your dinner trays will be up in just a few minutes. There's fresh water in the basin if you'd like to wash up. We'll bid you good night, then."

"Good night?" Milo repeated, looking incredulous. He waited until the twins closed the door behind them before pointing to the window. "It's barely five thirty! The sun hasn't even set!"

"That's what happens when you haven't left your house since Prohibition, I guess," I said. I reached down and tried to cool myself by flapping my shirt against my midsection, but it was heavy and limp from my sweat-soaked body. The air in the room was stagnant and stifling, despite the open window.

Hannah began walking around the room, examining it. "There's water in this pitcher!" she said in astonishment, pointing to a washstand with a white porcelain pitcher and bowl. "I think we're supposed to pour it into this bowl to wash our faces!" I couldn't tell from the squeak in her voice if she was horrified or fascinated. I suppose it could've been both.

A sudden sharp knocking came from the door I'd assumed was

our closet. I leapt back and screamed, as did Hannah. Milo shot back across the room like he'd been hooked on a fishing line.

"It's only me," came Finn's calm and steady voice from behind the door.

"Finn? How did you get in our closet?" I asked.

"I'm not in your closet," he said impatiently. The door swung open; Finn stood in a room almost identical to ours, except it was decorated in pale blues instead of garish purples. "Our rooms are adjoining. I thought you ought to know, in case you need anything from me in the middle of the night."

Milo's wisecrack shot through our connection like lightning. "Oh... I can think of a few things you might need from Finn in the middle of the night!" I suppose I should've been grateful that Milo didn't say the damn thing aloud, but I had to fight from blushing nonetheless.

"Thanks, Finn," I said a bit louder than was strictly necessary, given that the comment I was trying to block out was in my head.

"Hey, did you guys notice these runes?" Hannah asked. I turned to see her squatting in front of the windowsill. "These aren't Wards. Or at least, they aren't the usual Wards."

We all joined her at the window. Finn reached out and touched the runes. They hadn't merely been painted or drawn; they were branded into the wood, and sunken and blackened with age.

"I don't recognize them," I said.

"Of course you don't," said Hannah. "You never learned runes like you were supposed to."

"I know... some of them," I said defensively, but Hannah raised an eyebrow at me. I grinned sheepishly. "Okay, okay, I'm a rune delinquent. Do *you* know what they mean?"

"I might!" Finn announced excitedly, startling me so badly that I tumbled backward into a sitting position, before flopping awkwardly onto the plum-colored carpet. "Milo! Come over here and see if you can exit through this window."

Milo, who had been staring at the water pitcher as though it were the mouth of hell itself, looked up at the sound of his name. "Huh? Oh, sure." He flew at the window with a confident speed, expecting to glide right through the pane; instead, he bounced right off of it.

"What the—" Milo tried again. Again he couldn't cross through the glass, and instead tumbled backward toward the middle of the room.

"Reverse Wards," Finn said, slapping a hand against his thigh. "Meant to keep spirits in, not out. I remember reading about them for a test. Never thought I'd see them in use, though. Milo, try crossing into my room."

Milo approached the wall separating Finn's room from ours, moving a bit more cautiously this time. Sure enough, he couldn't enter Finn's room no matter how hard he tried.

Finn hopped up and examined the open doorway. "Try through here," he said.

Milo floated easily through the door into Finn's room and back again. "No problem here," he said.

Finn closed the door between our rooms. "Have a go at it now."

Milo tried but failed. "Nope, can't do it," he said. "Not unless the actual door is open."

Finn pointed to the panel on the door itself. Another rune was burned into the wood, in the exact spot where a peephole would usually be. "These Wards on these rooms are designed to make the spirits follow the same rules as living people, in terms of entering and leaving. If they want to come in, they need to use an open door, just like the rest of us."

"That's so strange," I said. "What's the point of that?"

"I'm not sure," Finn said slowly, "but I've got a theory. You up for a little Calling, Hannah?"

Hannah looked up, startled. "Calling? Here? Why?"

"You'll see. We'll have to go into the hallway, though."

Puzzled, we all followed Finn and convened outside our door; I closed it behind us as a defense against our room's purple nightmare.

"Hannah, go ahead and reach out a bit. Not too far, just within the house. See what you come up with," Finn said.

He kept his tone light and casual, and I knew Finn was doing it for Hannah's benefit. Calling dredged up a lot of painful memories for her; for a while after we'd defeated the Necromancers, she had refused to use Calling consciously.

Before we'd left Fairhaven yesterday, Hannah, Finn, and I had talked about her fears. We all agreed that while it was important for her to wield her gift sparingly and with caution, it was also important for her to overcome her fear of Calling; we never knew when we might truly need it.

Finn put a reassuring hand on Hannah's shoulder and squeezed it lightly. She looked at him and gave him a timorous smile. "Okay. I can do that. Just a little bit," she said, as much to herself as to Finn. Then she closed her eyes and reached out into the space around her, pulling at the invisible strings that would tie her to any spirit in the area—like casting out a thousand fishing lines and giving each a tug to see what was on the other end.

Hannah was quiet for a few moments, and then her mouth fell open. She let out a gasp that was half a laugh, then opened her eyes. "I can't believe it!" she said, looking back at Finn, who was nodding; apparently, Hannah had just confirmed whatever theory he'd formulated.

"What? What is it?" I asked eagerly.

Without answering, Hannah closed her eyes again. Every door along the hallway flew open at once, except for ours and Finn's. I leapt back with a yell.

Spirits, at least one from every room, flooded into the hallway, then turned as one to follow Hannah's irresistible Call. They came toward us, then hung motionless and ready for further instruction from Hannah; Hannah merely stood and watched them with half a smile on her face.

"Meet the guests at the Lafayette Boarding House," Finn said, laughing.

"You mean they... *what?*" I said weakly. "Are you seriously telling me that we're staying in a boarding house for *ghosts?*"

"I am indeed," Finn replied, still laughing. "Lu-Ann and Loretta Lafayette, purveyors of fine accommodations for the not-so-recently departed."

Suddenly it all made sense: The dust-covered furniture; the cobwebs; the uninhabited look of the entire house. Even as I pieced it together, I wondered why I was surprised. This *was* my life, after all.

I looked around again. A middle-aged couple hovered closest to us. The husband was dressed in a white suit, with a cravat around his neck. He sported a handlebar mustache and a truly epic set of sideburns. The wife had a perfect hourglass figure, complete with a waistline that could only be achieved by use of a corset.

"How long have these spirits been here?" I whispered.

"A long time," Hannah replied, reading them like books while they remained connected through her Calling. "Some for well over a hundred years!"

I turned to Finn. "Do you think the Lafayette sisters are keeping them here on purpose? Like, trapping them?"

I looked a bit further down the hall. An elderly gentleman was wearing a snappy set of spats, and had a fedora dangling from his left hand. The other spirits in the hall were similarly attired in outdated clothes—each outfit reflected the style of the era in which its owner had died.

"You'd have to ask Lu-Ann and Loretta," Finn replied. "But honestly, I very much doubt it. I think these spirits might be more comfortable in this society of the dead than amongst the living. Any number of spirits stay behind for a good long time, even if they have the chance to Cross. Many souls choose not to let go, you know that."

"Yeah, but we always *encourage* them to go. I mean, that's our job, to help them on their way—not to collect them like souvenirs. Encouraging them to stay like this might be just as bad as forcing them to stay," I said.

Hannah opened her eyes while at the same time cutting the mental threads that tied her to the surrounding spirits. As though a hypnotist had snapped his fingers to awaken them, the spirits looked around, confused for a moment, before retreating to their rooms.

"Catriona already knew what this place was like, remember? She tried to warn us before we got here. So the Council must know all about it—and I doubt they'd let this go on if Lu-Ann and Loretta were somehow standing in the way of spirits choosing to Cross," Hannah said, reasoning out loud; the uncertainty in her voice made it clear that there was plenty of room for doubt in her mind.

"I don't have a lot of faith in what the Council will or will not allow, to be honest," I replied. Let's be sure to mention it to someone back at Fairhaven when we get the chance, anyway."

"Good idea," Hannah said, with a look of slight relief on her face.

"Okay, okay! I'll make the rounds tonight and make sure no one's being held against their will," Milo said with a long-suffering sigh. "The floaters here look about as lively as a funeral procession. I'm pretty sure I'd rather watch paint dry than talk to them, but it's the right thing to do, I guess."

Hannah smiled slyly at him. "Thank you, Milo. You're a real martyr."

We walked back into our room. Before I shut the door, I heard the Millers back at it again, bickering over what year it was.

"But what does it *matter*, darling? What does any of that *matter*? I haven't the faintest idea what year it is, but I do know it's not *our* year. The years have gone by without us!" Dr. Miller sighed wearily.

His words sent a little shiver down my spine. I hoped the Millers were truly happy staying in this realm, regardless of their incessant bickering. Maybe they were just one of *those* couples—never happy unless they were at odds. But maybe, their stay at the Lafayette Boarding House wasn't entirely voluntary; I tried not to think about it as I pulled our door shut.

12

ACCESSORIZING

"**H**ANNAH STOP," I PLEADED. "Stop reading."

"I'm just reviewing the details in this last..."

I reached down and tugged the file out of her hand. Her grip on it was impressive considering the tininess of her hands.

We were sitting at a small table in the boarding house's front room, waiting for Iggy to pick us up. Finn was still upstairs getting dressed. Milo was off trying to wheedle some last-minute information from the spirit guests, who had turned out to be pretty tight-lipped around new spirits. The blossom-scented air wafting through the open windows was heavy and hot, even at 8:00 AM. I didn't even want to think of how sweaty and miserable I'd be when high noon hit New Orleans.

I tucked the file folder into the front pocket of my suitcase and zipped it closed. "You don't need that anymore, Hannah. You know this stuff. We both do."

"I know, but I just want to make sure."

"You're just making yourself even more nervous," I told her.

"I can't get any more nervous than I am right now, so you might as well give it back to me." Hannah lunged across me, making a grab for the suitcase, but I shoved it further away with my foot.

"There's not going to be a written test, Hannah. It's just our cover story."

Hannah dropped her head into her hands. "Oh God, I'm going to screw this up. I just know it Jess, I'm going to screw this up!"

"No, you won't! It'll be fine! The only thing we really need to get across to Campbell is that our family has a shitload of money, and that we're willing to throw fistfuls of it at him if he'll help us. As soon as he sees all those dollar signs, we'll be golden. A guy like Jeremiah Campbell isn't going to care about anything else."

Hannah took a deep, shaky breath and blew it out again. "You're right. I know you're right, I'm just... I'm not good at lying."

"Sure you are!" I said, perhaps a bit too brightly.

Hannah looked up at me, affronted. "Excuse me?"

"Well, you've been lying about seeing spirits all your life, haven't you?" I pointed out.

"Oh. Well, yeah, I suppose so—but I didn't exactly pull that off all the time. I mean, I wound up in New Beginnings, didn't I?"

I grimaced. "Don't think about that right now. That's all in the past." I paused for a moment, thinking how to outline our situation in a way that would be easier on my sister's nerves. "Okay, new perspective. All we're doing is telling a story. Just telling a story. If we tell it well, we're in. If we don't, well, we'll go back to the drawing board and try something else. But we can do it, I know we can."

Hannah smiled at me. "You're very positive all of a sudden."

I smiled back. "Don't worry, I won't make a habit of it," I promised.

"May we interest you in some refreshment?"

I jumped and yelped. Lu-Ann and Loretta had appeared soundlessly beside us. They were dressed this morning in identical gardening outfits, complete with wide-brimmed straw hats and heavy gardening gloves. Lu-Ann placed two teacups full of coffee delicately on the table in front of us. Loretta offered a plate of beignets from a tarnished silver tea tray.

"Um, thank you very much," I said, taking a beignet and a plate from the tray. Lu-Ann and Loretta nodded in tandem and walked into the front hall, where they paused in front of a blacked-out mirror, faced one another, then preceded to tie the ribbons on each other's hats and tuck loose wisps of each other's hair into place.

I gasped and inhaled a lungful of powdered sugar.

"What? What is it?" Hannah asked, patting me on the back as I coughed violently.

"I just realized... the mirror thing..." I spluttered.

"What? What about them?" Hannah asked, offering me a glass of water with a slice of lemon floating in it.

I chugged the water, cleared my throat, and said, "The mirrors! The spirits don't need or want them, since they don't appear in them, obviously. But Lu-Ann and Loretta don't need them either.

They don't need them because they literally act like each other's reflections. Look!"

Hannah turned her face to the hallway and watched the Lafayette twins primp each other. Her mouth fell open.

"Okay, they are officially the creepiest thing I've ever seen, and you know I've seen some horror-movie-worthy stuff," she whispered.

Oblivious to their appalled audience, the Lafayette sisters picked up their pruning shears from entryway table and walked outside. We watched from the window as they descended the stairs into their garden.

Between choking on the beignet and the spectacle of the Lafayette sisters, I was saved the trouble of having to distract Hannah by continuing my charade. The truth was, I was terrified too. The only other time I'd ever attempted anything that required this much outright acting was when Karen and I broke Hannah out of New Beginnings; in order to gain entrance, I'd pretended to be a strung-out teen in desperate need of psychological help. That day, I'd had some significant emotional investments—utter panic included—to motivate me. But today, we'd be relying on nothing but our own acting skills; like Hannah, I too was scared that I'd blow the whole operation. Plus, if we couldn't complete our first assignment as Trackers, would the Council keep us on? Then where would we be?

"It's a good thing we don't live in New Orleans," Hannah said, breaking into my troubled thoughts.

"I know, they are so... disturbing," I whispered, looking out the window where Lu-Ann and Loretta were crouching by a rose bush, pruning with a steady, synchronized rhythm. Despite their age and giant, rusty shears, they still managed to look like children playing a game of hide-and-seek.

"No, I mean, I would probably have a heart attack by the time I was thirty—I can't stop eating these beignets."

I tried to swallow and laugh at the same time; I choked again, expelling a small cloud of powdered sugar as I coughed. I was still sputtering as Finn walked into the room.

"Good morning," he said stiffly.

"Good morning," I replied. Hannah, her mouth packed with another beignet, could only wave.

At the sight of Finn, I felt the thumping of my heart speed up.

He was dressed in a black suit, cut perfectly to accent his broad shoulders. Underneath he wore a gray shirt; a half-tied tie dangled around his neck. For once, he was clean-shaven, and he'd pulled his usually unkempt hair into a ponytail at the nape of his neck.

"I, uh… need some help," Finn said awkwardly.

"With what?" I asked, mentally shaking myself. "Get a grip, Jess: Not happening," I thought.

Finn scratched his cheek in seeming embarrassment, then said, "This tie. I almost never wear them. Normally I can get it after a few goes, but…" He gestured to the blacked-out mirror behind him. "You see my problem?"

Hannah looked at Finn's tie, but shrugged and shook her head. "I've never tied one before. I'm no help, sorry!"

I stood up. "I'll help you." I walked up to Finn and, without looking up into his face, began fiddling with the tie.

After a moment of my fussing with his tie, he asked, "How, er, did you sleep?" A mundane enough question, but it filled the yawning chasm of silence in the tiny space between us.

"Badly. Really badly," I answered. I pulled his tie knot out entirely. "Sorry, I have to redo this completely."

"Why?"

"Well, you've got it pulled too far on this side, so—"

"No, I meant, why did you sleep poorly?" Finn asked.

"Oh." I felt a flush starting to creep up my neck and color my face. "Just being in a strange place, I guess. And all of those porcelain dolls staring at me."

Finn laughed quietly; I heard the gentle rumble of it in his chest. "I was up most of the night, too. I kept thinking I was going to roll over and find our hostesses hovering over me. Charming lot, those two."

I laughed, too. "They are truly the stuff of nightmares." I pulled the knot up to his throat. "There. Much better. Very professional."

"Why do you know how to do this?" Finn asked. "You never…" he trailed off, but I knew what he was going to say.

"Never had a dad around to practice on?" He opened his mouth to apologize, but I waved him down. "Don't. It's fine. In high school, I worked at a restaurant that had ties as part of the uniform. I got really good at it. There was also a really ugly bowler hat."

Finn chuckled. "You wore a bowler hat?"

"Yes. A red one. And suspenders, too. It was heinous. Let's not talk about it, okay? I can't believe I even just told you that." I was fiddling with tie unnecessarily now, smoothing the collar down around it, breathing in Finn's smell.

"No, it sounds brilliant! I might have to give Seamus a ring, see if we can't get the official Caomhnóir uniform changed." Living in America had been good for Finn in a way. He laughed a bit more easily now, and every now and then he'd attempt a joke. Even a lame one like this.

I laughed and looked up. He was looking down at me. There was so much in Finn's gaze that I could've gotten hopelessly, wonderfully lost falling into. I had to remind myself that finding my way back out would've been the hard part.

Finn took a hasty step back so that my hands were left stretched, embarrassingly, out in front of me.

"Thank you," he said stiffly. "Iggy ought to be here soon. I'll bring these bags out, shall I?"

My good old defenses kicked in and my embarrassment hardened into something resembling resentment. "Yeah. Thanks. Don't worry, I'm sure they'll have mirrors at Whispering Seraph."

Finn dropped his eyes to the bags piled by the door. He picked them all up at once and staggered out the door. I flopped back down into my chair and rolled my eyes at Hannah.

"I guess they should've made formal wear part of the Caomhnóir training," I said, pasting on a smirk.

"It's okay, Jess," Hannah replied gently. "You don't have to do that. It's just me."

The smirk slipped from my face, leaving it naked, vulnerable. "Yeah. I know."

"Car's here!" Finn shouted from outside.

"Milo, it's time to go." Hannah's voice hummed through our connection like the strum of a guitar.

"Coming, coming! I was about to give up anyway. Ugh, these floaters are *trés* boring—and I'm pretty sure they were even less interesting when they were alive."

I chugged the remainder of my coffee and—never one to waste good breakfast pastry—wrapped several more beignets in a napkin before following Hannah out the door.

I stopped short as I spotted the sleek, black sedan. "Hey, where's my sketchy van and donuts?" I asked to no one in particular.

Finn looked up from the trunk, where he was loading the suitcases. "What?"

"We're going undercover. I've seen the movies. Aren't we going to hang out in a van with blacked-out windows and eat donuts?"

"I have no bloody idea what you're on about," Finn replied. "Is this an American thing?"

"No, it's an 'I own a TV and don't live under a rock' thing. Never mind."

"Just get in the car, will you? We've got a massive number of details to review before we get to Whispering Seraph," Finn said over Iggy's snorts of laughter. "Iggy, you need to slide over. I'm driving. It's in the plan."

"Looks like you've brought your own donuts, Jess," Iggy chuckled, nodding at the beignet-filled napkin still in my hand. "Not much we can do about the van part, though."

I smiled at him. Iggy was always game for a laugh, thank goodness. He was probably the most affable person I'd ever met, even if he did usually look like he belonged in a hard-core motorcycle gang. I handed him a beignet, took one for myself, and crumpled up the napkin before stuffing it into my purse.

"We need to get moving." Finn scowled impatiently. "Shove over."

Iggy stuck the beignet in his mouth and scooted—without objection, but with considerable difficulty—into the passenger seat. I'd barely closed the car door before Finn peeled away from the curb. Lu-Ann and Loretta waved good-bye, with their lacy white handkerchiefs fluttering in unison like damsels in distress. Creepy, creepy damsels.

"How was your flight, Iggy?" Hannah asked.

"Easy-breezy, short stack!" he said genially. "Slept like a baby from take-off to landing. I can sleep anywhere, you know that."

"Yeah, including in the middle of an investigation when you're supposed to be manning the tech," I said, winking at him.

He threw his head back and roared with laughter. "Hey, if the ghost girls aren't going to keep things interesting, I'm gonna get some shut-eye."

"You really need to stop calling us that," I said. "I'll let it slide, though, since you look so snazzy."

Iggy's typical T-shirt and bandana had been replaced by a dark suit almost identical to Finn's. Even more astonishing was that Iggy had trimmed his beard to a semi-respectable length.

Iggy grimaced, tugging at the tie around his neck. "Haven't worn a suit since my pops died in '94. Hated it then, hate it now."

"You look very handsome Iggy," Hannah said, smiling.

Iggy turned around and grinned at her, revealing the great gap between his front teeth. "Thanks, short stack, but I won't be making a habit of it. I feel like a stiff."

"No one would believe you work security detail if you're wearing a Rolling Stones T-shirt—especially one that's nearly as old as Stones themselves," Finn said, pulling his seatbelt across himself as he drove. "We all need to look the part. Speaking of which," and he glanced at me in the rearview, "well done staying in bounds with the dress code. I wasn't sure you were going to."

I squirmed under his gaze and began smoothing the hemline of my Gucci dress, which cost more than I made in a month at my two jobs combined. "I know how important this is, I'm not going to screw it up over fashion," I said defensively—all the more so because I could feel the blood rushing to my cheeks. "And not a word out of you, please," I said through my connection to Milo, who had chosen the dress and had gone into paroxysms of glee when I'd stepped out of the bathroom that morning wearing it.

"No, we'll just find some other way to screw it up," Hannah said slightly hysterically.

I saw Finn scowl in the mirror. "Is there a problem? Hannah, are you alright?"

"Hannah's just a little nervous about convincing Campbell of our cover story," I told him.

"Just write him a check with plenty of noughts at the end. That will be all the convincing he needs," he replied.

I turned to Hannah, trying to smile reassuringly. "See? Isn't that exactly what I said?"

Hannah made a movement that was half-shrug, half-nod. It was probably as good as we were going to get out of her with her nerves this highly strung.

"Jess," buzzed Milo in my head, "I want to do some breathing exercises with Hannah, but I need your help... Iggy can't really know I'm here. Just repeat what I say." Then Milo addressed Hannah. "Sweetness, close those baby browns and follow Jess' voice."

Milo changed the connection so that only I could hear him. I repeated his calming words to Hannah and directed her breathing per Milo's technique, with Iggy none the wiser.

We'd told Iggy a sort of half-truth about Milo, even though Finn had objected. But we figured that if both Iggy and Milo were going to be included in this plan, we'd better have a cover: We'd said that Annabelle had helped Hannah make contact with a spirit who had—because of Hannah's Sensitivity—attached himself to her. Iggy couldn't know anything about any Durupinen-level stuff, so we merely told him that Milo was willing to help Hannah however he could. To secure the lie, we'd also said that Annabelle had taught Hannah how to communicate with Milo whenever she needed to. Iggy, overwhelmingly thrilled at the idea of real spirit activity, had immediately launched into a million questions, but they all concerned EVPs and tech stuff; any questions about why Hannah suddenly had this spirit attached to her simply never occurred to him.

After a few minutes of guided breathing, Hannah had calmed down a good bit. The technique was apparently very effective on Iggy too—he'd fallen fast asleep in the passenger seat.

"Milo," said Finn in a hushed tone, "come up here and see if he's properly asleep."

Milo uncurled himself from Hannah and floated forward, examining Iggy. "Yep, out cold!" he announced, just as Iggy began snoring softly.

"Right. Before we get there, I have one more accessory for both of you," Finn said to us quietly. He tossed two small square boxes into the back seat. I pulled the top off of mine to reveal a simple silver bracelet made of two intertwined, ropelike strands. A single, highly polished, oval rose quartz dangled from it.

"It's... really pretty," I said, not really sure how to respond. I looked over and saw Hannah removing an identical bracelet from her box.

"You're not to wear it because it's pretty," Finn said a bit impatiently. "You're to wear it because it's been imbued with a Casting. Catriona gave me one for each of you before she left."

"Oh," I said, turning the bracelet over in my hand. "What does it do?"

"It's called Masking," Finn explained. "It's meant to camouflage your connection to the Gateway, so that the spirits at Whispering Seraph—if there are any—don't sense it."

"Really? I didn't know there was a Casting that could do that," I replied, keeping my voice low.

"Masking doesn't last long, and it shouldn't be used often," Finn said. "From the outside, Masking works similarly to a Binding—although it doesn't prevent a Gateway from being opened should the Masked Durupinen choose to perform a Crossing. But, as with a Binding, the spirits won't be able to sense your Gateway."

"Wow," Hannah said, sliding the bracelet on. "I wish we could wear these all the time. It would be nice to control when Visitations happen."

Your bracelets are for Durupinen, but spirits can use Maskings, too." Finn said. "We're not properly sure how they do it, but we do know that there's a way spirits can Mask themselves. The little information we have points to it being the same Casting—or one quite close to it. I did a study on Masking the term before the two of you arrived at Fairhaven."

"You were at Fairhaven before us?" I asked, genuinely perplexed.

"Of course he was," Hannah answered for him. "Didn't you know the Caomhnóir start a semester before us? It's like their version of basic training."

Finn, too focused on the mission at hand for a stroll down memory lane, continued on. "Unfortunately, the more you use a Masking, the less effective it becomes—until it stops working altogether. If this job at Whispering Seraph takes longer than three or four days, we won't be able to count on the Masking bracelets to hide you any longer."

"So, what do we do then?" I asked.

"We'll cross that bridge when we get to it—if indeed we do get to it. I, for one, intend to be long done with this assignment by the time that Casting wears off," Finn said firmly, as though his affirmation ensured our swift and successful exit from Campbell's plantation.

"Oh, well, if you *intend* it, then I guess we have nothing to worry about," I grumbled, catching his glare in the rear view mirror and returning it. Even as I watched, his gaze softened so that we both had to look away; he refocused on the road and I turned to watch the rows of historic houses now flashing past.

Looking into each other's eyes was more complicated than it used to be.

I settled against the back of the seat, grabbed Hannah's hand without a word, and tried to relax. It was an hour ride from the city to Campbell's Sanctuary at Whispering Seraph.

13

JEREMIAH'S ANGEL

RIVING THROUGH THE GATES of Jeremiah Campbell's property was like stepping into the nostalgic daydream of a Tennessee Williams heroine: The place practically reeked of Southern aristocracy. After gaining clearance from the guard, we entered the property through a set of ornate wrought iron gates, and drove up a long driveway lined with enormous Southern sugar maple trees; great drooping tendrils of Spanish moss hung from their branches. The house itself loomed at the end of the driveway like a monarch awaiting visiting dignitaries. Whispering Seraph was a quintessential plantation house, propped up into a military posture by a row of Doric columns. Long, shuttered windows and a wide front porch that ran the length of the house's imposing facade completed the effect. Behind the mansion, the lawns swept back, dotted with benches and fountains; a pond with a boathouse and a dock jutting out over it was visible in the distance. A smaller pond sat glimmering in front of the house. Whispering Seraph was breathtaking; I wouldn't have been surprised to see Scarlett O'Hara storming out the front doors in a fit of passion.

At first glance, we appeared to have stepped back in time. As we got closer though, the carefully hidden modern touches began to appear: Security cameras followed our car with their electronic eyes; rows of golf carts were lined up like waiting steeds inside of an enormous open barn; a satellite dish was tucked discretely behind the massive brick chimney.

"Wow, I guess we now know how the other half lives," I said.

"Oh, I was *so* meant to be part of the other half," Milo whispered into our heads while staring out the window in awe.

"I bet they only serve organic vegan food here," said Iggy with a horrified shudder.

"Actually, the brochure advertised traditional Southern cooking, with all the comfort foods included," I said. "So we'll eat well at least."

"If he lets us in," Hannah said. "We haven't passed the screening yet, remember? I don't think we'll be getting any comfort food until then."

"Well then, let's nail this, because I'm out of beignets—which is, quite frankly, a travesty. I could go for some home-style Southern cooking," I said, with much more bravado than I felt. Now that we were staring at Campbell's plantation, the truth was that I was much more intimidated than I had prepared myself for. This place was a fortress: Infiltrating it would be no small task.

Campbell was expecting us—we'd made our appointment through the official channels. The security guards waved us right up the driveway and into a small parking lot around the far side of the house. Finn killed the engine and we exited the car; we each sported our own pair of oversized sunglasses. We made our way to the front steps, where a sunnily beaming woman in a crisp white pantsuit invited us inside.

"Welcome to the Sanctuary at Whispering Seraph, Ms. Taylor and Ms. Taylor. We've been expecting you. If you'll come this way." The woman's voice was so calming that she might've been singing a lullaby.

Obediently, we followed her into an elegant foyer with a grand staircase. A number of large paintings, probably commissioned works from successful artists, hung on the walls. I knew it was important to try to give off an air of indifference—if we really were as rich as we claimed, we would've frequented places more opulent than this. To stop myself from staring, I pulled out my phone and pretended to be texting. In actuality, I was silently snapping as many pictures as I could—if Campbell didn't invite us to stay, I might not get another chance.

The woman ushered us into a formal parlor with high ceilings, restored antique furniture, and a fireplace flanked by columns that imitated the ones on the outside of the house. Hannah and I sat down, but neither of us removed our sunglasses; it was much easier to keep hiding behind them.

"Mr. Campbell will be right with you," the woman said. She glanced at Finn and Iggy, who stood imposingly by the door with their chests thrown out and their arms crossed. "Do you prefer having your security stay with you while you meet with Mr. Campbell?"

"Yes," Hannah and I cried together, much too loudly.

"Yes," I repeated, in a calmer voice. "Our father insists on it when we're traveling without him. I hope that won't be a problem?"

"No, certainly not," the woman said, nodding at Iggy. She turned back to us, gesturing to a tea cart in the corner. "Can I offer you some refreshment? Iced tea?"

Hannah shook her head but I accepted. "No sweetener, please, and make sure it's cold."

"Of course," the woman said, pouring me a glass before heaping ice into it. She handed it to me and placed a lace-edged napkin on the table in front of me. "Mr. Campbell will be right with you." Then she backed out of the room, closing the large, polished, French doors behind her.

Hannah pulled off her sunglasses and stared at me. "What are you doing? Don't talk to her like that, we'll get in trouble!"

"No, no, it's smart," Milo said, giving me an approving smile. "She's acting like a VIP. You think the wealthy come here without personal demands? I bet Talia Simms carries a whole list of crazy things around with her wherever she goes." He sighed before adding dreamily, "I know I would."

"Yes, but we aren't famous movie stars, and we shouldn't be rude," Hannah said. She looked at Finn for guidance.

"I think it's fine. Don't talk to Campbell like that, though."

"I'm not an idiot," I snapped. To calm my mounting nerves, I took a large swig of my iced tea—and inadvertently gave myself a brain freeze headache. Well, my drink was cold, anyway; the woman knew how to follow instructions.

The door beside the fireplace swung open. I squinted through my brain freeze and watched Jeremiah Campbell stroll into the room toward us. He was tall and square-jawed, with chiseled features, thick salt-and-pepper hair, and the kind of smile you rarely saw outside of headshots and commercials.

"Ms. Taylor and Ms. Taylor. How very charming to meet you both," he said, reaching out a bronzed, perfectly manicured hand. "And let me first say, before we exchange any more pleasantries, how very sorry I am for whatever loss may have brought you here."

He had a smooth and sultry Southern drawl; the rhythm of it was pleasant and soothing, almost hypnotic. For a moment, all I could do was nod and stare at him while he shook my hand.

I pulled myself together. "Thank you," I replied. "It's been... hard."

"Oh, nothing harder, nothing harder in this world," he agreed with a solemn nod of his head. "Now, please do sit down again and make yourselves just as comfortable as you can. I see my manager Maya has offered you some refreshment. Do y'all require anything else—anything at all—before we start our interview? Please don't hesitate to ask. I assure you, it would be no trouble."

"No, thank you," I said, looking over at Hannah, who shook her head mutely. She seemed stunned, or else too nervous, to answer for herself.

"Very well, then, if you're quite sure."

Campbell took a seat facing us. "I do hope it's alright if we chat here. I generally handle these sorts of things in the office, but this is much more friendly, don't you agree? No need to put a desk between us—we'll get to know each other that much better." He smiled again.

I twitched my mouth into a smile in return. Behind me, Iggy cleared his throat quietly.

"Now, first of all, let me tell you just a little bit about myself," Campbell began, plucking a bit of lint from his cuff and flicking it gently to the carpet. "I like to start this way, you see, not because I particularly enjoy talking about myself, but because, personally, I find it so much easier to open up to someone who has first opened up to me. So I think it's most important for you to have a very clear understanding of who I am and what we do here at Whispering Seraph's Sanctuary—and not just the kind of information in the brochure. Although," he gave a small laugh, "I do hope you found our literature to be helpful and informative?"

"Yes," I replied. I cleared my throat, which felt dry despite the iced tea. "That's why we're here."

"That's just fine then," Campbell said. "Well, I had a very religious family, as one might expect, growing up in the Bible Belt, but I've never been a particularly religious man. I can't say why, exactly, that is. Maybe it's because, admittedly, I've led a charmed life, for the most part. I've been very successful in my relationships and business ventures. I was born into a solid Southern family, and I haven't faced very many struggles—perhaps that's why I never felt the true need for spiritual guidance in my life. I say this not to boast—it's just that most of the good things in my life have fallen into my lap, and I don't deny that. Happy circumstances, as it were. Good education, a well-connected family, that sort of thing. Y'all understand where I'm coming from, here?"

"Yes," I said, and Hannah nodded again. We were impersonating wealthy heiresses, after all—they would know about being born into a charmed life. "I... that is to say, we, have been very lucky as well."

"Well, yes," Campbell said, and his smile bloomed as he reached a hand out toward us. "We are quite alike in this way, aren't we?" I took his hand—largely so Hannah didn't have to—and allowed him to give it a friendly squeeze. "I spent fifty-seven years of my life overly concerned with the material, while barely sparing a thought for what we might call spiritual concerns. I never would've claimed a deep connection to those who have passed on. In fact—and I'm ashamed to admit this—but I'm not sure I truly believed in life after death. It's a thought that still torments me, knowing what I know now."

Campbell hung his head for a moment, as though in silent contemplation of this past misdeed. Hannah and I both watched him, literally mesmerized by his charm, seeming openness, and whatever show he was putting on in this moment.

He exhaled and looked up again, although his dazzling smile seemed somehow quieter now. "I may never know the reason I was chosen. Surely, there were others of much deeper faith—those far more deserving of this task—but I can't ever hope to fathom any of that. The Lord, as they say, works in mysterious ways. But the fact of the matter is, one day I woke up with a wondrous connection, a connection that I gave up quite literally everything in my life to follow. I have striven to use it for good; it's a connection I will use to help you both, if we agree that it will be mutually beneficial for all of us."

He smiled at us both again, encouraging us to contribute to the conversation. I swallowed hard. "We would love that. We... we need your help." I took Hannah's hand; I hoped it would look to Campbell as if I were reaching out to her for support, rather than trying to calm her nerves.

"Yes, let's talk about that. I'd very much like to know what brought you here today. Now that you know a bit about me, I hope you'll be inclined to tell me a bit about yourselves?"

Hannah and I looked at each other; I knew that she was truly panicking now. I suddenly realized her anxiety might work for us—Campbell would probably think she was giving into her grief.

Here goes everything. As excited as I had been a few days ago about being a Tracker, I was decidedly less than enthused now; what if this guy saw straight through us?

I turned back to Campbell and took a deep breath. "Well, you have our application, so you know a lot about us already," I said, taking off my sunglasses and forcing myself to meet his eye. "Look, I know we're a lot like you were. We haven't had a lot of struggles. Maybe that's why we're having so much trouble dealing with what's happened."

Helpfully, Hannah pulled herself together enough to nod at this point.

Campbell was nodding too, in a way that suggested he not only understood what I was saying, but that he had anticipated every word of it. "And tell me ladies, what, exactly, has happened? In your own words—and do take your time—tell me your experience," he said, with all sorts of empathy and patience in his voice. If he were faking it, he was very, very good.

"We lost our best friend," I said bluntly. "He died a few months ago, but we think he might still be here with us."

"I see," Campbell said, clasping his hands together and bringing his two pointer fingers to rest thoughtfully against his lips. "And what is it that makes you think your friend is still with you?"

We were prepared to answer this question, both verbally and with help from Milo's energy. Through our connection, I could feel Milo's energy buzzing all the more excitedly, offering himself up for detection; in my peripheral vision, I could see that his form was glowing more brightly now. Throughout our interview, I'd been watching Campbell closely for any indication of his being able to sense Milo; Campbell had given no such acknowledgment. But now that Milo was revving himself up, I knew that, behind his sunglasses, Finn was now on ultra-high alert for any inking of Campbell's "gift."

"It's little things, I guess. Lights flickering on and off. Doors opening and closing. The night before we called you, our TV turned itself to Milo's favorite show three times... *after* we'd shut it off. Or sometimes, we find things in different places from where we left them—especially gifts he'd given us. These bracelets, for example," and here I held my wrist up, showing him the Masking bracelet, "Milo gave them to us as a birthday gift. Yesterday morning, before we left, they were laid out on our vanities—with no explanation."

"And you feel certain that these experiences are due to Milo's presence, and not to something else? Something entirely explainable... or even merely coincidence?" Campbell prodded carefully. "I don't mean to offend you. It is simply one of those questions that I must—in good conscience—ask anyone who seeks my help."

"No, no, I get that. I'm not offended. And no, I just don't think it can be a coincidence."

Campbell turned to Hannah. "And you, Ms. Taylor?"

"No," Hannah said, her voice a tiny squeak. "It's Milo. It has to be."

I jumped in, attempting to spare my sister from further direct questions. "You have to understand, Mr. Campbell, that we were almost never apart. Milo even lived with us for the last year he was alive. The three of us did everything together, like we were triplets instead of twins. Do you know what I mean?"

Campbell shook his head sadly. "No, I cannot truthfully say that I do. I don't believe I could ever hope to comprehend the level of your connection, nor fully appreciate the depth of your grief. I won't insult you by pretending I can understand what you are going through."

Shit. He was good, I had to give it to him.

"Many, many people believe they are haunted," Campbell went on. "I apologize for using what might feel like an indelicate term, but I have yet to find another that fits. If your friend is indeed with you, he's occupying a space in your life—a space that needs to be free and clear for you to move forward and heal. Now I must tell you both that most people who believe they're haunted are mistaken. It isn't their fault—they aren't crazy or delusional. They're merely victims of desperate hopes and wishful thinking. I don't want to be harsh, but have you considered that this might be the case for you?"

"Of course we have!" I cried, playing my part. "We don't want to be in this situation. I'm sure a lot of the people you meet are just hoping and praying that they've got a ghost, but that's not us. Or at least, that's not me."

I threw a look at Hannah. She picked up her cue and scowled at me. "Shut up, Jess."

"No!" I snapped back at her. "He needs to hear this." I turned to Campbell. "Hannah took it a lot harder than I did when Milo died. Now she tries to talk to him, to encourage him to stay around. It's not healthy."

Hannah looked down at her feet; it played as shame, but I could only assume she wanted to avoid Campbell's probing gaze. "It's not me. It's him. He's still here! I can't help it if he's still here."

"Then why won't you tell him to go!" I asked her. "I loved him too, but why don't you explain that he needs to... I don't know... find peace, or whatever?"

"I can't tell him that!" Hannah snapped; her tone was convincingly affronted. "What if he needs our help? What if there's something really important he's trying to tell us?"

"What could he possibly want to tell us that we don't already know?" I cried. "We grew up with him. We lived with him. Look, I'm sorry, but it just doesn't make sense!"

"Ladies, please," Campbell began, cutting through our feigned argument with his calm and soothing manner, "Let me put this argument to rest for you." He took a deep breath, and then—leaning forward in a conspiratorial sort of way—continued on. "Would you mind terribly if I attempted to connect with Milo now? It will serve two very important purposes—it will help me establish if he is indeed with you, and it will also give you a chance to validate my gift for yourselves. May I?"

My heart began to hammer so hard I thought Campbell would surely hear it. "Yes, of course you can. That's why we're here!" I told him, trying to look relieved.

"Very well. I will first ask you to encourage Milo to communicate with me. We all need to work together. There will be little I can do if he refuses to speak with me," Campbell said, placing a hand over his heart; he was the picture of perfect apologetic humility.

This was going to be the tricky part: How much would we have to fake, and could we do so convincingly enough to be invited to stay? I'd been scanning the room for spots where microphones or projectors could be hidden, and I knew Finn had been doing the same. So far, I'd seen no tech planted in the room. What was Campbell's game?

154

"Um, okay," I replied. "I, uh, guess I don't really know how to do that. Do I just... talk? Will he hear me?"

"If he is truly here, yes, I think he will be able to hear you," Campbell replied, smiling encouragingly.

I grimaced. "I don't know. Hannah's usually the one who tries to communicate with him. Shouldn't she do it?"

"If you'd like," Campbell said, looking at Hannah now.

Oddly enough, Hannah seemed to gather a sense of confidence from Campbell's encouragement. Whether this guy was legitimate or not, he was incredibly goddamn persuasive. The longer he talked, the more intricate his web of trust became—and we were most definitely the flies in this scenario.

Behind me, Finn gave a tiny, throat-clearing cough. Iggy shifted slightly from one foot to the other. The tension was starting to creep back toward them, like a noxious fume we were all now breathing.

Hannah sat up a little straighter and cast her gaze to the ceiling, scanning it as though Milo might be rocketing around the chandelier. Of course, we knew that Milo was sitting in the chair beside her, but Hannah had to put on a show.

"Milo?" she called with convincing hesitancy. "If you're here right now, and I think you are, could you please listen to Mr. Campbell? Try to answer his questions if you can, okay? He's trying to help us, but none of that will matter if he can't talk to you."

"You got it, sweetness!" Milo shouted slowly and very loudly. Evidently, he didn't have much faith that Campbell would be able to hear him: Milo delivered his answer as though Campbell were standing at the opposite end of a football field.

"Excellent. Just allow me a moment to prepare, and I will attempt to make contact," Campbell said.

Campbell closed his eyes and lifted his face to the ceiling. He raised his arms into the air, as though in humble supplication, and began murmuring under his breath. Hannah and I both leaned forward, trying to catch what he was saying, but I couldn't make anything out. This went on for about thirty seconds. I chanced a glance over at Milo, who looked back at me and shrugged as though to say, "Nothing's happening over here!"

I turned to Hannah and shook my head. This guy was as big a fraud as the others. What were the Durupinen so worried about?

§

A strange swooping something engulfed the room—a fog or a cloud so huge that it momentarily blocked the light streaming through the windows. The temperature in the room dropped by several degrees, and a heaviness settled over everything. I felt slow and sluggish, almost dizzy. My vision filmed over so that I was looking at everything through a haze, like a half-waking dream.

I looked over at Hannah. She had her hands pressed to her head as though she were suffering from a terrible headache. Finn was shaking his head as if to clear it. Iggy stood just as he had before. I'd seen him flinch as the cloud had blocked out the sunlight, but now, as I tried to focus on him, he reached up a hand a scratched his nose; it was clear that Iggy wasn't feeling anything strange, apart from perhaps the shift in temperature.

The new thing in the room—the fog or the cloud or whatever it was—settled around Campbell, wrapping itself around his head and shoulders, barely visible and yet irresistibly drawing my eye. Campbell opened his eyes and smiled at us with that same brilliant smile of his. Then he looked toward the place where Milo was sitting.

"Hello, Milo," said Campbell warmly.

Milo's jaw dropped. "Uh, hi?" The surprise in Milo's voice was real; he didn't need to fake anything.

"He's here," Campbell said, addressing Hannah and me. I tried to pull myself together and look normal; if Iggy couldn't sense anything strange then we shouldn't acknowledge the cloud-like being either, or we might blow our cover.

"Really?" I asked, trying to sound skeptical.

"Oh, yes," He's here beside Hannah," Campbell said, gesturing to the space where Milo sat. Hannah had taken her hands down from her head, but her face was still twisted with discomfort.

"How do you know?" I asked. "Can you see him?"

"In a manner of speaking," Campbell replied. He turned back to Milo and addressed him in a loud, clear voice. "Milo, I know you're here, and that you've chosen to stay behind with your friends. They have sensed you, but they cannot talk with you the way that I can. I want to prove to them that you are indeed here. Can you tell me something you want your friends to know, perhaps something private or personal?"

We'd prepped Milo for this type of question. Milo threw a nervous glance at me, then spoke to Campbell in the same tone Campbell had just used with him. "Um, yeah, okay," he began. "Tell them I don't want to leave them, because you can't just have two musketeers."

Campbell made no indication that he'd heard Milo, but once Milo had finished speaking, Campbell inclined his head to the right, and the fog embracing him pulsed with energy and seemed to swirl and thicken. He listened for a moment, nodded, and then said, "He says he doesn't want to leave you because there can't only be two musketeers. Does that mean anything to you?"

Neither Hannah nor I had to feign our shock. We gaped, first at Campbell, and then at each other.

"Oh my God," I cried. "We always called ourselves the three musketeers. Always."

At my pronouncement, the cloud form dissipated; it unwound itself from Campbell's body and lifted from the room. My vision cleared, as did the groggy feeling in my head. Hannah began blinking spastically, as if willing the last of her own headache away.

"I'm sorry, but Milo seems to have gone for the moment," Campbell said.

Hannah and I both looked at Milo: He was still in his seat, wide-eyed. Lost for an explanation, he turned to me and shrugged his shoulders, clearly afraid to speak aloud again.

Now that the fog was gone, it seemed Campbell was incapable of sensing Milo anymore. "That must've been quite a shock for y'all. Are you alright?" Campbell asked, composing himself into a picture of absolute concern. He walked over to the tea cart, then returned with two glasses of water, which he handed to us. We each took a glass and chugged it, still reeling from whatever the hell had just happened.

"There's no way you could've known that," I said, sputtering a little on the last gulp of water. "There's no way—unless he really was here. Unless he told you himself."

Hannah chimed in quickly, determined to stick to our script. "He really is here, isn't he? I was right!"

Campbell ran a hand through his thick graying hair and heaved a sigh. "Yes, you were right. For my own part, I am perfectly satisfied that you are indeed haunted, and that y'all would benefit greatly from some time here at Whispering Seraph. By working together, we could help your friend Milo find the peace he needs—and help the both of you move forward. I have every confidence we could make that happen. But what about you? You must surely have had your skepticisms before you arrived. Have I alleviated them for you?"

"Yes!" Hannah and I said at once. We still had plenty of skepticism, but now there was a whole new world of questions surrounding Jeremiah Campbell.

"Please, Mr. Campbell, can you—"

"Hannah, please, I must insist you call me Jeremiah. We have no use for formalities during such an intimate process."

Hannah blushed. "Right. Well, Mr.... um, Jeremiah... can you please let us stay? You're the only person who can help us. I don't know what we'll do if you say no!"

Campbell spread his arms in a wide, welcoming gesture. "Of course, it's essential that you stay. However," and he dropped his arms and walked over to his desk, "there is the rather indelicate matter of finances to discuss." He pulled out a light blue file from his desk drawer. "I want to be quite clear that I do not provide these services for my own financial gain."

It took every fiber of my being not to roll my eyes as Campbell looked sternly from one of us to the other, as if trying to drive home his point. "This blessing I've been given is meant to be shared, to help others. But in order for me to do that, I need to continue the upkeep and running of Whispering Seraph. I must pay my staff for their good work. I must continue my vital renovations to the house, which ensure my guests' privacy while I'm helping them find the peace they need."

"Yes, we understand all of that," I said, jumping in before Campbell's head exploded from his own self-martyrdom. "This place is incredible. It's one of the reasons we decided to come and see you. You've been in touch with our mother, right?"

"We have spoken, yes," Campbell said. "A charming woman."

I scoffed silently. Catriona was anything but charming in my mind, but I had the feeling she was an unparalleled actress when she needed to be.

"She wants us to get past this. It's been... disruptive for the whole family. Money is not a concern," I said, waving a hand airily. "If you're willing to let us stay, our mother's business manager will wire the first payment right away. Just have your staff send her your information."

Campbell smiled again, more brightly than ever. "Well, then. I guess that settles things. Isn't it just lovely when these things work out?"

We nodded, returning his smile.

"Very well, then. Maya will be pleased to settle all the additional details." With this, Campbell walked over to us; we both stood up nervously. He placed a hand on each of our shoulders. I felt not an inkling of spirit connectivity buzzing within him. "I want to assure you both, there's nothing to be afraid of anymore. You are in the right place to find the answers you seek." His tone, as ever, was smooth and reassuring. If we'd been actually grieving, if we were actually in mourning and perhaps scared out of our wits, his reassurance would've been worth every cent in our bank account.

I tried to smile, but I just couldn't. I wanted him to leave; I was itching for all of us to discuss what the hell had just happened.

"Thank you," Hannah said breathlessly.

Campbell gave each of our shoulders a squeeze, and then backed himself—with one last gracious bow—through the door he had entered from. As he shut the door behind him, everyone seemed to deflate, heaving out deep sighs. Without knowing it, we'd all been holding our collective breath, so to speak, since Campbell had come into the room.

Hannah stumbled back and collapsed into her chair. Iggy was patting absently at his pockets, feeling for a cigarette he knew he couldn't indulge in yet. Finn was shaking his head like he had water in his ear. And I... I didn't know what to do with myself at all.

"What the actual—" Milo began, but was cut off by the prompt appearance of Maya, the same woman who had shown us into the room to begin with. She came bearing two clipboards full of paperwork and a broad, white-toothed smile. I wondered if Campbell screened his job applicants based on the sheen of their tooth enamel.

"Glad to hear y'all will be staying with us," Maya said warmly. "Just a few details, and then we can get you settled in, nice and cozy. Will you need to have your things brought over?"

"We'll send Iggy for them," I said. "Everything we need is at the hotel."

"Perfect!" she declared brightly. "There are some forms to fill out, as well as some privacy agreements to sign. Please look everything over carefully and let me know if you have any questions. If you'd like to have a lawyer look at anything, we have one on staff—or we could fax the paperwork over to yours. Also, Jeremiah likes to assure all guests that we have ample security on the grounds. We do not generally allow for additional personal security—"

Finn started forward, looking alarmed, but I gave him a sharp look and he stopped short in the middle of the room.

"My parents never would've let us come down if they thought our detail wouldn't be allowed," I said, adopting a slightly-entitled tone. "I really can't imagine their agreeing to our stay if we can't have our own security. Isn't there anything you can do?"

"Well, I'm sure we can work something out," said Maya with another ingratiating smile. "We have made exceptions in the past, under very special circumstances." We all understood that "working something out" would simply mean more money; "special circumstances" meant "mind-bogglingly rich."

"Good," Hannah said quietly. "This is one of those circumstances." She was catching on to this VIP thing.

Maya turned to Finn and Iggy. "Gentlemen, there will be protocol to follow, as I am sure you will understand. A full list of prohibited practices and devices can be found here." She handed a folder to Finn, who took it without comment. "Just ring the bell when you've finished, and we'll get you settled into your suite." She pointed to a small silver buzzer that I hadn't noticed before. Then she backed out of the room again, without ever once letting that perfect smile slip from her face.

"No, but seriously, what the hell—" I began.

"Not here," Finn said curtly. "The car. Now."

§

"Well, I guess we can all agree there is something very strange going on with Campbell," I said, as soon as the car door had slammed shut behind us. We'd had Iggy stay outside the car, stationed as if he were guarding us. If any of Campbell's staff questioned our sudden retreat to the sedan, we'd just have to pass it off as a quirk of the super wealthy. Surely, the mega-rich did far stranger things on a daily basis.

"You can say that again," Hannah said. "Could everyone see what happened to him when he connected with Milo?"

"Yeah," I said, nodding and shivering simultaneously. "What the hell was that cloud thing?"

"I have no idea, but I've never seen anything quite like it before," Finn declared.

Hannah shuddered, as though thinking of the cloud-being repulsed her. "I guess that... that... *thing* is what he calls his angel. How would you describe it? It was some sort of..."

"Creepy fog?" I offered.

"Energy cloud?" Milo suggested.

"I guess so," Hannah said. "That was all I could see. It definitely had an energy of its own. I could feel it when it entered the room, but... I've never felt anything quite like it in my life. It wasn't a spirit—or if it was, there was something very wrong with it."

"And once it came into the room, Campbell said he could see Milo," Finn said.

"Actually, I don't think he could," said Milo.

We all turned to Milo. "What do you mean?" asked Hannah. "He knew right where you were. He looked right at you."

"Not exactly," Milo said. "He looked in my direction, but he wasn't looking in exactly the right place. He was staring at a spot maybe a foot to the right. He knew my general location, but I don't think he could actually see me."

Hannah frowned. "Really?"

"Yeah," Milo said. "I think that fog-cloud thing told him where I was, and he... just looked where it told him to look."

We all digested this for a moment. As I processed, I realized something else about the experience that now made a little more sense.

"He couldn't really hear you either, I don't think," I said. "There was a delay between when you spoke and when he registered what you said. Maybe that fog-creature was the one who could hear you, and relayed your answers to Campbell?"

Milo nodded. "Yeah. Yeah, that would explain it. He never acknowledged me before that thing came into the room."

Finn ran a hand through his hair, as he always did when he was contemplating something; he mussed up his specially groomed ponytail in the process. "Okay, so it isn't really Campbell who senses the spirits? It's this... other thing?"

"I think so," I said. "Based on what we saw, that would make sense."

"Based on what we saw, nothing makes sense!" Finn cried. "Are we sure that thing isn't a spirit? We could all see it, even though Iggy couldn't—which holds true for other spirits."

"No, I don't think it could be a spirit," Hannah said slowly, chewing on a lock of her hair. "That wasn't what I felt... it wasn't a true spirit. This was different. I felt like I'd been... drugged, or something. I could hardly see straight, my head was pounding. I thought I was going to pass out, I was so dizzy! Did anyone else feel it?"

"I did," I said. "No headache, but definitely the dizziness... and my vision was blurred, too."

"Me as well," Finn said. "Perhaps it was an Empathic experience? They can be properly intense, from what I understand."

"No," Hannah said, shaking her head. "I've had plenty of those—they're emotionally based. Even if they affect you physically, the primary sensation is the emotion itself. I had no emotional connection to whatever that thing was. None at all."

Our friend Mackie, who'd been one of the very few to befriend us at Fairhaven, was an Empath—a Durupinen who experienced spirits through an especially intense emotional connection. Mackie had been reduced to shuddering and tears after many a Crossing, and the pain she'd sensed the night we Uncaged the Silent Child had left her writhing uncontrollably in agony. We'd seen firsthand the intensity of an Empath's connection.

"Okay, so if it wasn't a spirit, then what was it?" Finn asked, throwing his hands impatiently up in the air.

We all sat silently in contemplation. We all knew there were beings out there who were... other than human or spirit. The Wraiths, for instance. Elementals, too. And the Necromancers had taught us that spirits could—through dark Castings—be dismantled and reassembled into truly perverted beings that weren't exactly spirits anymore. Even I, when Walking, could be counted among these other beings—Walkers were neither merely human nor merely spirit, after all. But beyond these... what else was there?

"We are way out of bounds here. We have no experience with this," said Finn. "If we don't know what that thing is, how can we so much as begin to deal with it?"

"We need to get a message to Catriona," I said. "She'll know what to do."

"You think she's had experience with whatever this thing is?" Hannah asked.

"If not, she'll know where to find the answers," I replied.

"Well, she won't be hearing anything from me," Finn grumbled. He had flipped open the folder Maya had given him and was scanning the private-security policies. "No walkie-talkies, no Bluetooth, no mobiles, no laptops or tablets—this is mad, we can't agree to this!" He was practically shouting now. "How are we supposed to protect you if Iggy and I can't communicate with each other, let alone with the outside world? And there will be no way for us to report back to Catriona!"

"No way for us to interfere with his technological equipment either, if he's using the same kind of smoke and mirrors as Freeman," Hannah pointed out. "Do you think he could've created that cloud thing with some kind of a trick?"

"I think we can rule out smoke and mirrors at this point," I reasoned. "For one thing, how could he create something that only the Sensitives in the room could see? If it were a trick he'd created, Iggy would've reacted to it, too. I mean, I know he saw the sunlight dim, but he didn't react to anything else. No, something more bizarre than parlor tricks is going on here. But if we want to stay and get to the bottom of it, we're going to have to follow Campbell's rules."

Finn shook the folder in my face. "How are we supposed to agree to these?"

"Well..." I began, already knowing I would regret making this suggestion, "you and Iggy don't have to stay."

Milo groaned. "Here we go. Let the drama begin," he muttered.

"Pardon?" Finn growled. "What do you mean, we don't have to stay?"

"Well, just consider it," I said. "There are armed guards and security cameras all over the place. The whole property is gated and walled. We'll be perfectly safe here. We could do the investigating then relay the information to you. You'd be free to communicate as much as you need to with Catriona and the other Trackers—and you'd also be able to do more research on your own, without all the restrictions."

"Ignoring for a moment that this is the worst idea you've ever had, just how are you going to communicate with us?" asked Finn. "You have the same restrictions on technology as we do, except for mobiles—and we all know how spotty those can be. There can't be only one channel through which I can reach you."

I pointed to Milo. "We've got a built-in communication system. We can send Milo with any information you need to have."

"Whoa, whoa, when did I become the messenger boy?" Milo asked indignantly.

"Remember what Catriona said," I began. "If we're on a mission, you're on a mission. You agreed to that, remember?"

Milo crossed his arms and pouted. Everyone ignored him.

"There then, you've solved the problem for us," Finn said smugly. "If you can send Milo out to communicate with us, then he can communicate with Catriona just as well. I'm staying. It's not going to be that easy to get rid of me, Jess."

"I'm not trying to get rid of you! I just thought..."

"You just thought you'd have better luck here without me breathing down your neck, insisting you make safe choices," Finn snarled, cutting me off before I could explain myself. "I'm not a fool, Jess. I know full well that you prefer doing things your own way, but until we understand exactly what that cloud-thing is, there's no chance in hell I'm going leaving you and Hannah unprotected. Conversation closed."

I didn't even bother starting an argument—which was a new approach for me. I wasn't trying to get rid of Finn, I really wasn't. I was past the point of wanting to get rid of him. If anything, I wanted him around much more than was healthy for our strictly platonic relationship.

I took a deep breath to keep my voice calm and even. I kept my eyes focused on my hands, which were now folded in my lap. "Actually I've been thinking it might be smart to investigate from the inside and the outside at the same time. You and Iggy could stake out Whispering Seraph from the perimeter, using the team's technology. You could blanket the place with satellites and camera-drones. Hannah and I could use that intel to inform our moves while we're inside. To keep us *safer*." I placed a delicate emphasis on this last word.

No one spoke. I looked up, expecting to see Finn glaring at me, or else building up to an explosion, but he was just staring at me with his mouth open. In fact, everyone was staring at me.

"What?" I asked, a bit defensively.

"That's... actually a properly good idea," Finn said.

"You don't need to sound so surprised," I said, scowling. "I've been known to have one or two of those."

"That still doesn't mean I'm willing to have the two of you in here without protection, though," Finn said. "Perhaps Iggy could handle the surveillance while I stayed inside with you."

Hannah shook her head. "It's too big of a job for one person. There's no way Iggy could set that much tech up by himself... and just going through all that footage would be a full-time job." I knew Hannah was right; as a grad student, she'd spent whole weekends under mountains of case studies.

"Could you get the rest of the team down here?" asked Finn. "The Trackers can pay them. I'll requisition the additional funding from Catriona."

"I have a hard time imagining the team saying no to an all-expenses-paid trip to one of the most haunted cities in the country," I said.

"Great. Let's get Iggy in here, ask him what he thinks," replied Finn.

"Wait!" cried Hannah. "We still need someone on the outside who can communicate with Milo. He can't deliver messages to the team if they can't even see him."

"See if Annabelle can make it, too," Finn suggested.

"We can't ask her to do that, this is her busiest time of year," I said. "Let's ask Lu-Ann and Loretta to help instead. The team can set up tech command at their boarding house. That way one of the Lafayette twins will always be around to take messages from Milo."

"Oh great, daily chats with the twins from *The Shining*. I can hardly wait." Milo grumbled.

Hannah opened her door and waved Iggy into the car. He slid into the front passenger seat, exhaling loudly as the first gush of the car's A/C blasted across him. I felt a pang of guilt from having kept him out in the heat.

We outlined our plan; Iggy was ecstatic, as I expected. "We're going to throw everything we've got at it!" he cried. "I bet the guys can fly down tomorrow. We've got a hell of a lot of new long-range tech we've been raring to use... this place'll be perfect."

"Good. Well. That's all sorted, then," Finn said. "Let's get this investigation properly underway."

14

NIGHT SWIMMING

ANNAH AND I CAREFULLY PLAYED OUR PARTS for the next few hours. It was utterly exhausting. We nodded and smiled as we signed about a hundred different waivers, agreements, and contracts—a veritable mountain of paperwork—while pretending we understood all the legalese. Finn and Iggy stood at attention the whole time, playing their roles as security perfectly. Then Hannah and I sat through a long and self-indulgent welcome video, narrated by Campbell himself, which explained the various elements that would make up our retreat. The only part of the video which really piqued our interest was the short section about Whispering Seraph itself.

As we watched, Campbell smiled serenely at us from the TV screen. "As a former real estate man, I'd like to be able to say that I found Whispering Seraph, but really, it was Whispering Seraph that found me. The property came to me in a dream, a vision bestowed on me by my angel. It was then I knew this was the place I needed to be," he said, gesturing grandly as he stood at the end of the long, tree-lined drive with the house and grounds sprawling out behind him. "You can feel it in the air here; the connection with the spirit world is strong. This is a property with a great deal of history; its stories are walking around, unseen by the naked eye, but screaming loud as can be for those who have the courage to listen. And now you've brought your own story here too. We will reveal its mysteries together."

Maya brought us a late lunch on a tray as we wrapped up the registration process. She apologized profusely for the mountain for forms. After lunch, she took the four of us—five of us really, with Milo in silent tow—on a tour of the grounds. It was almost unbearably hot, but we all stayed alert and watchful. Iggy, I knew, was focused on the property's tech; I could see him taking mental notes of the security cameras, keypads, alarm systems, and the motion sensors. The rest of us we were on the watch for anything that might be Durupinen related in any way—a rune, traces of a spent Circle, anything. By the time we reached the front porch again—a full hour and a half later—we were drenched in sweat from head to toe; we hadn't found a shred of Durupinen-related evidence.

A woman with a tray of drinks stood just inside the door, and we all gulped tall glasses of lemonade while Maya concluded her tour script.

"And now, I'll show you up to your suite, where I hope you'll find everything to your liking. If anything needs to be adjusted to suit your needs, please do let me know—we will take care of it at once," she said. Then she turned to Finn and Iggy. "Gentlemen, you may follow so that you know where the ladies will be staying, and then Mr. Carey, sir, I'll show you to the security quarters for your own accommodations."

"Thank you," Finn said stiffly, and I fought a bubble of laughter that was trying to escape me. Poor Finn—it was like we were flying first class while he was stuck in the cargo hold.

Our room was on the second floor, overlooking the expansive front lawn. When we first entered the house, I'd never been so happy to walk into an air-conditioned space in my entire life—and I was even happier when Maya said we didn't have to leave our wonderfully cool room for dinner. The kitchen would prepare anything we wanted from an extensive room service menu.

"Not going to lie," I said after Maya let herself out. "I could seriously get used to this Tracker gig." I flopped onto the nearest bed and was almost swallowed by the goose-down duvet. "Do you think I could conduct the entire investigation from this bed right here?"

"Well, you could try, but I think you could kiss your Tracker status good-bye," Milo said. "This place is off the hook, though. Massages and manicures on demand! Hey, I wonder if they have style consultants, too."

"Hannah, could you Call a shitload of spirits to come and unpack our stuff?" I asked.

"Not funny," came Hannah's flat reply from the other side of the room.

"It was a little funny," I muttered. I sat up and saw Hannah crouching by the window.

"What are you doing?" I asked.

"What are we supposed to be doing right now? I'm Warding our room!" Hannah said impatiently. "Catriona said to do it right away—and I'm not taking any chances, especially now that we've seen that smoke-cloud angel thing. Do you want to wake up and find that thing hovering over you?" She shivered violently.

"Definitely not. I'll help you. But then we're ordering dinner. And remember, the Durupinen are paying, so let's order something stuffed with lobster, okay?"

Spurred on by the thought of the unknown angel—and admittedly, by the lobster—we Warded our room in record time, and then spent the next couple of hours unpacking and eating an incredible dinner. Milo blinked out while we ate—he didn't generally stick around during mealtimes. But by the time we'd finished, rather than wanting to fall into bed, I found myself getting antsy, almost agitated.

I stood up. "Okay, as nice as it would be to drift off into a food coma right now, we've got work to do. I'm going exploring."

Hannah looked startled. "Really? Why? We just got a tour. I mean, are we even allowed to?"

I shrugged. "We're guests here now, remember? Campbell told us to make ourselves at home. I think that means we're allowed to check the place out."

Hannah bit her lip. "Oh, um... I don't... should we?"

I threw my hands up impatiently and marched toward the door. "Forget it, I'll go by myself."

"No, I... I just want to... I can come with you, if you want." Hannah said it earnestly, but I could hear a tiny tremor in her voice that begged, by its very presence, for me not to ask this of her. I was perplexed for a moment—this wasn't a prison after all—but then I suddenly realized why she was so scared.

"Hannah," I began gently. "This isn't like New Beginnings, or any of those other places. We chose to come here. We can leave anytime. No meds. No doctors. This is our choice, remember that."

She dropped her eyes to her hands, which were twisting agitatedly in her lap. "I know that, Jess. But, um... thanks for the reminder."

"Good. And if anything about this place is too much, just say the word and we're out of here," I said, placing one hand on the doorknob. "And the Durupinen can stick this Tracker gig right up their collective ass if they don't like it. Whatever happens, I don't want you to ever feel like you're back in one of those places, you understand?"

Although Hannah's gaze remained on her own hands, her mouth twitched into the merest suggestion of a smile. "Yeah, I understand." Then a tiny giggle bubbled up out of her throat.

"What?" I asked. Everything I'd said was sincere; I didn't see what was funny.

"What's a collective ass?" Another giggle escaped her.

"Oh, shut up," I said, feigning annoyance but feeling nothing but gladness at the sound of her laugh. "Call Milo if you need him, but I'm sure he'll be back soon. I'll see you in a bit," I said, and walked out the door; I pulled it shut behind me quickly, before Hannah could convince herself to change her mind. I needed some time to think; being by myself was for the best right now.

I set off down the hallway and toward the grand staircase, but I soon stopped paying attention to where I was going; my mind just couldn't make sense of this situation. Jeremiah Campbell had some special abilities, there was no denying that. As much as I wanted to believe he was just another scam artist, I had to accept that this wasn't true. I didn't have the faintest idea how Campbell was connecting with spirits, but nonetheless he did have a legitimate spirit connection. But what the hell was that angel thing?

Before Catriona had dumped us with the Lafayette twins, she'd received solid confirmation from the Trackers: Campbell had no traceable Durupinen or Caomhnóir blood in his ancestry. So how had he wound up on an old Durupinen property? Had his "angel" really led him to this place?

I began to wonder: Was it so impossible that someone completely unconnected to the Durupinen could communicate with the spirit world? Could refusing to believe that others might have abilities like ours be yet another example of the Durupinen's willful arrogance? That arrogance had nearly destroyed us all three years ago—the Council's refusal to acknowledge the resurfacing of the Necromancers had led to the fulfillment of the Prophecy. Why did we have to have a monopoly on spirit communication? Why couldn't there be others who had spirit connections as powerful and meaningful as our own?

WHISPERS OF THE WALKER

I stopped dead as a wall of warm, heavy air seemed to smack me right in the face. I had walked out onto the front porch without even paying attention to where my feet had been taking me; someone had left the door to the porch wide open. The sweeping lawn sprawled out before me, smooth and velvety beneath the canopy of massive trees and their trailings of Spanish moss. I took a deep breath, but the air, heavy with moisture, felt sluggish in my lungs, as though the humidity had smothered the oxygen. I looked at my watch; it was nearly 11:00 PM, but the temperature had fallen only slightly—it had to be at least seventy-five degrees still.

I crossed the massive porch and continued down the steps and out across the grounds. There was an eerie beauty to the Louisiana night, a tranquility that even the sounds of the night couldn't quite seem to penetrate. The stars shone brightly, and although the moon wasn't quite full, a halo enveloped it. Here and there between the trees, the dull glow of a spirit flickered past; much like at Fairhaven, the spirits didn't seem out of place here, they simply belonged to the landscape. The lines blurred so easily here, an overlapping of realms as natural as the meeting of the ocean and the shore. What was it about places like this that made them havens for the dead in the world of the living? Was it because of the place itself, like a geographic anomaly, or was it further confirmation that Campbell was exactly what he claimed to be?

A loud splashing sound halted me in my tracks. Once again, my thoughts had carried me further than my feet had realized; I was now only a yard or two from the pond, standing in tall, unmanicured grass. The stillness that had stolen over me evaporated; an electric crackling of fear now replaced it. What had made that splash? I was in Louisiana now—weren't the waters here teeming with alligators?

I spun around frantically, hopping from one foot to the other in a terrified, spastic version of an Irish jig. I was sure I was about to be devoured, but all was still again. I scanned the surface of the pond and the tall grass around me. I laughed out loud: Three minutes alone in the Louisiana night and I'd nearly given myself a heart attack. I was such a city girl.

Praying no one in the compound had witnessed my freak-out, I started to turn back to the house, but I tripped and tumbled to the ground. I threw my hands out in front of me to break the fall, but landed hard enough. Still envisioning massive jaws poised to swallow me whole, I scrambled into a sitting position and looked frantically around for what had caused me to trip.

A pile of clothes lay abandoned in the grass. My attacker was nothing more than the strap of a gold sandal twisted around my ankle. I laughed at my own panic and bent down to free myself. I noted the white cottony maxi dress and the heavy, studded leather belt that lay curled on top of it like a couture snake.

Something else lay glimmering among fabric; it was a long, gold chain with a glittering ring attached to it. I picked it up.

"Find her. Find her. She's out there." The voice shot into my head as clearly as my own thoughts.

I dropped the ring as though it had burned me. I spun around looking for the owner of the voice, but I couldn't see anyone, spirit or human.

"Hello?"

Nothing.

"Is someone there? I can hear you. Do you need my help?"

"No. Help her. She needs your help."

"Who?" I asked. "Help who?"

My eyes, in their frantic search for the owner of the voice, had fallen on the surface of the pond. There, a long, dark shape floated in moon's shining trail of light. I squinted, focusing hard. What looked like long hair billowed around the shape's head.

A woman. A perfectly still—possibly dead—woman.

I didn't stop to think. I sprang to my feet, pelted for the water's edge, and flung myself into the shallow, weedy pond. I half-swam, half-waded out toward the woman. As I pushed off against the pond's slimy bottom, its muck sucked away both of my shoes. I splashed and flailed in my desperation to reach the woman, who remained utterly motionless.

I fought past tangles of weeds, cursing the weight of my soaked clothes. As the pond's bottom fell away, I dove forward and swam the last few yards. I reached out a violently shaking hand and grabbed the woman's wrist, yanking her toward me. She flailed as I grabbed her—she was, thankfully, alive. Flipping her over revealed a face I knew well, although I'd only seen it in photographs.

It was Talia Simms.

I began tugging her back toward the shore, but even as I did so, she started coughing and sputtering. Since she was obviously breathing, some of my blind panic started to dissipate—only to be replaced by the very specific panic that we'd be eaten by an alligator before we could reach the shore. I waded through the remaining shallows, and Talia, wrestling her arm from my grip, did the same, until we both lay, panting and coughing, on the grass.

"What... the hell... are you doing!" Talia sputtered, before retching out a mouthful of pond water.

"What?" I asked, with my voice barely audible over my own wheezing.

"Were you trying to kill me?" she gasped.

I scrambled into a sitting position so that I could see Talia properly. She lay on her side with her sopping hair stuck all over her face, dressed only in a tank top and underwear. Mascara ran down her face in dark trails, like lines on a roadmap.

"What? Of course not! I saw you in the water, and... I was trying to save you!" I cried.

Talia sat up, pushing the hair from her face and glaring fiercely at me. "I didn't need to be saved! I wasn't drowning... at least not until you scared the shit out of me and I swallowed half the pond!"

"I... what?" I asked. "You were face-down in the water! You weren't moving! At midnight! What was I supposed to think?"

"I was... floating!" she said, dropping her gaze. "I... it was peaceful and quiet. Or at least it was until you came barreling into the water!"

"I... you..." I sputtered, not sure whether I was angry or relieved. "Well, you shouldn't do that in the middle of the night! Anyone who sees you will probably panic!"

"There was no one out here when I came out," she muttered. As she did so, she suddenly realized she wasn't wearing her clothes; blushing violently, she scrambled to her feet and ran over to scoop them up.

"Who are you, anyway?" she asked. "How did you get in here? I've never seen you here before."

"I've never seen you here before either," I said, watching her fumble around in her haste to re-dress. "I just got here today."

But Talia wasn't listening to me. She was searching, with an increasing franticness, through the folds of her dress; then her head shot up, revealing a fierce expression.

"What did you do with it?"

"With what?" I asked, perplexed.

"There was a necklace over here with a ring on it. What did you do with it?" Her voice rose into a hysterical panic. "Did you take it? You took it, didn't you?"

"No! No, of course not!" I said, walking over to join her. "I tripped over your sandal in the dark, and found the necklace with your clothes. I dropped it when I saw you in the water. It should be somewhere right... yes, here it is," I said, spotting the chain curled in the grass. I picked it up and held it out to Talia, who snatched it from my hand with a cry of relief. She pulled the chain over her head and tucked the ring down inside her dress.

"You shouldn't have touched it!" she spat at me.

Finally, my anger truly bubbled to the surface, burning through what remained of my shock. "Yeah, well, the next time I see you apparently dead, I'll just walk on by. And just a little tip, Louisiana isn't the safest place to have a Zen moment in the water at night, unless you consider alligator wrestling a form of relaxation. Namaste, bitch."

With that, I turned on my now-shoeless heel and marched back to the house. When I turned to close the door behind me, I could still see Talia sitting in the grass exactly where I'd left her. I couldn't be sure, but I thought a figure might have appeared beside her—a figure just a shade blacker than the deepening darkness.

§

I stalked back into our room, where Hannah was diligently reading a book. Milo was using his electromagnetic pull to flip through the channels on the television; he flicked his finger in a bored sort of way as the channels changed. They both looked up as I slammed the door behind me.

"Jess! Why are you all wet?" Hannah asked, tossing her book aside.

"What the hell happened to you?" Milo said over her, dropping his finger and inadvertently turning the television off.

I caught a glimpse of myself in the full-length mirror in the corner. I was, of course, a muddy, dripping mess.

"I just met Talia Simms," I announced angrily. I walked across to the bathroom, pulling my sopping clothes off as I went. I dropped them into a pile on the bathroom floor and turned on the shower. Water gushed from everywhere as a dozen showerheads, hidden in the walls, sprang to life. I stepped in and slid the door shut.

"Oh my sweet heaven, you are kidding me?" Milo said, appearing instantly inside the stall. "Tell me everything. What did she say? What did you say? Wait. Okay, just set the scene for me. What was she wearing?"

"Milo! Will you get out of my shower? I'm trying to... holy crap that feels good!" I said, as the massaging jets began turning my tense muscles to jelly. For a moment, I completely forgot my anger at Milo's intrusion.

"Details! I need them! Spill!" Milo cried. "Just tell me what she was wearing. Could you see any labels?"

"Underwear. And a tank top."

Milo squinted at me, trying to decide if I were joking or not. "And over that she was wearing...?"

"Nothing. That was it," I said, trying to cover my own nakedness with my loofah mitt.

Milo folded his arms. "So what did you do, break into her room? Hide out in her bathroom like a psycho stalker?"

"Do you really want to ask me that question when you're literally invading my shower? While I'm stark naked?" I yelled.

Milo rolled his eyes, "Relax Jess, it's not like I'm *interested*."

"Dead or not, gay or not—you're not getting another detail out of me until I get some privacy!" I snapped.

Milo blinked out of view, then reappeared outside of the stall's glass door, which was now mostly clouded over with steam. "Better?" he asked.

"Better." I picked up the shampoo and squeezed a dollop into my hands. "Sweet lord this stuff smells incredible—like unicorns and stardust!" I looked more closely at the bottle. "It's French. Is this what French people smell like? We're moving to France."

"Jessica Ballard!" cried Milo, as if he'd caught me stealing from his wallet red-handed. "Stay on topic! You met Talia Simms in her underwear? Explain! Now!"

I put down the shampoo and launched into a tirade about my encounter with Talia, although my anger ebbed considerably thanks to the French beauty products and the intensely hot water; I kept ratcheting the temperature up until I was pretty sure I would scald the top layer of my skin off. I finished my story and stepped out of the stall to find a towel. What I found first was Milo sputtering incoherently.

"But... she... you... does this mean you two won't be best friends?" he whimpered.

"I think it's safe to say we won't be getting matching tattoos, if that's what you mean," I replied, as I wrapped myself in a spa-quality bathrobe and shuffled out of the bathroom. "Hannah come over here and smell me!" I called. "I smell all Parisian!"

Milo was so incensed that his form began flickering. "Jess, you've spoiled everything!" he shouted. "How are we supposed to become a part of Talia Simms' entourage? You practically drowned her!"

"Okay, first of all, I'm pretty sure being alive is a necessary qualification for being in a celebrity entourage, and that leaves you out. Secondly, as I already explained, I wasn't trying to drown her—I was trying to save her. And if she doesn't want to be rescued, she should probably stop impersonating drowned corpses in public."

"She's Talia Simms, she can do whatever she wants," said Milo, with his arms crossed like a truculent child.

"Yeah, she seems to be under that impression, too," I said. "What I'm more interested in, though, is figuring out who told me to save her. Because whoever it was was pretty insistent that she needed help."

"Didn't you see anyone?" Hannah asked. She had listened to our exchange through her connection with Milo without a word, digesting it in her characteristically quiet, thoughtful manner.

"No," I answered, before flipping my head over so I could towel my hair dry. "I think the voice might've been male, though. It all happened pretty quickly. I was too focused on rescuing Talia to concentrate much on the spirit presence."

"Well, it's pretty obvious who it was, isn't it?" Milo said. When we stared at him in response, he heaved a dramatic sigh. "Grayson Allard! Her boyfriend!"

"Oh, right," I said. "I almost forgot about him. Yeah, that would make sense. I don't think we can just assume that, though. Not without proof."

"Who else could it possibly be?" Milo asked. "They were in love! A perfect Hollywood couple! When they stood next to each other, they were so gorgeous you could feel your brain starting to melt—almost like trying to stare directly into the sun. And then he died, and even his death was perfect..."

I put up a hand. "I'm going to stop you right there," I said. "What the hell does 'his death was perfect' mean? He died in motorcycle crash! It was horrible!"

"Of course it was horrible, but it was just so... James Dean! It was almost like he was too gorgeous—and their romance too perfect—to be allowed to exist, you know?"

I shook my head at him, lost for words. Milo had watched one too many reality TV shows, bless him, and was starting to forget what actual reality was like for normal people.

"It could certainly be him, but we won't know for sure until he shows himself," Hannah said. "And no, I won't Call him. If nothing else, it's too risky while we're undercover."

There was no arguing with the logic of this. Drawing attention to ourselves now would be incredibly stupid. We needed to blend as best we could into a group of people we had absolutely nothing in common with—nothing, except for a healthy belief in the paranormal.

"Of course not, Hannah. We're not even close to considering Calling, *or* Walking. Only in emergencies. We made that point clear to Catriona before we came here."

"So the only real choice that leaves us," Hannah went on, "is to hang around Talia and wait for him to show up again."

"Haven't you been listening?" Milo cried. "We can't hang out with her now! Jess almost drowned her! I bet Talia's bodyguard tackles Jess the next time she comes within fifty feet! Celebrities have taken out restraining orders for less."

"Yeah, especially since she thinks I was stealing her jewelry," I added.

"What? Why would she think that?" Hannah asked.

"She had this ring on a necklace on top of her pile of clothes. I was looking at it when I saw her in the pond, and dropped it in the grass. It took us a minute to find it when we came out of the water. She was hysterical about it."

Milo's pressed his hand over his heart as though he were having a ghostly version of a heart attack. "What kind of ring? What did it look like?"

I shrugged. "I didn't get a great look at it, but it was gold and had a big pale stone set in it. It was kind of heavy."

"A big pale stone? Like a diamond?"

"I don't know. I guess it could've been."

Milo looked from Hannah to me with his mouth hanging open. "Am I seriously the biggest girlie girl in this room?"

"Yes," Hannah and I said together.

"It's obvious! It was an engagement ring! From Grayson! She flipped out when it was missing because he gave it to her before he died!"

"I don't remember hearing they were engaged," I said doubtfully. "Don't you think that would've been in the news? The tabloids would've gone even crazier because that makes their story even more tragic."

"It was a secret engagement!" Milo squealed, his voice so shrill that Hannah winced. "It must've happened right before he died! Either they were keeping it under wraps for privacy, or they hadn't had a chance to announce it! When Talia saw that you found the ring, she freaked out because she thought you would tell the world!"

I considered this. Part of me thought Milo had read one too many gossip magazines, which was probably true. But the other part of me thought his theory made a lot of sense. Talia should've been more upset about being dragged half-naked out of the water, but her most vehement reaction had definitely been to the ring.

I wasn't about to encourage Milo in his crazy fanboy theories, so I changed the subject. "I'm not so sure I buy her story that she was just relaxing out there. I obviously didn't do a very good job of it, but someone needs to keep an eye on her while she's here. I think it's likely that I stopped her from doing something drastic, even if she hadn't entirely made her decision yet."

"Hopefully you shocked her out of it—at least for tonight, anyway," said Hannah. "Maybe you can try to find her in the morning and apologize."

I felt as though I were being forced to swallow something vile. "Sure," I said, through gritted teeth. "Sure, I could do that."

Hannah looked slightly alarmed by the look on my face. "But maybe try to look a little less... murder-y when you do it, okay? If you come at her looking like that she'll think you really are out to kill her."

"Right. Okay. No problem. Speaking of tomorrow, do we have a game plan?" I asked.

"The most important thing is to try to get some time with Campbell, if we can. We need to see him make another spirit connection," Hannah said. She reached over to the nightstand and grabbed Campbell's brochure. "This schedule says that he'll be holding a session called 'Communing with the Lost' at 9:00 AM; we should obviously go to that."

"Good idea. What's he doing after that?" I asked. "We should try to keep him in our sights all day long."

"It doesn't say. That's the only scheduled activity that mentions him by name. The others are all more generic—'Cleansing Meditation;' 'Healing Rifts;' 'Spiritual Music.' He could be at any of them, I guess," Hannah said, flipping the paper over.

"Or none of them," I pointed out. "We might need to split up, but we'll cross that bridge when we get to it."

Hannah nodded and began smoothing her bed excessively, a holdover from the OCD-like tendencies she had developed while bouncing between mental hospitals and group homes. They resurfaced whenever she was particularly nervous about something.

I went on, "We should also try to talk to some of the other guests, especially the ones who have been here for a while. Their experiences with Campbell might give us some important clues."

"I guess I can socialize on the flip side, see if I can connect with any of the floaters," Milo offered. "They'll have their own experiences, and since you two can't be seen talking to them..." Milo shrugged in an aggrieved sort of way, as though he were sacrificing himself by volunteering for this task.

"You have to stick to the story, though, even with the spirits," Hannah reminded him. "You can't let them know what we're really doing here, because if Campbell really can communicate with them, they could blow our cover."

Milo rolled his eyes. "Obvi."

"And make sure you remember there are other spirits to talk to besides Talia's ghost," Hannah added. "I know you want to find out if it's Grayson Allard, but stalking is stalking... even if both of you are dead."

As she said Grayson's name, a sudden familiar tingling jumped into my fingertips, like an itch that I just couldn't resist scratching. I jumped up and pulled my sketchpad and pencil from the bedside table and plopped down next to Hannah on the bed.

"Speaking of movie stars who may or may not be haunting Talia Simms," I said, "my Muse fingers are a-tingling, so let's see who the mystery man really is." I flipped past the sketch of our resident spirit back home in Salem and found a fresh, blank page.

"Ooh, are you getting something?" Hannah asked, scooting in closer so she could watch me work.

"Yeah, as soon as you said Grayson's name," I replied. "I'm not convinced we connected for long enough to get anything good, but I'll give it a try."

I closed my eyes and felt my way out into the space around me, following the energy as it ran from the tips of my fingers, up through my body, and out through my connection to the spirit realm. I found what I was looking for—a bright, pulsing spot that was calling to me and sending those irresistible pulses of pure essence shooting back into me. I focused in, breathing deeply, clearing all other thoughts and emotions; everything I could divine about this spirit needed to travel unfettered from his being to my fingers. I could feel my hand, independent of my control, flying over the page. When I finally opened my eyes, my sketch revealed a face that I knew very well.

"I told you it was him!" Milo cried. "He's here! Grayson's here and I might actually get to talk to him. I feel like I've been training my entire afterlife for this moment!"

The face that stared back at me from the page was ruggedly handsome—stubbled chin, closely cropped hair, and intense, piercing eyes that held such a sadness that I found myself unable to look directly into them.

"Well, he's here, but he's keeping his head down," I said. "I think the only reason he even attempted to communicate was because he thought Talia was in danger. I don't think you're going to find him very sociable, Milo. If you find him at all, I mean."

"You underestimate my mesmerism," Milo said confidently. "I'm captivating, trust me."

"You trust *me*, Milo," I said, and I couldn't help but smile at him. "I underestimate absolutely nothing about you."

15

SILENCED

B Y MORNING, AFTER A MUCH-NEEDED full night's sleep on the most comfortable—and probably the most expensive—bed I'd ever had the privilege to sleep in, I had gained enough perspective to realize that apologizing to Talia was the most reasonable thing to do. She may have overreacted, but then again, I was known to be a tad emotional sometimes, too.

Well, maybe more than a tad. Okay, fine, I regularly flew off the handle.

In any case, I made peace with the idea of making peace, and resolved to find Talia as soon as we went downstairs for the "Morning Social Hour and Breakfast."

As soon as I stepped out onto the porch, it became clear that I would not have a chance to find Talia. Nor would I be able to socialize or have breakfast first—Talia's personal assistant flew at me like a bat out of hell the instant I arrived. She had a face like a squirrel and an unnaturally high, fast voice, almost like someone had put her on permanent fast forward.

"Ms. Simms has requested that you look over these documents and sign them," the woman said, thrusting a stapled packet under my nose.

"I... what?" I was ready for any number of things this morning—being served papers was not one of them.

"Ms. Simms requests that you sign these papers. It's a privacy agreement, which stipulates that you will not disclose any information about last night's encounter—including any pictures or other forms of media you may have used to document said encounter—and that you will agree to immediately take down any social or electronic media posts that you may have shared. We can arrange generous compensation if necessary."

I glimpsed at Talia over the woman's shoulder. She was sitting at a table in the corner, staring down at a small bowl of fruit as though she had absolutely no idea what she was meant to do with it. Her shoulders were stiff; I was sure she was listening to us.

My gut reaction was to shove the packet into the woman's face and rip it in half, then whip out my phone and tweet every detail I could think of to the entire world. Instead, I took a deep breath and forced my face into a smile. "I thought everything that went on here was already secret because of Mr. Campbell's privacy policies?"

The girl shook her head. "His policies apply specifically to organized activities and events. Your encounter with Ms. Simms falls into the category of leisure time, and therefore is not technically protected in the terms set forth in Mr. Campbell's contracts."

"Oh, I see..." I replied, to fill the tense space between us. Meeting Talia Simms was among the least leisurely experiences of my life, but I decided not to challenge the term. I worked to keep my smile in place and said, "Do you have a pen?"

The girl opened her mouth to unleash the second half of her speech but then, clearly taken aback, closed it again. Perhaps no one had ever agreed so readily to this kind of proposal. The woman had obviously been ready to haggle about a payoff, or else threaten me with legal action. A bit flustered, she produced a pen from her purse and held it out to me.

I took the packet and flipped through to the last page. "Is this where I sign? She doesn't need to pay me. I'm not looking for publicity, you know. I just wanted to make sure she wasn't... well, dead." I signed, then handed the pen and the papers back to the assistant.

The woman blinked and then practically snatched the papers back from me, lest I change my mind. She marched back to Talia's table, where she sat down smartly and the two of them quickly began conferring. I turned my back on them and walked over to a table bathed in the early-morning sunlight. Hannah sat down beside me, smirking.

"What?" I asked, snatching up a croissant out of a basket and taking a huge bite. It was still warm.

"That was unexpectedly diplomatic of you," she said. "Very well played."

I leaned forward slightly and waved my hand in a theatrical little bow. "Maybe I should be the one with the Oscar."

Milo was paying no attention to our conversation whatsoever. He was craning his neck and gawking obnoxiously at Talia from his seat beside Hannah. "Oh my God, oh my God. She's here, she's actually here. Be cool, Milo, be cool," he muttered quietly under his breath.

"It doesn't matter whether you're cool or not," I told him, using our connection so no one would see me talking to thin air. "You could walk right up to her and fanboy all over her. She wouldn't notice."

Milo was too starstruck to retort. He just muttered something that might have been, "I bet she smells like summer rain and Beyoncé."

I turned to Hannah, keeping my voice low. "I don't see Grayson or any other spirits around here. Do you?"

Hannah shook her head. "No, but I'm sensing at least six or seven, though. You?"

I focused in on the familiar buzz that filled any space latent with spirit energy. For Hannah and me, this buzzing was as much part of our daily soundtracks as the wind, or cars driving by on the street, and no more alarming than a familiar song playing quietly in the background. We had learned as Apprentices to tune out this energy until we chose, consciously, to pay attention to it.

Yes, there were at least half a dozen spirits present on the porch. An emo teenager, filled with rage, spewed unheard profanities at his mother; a woman in her late sixties chastised her unwitting husband for eating too much bacon; a child complained loudly that he couldn't eat the food and that it wasn't fair, while his energy itself screamed, "Why won't you look at me, mommy?" Even as I plucked their voices from the fabric of the buzzing, my fingers itched to commit their faces to paper. I couldn't see any of them with my eyes, at least for the moment, but I could see them with the visual part of my brain—the part which crafted the images I drew with such detail and care.

Partly to calm the itching in my fingertips, I began fingering the rose quartz on my wrist. Breakfast offered the first real test of our Masking bracelets—yesterday Hannah and I had seen a spirit here or there, usually from afar, but now we had at least a half dozen spirits with us on the porch. Thankfully, the bracelets were working perfectly for the time being; Grayson had given no indication last night of his sensing my Gateway, and now, none of the spirits here with us noticed anything special about us. Not a single one materialized and started hovering around us curiously, as often happened when a spirit first detected our Gateway. We were "invisible" for the time being; it felt strange, in a way.

I didn't know yet what Campbell was up to in luring all these wealthy people to this property, but he certainly didn't choose them just for their money. Every single one of these people was legitimately haunted.

A blonde waitress appeared at our table, interrupting my spirit inventory. She was dressed in a uniform that made her look as if she'd stepped out of an Edwardian British drama—right down to her high, stiff collar and lace-trimmed apron. She deftly swung several platters off of her silver tray and placed them before us. They were laden with heaps of eggs, bacon, biscuits, home fries, and fruit salad. I barely allowed myself a moment's curiosity—How many of the body-image-crazed celebrities here actually ate this kind of stuff?—before loading up my plate, grabbing a fork, and tucking in.

"You know," I said, through a mouthful of egg, "I definitely don't have the willpower to be a celebrity. All of my tabloid photos would be of me stuffing my face."

"Well, stuff it quickly," Hannah replied, "because the first communication session starts in fifteen minutes."

§

After dining on the airy and sunlit dining porch, the drawing room seemed unnaturally dark. The curtains were all drawn; I suspected there were black-out shades behind them too, for no light crept in around the edges. A low fire crackled invitingly in the white marble fireplace, and tiny flames danced on candles that had been nestled among the bookshelves. The room ought to have been uncomfortably warm, but I could hear the hum of the air conditioning as it fought valiantly to keep things cool.

The first row of chairs was already full of rapt and waiting guests. Like us, several others had made their way to the drawing room from breakfast; most of these guests were now wandering the room, taking in the art on the walls, or else laying claim to chairs with their belongings. I took the opportunity to scan the room for anything even vaguely Durupinen related, while keeping an eye out for any hidden tech; I could find nothing.

At the front of the room, a single chair stood on a platform beside a grand piano. "Is he going to sing show tunes to the spirits?" I asked. "If he comes out in a velvet tux like one of those cruise ship performers, I'm leaving."

Hannah shrugged. "Let's find some seats."

"Maybe closer to the back," I suggested. "I want to keep both the guests and the spirits in view."

We slid into two chairs in the back corner of the last row, leaving at least three chairs between us the other guests. At Hannah's suggestion, Milo began to drift around the room; he had agreed that it would be a good idea for him to attempt communicating with the other "floaters."

As Milo began his first lap, Talia entered with a wide-brimmed hat draped low over her face. She skirted a woman who tried to speak to her, and took a seat on the other side of the room, in one of the back rows; she immediately assumed a body language so guarded that no one else dared approach her, although several people pointed.

"I'm still not picking up on Grayson, are you?" I whispered to Hannah.

"No," Hannah whispered back. "I'm not sensing any spirits near Talia right now." Then through our connection, I asked Milo, "Is there anyone around Talia?"

"Nope." He replied. "Lots of deadside cruisers here, though—and they're all pretty eager to talk. I'll let you know what I find out."

Suddenly, the lights—and indeed the very flames in the hearth and on the candles themselves—dimmed to a dull glow. The crowd gasped collectively. I looked around the room and realized that every single guest at Whispering Seraph must've been in the room with us.

"Okay, that was weird," I muttered, making a note to examine both the candles and the fireplace when the session was over. Surely they were gas-fueled or something like that; a flick of a switch could create instant ambiance.

An unnatural hush fell over the room as thirty or so upturned faces swiveled, in almost perfect synchronicity, to the platform at the front.

Campbell made us wait; he drew out the moments before his

appearance until the anticipation built to an almost unbearable degree. The guests were kept waiting for so long that they started to speculate, in a volley of whispers, as to whether Campbell was really coming out, before vehemently shushing each other in the hopes that he might suddenly appear. This cycle repeated itself three or four times until the crowd nearly reached its breaking point.

Toward the front of the room, the spirit of an elderly gentleman, thin and spry despite his age, had begun mocking the crowd, shouting that Campbell was a coward, that he wasn't coming at all, that the guests all should leave. It was almost impossible for Hannah and me not to giggle a bit at his antics—certainly he was being serious, but his theatrics were over the top. But in an audience this tense, we didn't dare laugh—it would give us away in an instant.

Just when I truly thought the audience was about to give up and leave, the door behind the platform swung open and Campbell strode forth, with both arms in the air like he was freaking Evita about to address Argentinean masses. I failed to stifle a derisive laugh, but fortunately my snicker was swallowed by the crowd's tumult; the other guests were cheering, clapping, and shrieking Campbell's name. A few were even reaching upward, with their arms stretched wide, shouting prayers and blessings upon him.

I concentrated on stemming a rising tide of irrational panic within me; overtly devout and raucous demonstrations of faith always made me want to run for the hills. It wasn't that I couldn't respect religious people—even the fervently religious. The line, for me, was when the faithful began throwing their canes and crutches aside, claiming that prayer had healed them. That kind of shit scared the living daylights out of me.

Campbell showed no signs of fear, though. Indeed, his face was alight with joy; he was obviously basking in the attention. His chest expanded over and over again, as though the adulation of the crowd were oxygen.

"Ugh, just look at him," I whispered under the din. "Is he getting off on this, or what?"

"Forget him," Hannah said. "Look at the spirits!"

I looked around, as subtly as I could, locating the spirits; their reaction to Campbell's appearance wasn't nearly as universally enthusiastic. Several looked quite excited to see Campbell and were clapping and cheering along with their living companions. But a few looked quite wary. One spirit had crossed his arms defensively over his chest, with his chin jutted out defiantly. Another spirit, the angry teenager who we'd sensed at breakfast, was pointing and shouting slurs at Campbell.

"Why won't you give them my whole message you bastard! Why are you lying to them?" the teenager shrieked over the applause.

"Whoa. The spirit contingent is quite split on Campbell, aren't they?" I muttered in Hannah's ear.

"Mm-hmm," she agreed, clapping to blend in with the others.

Finally, after a thorough ego boost, Campbell put his arms up: The hush that came over the group seemed as if it had dropped onto their heads from Campbell's open hands. The spirits, too, fell silent.

"Good morning to you all, spirit and living alike," Campbell opened. "To some of you," and here he took a moment to make eye contact with several different guests, while keeping his stunning smile firmly in place, "welcome back to the Sanctuary at Whispering Seraph. To others, we welcome you for the very first time." At this, Campbell looked directly at Hannah and me. Hannah smiled shyly, nodding at the group—some of whom had turned in their seats to look at us. I flicked a hand awkwardly in acknowledgment of the attention, but dropped my eyes quickly to the floor. I had a part to play as the reluctant sister—a part for which I was well cast.

"I have such gratitude in my heart, seeing y'all here, and I'll tell you why," Campbell went on, with one hand clutching passionately at his crisp white linen shirt. "Because it means that I get to use this gift I've been blessed with. Get to use it for one more day. Get the incredible opportunity to help everyone in this room find connection and peace. There is no greater thing in this world than helping others. It's our purpose. It's at the core of our humanity. It's its own reward—the only reward you or I will ever need."

"Yeah, that and the disgusting amounts of money you squeeze from these poor, desperate people, you hypocrite," I thought to myself; a bitter laugh from one of the spirits let me know I wasn't the only one in the room who felt this way.

As surreptitiously as I could, I scanned the room once more. Every living audience member was positively lapping up Campbell's bullshit. If Talia moved any closer to the edge of her seat, she'd fall off of it. Her expression was twisted with emotion, with a gleam of hope in her eyes. If I didn't know better, I would've thought she were being filmed for one of her movies. There was still no trace of Grayson, despite his having been so protective the previous night. In fact, as I took a quick headcount, I realized Talia was the only person in the room who didn't have a spirit attached to her.

My anger at Talia trickled away; my rage was sapped by seeing her tears while knowing that there was no one there beside her silently wishing to reach out and dry them. As I watched her, all I could feel was terribly sad and sorry for her.

Almost as though she'd heard this thought, Talia turned and caught me staring at her. She dragged the back of her hand angrily across her face, wiping away her tears, then glared at me before whipping her head around to face the front. She snapped her head so quickly that her hair swung around the back of her head in a single curtain, like a door slamming shut between us.

Right, okay, so maybe a little of my anger was back.

"Before I start, I want to remind everyone," Campbell continued, in a voice saturated with regret, "that I have no control over which spirits are here and which are not. I have no control over what they say to me, or what they may choose not to say. I'm merely a conduit. I can only continue if everyone agrees to remember this."

Fervent nods and answering cries of "Yes!" "Of course!" and "We understand!" came from the crowd.

A shiver ran down my spine: This was starting to feel more and more like a cult than a retreat. Then again, I doubted cults advertised themselves as cults—I doubted their brochures said, "Join us for relaxation, community-building, and a good brainwashing." Milo must have picked up on my thought through our connection because I heard him stifle a snort.

"Y'all know how my gift came to me—Y'all know it isn't really my gift at all." Campbell went on humbly, "It belongs to my angel, who comes to me with messages from those we've lost. I may never know why I was chosen. But I do know this: Everyone in this room was chosen, too. We've found each other, and that was no accident. I don't believe in accidents. Only Providence, do y'all understand me?"

Again came a sycophantic chorus of answers, with the audience's heads bowing in unison like flowers all caught in the same irresistible breeze.

I glanced at Hannah again. Her face was twisted with distaste, as if her mouth were full of something bitter. I nudged her with my foot; with a start, she quickly recomposed her expression into one of polite interest. We couldn't let our ruse slip, no matter how badly I wanted to punch Campbell right in his too-shiny teeth.

"And Providence knows that we're all here for a reason, so let's get down to it. There are loved ones here who wish to speak, and I'm ready to let them be heard!" At this, Campbell threw back his head, closed his eyes, and opened his arms as if he were welcoming a dear friend.

Just like yesterday, a great dark swooping something descended over the room, like the shadow of a bird of prey. It was more than just darkness, though; for Hannah and me, the strange disorienting pressure returned. My head swam and ached, but I fought against it. I kept my face as impassive as I could as I focused all of my energy on studying the cloud thing now circling us like a hawk.

There was a rippling to the cloud, a sort of billowing motion, as though a wind none of us could feel were filling its sails. The cloud still had no defined form... no limbs, or head, or—as one might expect from a so-called angel—wings. The cloud, an amorphous blob of dense energy, shifted and flowed, finally swirling itself around Campbell; it came to rest on his shoulders.

Campbell couldn't see his angel, that much was clear. He didn't seem to know where it was in the room until the moment it came to rest on him. But every spirit had been following the cloud's progress; their collective energy was buzzing through me, humming with trepidation, agitation, and fear. None of the living people in the room seemed to sense the cloud at all, however. Aside from a shiver here or there—the temperature in the room had cooled appreciably when the cloud entered—they just waited, watching Campbell intently, utterly ignorant of the paranormal, serpentine *something* now winding itself around their beloved guru.

That serpentine something was now hissing into Campbell's ear, from the look of it. I burned with frustration; I wanted to know what, if anything, the angel-being was saying. I wanted to tell Milo to try to get closer, but I'd closed our connection after I'd heard him snort a few moments ago; we'd already agreed that using our connection while the angel was present would be a bad idea. What if the angel, or whatever it was, could pick up on it? What if it realized we could communicate with spirits, too? Worse still, what would happen if it told Campbell about us?

Campbell, meanwhile, had inclined his head lovingly toward this creature, as though in an embrace. I leaned forward, straining every sensory and extra-sensory muscle I had, trying to hear or sense what the "angel" was saying. I gleaned nothing, and instead had to concentrate on fighting my headache and dizziness, which were both building steadily.

"Marigold!" Campbell shouted suddenly. "Marigold Jackson! Your beloved husband Harold is with you again today. He sits beside you, in that very chair. Although it appears empty to you, I assure you it's anything but!"

Every head whipped around in fascination at the woman named Marigold. She was perhaps in her late fifties, and well preserved, no doubt, by a good deal of skillfully executed plastic surgery. Clutching convulsively at a string of pearls around her neck, she turned, with her eyes full of tears, to stare into the air beside her—air which I could clearly see was indeed occupied by the spirit of a man with a mustache, a receding hairline, and an indignant expression.

"Don't you talk to her!" he shouted in a Texas drawl, shaking an angry fist at Campbell. "Pick on someone else, why don't you, and leave my wife alone!"

Marigold, oblivious to her husband's protests, cried, "Harold! Oh, Harold, I just knew you were here. I could sense it. I could just sense it!" She dug into her purse, extracted a wad of tissues, and began sniffing noisily into them.

"Harold, if there's anything you'd like to say to your wife, she's here! She's listening," Campbell urged. His expression was eager and open, and he was looking in the direction of the chair Harold was indeed occupying. However, it was quite obvious Campbell had no idea that Harold, as he continued to shake his angry fist, was not sitting in that chair, but standing upon it.

"I've got something I'd like to say to *you!*" Harold shouted. "You've got some nerve, tricking my wife into coming here and squandering all our money on your parlor tricks! She never had any sense when it came to money, that's nothing new! Jewelry, shoes, that ridiculous elliptical exercise contraption she bought off the TV! She probably won't even touch the damn thing! But that's nothing compared to this foolishness! You're nothing but a swindler, that's what you are! A low-down swindler who oughta be in jail!"

Some of the other spirits were protesting now too, shouting their support for Harold's tirade. Campbell seemed oblivious to all of it; he was listening intently to his "angel." A moment or two later, though, Campbell chuckled and shook his head.

"Now Marigold," Campbell began, shaking his finger at her as if she were a naughty puppy, "Harold asks you to have a bit more sense with how you're spending your money! He says he's not convinced you'll even use the elliptical machine you bought off the TV!"

Marigold's mouth fell open, then she began to laugh through her tears. She faced Harold again, although her eyes were focused on his sizable belly rather than his face. "Oh, my stars! I'm sorry, cupcake, but the before-and-after pictures were mighty impressive."

Almost everyone among the living laughed, Campbell included.

"That's not what I meant!" Harold shouted to Campbell over the laughter. "You know that's not how I meant it!"

Campbell put his hands up to quiet the continued laughter. "I'm glad we can find humor even amid our grief, but let's not lose sight of the fact that Harold is watching out for you Marigold. Even now, he wants to make sure you're taken care of."

Marigold's eyes filled with tears again, although the smile remained on her face. "That's my Harold. He always took such good care of me!"

"Well, now you need to take good care of yourself, Marigold," Campbell said solemnly. "That's what Harold wants now. So rein in those frivolous purchases, young lady! Harold left you quite comfortable, but you mustn't expend your resources on home shopping channels, alright?"

Marigold continued to laugh and cry simultaneously. Harold sat down, muttering under his breath. I picked out the words "durn snake-oil salesman" before he faded completely from sight.

"Good then," Campbell said, with his winning smile still lighting his features. "Let's see who else is with us—hidden from our sight, but never from our hearts." As he closed his eyes once more, I leaned forward, catching Milo's eye; I raised my eyebrows at him.

"Oh, right!" he said loudly, suddenly remembering that he was supposed to try to get himself noticed. He stood up and started waving his arms; his calls joined those of the other spirits vying for Campbell's attention.

"Hey! Mr. Campbell! Over here! I need to talk to Hannah! Please, Mr. Campbell, I have an important message for her!" Milo was truly made for this role; no one could demand attention quite like he could.

Campbell, his eyes closed, sat listening intently for a moment. Then he opened his eyes again and looked right at me. My heart skipped a beat before I realized Campbell was actually looking just next to me, where Milo had positioned himself.

"Let's all welcome our newest guests, Hannah and Jessica Taylor!" announced Campbell, with what sounded very convincingly like true warmth in his voice. "And of course, their dear friend, Milo Chang."

Everyone turned to us, offering greetings. An elderly man several rows ahead of us actually got up and came over to shake our hands. Panicking in the sudden spotlight—and unable to think of a valid reason for using force against a little old man—I plastered on a smile and let him wring my hand enthusiastically.

"I hope our proceedings this morning have gone a step further towards convincing you that you are in the right place," Campbell said, looking at us expectantly.

"Thank you," I muttered in a tiny voice. Hannah, barely audible, echoed me.

"I know you've come here after the terrible loss of your friend Milo. I'm so privileged to be the one to help cast off the veil of darkness in your lives!" And here Campbell walked to the nearest window and threw back the curtain with a flourish, causing the morning sunlight to stream into the room. "Your friend Milo has indeed joined us, and it seems he's quite eager to speak with you!"

Hannah snapped into action, gazing around as though she couldn't see Milo next to me.

"Milo? Your dear friends are eager for your message. What have you come to share with them today?" Campbell asked, staring at the place where Milo indeed was.

Milo took a deep breath he didn't actually need, and spoke his rehearsed words loudly and clearly, "I need Hannah to know something. I'm not mad at her, about the fight we had before I died. I know she feels guilty, but she shouldn't. I loved her like a sister—and siblings always fight a little. It was just a stupid disagreement about a boy who really doesn't matter. Can you tell her that? Please? She's torturing herself. She really shouldn't be doing that... she'll make herself sick! Once I know she's forgiven herself, I can move on."

Everyone waited in the silence as Campbell received Milo's message through the mouthpiece of his angel.

"Milo's message is for you, Hannah," Campbell said, extending his arms toward her as though he half-expected her to run into them. "He knows you're feeling guilty about the argument you had before he died. He says that it wasn't important—just a silly fight about a boy who doesn't matter. He's insisting that you stop torturing yourself before you make yourself sick."

Hannah covered her face with her hands to hide her utter lack of emotion; it would've been nice if she could've produced a few crocodile tears, but that sort of thing just wasn't in her. I flung an arm around her shoulders and pretended to comfort her amid the crowd's applause and "hallelujahs!"

"You see the peace and joy this place can bring!" Campbell cried out. "I hope this means the Taylor girls will be with us for quite some time now! What a blessing to stay connected with those we love, even after they've left the living world!"

"But Mr. Campbell," Milo pleaded, "can you ask her if she'll forgive herself? She needs to, for both of us to move on!" But Campbell, flushed and euphoric by his own success, had already moved on; he closed his eyes and swayed on the spot, waiting for his angel to find him another spirit.

"Is... do you think he's okay?" I whispered to Hannah, under the guise of continuing to comfort her. Campbell's face was getting rosier by the minute. He was sweating profusely and his eyes, when he opened them, had taken on a glassy quality, like someone with a raging fever. "He looks sick."

"I don't know, but if he doesn't wrap this up soon, *I'm* going to be sick," Hannah mumbled back to me. "I think my head might explode if we don't get away from that angel thing soon. I can barely see."

"Yeah, me too. Just try to hang in a little longer." We probably could've excused ourselves under the guise of emotional distress, but I didn't want to miss any of this session; this could be our only chance to really watch Campbell in action.

"Another message!" Campbell cried, raising a trembling finger and pointing toward the back of the room. Talia let out a soft cry of joy and looked expectantly around, but the name that Campbell called out next was not hers.

"Moira and Tom Owens! Kyle is here with us today and is eager to speak with you!" Campbell cried. The rest of the guests—and the spirits—quieted down at once, eager to hear the next message.

I was far more interested in Talia than I was in whatever message Campbell had for Moira and Tom Owens. I watched as Talia tore her face from her trembling hands, behind which she'd been sobbing silently, and attempted to pull herself together. I forced myself to turn back toward Campbell before Talia caught me staring again.

As I turned to the front of the room, a sudden movement in the window behind Campbell caught my eye. There stood Grayson Allard, his face twisted in absolute agony, watching Talia. It was clear he wanted to go to her and comfort her, but he seemed unable to enter the room, as if he were somehow barred. Why didn't he just come in? There were no Wards that I could see, and Warding against only one specific spirit was truly high-level Durupinen stuff—I honestly didn't think Campbell could manage it without Fairhaven-type training. Then I saw Grayson look up at Campbell; his eyes flashed with such unmitigated rage that it actually took my breath away.

"What's wrong?" Hannah whispered to me under the continued applause.

"It's... I'll tell you later," I muttered, turning my focus back to the Owenses. Moira and Tom were a couple in their late forties; they were both pale and drawn, and were and clutching at each other's hands. When their names had been called, they had both closed their eyes and started praying aloud, "Oh thank you, Lord! Thank you!"

Kyle was the emo-teen who'd been shouting periodically at Campbell throughout this "Communing with the Lost" session. He was tall and thin, with a goth ensemble which rivaled my own usual attire. When Kyle had heard Campbell call his name, he'd flown forward, coming to rest about a foot in front of Campbell's platform. The hostility radiating from his form was nearly as intense as what I'd just seen on Grayson Allard's face. In fact, there was now so much spirit negativity around me that I was starting to feel it affecting my own mood; it was seeping into me like an infection.

194

Kyle hovered confrontationally in front of Campbell. "Yeah, you want a message from the other side, bro?" he screeched, then shot across the room so that he was mere inches from his father's face. "You see these tears dripping down their faces? You see this remorse? It's all bullshit, you understand me? Total bullshit! They didn't love me! Every single day of my life, all they did was tell me just how much of a disappointment I was." Kyle's was so upset that he was vibrating, with his edges blurring out of focus, as he flung his accusations at his oblivious parents.

"I was never smart enough, never athletic enough! My friends weren't good enough. Nothing I did was ever good enough! It was their fault I got in that car! It was their fucking fault—I was too angry to think straight! If they would've laid off me just that once—listened to a single goddamned word I had to say—I wouldn't be stuck here, missing out on the rest of my life! I'M NOT SUPPOSED TO BE DEAD YET!"

As Kyle ranted, Campbell, nodding slowly, was listening to his angel. Then he turned to Kyle's parents, his face transfigured into solemnness. "Kyle says he knows he was going too fast in that car. He says he was too upset and wasn't thinking clearly. He regrets it deeply, no longer being here to experience life with you."

Moira and Tom were sobbing, and babbling to the son they couldn't see. The other audience members began applauding wildly again. My ears were absolutely ringing with anger at the way Campbell had twisted Kyle's message. Poor Kyle, whose words fell on deaf ears even after death, was now cursing at the top of his lungs; he'd become a blur of red hot rage. Hannah and I looked at each other.

"Jess, something's happening... brace yourself," Hannah whispered under her breath.

But I didn't need telling. We'd both felt it before. The building up of spirit energy, like steam in a kettle, like too much hot air in a balloon. I felt it concentrating behind me; I turned just in time to see two figures barreling into the room. The first was Grayson Allard, who flew right at Talia, knocking her from her seat. With my heart in my mouth, I realized the second figure was Finn—and he was running right at us.

16

BEHIND THE MASK

THE BACK WINDOWS EXPLODED in a hailstorm of glass, which sliced through the thick curtains as if they weren't even there. Needling shards flew everywhere. Finn had leapt on top of us just in time, pulling us both to the ground and shielding us from the debris. All around us, people had dropped to the floor with their arms over their heads; a few were still screaming. Lying on my stomach, I arched my neck just enough to see Campbell on his knees beneath his grand piano, cowering as though a bomb had gone off.

Well, a bomb *had* gone off. An enraged, disembodied spirit-bomb.

"Are you okay? Are you hurt?" Finn's face was pressed to my hair, with his lips against my ear. A shudder ran through my entire body that had nothing to do with the stress of the explosion and everything to do with his unbearable closeness. For one wild instant, I forgot everything except his mouth's being a fraction of an inch away from the curve of my neck. His panting breaths raised goose bumps all over my body. "*Please*," I thought, "*Please* just turn me around and kiss me right now."

Then I remembered where I was and mentally dope-slapped myself back into reality.

"I'm fine, I'm fine. Get off us!" I gasped.

Finn jumped nimbly up and extended a hand to both Hannah and me, pulling us both to our feet simultaneously.

"How did you know the explosion was coming?" I asked him, avoiding his gaze as I rubbed the goose bumps from my forearms. "You were halfway across the room before it even happened."

"I felt it building up. Didn't you?" Finn answered, still panting a little.

"We knew something was going to happen, yeah," Hannah said.

All around us, frightened guests were helping each other up and brushing bits of glass off of their clothes. I scanned the spirit population for any sign of Kyle, but he had vanished. And so had Grayson Allard.

Talia crouched on the floor alone, looking wildly around for the person who'd shielded her from the blast. Not a single shard of glass lay within a foot of her; it was as though Grayson had created a protective bubble around her with his energy.

Burly men in Whispering Seraph staff shirts came running from all directions, calling out instructions to each other and shouting for Campbell.

"I'm here, I'm here," Campbell called in a shaky voice as he crawled out from beneath the piano. Two of the security staff ran to him and tried to help him to his feet, but he batted their hands away. "Leave me alone. I'm fine, perfectly fine! Help the guests! Is everyone alright? Is anyone hurt?"

Miraculously, it didn't seem as if anybody was injured. There was no blood on any of the frightened faces in the crowd. Campbell dropped his gaze a moment, muttering under his breath, and then realized his angel had taken flight. He took a long breath, then looked around the drawing room before letting out a deep, confident laugh. The sound was so unexpected that several people began staring at him as though they thought he, too, might explode.

"Well, that wasn't very polite, now was it?" Campbell said, still laughing.

The crowd, agog, was clearly bewildered as to what Campbell found so very humorous in this moment.

"I really must apologize. I didn't foresee that kind of enthusiasm in one of my communication sessions, but I suppose that's what I get for opening our doors so wide. Please, before y'all start packing your bags, let me explain what's happened here."

All around us, expressions began to calm at the soothing, self-assured tone of Campbell's voice. As the crowd relaxed a measure, he continued, "It seems we had so many eager spirits here—so many waiting for their turn—that we experienced a short-circuit. Just too much of a good thing! We blew a spirit fuse!"

Campbell laughed again—and this time, a few of the guests laughed along with him. I couldn't force myself to join in. Neither, it seemed, could Talia, whose own security had arrived and was now towering over her as she settled back into her seat. Her eyes were still darting around the room, and she was vigorously rubbing at a spot on her upper arm; it was the spot, no doubt, where Grayson's spirit form had made contact with her.

Campbell went on. "This is one of the pitfalls of dealing with spirits, my dear friends. It can be terribly unpredictable. There's still so much we don't understand. I won't pretend to have all the answers. But I will never stop offering myself up as the conduit between you and your loved ones, as long as you still want to speak with them."

Applause rang through the room, punctuated by shouts of 'Thank you!' and "Bless you!"

"Now, that's what I wanted to hear! I'll go sit down with my events coordinator and devise a new schedule. We'll arrange for smaller, more private, communication sessions throughout the remainder of the retreat, to keep this short-circuiting from happening again. In the meantime, I must ask that everyone please take a moment to allow my staff to check you over and make sure you really are alright. We have a nurse on staff, if need be. We'll end the session here today." And, waving over his shoulder to the adulating group, Campbell slipped out the door behind the platform.

I'm going to follow him," Finn whispered, watching Campbell disappear.

"I want to come with you," I said.

I expected him to scoff. I expected him to insist I stay behind because it might be dangerous. Instead, Finn surprised me by saying, "Let's go, then. Out the French doors."

I didn't bother to discuss his chosen route, in case he changed his mind. I grabbed Hannah's arm and whispered to her, "Finn and I are going to follow Campbell. We'll meet you back in the room."

Hannah's eyes widened, but she didn't protest. "O-okay. Milo and I will keep an eye on the spirits in here, and see if we can figure anything out."

"Great," I said, squeezing her hand in encouragement. Then I hurried after Finn, who had already edged his way to the perimeter of the room and was heading toward the door.

I caught up to Finn, then stayed close on his heels. "Shouldn't we try to follow Campbell through the door behind the platform?" I asked. "We're going to lose him."

"His security will notice us if we go that way," Finn replied. "If we cut across the porch and through the entry hall, there's a hallway behind the staircase. That's where he's headed."

"How do you know that?" I asked.

"Memorized the floor plan before we got here," Finn said flatly.

"Oh. Right. Cool." I should've guessed.

We slipped through the French doors without attracting anyone's attention. We darted across the entry hall and made it to the passage behind the staircase without meeting a single person. In front of us, a corridor stretched out, lined with doors on both sides and lit with small but elaborate chandeliers—like clusters of sparkling grapes set into the ceiling.

"Which one?" I asked, gesturing hopelessly ahead of us.

"I memorized the floor plan, Jess, but I'm not psychic," said Finn, with an impatient bite in his voice. "Now we search. You take the right side, I'll take the left."

We tiptoed down the hallway, which was thankfully carpeted, stopping every few feet to listen at each door. No sounds came from behind the first four doors, but just as I was approaching the fifth, Finn hissed, "Jess! He's in here!"

I stole across to the very last door on the left and pressed my ear to the cool wood, so that Finn and I were staring into each other's faces as we listened. Thank goodness for the old South's grand constructions: The high ceilings and hardwood bounced Campbell's voice right out to us.

"Please, you must tell me what happened in there!" Campbell cried. A few moments of silence passed, and then he said, "You can't call that nothing! Someone could've been killed!"

More silence. I pressed my ear harder to the door, but couldn't make out another voice.

"On the phone?" Finn mouthed to me.

I shrugged my shoulders in reply, not wanting to chance being overheard.

"I don't mean to question you," came Campbell's voice. "Yes, I trust you—I do, I swear it! But I'm very uneasy about—"

Campbell broke off, presumably to listen again. I concentrated still harder, trying to hear the other voice. As I focused in, a wave of dizziness washed over me. Suddenly, it clicked.

"The angel!" I whispered to Finn. "He's talking to the angel! It's in there with him right now!"

I saw the realization light up in Finn's eyes and he smiled. "You're right!"

Campbell's voice was calmer now, more subdued. "Yes, of course. As long as we aren't keeping them here against their will. I couldn't go on with this if I thought—" Another long pause. "Yes, my angel. Yes, thank you. You can count on me. I won't fail you."

A cold something tingled up my spine. What was this being he was talking to? Because I was damn sure it was no angel.

"What are you doing?" cried a wary voice suddenly.

With my heart in my mouth, I leapt away from the door and bumped right into Talia.

"Damn it, Talia, you scared me!" I growled. "Keep your voice down!"

I took her by the arm and pulled around the corner. Finn followed.

"Let go of me!" Talia hissed, yanking her arm out of my grip. "You didn't answer my question!"

"I was... we were just... I came to talk to Campbell. My security is very concerned; he was expressly forbidden from that room—a room that just happened to explode." I cocked my thumb over my shoulder at Finn, whose face wore its usual curmudgeonly expression.

"Quite right," said Finn. "My first duty is to Ms. Taylor. Not to Campbell's rules."

I jumped in before Finn could go on. Were security guards supposed to address their employer's acquaintances directly? "We were going to knock," I said to Talia, "but then Mr. Campbell started shouting at someone, so..." I shrugged as though to suggest that eavesdropping was the natural next step.

Talia looked at Finn and dropped her guard a little. "Oh yes, I'm going to have to talk my security down off a ledge too, I think."

"So is that why you're here? Security?" I asked.

Talia snapped her head back toward me and glared as though she found the question impertinent. "None of your business," she spat.

I gave her the haughtiest look I could muster. "You know, you might be used to being the queen of the castle in Hollywood, but no one here is intimidated by you. Everyone here has as much wealth and influence as you'll ever have, so you can get down off of that high horse. Your fame means nothing to me."

I looked over at Finn and snapped my fingers at him. "Let's go, Finn. I have a massage appointment in the spa."

Finn stared at me blankly for an instant, too shocked—and perhaps hurt—by my behavior to so much as answer back. In the next instant, the light of recognition glimmered in his eyes. I was not Jess Ballard, the woman with whom he had an extremely complicated relationship, I was "Ms. Taylor," child of luxury and privilege, ruler of her own little kingdom.

Finn inclined his head at me before following me down the hall at a swift march. "Well done," he said, after we'd put a little distance between us and Talia. "Very convincing. Quintessential entitled prat."

"Thanks," I murmured back. "Now don't distract me, I'm trying to pull off a dramatic exit."

"Are we really going to the spa?" he whispered.

"No, of course not." I hissed. "I don't even know where the spa is. Just keep walking like we know where we're going."

We marched straight down the hallway. Only as I turned the corner back to the entryway did I glimpse Talia standing in the hallway, staring blankly after us. In that moment, she looked very small, and very alone.

Finn trailed behind me as far as the front doors, but instead of heading up to my room, he charged straight out onto the porch, down the steps, and out onto the grounds. I decided to follow him. If Hannah needed me, she could always have Milo buzz into my head.

"Where are we going?" I asked, jogging to keep up with Finn.

"To one of the blind spots. I don't want to be overheard," he replied.

"Blind spots?"

"From the security cameras. Iggy sent me a satellite photo with all of them marked off. There's one just over here."

"So he's all set up at the Boarding House?" I asked breathlessly.

"Yes. He's got the all the tech set up in his room. He couldn't be happier with the arrangements, given how haunted the place is. He's not even off-put by the Lafayette twins. Catriona ordered that they put a Casting on themselves—and on the boarding house—so that all appears a bit more normal. In fact, our biggest challenge with this case may be getting Iggy to leave when we're finished."

Finn parted the curtain of Spanish moss on an enormous tree

that branched out over the garage. He took a seat on a small stone bench on the garage's far side; from this vantage point we could no longer see Whispering Seraph. I sat down beside him; the bench was about a foot lower than I would've liked it to be, and our knees jutted out awkwardly, causing them to brush together.

"Right then," Finn said. "Tell me everything you can about what happened in the session."

I explained everything, from Campbell's rhetoric, to the responses of the crowd—both living and dead—to Grayson's appearance in the window and his shielding of Talia. As I proceeded, Finn's expression grew darker and darker, until it seemed as if a cartoon rain cloud had gathered over his head.

"And then Kyle lost his shit, and the place exploded!" I finished.

Finn stood up and began to pace agitatedly. "So Campbell isn't delivering the spirits' entire messages. He's only relaying the comforting and amusing bits. No wonder the spirits are angry."

"Yes, but I don't think Campbell realizes that's what he's doing," I said.

Finn stopped pacing and scowled at me. "How could he not know? That doesn't make sense."

"It does if he's not hearing the whole message in the first place," I said. "Look, we've already figured out that Campbell can't hear the spirits himself. Remember, it was the angel thing who could hear Milo, and who relayed Milo's message. Campbell was just repeating what the angel told him."

"Right, so..." Finn said slowly, as though waiting for a punch line.

"So the angel is editing the messages!" I cried. "For whatever reason, it doesn't want Campbell to get the whole message either."

"But what's the point of that?" Finn asked. "Why would the angel want to do that?"

"Not a clue," I replied. "We have no idea what the thing even is, let alone what its motives are."

Finn paused for a moment, then asked thoughtfully, "So what kind of information is it omitting? Is there a pattern to it?" he asked, ever logical. He sat down beside me again. "Tell me exactly what he left out, spirit by spirit."

"Well, with Harold, it was pretty obviously about dollar signs. Harold wanted his wife to stop blowing her money in general, but his biggest concern was the amount Marigold is shelling out to stay here. But when Campbell delivered the message, he conveniently left out the retreat's fees."

"Okay," Finn said. "That's a pretty obvious motive, in that it keeps Campbell in business. Although, what an angel would want with money, I can't properly imagine. What else?"

"Next was Milo," I said. "He delivered Milo's message almost word-for-word. The only thing he left out was the part about forgiveness. Remember the script we wrote for Milo? He said that if Hannah forgave herself, he could move on. But Campbell skipped that part, even when Milo insisted."

"Hmm, okay," Finn said. "In a more roundabout way, that's also about money, isn't it? If Milo stays around, you and Hannah will want to keep communicating with him—and that means more retreats and more money in Campbell's pocket. And what about the last one? Kyle, was that his name?"

"Yeah. His message got twisted way more than the others. That poor kid really hates his parents—he flat-out blamed them for his death, and for missing out on the rest of his life. But Campbell—well, the angel—ignored all of that and spouted some bullshit about Kyle missing his parents and regretting the car accident. Understandably, that's when Kyle lost it."

"So," Finn said, "the angel tells people what they want to hear—or at least just enough to keep them coming back for more. And the more cash they shell out, the more Whispering Seraph can keep expanding!"

"But how much more could Campbell possibly want to do to this place?" I asked. "It's palatial! It's the definition of luxury itself! Yoga, spas, swimming pools, gourmet food, the works! I mean, here in this heat, this retreat's even got a giant fire pit!" I said, gesturing to the circular stone structure about a dozen yards away. Its sunken center was already stacked high with firewood. "For God's sake, who the hell wants to roast marshmallows when it's eight hundred degrees out? But you can, if you want! Because this place has everything!"

"And I'm sure it costs a small fortune to keep this all running," Finn said. "But even so, he's not finished. He's got permits on file with the county to expand further. And he can't do that without a substantial stream of income."

"So the angel wants him to keep building?" I asked.

"So it would seem," Finn replied.

"Well, the angel better come up with a new game plan, or else start recruiting some new guests. Kyle wasn't the only angry spirit there today—and he certainly won't be the last to lose his cool if this keeps up!"

Finn nodded. "I'll report back to Catriona tonight, but if things continue this way, we may be forced to shut this place down through Castings. That will mean breaking our cover, but this pot is properly ready to boil over."

This was exactly the kind of situation Finn hated—unnecessarily dangerous and unpredictable. I could see his Caomhnóir instincts kicking into overdrive. I knew I had to choose my next words carefully, or else he'd pull us out of this place faster than a parent removing a tantrumming child from a black-tie wedding.

"I agree we should let Catriona know everything that's happening, but let's not panic. If we shut the place down, we may never find out what this angel is, or what its agenda may be. I think we should proceed—but cautiously, of course." I added these last words in reaction to the look on Finn's face; I had to head him off before he interrupted. "We can monitor things closely, but we're only just starting to dig. It would be a shame to give up too soon."

Finn chewed his lip pensively. "You've properly Warded your room?"

"As soon as we got here," I replied calmly.

"And you're carrying your Casting bag at all times?"

In answer, I patted my purse, where my little black velvet bag bulged with all the materials we would need for any and all Castings.

Finn narrowed his eyes at me. "You're humoring me."

"I like to think of it as trying to work together," I said. "I'm becoming reasonable and cooperative in my old age."

Finn actually smiled. Not a grudging, involuntary smile, but a genuine grin. "Alright, then, points to you, but only because I was raised to never disrespect a pensioner."

I smiled back. "Thank you. And I'm serious, I'm not humoring you. We'll be really careful. And if things get out of hand, we're out of here. I don't owe anything to the Durupinen, whatever Finvarra might think. I'm not risking my life for them."

"You didn't owe them anything the last time you risked your life for them, either," Finn pointed out.

"I didn't risk it for them. I risked for Hannah and Savvy and—"

For you. I risked it for you, too. And I would've lost everything if your words hadn't brought me back, my soul whispered. My mouth, however—after a potentially traitorous hitch—continued on as if my soul had remained silent.

"For my friends." I finished. "Some of whom happen to be Durupinen. That's not the same thing."

Finn didn't notice my awkward pause, or if he did, he didn't let on. "Fair enough. But I know you—and by now the Durupinen know you, too. You won't let Campbell take advantage of the people here. You won't let these people suffer if you can stop it. And you'll probably risk your life in the process."

I smiled as innocently as possible. "Not on purpose."

Finn laughed—a free, raucous sound—and then jerked his head in the direction of the main house. "Let's head back to your room. We need to coordinate with Hannah and Milo, and decide what our next move is."

17

DISCOVERED

Y OGA. GROSS. An hour designed to remind me just how uncoordinated, non-athletic, and un-Zen I truly am. Why couldn't I just go hide in my room?

Unfortunately staying in my room wasn't an option, so here I was in Whispering Seraph's yoga studio, with my arms over my head, struggling in vain to balance on one foot while the other was fighting valiantly to stay tucked behind my knee. The instructor looked so calm that she could have fallen into a light doze, yet it was all I could do to remind myself not to curse out loud.

"Ouch. SHIT! Oh, sorry!" So much for not cursing aloud.

My apology was addressed to the woman beside me as I nearly toppled onto her. Giving up in earnest, I sat myself on my mat and began massaging my now-cramped calf. The instructor took a break from her lovely dream state to throw me a dirty look, which I returned earnestly.

"Oh, don't you worry your pretty little head about me, honey," the woman said, flopping down beside me. "I ain't no nun. I've heard a cuss or two in my life—just don't expect me to admit to any myself. My poor mama would roll over in her grave."

I smiled up at Marigold Jackson, whose foundation was starting to drip from her face. The spirit of Harold was nowhere to be seen—perhaps he shared my opinion of yoga. "Thanks, I replied. "I'm just no good at this kind of thing. I don't even know why I'm here, to be honest. Well, I don't mean here," I clarified, gesturing grandly around to suggest all of Whispering Seraph. "I guess I just don't see how yoga is supposed to help."

"Come on, sugar," said Marigold as the instructor shushed us. "Let's head on over to the juice bar."

Well, I guess my assignment of "getting to know some of the other guests better" would be easier than I thought. Marigold and

I rolled up our mats and walked out the back door. We passed through the sun-soaked lobby to the juice bar. The bar was deserted, except for a smiling attendant.

"What can I get for you ladies?" he asked, throwing a white hand towel over his shoulder before placing two tall glasses onto the countertop.

"How about a bourbon straight up?" Marigold asked.

The young man's smiled slipped slightly. "We don't serve alcohol, ma'am. It's a widely recognized depressant, and our policy on hard alcohol is—"

"You're a widely recognized depressant," said Marigold, with a dismissive wave of her hand. "Two Berry Blasts, then, cowboy—and make it quick, we're melting into puddles of gorgeous over here."

The attendant began juicing armloads of fruit with alarming speed. Marigold turned to me, fanning herself with a laminated drink list. "So, you're brand new, right? It's Hannah, isn't it?"

"No, Hannah's my sister. I'm Jessica. Jess for short."

"Oh, that's right. I'm sorry, Jess. When did y'all get here?"

"Just yesterday."

"I thought so," Marigold said, with the air of someone who'd seen hundreds come and go through Whispering Seraph.

"You're the first person who's bothered to introduce herself to me. I get the sense people like to keep to themselves around here," I said.

Marigold rolled her eyes. "This isn't the place to come to if you're looking to make friends. Some of 'em are downright ashamed to be here, embarrassed to admit they believe in ghosts. You'll never see that movie star with her sunglasses off, as if we all don't know exactly who she is. Most of the rest are too rich to care about anyone but themselves. And I suppose a few are just too blue, poor things, to muster up enough effort for socializing. It's a strange group, but then again, it's a strange place."

"When did you get here?" I asked.

"Oh, I've been here nearly three months now," Marigold said offhandedly. "I was the first-ever guest here. Jeremiah held a gathering at his home back in Charleston; he connected with Harold right away, before we'd even had a chance to sit down around the table. I knew then I'd follow Jeremiah Campbell wherever he went."

As she spoke, I did the mental math of what a three-month stay at Whispering Seraph would cost and felt a bit faint. This woman was loaded—no mistake.

The attendant placed two tall, deeply red beverages in front of us, each topped with a skewer of sliced fruit. Marigold tossed a twenty-dollar bill onto the counter, completely ignoring the attendant's feeble protests about not being allowed to accept tips, then we crossed the lobby into a kind of solarium, where we sat down on a pair of wicker chairs.

"What do you think of this place so far?" she asked me.

"Well, I think I'd like fewer exploding windows and less focus on my flexibility, but other than that it's pretty amazing," I replied.

Marigold laughed. "Yes, that was really something this morning, wasn't it? Never a dull moment around here."

"You mean that kind of thing has happened before?" I asked in disbelief.

"Well, no, nothing like that," Marigold said. "But this isn't exactly a run-of-the-mill retreat, now is it? Lights flicker, candles flare, doors slam shut—that sort of thing. It's pretty exciting, wondering what's going to happen next."

"I guess, for some people," I said. "I like a little more predictability in my life."

We sipped our drinks. They tasted like strawberries and ginger and seaweed-based health supplements.

"You lost a friend of yours, did I understand that right?" Marigold asked.

"Yeah. Milo. He was our best friend. I still can't actually believe it," I said.

"Oh honey, no one here can quite believe it. Why do you think we're trying so hard to stay in contact?"

"So when do you think you'll be done?" I asked.

Marigold frowned. "Done with what?"

"Whispering Seraph. How will you know when you've got what you need?"

"Oh, sugar, I don't know," Marion replied with a heavy sigh. "It's almost become a way of life now. I expect I'll stay until my Harold is finally at peace."

My blood boiled. I fought against letting my anger show on my face, although I'm sure some red crept into my cheeks. Harold wanted nothing more than for his wife to stop throwing her money away on this place, yet as long as Campbell—or his angel—kept delivering partial messages, Marigold would stay. Utterly sickening.

"Well, you've been here the longest, so maybe you can explain something to me, because I'm a little confused about it," I said, remembering that I was supposed to be the "reluctant" twin.

"Sure thing, sugar, fire away," Marigold replied.

"Do you think the ghosts are happy?"

Marigold furrowed her brow as though the question made no sense. "I'm not sure what you're getting at."

"Well, I don't know a lot about this spirit stuff," I said, acknowledging in my head the enormity of the lie, "but they're not supposed to be here, right? Shouldn't we be trying to help them... I don't know, move on? Cross over? Go to heaven?"

Marigold looked a little unsettled for a moment. "I don't know," she replied. "If they want to stay with us, why shouldn't they be allowed to?"

I shrugged. "I'm not sure. Maybe they should. I was just thinking about it and... well, I guess it would be pretty easy to keep them here just for us."

"Are you calling me selfish?" Marigold asked, with her voice rising a bit.

"Not at all," I said as gently as I could—I certainly wasn't judging this woman for wanting to keep the man she loved close to her. How could anyone ever condemn another for love? Love, on its own, was never a crime.

"Please don't get angry. That's not what I mean. I'm just afraid that this place is all about holding on... when maybe it should be about letting go."

Marigold didn't have a response to this, and so she looked for it in her juice glass. Just over her shoulder, the door opened and several other people walked into the solarium; the yoga class had finally ended. Tom and Moira Owens brought up the back of the group, and there, floating in their wake, screaming a steady stream of profanity as though using it to propel himself forward, was Kyle.

Discovery—it happened in less than a second. Kyle screamed in frustration; the sound made me jump. As I looked up, we caught each other's eye.

His mouth fell open.

"Shit."

Quickly I dropped my eyes to my lap, which I realized was now slopped in Berry Blast. I was speckled all over with bright red juice; I must've looked like a crime scene.

"Oh, honey, you've gone and spoiled your clothes!" Marigold tutted, handing me a napkin.

"Thanks," I said, taking it from her and blotting myself. From the corner of my eye, I could see Kyle still staring at me.

"You can see me," he said. It wasn't a question.

"You'll never get that out, sugar, it's got beet juice in it," said Marigold. "Although there was this stain remover I saw on TV..."

I could barely focus on the rest of her sentence. Kyle had appeared behind her, waving both arms frantically over his head as if I were a plane he was signaling to land.

"HEY! HEY! Right here! I'm right here! I know you can see me!" he shouted.

"...spilled a whole bottle of red wine on this white carpet, and then a jar of marinara sauce, and—"

"LOOK AT ME AGAIN!" Kyle screamed. "Damn it! Don't pretend you can't hear me!"

On our table, a glass bowl full of fresh-cut peonies began to tremble. There was no way around it; I was going to have to talk to Kyle—and quickly—before he exploded again.

"Marigold, you'll have to excuse me. I'm going to the restroom to try to get this out," I said, jumping to my feet and cutting across her. "I can't believe I was such a klutz. Do you want anything else from the juice bar before I go?"

"What? Oh, no honey, I'm fine," she replied, looking a little disappointed that I wasn't more interested in her one-woman infomercial.

"Okay, I'll be right back. Sorry, I just don't want it to set."

I turned and found Kyle planted right in my path. I couldn't detour around him without drawing attention to myself; as much as I hated the idea, I had no choice but to walk straight through him.

Pushing through Kyle was like being doused with frigid, angry water from the inside; I could feel it running down the inside of my skin and then ebbing away as I left him behind me. I couldn't repress a violent shiver. Kyle didn't miss it.

"Ha! You felt that! Look at me! Look at me! You just saw me, I know you did! Why won't you answer me?"

I came to a sudden halt in the middle of the lobby, which Kyle wasn't expecting. He floated right into my space again, coming so near that I could feel the chill of him again. He was so close that, although I spoke with barely a breath of sound, he could hear every word. "Because we're in public, Kyle, now *be cool* and shut up. We need a place where no one can see us!"

"Wha—oh!"

Kyle immediately began behaving himself, floating silently behind me. But I could still feel the buzz of his excitement—licks of electricity that raised the hairs on the back of my neck. I walked right past the juice bar and into the women's restroom, locking the door behind me. I spun around.

Kyle seemed to shrink and pale slightly as I faced him with whatever my fury had scribbled all over my face, but he stood his ground. Well, floated his ground, more accurately.

"You can see me," he said again, although not as forcefully as before.

"Yes, we've established that," I snapped. "Way to almost ruin everything there, Kyle."

"What did I ruin?"

"That's none of your business."

He tried a new question. "Did I do something to make you see me?"

"No, I can always see spirits. It's a very annoying talent of mine," I replied, trying to give him as little information as I could possibly get away with.

Kyle's eyes widened. "Really? All of them? The other ghosts here, too?"

"Unfortunately, yes. All of them," I sighed.

"And you can understand everything I'm saying?" he asked, as his shock slowly transformed into eagerness.

"Yes, I can understand everything you're saying," I repeated, somewhat wearily.

"This is amazing! Listen, I need you to come with me. I need to tell my parents—"

"Hold it right there," I said, putting my hand up to silence him. "I'm not telling your parents anything. I'm not a messenger pigeon. That's not why I'm here."

"But you have to!" Kyle said, starting to fire up again. "That asshole Campbell is useless—he's just taking my parents' money and twisting my words around to make them feel better!"

"I know. I heard it. All of it." I replied, not without sympathy.

"So then..." Kyle opened and closed his mouth a few times, unable to immediately wrangle his thoughts into words. "What are you doing here? If you can see ghosts, you don't need Campbell's help."

Shit. I was hoping he wouldn't realize that. This was bad; I was going to have to tell Kyle far more than was safe for our mission. "You're right, I don't. I'm here to shut him down," I answered.

Kyle froze. His energy, which had been pulsating toward me in angry waves just a few moments before, was still now.

"I've got a sort of... an obligation to make sure people like Campbell can't take advantage of people like your parents. I've made it a personal mission, actually."

"Why do you—"

"Because Campbell, and others like him, make it a lot harder for me to do my real job."

"Your real job? What's your real job?"

I didn't answer. I'd already told Kyle way too much; Finn was going to kill me.

As if Kyle had heard this last thought, he raised an eyebrow at me, then threw his head back. "Hey! Other ghosts! There's someone here who can—"

"Shut up! I'll tell you, just—stop shouting!" I cried, caving immediately to his manipulation.

I sighed. Kyle obviously wasn't going to let this go until I gave him a really good reason to. So much for my undercover skills.

"Look, stop focusing on your own anger for a minute and instead focus on me. Put your emotions aside and look me in the eye. Really concentrate," I said.

Kyle calmed himself and did as I instructed. As he focused in, I slipped the Masking bracelet from my wrist. I felt the Casting, like the finest, most gossamer of veils, slip away from my being.

The very instant I was free of the Casting, Kyle's eyes widened. He gasped and shot backward, as though I had scalded him. Then slowly, hesitantly—as if he were approaching an animal that might attack at the slightest provocation—he floated toward me again. A slow smile spread over his features; all his anger and resentment disappeared. He looked, for the first time, like the fresh-faced kid he really was.

"You... you're... I can see the way home," he whispered.

"What you're feeling is called the Gateway," I told him, "and I'm one of the people who can help guide you through it, when you're ready to Cross over."

"I thought I missed it," Kyle whispered. "I thought I was stuck here. For good."

"No, you're not. You can still move on if you want to, but you'll need my help to do it." I said, as I slid the Masking bracelet back onto my wrist. Kyle's smile faded at once, like I'd shut a light off inside him.

"Why did you cover it up?" he asked, with a longing in his voice—a longing I recognized as easily as my own reflection.

"I have to keep it hidden from the other spirits here, so that they don't discover what I am."

"But why would you keep that from us? Don't you want to help us?" Kyle asked.

"Yes, of course I do," I said. "And I will, when the time is right. I'll give all of you the chance to Cross if you want to. But right now Campbell is my priority. He's not just getting rich off the living while pissing off the spirits. There's something else going on here, something... bigger."

Kyle was intrigued enough to refocus on my words for a moment rather than concentrating on what he'd sensed about me. "What do you mean bigger?"

"I'm not sure," I said. "There is more to that angel and to this place than meets the eye. There's a bigger plan, maybe even something dangerous, but I don't know what it is yet. I need to stay undercover until we sort it out."

"There's someone else here who can see me too?" Kyle asked. "Is it that girl you're with?" Is that who you mean by 'we?'"

"My sister and I, and the people we're working with, yes. Don't bother wasting your time asking me anything else about them, because I can't tell you. But the point is, the other spirits—and especially Campbell himself—can't know about this. If he realizes what I am, our one chance to shut this place down will be ruined!"

"So what do I get, then?"

I frowned. "What do you get?"

"In return for keeping your secret," Kyle said, with a smirk tugging at the corner of his mouth.

"You're joking, right?" The nerve of this kid.

"I'll keep my mouth shut around the other ghosts, and around

Campbell too, if you promise to give my parents my message before I go," Kyle said, crossing his arms.

"Or... how about I open up the Gateway here in this bathroom and let it suck you through to the other side right now?"

Kyle's smirk faltered. "That's not how it works. I'll bet anything that's not how it works!"

"You sure about that, Kyle? Should we try it and see?" I asked, hovering my hand over my bracelet while silently praying he wouldn't call my bluff.

"Okay, okay!" Kyle said, backing down as he nervously watched my fingers pulling at the quartz stone. "I just... I really need my parents to understand. Can you help me with that before you leave here? Please?"

I dropped my wrist to my side again. "I will, but don't expect me to torture them on your behalf. I've heard your constant yelling and cursing around them. You've got real stuff to say to them, and that's fair. I get that. I had some pretty real stuff to say to my mom, too. But you need to think really long and hard about how you want to say it. Regrets are just as easy to acquire after you're dead, but they're usually harder to fix."

Kyle considered this. "I... okay. I'll think about it."

"Good. And in the meantime, not a word to the other spirits."

"Fine. Do you need... I mean... can I help at all? With busting Campbell?"

I smiled a little at him for the first time. "If I need a hand, you'll be the first ghost I ask."

18

WARDS

"**S**O HE ACTUALLY TRIED TO BLACKMAIL YOU?" asked Hannah incredulously. "Well, that's a first!"

"No kidding. Threats? Sure. Bribes? Frequently. But blackmail? Not until today," I said.

We were back in our room, and I was relaying every detail of my encounter with Kyle to Hannah and Milo. We were changing for dinner, which, much to my dismay, was a formal affair. I looked at the four dresses laid out on the bed, wanting nothing more than to set fire to all of them.

"So now he knows everything?" Hannah asked, wringing her hands. "Oh, no. That's really not good, Jess. He could totally blow our cover!"

"I know that, Hannah!"

"What should we do? Do you think we need to get out now, or should we stay and hope he's as good as his word?" she asked.

"I think he meant it when he said he would keep our secret, so I think we should stay, for now. But I also think he's impulsive and unpredictable—we should keep a really close watch on him."

"Agreed," Milo said, floating back and forth over my outfits, "That boy is one unstable floater. I honestly don't even know how he keeps his form. He's half-ready to explode at any given moment."

"I know, he's in rough shape," I said, "which is why I was sort of... hoping you'd take him under your wings a little bit."

Milo looked up from the clothes and raised an eyebrow at me. "Wings? My wings? You know I only spread these babies for special occasions."

"I know. Did I mention they are beautiful, sparkly, and fabulous wings?" I said, batting my eyelashes at him.

Momentarily placated, Milo replied, "The winged goddess is listening, proceed."

"You've seen how much anger that kid has toward his parents," I said. "And I'm no Empath, but I can tell that a lot of that anger comes from pain. A deep, deep hurt, you know?"

Milo's smile vanished. "Yeah. I know."

"He needs to work through it, Milo, or he'll never move on. He'll just stay here, screaming without a voice at parents who didn't want to hear him when he was alive, and can't hear him now. He needs someone to talk to, and I think you are the best option."

Milo rolled his eyes as he fought between his need to be endlessly sassy and his cleverly disguised well of deep, painful emotions. "Ugh, girl why have you gotten so *real* on me all of a sudden? We were accessorizing! I was in my happy place!" He gestured down to the piles of expensive clothing and shoes.

"I know. Sorry," I said. To lighten things up, and sort of as an apology for steering him just a little too close to his own parental baggage, my next words became a custom-made-for-Milo gift. "What if I let you pick out the dress for tonight, no questions asked?"

Milo smirked at me. "And the accessories?"

"And the accessories," I promised, solemnly putting up three fingers in a Boy Scouts-style salute.

"Okay, okay, I will mentor the angsty floater," said Milo, with a dramatic sound halfway between a groan and a sigh. "And you're wearing the green dress with the gold lace-up heels and the gold clutch. Now point me toward the jewelry."

A few minutes before we needed to head downstairs for dinner, and thirty seconds after almost breaking my ankle for the fourth time, there was a knock on our door. I opened it to see Finn standing there, with a set of keys in hand.

"I was hoping to... wow," he said, before he could stop himself. A little breathlessly, he looked me over from head to foot.

"Still sticking to the dress code, as ordered," I said, fighting against the blush now infusing my cheeks. A blush, which I now realized, was coloring Finn's face as well.

"I... yes, of course. Right." Finn shook his head a little and resettled his face into his characteristic scowl. "I do apologize, I only meant... you look quite... nice."

"Milo picked it out," I said, as though I could thrust the awkwardness of the moment onto Milo, just so that it would stop suffocating me.

"You don't have to say it, I'm a genius," Milo called from the bathroom, where he was instructing Hannah on how to arrange her hair.

"Right. I only meant to say that I'm headed back to the Lafayette Boarding House for a bit. Iggy has some more information for me on the property, and I'm going to take a call from Catriona on the way, to update her and get any further instructions. I'll be back later tonight."

"Oh, okay," I said. "Well, good luck."

"You'll all be alright until I get back?"

"It's just dinner, Finn. We can handle it," I replied.

"Yes. Well, I'll just leave you to it, then, shall I?" he said, and, nodding to Hannah and Milo as they emerged from the bathroom, he turned and marched down the corridor.

I shut the door on his retreat, because the image of him walking away from me was—to be honest—a little too metaphorically accurate. Hannah stood in the bathroom doorway, with her hair freshly braided, looking very pretty in a purple dress with tasteful Hawaiian flowers printed on it.

"Finn's leaving?" she asked, with an anxious edge to her voice.

"Yes, but he'll be back later tonight," I said, as dismissively as I could. "Looking good, Hannah—and I'm not just saying that because you're my twin. Is that... eyeliner I spy?"

She pointed at Milo. "It's his fault."

"And you're welcome," Milo sang.

"Okay then, makeovers complete... so let's get this over with. I've only got another hour or so before my feet explode out of these shoes," I said. "Do we have a game plan?"

"Mingle and chat, learn as much about the guests, the property, and Campbell as we can," Hannah recited, as though reading from the back of a flash card.

"And who's better at mingling and chatting than us?" I said, flinging my arm around her shoulder. "The socially awkward twins! Let's go rock this exercise in futility!" I shouted as our battle cry, before opening the door.

We walked right into the icy cold blast that was Kyle Owens, who was hovering just outside our doorway.

Hannah and I both leapt back, gasping in shock, then immediately tried to recover ourselves. We glanced up and down the hallway, which thankfully was entirely deserted by the living.

"Kyle, what are you doing here? I told you to leave us alone, or you're going to blow our cover!" I hissed.

"I know, I know, I'm sorry! But I made sure no one was around, didn't I?" he said defensively. "I have to tell you something!"

"Okay okay, whatever, just get in here," I said.

"I can't! I tried to come in, but something kept blocking me!" Kyle replied.

"Oh, right, the Wards," I muttered. A sudden sound, like the opening of a door, threw me into panic mode. "Come this way, hurry!" I said, and ran, with what I could only assume was the grace of a flamingo, across the hallway and into the utility closet directly across from our room. Hannah followed, and after I shut the door, Milo and Kyle flew through it to join us among the cleaning supplies.

"What the hell are Wards?" Kyle asked.

"Never mind, Kyle. All it means is that you can't go into our room," Hannah answered in a whisper. "What did you want to tell us?"

"I wanted to make sure you were coming down to dinner. I heard one of the staff say that Campbell was going to make a speech, and I thought you'd want to see it," Kyle answered.

"Then I'm really happy that I'm in this supply closet right now instead of downstairs," I growled.

"Hey, the closet was your idea not mine," Kyle said, crossing his arms. "I was just trying to help."

"I know. You're right. I'm sorry. So let's get out of here before we miss Campbell's speech. Milo, can you check if the coast is clear?"

"Oh sweetness, coming out of the closet is my specialty!" Milo said with a dazzling grin. He poked his head through the door and pulled it back in. "We're cleared for take-off!"

"Good." I threw the door open and marched awkwardly back out into the hallway. These heels were going to kill me.

"So are those Ward things why I can't get into the basement either?" Kyle asked as we walked toward the staircase.

I stopped abruptly. "You can't get into the basement?"

"Nope. I tried to follow Campbell down there once, but I couldn't do it. It was like an actual solid wall, for the first time since I died. It was really weird," Kyle said.

My sister and I exchanged a look that was equal parts shock and alarm. Wards here? At Whispering Seraph?

"Is there any other way to keep spirits out of a space, other than Wards?" I asked Hannah, whose eyes were now wide with concern.

Hannah shook her head. "I don't think so. Not that I know of."

My next step would've been to ask Finn, but he was inconveniently absent, so I did the next logical thing. "Kyle," I said, "can you take us to see that basement door?"

"What, now?" Hannah asked, looking alarmed.

"Yes, now! It's the perfect time! Campbell is going to give a speech, so he'll be in the dining room."

"Yes, but we need to be in the dining room, too! We need to hear that speech, whatever it is!" Hannah pointed out. "Why don't we just wait until later?"

I bit my lip. Hannah was right. There weren't enough people staying at this place that our absence would go totally unnoticed. Plus, there were assigned tables for dinner.

"Okay. You and Milo go to the dining room. I'll follow Kyle to the basement stairs, just so we know where it is. I'll be right behind you. Two minutes behind you, okay?" I said. Hannah had already opened her mouth to argue, so I added quickly, "Just tell them I had to change my shoes or something. God knows that's true enough."

I squeezed Hannah's hand, and—before she could say another word—I followed an eager Kyle down the stairs. I dodged a handful of people chatting in the lobby, then we ducked down a hallway I'd never been in before.

"I feel like a spy," Kyle said excitedly. "Like an FBI guy, or James Bond. Something like that."

"Whatever floats your boat, Kyle," I murmured. A woman backed out of the closest door, carrying a tray of bread baskets. When she saw me, she did a sort of half-curtsy, while being careful not to send rolls tumbling all over the floor. Thankfully, she didn't stop to ask what I was doing. I just smiled at her and kept walking.

"Are we almost there?" I asked, as we turned a corner into a darker, narrower hallway.

"Yeah, it's just around this corner," Kyle said.

Kyle became harder to see in the half-light, but I followed him to the end of this last hallway. At the very end of the passage, a large, unpainted door stood like a sentinel guarding the basement.

"That's it," Kyle said, with a disproportionate amount of triumph. He was a little too into this spy thing—this wasn't a game, after all—but I let it go for the moment.

I kept walking until I stood about four feet in front of the door. I looked it over from top to bottom. It seemed, on first examination, to be utterly unremarkable. Just a door, nothing more.

"Kyle, let me see you try to go through it," I said.

"Sure," he replied, and flung himself at the door with unnecessary force. He bounced away from it as if it were made of rubber. "See?" he said. "Nothing!"

"Have you tried sinking down through the floor?" I asked.

Kyle's eyes widened. "Huh? No, I didn't think of that! Wow, that would've been easier than bouncing off this door for an hour!" He aimed himself at the floor and tried to dive through it. Again he bounced backward, unable to pass through.

"Okay, so it's not just the door. It's the whole basement. Campbell doesn't want spirits down there at all," I said, much more to myself than to Kyle.

I took a few more tentative steps toward the door, closing the distance warily while half-expecting that I'd be flung backward as well. But the door's only defense against me, as far as I could tell, was a normal one: It was padlocked shut.

I examined the lock, then looked at the door itself more closely. I ran my fingers over the wood, from top to bottom, willing my senses to somehow detect the presence of a Casting.

"Did you find it? Does it have Wards on it?" Kyle asked in a stage whisper.

"I can't tell. There might be..." I had just begun to feel something, just the slightest trembling, the lightest tingling of energy. Was I imagining it?

I traced my fingers more closely along the grain, following the wood's natural lines up to the edge of the padlock. And—without knowing why, but feeling compelled to just the same—I pushed the lock aside. A tiny, lightly carved rune in the shape of an eye stared up at me. I'd finally found the solid Durupinen connection we'd been searching for.

"Oh my God," I whispered.

"What? What is it?" Kyle cried.

"Ms. Taylor? Is that you?" asked a man's voice.

I dropped the padlock in shock and spun around. Jeremiah Campbell stood in the hallway behind me; his expression was both mystified and slightly amused. To his left, the door through which he had evidently just emerged was swinging closed. Thankfully, he was alone; his angel was nowhere in sight.

I felt Kyle's energy dissipate as he, in his own panic, vanished from my side.

"What are you doing all the way back here?" Campbell asked. Did I imagine it, or was there an accusatory note in his voice?

I froze as dread overtook me. I had no excuse. I had no cover story. The jig was up; we were going to be thrown from the gates of Whispering Seraph, and Campbell and his angel would continue sucking his devotees dry. I thrust a smile onto my face, hoping to buy myself a second to pull myself together.

I recomposed that smile into one of relief. "Mr. Campbell! Oh, thank goodness you're here!" I said, walking straight up to him and taking his hands in mine. He looked startled but didn't pull away.

"Ms. Taylor, what—"

"I am so completely lost!"

"Lost?" he said, bewildered.

"So lost. Big surprise—I've probably got the worst sense of direction ever," I said, adding a self-deprecating roll of the eyes. "Honestly, if I walk out of a store in the mall, I have to look for stores I've already been in so I can tell which way I'm going," I babbled, drawing on every "helpless woman" stereotype I could think of. "It's pathetic, really. Milo used to give me hell about it." I paused here, as though mentioning Milo caused me pain.

"There now, you know he's here with you," Campbell said, unable to restrain himself from snapping immediately into his role as a spiritual comforter, even under these odd circumstances.

"I know that now, thanks to you," I replied, and took a deep breath before continuing. "I was on my way down to dinner, and I decided to stop in the powder room first—only I couldn't find it. Then I went completely the wrong way trying to head back to the lobby. So finally I followed a woman carrying a tray, thinking she was probably headed to the dining room. But she disappeared into a kitchen, I think, and so I just kept walking and... wound up here."

I finished my explanation, relieved that I'd managed to get through it without choking on my own words. I'd battled both the living and the dead; lived as a fugitive in the Traveler camp; rescued my sister and defeated the Necromancers; Crossed through the Gateway and back; toppled Freeman's empire; and now I was the only living Walker on this planet, as well as an elite Durupinen

Tracker. And those were just my career highlights. Did this guy really think I couldn't navigate a hallway?

Snapping me back into my role, Campbell, with the slightest suggestion of a condescending smile, asked, "And you thought the dining room might be behind a locked door?"

"Well, no—by that point I was just kind of panicking," I said with a shaky laugh. I swallowed my pride even further. "I thought it might be an emergency exit or something. Like I said, thank goodness you're here. I get major anxiety when I'm lost, especially when I'm all by myself. Will you please rescue me, and escort me back to civilization?" I flashed him my very best set of puppy dog eyes, to reinforce my "helplessness."

Campbell's expression cleared with his acceptance of my damsel-in-distress routine, and he gestured chivalrously back up the hallway. He offered me his arm, then began leading the way with a confident stride.

Holy shit, he bought it. Shout out to patriarchal stereotypes for making that one possible.

"I'm sorry you lost your way. I still haven't even been down in that basement, and I've been here for nearly six months. Couldn't even tell you what's down there," Campbell said. "I realize I should know, but I've never liked basements much."

"Me neither," I said, biting my tongue so that I wouldn't accuse him of lying through his unnaturally bleached teeth. No one Warded a room they never intended to enter.

"These big old Southern homes can be a bit like rabbit warrens. Charming if you know where you're going, but a bit confusing to the outsider," Campbell drawled as we strolled along.

"Yes, I've seen that for myself. I really should carry around that map you provided with our schedules," I said with an ingratiating smile.

"They do come in handy at first, but I'm sure you'll get your bearings in no time. Just give it another day or two. In the meantime, I shall be glad that you forgot it, as it has enabled us to have this nice little chat."

I swallowed back the impulse to slide my arm out of his, and instead nodded as demurely as I could. Campbell was now teetering on the precipice between Southern charm and lecherous old man, but I could hardly disengage now. I decided to let him keep talking, since he was so very fond of it.

"How are you enjoying your stay so far? You and your sister?" he asked me cordially.

"Oh...well, everything's been really lovely. I'm not really sure if 'enjoy' is the word I'd use, just because of the reason we're here, but..." I trailed off, again hoping that implied emotion would take the pressure off of having to say too much.

"Naturally, yes," Campbell said. "I really must be more careful with my choice of words. I merely meant to inquire after the comfort of your accommodations and the quality of the support staff. Has it all been satisfactory?"

Smooth as butter, this creep. "Yes, it's all been great, thank you," I said with a smile.

"Excellent, excellent. That's what I like to hear. We do give guests a chance to fill out formal surveys at the conclusion of their stay, but I like to check in just the same, in case there is anything more I can do while y'all are here," Campbell said.

"Well, now that you mention it, do you think we could have fewer explosions?" I said with half a laugh. "I had to talk my security guard off of a ledge after this morning. He even wanted to call my parents."

Here Campbell's serene expression faltered just slightly, and I remembered his pleading with his angel for an explanation. "Yes, that was most unfortunate. But it's important to remember, Ms. Taylor, that we are delving into the unknown when we interact with the spirits. There is so very much we don't know, but we must be brave in our attempts or else we deny ourselves a wonderful opportunity. How else are we to experience far beyond what we ever thought possible?"

"That's basically what Hannah said," I lied. "She thinks we should be willing to deal with a little breaking glass if it means we get to talk to Milo. She said the scary stuff is worth it if it means he can speak to us."

"And is it?" Campbell asked.

I smiled. "It was nice to hear from him." Here I paused, before adding a final, finishing flourish designed to pander to Campbell's ego. "And you're so brave, Mr. Campbell. I think I'd die of fright if an angel came to me and gave me the power to talk to ghosts."

Campbell ate that shit up. He smiled even wider for a moment, before turning humble. "I can't pretend I didn't feel some fear. But the blessing, Ms. Taylor, the blessing of it all! It far outweighed my doubts and fears," he said—although I noticed that he, for the first time, dropped his gaze away from me as his smile flickered for just a moment.

So Jeremiah Campbell had some lingering doubts, did he? That was interesting.

"And I'm hoping to spread those blessings even further after tonight. I hope you and your sister will consider supporting me in that endeavor."

"What do you mean? Spread blessings how?" I asked.

"Oh, you'll see very shortly. I'm planning to address the guests this evening at dinner. It is truly exciting stuff, though, as I'm sure you will agree."

"I can't wait to hear all about it," I said, even as my heart began to race.

§

Applause erupted all around us as we entered the dining room. I could barely keep the smile from slipping off of my face—so many pairs of eyes were not only on Campbell, but on me, too, as I dangled from his arm like an accessory. How humiliating—undercover work was harder than I thought.

The dining room was perhaps the grandest of Whispering Seraph's rooms. Campbell had converted the mansion's ballroom into a space used alternately for large presentations and formal dinners. The high ceilings and original chandeliers had been restored to their original glory; the marble floor, polished to a perfect luster, almost gave the impression that we were walking on water.

Luckily, Hannah and I had been assigned to a table close to the back of the room, and Campbell walked me straight to it. He pulled out my chair, then planted a kiss on my hand as I sat down. I continued to smile and joined in with the applause, even as Hannah and Milo, who were clapping themselves, stared at me with a hundred questions blazing in their eyes.

I leaned into Hannah, keeping my smile carefully plastered to my face. "Don't react—we need to get through this dinner," I warned her, "but I've found a rune." And Hannah, God love her, smiled politely as if I'd merely made an excuse for being late.

I turned and watched Campbell as took his seat at the table

closest to the front of the room, where he was joined by Marigold and another woman I hadn't yet met but who was absolutely dripping with expensive jewelry. Campbell picked up a glass of wine and started chatting; it seemed he was saving his big announcement, whatever it was, for later on.

Letting out a sigh of relief, I reached for my napkin and saw a hand resting a few inches in front of it. Being completely unaware that anyone had been seated on my other side, I looked up and found the owner of the hand looking right at me.

"Hello," Talia said coolly.

Milo was not-so-silently losing his shit on my other side. I wish I could've found a way to step on his non-corporeal foot, or at least to tell him to chill the hell out, but we were now on a strict "no-connection" policy when Campbell was present. So instead, I sat myself up a little straighter in my seat in an attempt to be dignified enough for both of us.

"Hi, Talia," I said, trying to manage a friendly smile.

Talia looked effortlessly chic, of course, in her white halter-topped pantsuit with a plunging neckline; a jade-studded cuff bracelet adorned her wrist. I'd never seen anyone with skin that perfect up close, with the possible exception of some of the Durupinen at the height of their Leeching. Talia's face, though, while stunning, did not return my smile.

I looked over at Hannah, who, alarmed by my discovery of the rune, seemed to be trying to blend into the wall behind her as she puzzled things through. "Were you two already formally introduced?" I asked. "Talia Simms, this is my sister Hannah Taylor."

Talia gave Hannah a begrudging nod and a shadow of a smile before she refocused her narrowed eyes on me. She didn't lose another moment before explaining exactly what her dirty look was for.

"You signed the agreement."

"What?" I asked, caught so off guard that at first that I didn't remember what she was talking about. "Oh, the non-disclosure thing? Yeah, I did."

"Why?"

"Why, what?" I asked.

Talia flapped her hands at me impatiently. "Why did you sign it?"

"I guess I just wanted you to know that I wasn't interested in selling you out." I pulled my napkin onto my lap and looked around. "Could you pass the rolls, please?"

Talia blinked, and then, automatically, reached a hand out toward the basket of rolls and pushed it within my reach. "Why not? Haven't you read a magazine in the last six months? Everyone sells me out."

"Maybe that's true in Hollywood, but not everywhere. And definitely not here. We're all just trying to heal. I don't think anyone here cares about gossip—at least not much. I certainly don't."

Talia glared at me as I buttered my roll, but—as I bit into it—her glare melted into a look of confusion.

"You could make quite a lot of money, you know. Not just from me, but from the paparazzi. You've got the kind of story they can't wait to get their hands on. Grieving actress attempts suicide by skinny dipping! Complete with a firsthand description of me half naked? Any tabloid would offer you thousands of dollars. Maybe more."

"That might be true, but I'm not interested," I answered, trying to sound as disinterested as possible. Thousands of dollars would cover our rent for months.

"Not interested enough to turn your back on thousands?" Talia asked, perplexed.

I shrugged. "We're very comfortable. Or at least, our parents are. Isn't that a prerequisite for coming here? But not everyone cares that much about money, you know."

She laughed bitterly. "Spoken like someone who has plenty of it. Alright then, if not money, what about your fifteen minutes of fame? It's a lot of free publicity when you've got a story like this."

"Fame is just about the last thing I want," I said. "You should be able to understand that, at least. I bet there are plenty of days you wish no one knew who you were. Especially..."

I didn't want to torture her by finishing the sentence. We both knew what I meant. Especially now. Especially after Grayson.

Neither of us spoke as a waiter appeared between us, placing a beautifully plated endive salad in front of each of us. Talia watched as he then served Hannah, who was trying desperately to look anywhere but at the two of us. Talia waited until the waiter put another table between us before continuing.

"You're not even going to tell them about the ring?" she pressed.

Although she had dropped her voice to nearly a whisper, I could still hear the tremble in it.

Damn, Milo was right: It was an engagement ring. I could almost taste his smugness even with our connection firmly closed. For Talia's benefit, however, I played dumb.

"What, so tabloids will pay just to find out how you accessorize? Wow, people really will read anything, won't they?" I took a bite of my salad and chewed it slowly.

I couldn't tell whether Talia believed the ruse, but she certainly appreciated it. Her shoulders relaxed for the first time.

"Now, I've got a question for you," I said upon swallowing. "I am allowed to ask questions, aren't I?"

She looked almost sheepish. "Yes."

"Why do you keep suggesting reasons for my running to the papers? You're starting to sound like you actually want me to."

Talia dropped her eyes to her untouched food. "Of course I don't want you to... I'm glad you signed it. I just... I guess I just still don't understand why you did it."

"Well, you don't have to understand it. I'm not going to tell anyone, okay? Anyway, I don't think your going for a swim is that interesting of a story, to be honest, although I certainly wouldn't wear my jewels in a pond! I'm sure some new-monied Kardashian type just invented a collagen-and-kale self-cleanse that everyone will be much more interested in."

Talia actually smiled a real smile. It was dazzling. Milo basically imploded. It was getting harder and harder to pretend he wasn't here.

I took advantage of the moment and leaned across to her. "I'm serious. I'm not your enemy. I hope you find what you need here. And at the risk of sounding like a celebrity stalker, you can talk to me, if you need to. I'm snarky, but I'm a good listener."

It was as though a wall came crashing down behind her eyes. I watched it tumble, watched the warmth flood her face.

"I'm so sorry," she began. "I'm so sorry for the way I spoke to you. I'm not really one of those actors who talks to people like that. I just... I'm not myself, I can't—"

I put a hand up. "Forgiven. And I'm sorry for how I talked to you, too. I wallow in sarcasm the way other people wallow in misery. I'd like to say I don't usually talk like that, but I do. All the time. I'm working on it."

"Ain't that the truth," Milo muttered.

Hannah finally chimed in. "She really is getting better about it," she said breathlessly. And then, unable to help herself, she added, "Can I just say I thought you were incredible in *The Broken Dream Diner?*"

"Thank you very much," Talia said. "That was one of my favorite projects."

We carried on a very pleasant conversation during the rest of dinner, punctuated by Milo's disjointed outbursts of "Slay!" and "Queen!" We kept to fairly innocuous topics, never delving into anything too uncomfortable. I tried to keep a running tally in my head of the lies I had to make up to keep in line with our cover story, but I knew that Hannah would help me keep them straight. A low-level current of guilt ran beneath it all, because I felt like shit for lying to a woman who was only just beginning to trust me.

Tuning out the spirits' voices was easier amid the dining room's constant hum of conversation than it was in relative silence, but it was still a challenge. The little boy from breakfast was demanding, in increasingly hysterical tones, that his parents order him an ice cream. An elderly couple was reliving their halcyon days by jitterbugging enthusiastically around the open floor space in the center of the room. Harold was blustering forcefully; first he demanded that Campbell stop flirting with Marigold, then he repeatedly ordered Campbell to go straight to his vault to begin repaying the money he'd swindled from her. Only Kyle was uncharacteristically quiet. He sat across from his parents, with a pensive frown on his face, watching them as they ate and chatted. Grayson was conspicuously absent.

As waiters with tiered dessert carts began making their rounds to the tables, Campbell finally rose to his feet and strolled to a podium at the front of the room. An easel stood beside it, draped with a red velvet cloth that bore a large rectangular symbol. A hush fell over the guests as suddenly and completely as if he'd flicked a switch. We were his captives and he knew it.

"Here we go," I muttered to Hannah, who had begun twisting her napkin in her lap.

"Good evening, my friends!" Campbell said. "I'm so happy to have you all here, to celebrate the beginning of yet another retreat session at the Sanctuary at Whispering Seraph. For some of you, this is your first time here. I hope it will not be your last."

"Such a strange thing to wish," I said to Hannah.

She kept her eyes on Campbell, but nodded nonetheless. "If the real hope is to bring people peace, shouldn't he want us to find it and leave?" she said. It wasn't really a question; Hannah was right and we both knew it.

As I turned back to Campbell, I found Talia staring at me with a strange expression. She'd heard what Hannah and I had said, and she appeared disturbed by it. She opened her mouth as though to comment, but closed it again as Campbell's voice rang out again over the murmurs of adulation.

"Whispering Seraph is already a lot of things to a lot of the people in this room. A retreat. A spiritual center. Sometimes a day spa—I'm looking at you Eileen, I know you love those hot-stone massages, darling," he chuckled, winking at the bejeweled woman sitting at his table.

"You know it, Jeremiah, love!" she called, raising her glass. The crowd tittered.

"Most importantly, I know Whispering Seraph is a place of connection and recovery. Of renewal. Of connections with those we thought had left us forever. And I am so thrilled to share with you tonight a new vision for what Whispering Seraph could become—a haven where even more people can open their hearts and begin healing. It's a vision that came to me in a dream, brought to me by the same angel who has blessed me with the remarkable gift that I share with all of you. A design, the angel tells me, that will ensure a clearer, more continuous connection with those we've lost."

Hannah and I looked at each other, perplexed and—increasingly—alarmed. A design that could better connect with the spirits? A rune on the basement door? What the hell was going on? My heart began to pound. We were in over our heads here... *way* over our heads.

"I am revealing my vision here first because you are my Whispering Seraph family," Campbell continued. "You are the ones who know the power of this place and what it can do for you. I hope you will join me. I hope you will consider doing what you can to help make this vision a reality." Here Campbell paused dramatically. "And so, without further ado, I present to you Whispering Seraph's final phase!"

The velvet drape fell from the easel with a delicate swish and a quiet thud. The room erupted into enthusiastic applause.

No one heard my gasp. No one noticed as Hannah's champagne flute slipped from her fingers and shattered into diamond-bright shards at her feet.

The new Whispering Seraph was one enormous and unmistakable Summoning Circle.

19

DRAWN TO TROUBLE

WE PLAYED OUR PART THROUGH THE REST OF DINNER. We smiled. We schmoozed. We pretended to care about expensive French wines and cheeses. Campbell, with his charm turned up to the max, made a personal visit to each table, eliciting promises for donations. At his visit to our table, Hannah and I both exclaimed over how beautiful the new plans were, and I made a non-committal remark about squeezing our father for a donation.

After dessert, when the other guests started milling around the dining room, I made my way over to the easel where the new plans for Whispering Seraph sat prominently on display. I pulled my phone from my purse, casually flicked on its camera, and waited patiently for the right moment to snap a few pictures.

I didn't have to wait long. Marigold, who had indulged in more than her fair share of wine, dragged another guest over to the piano; she belted out "Don't Rain on My Parade" while the other guest accompanied her. With all eyes on Marigold, I snapped several quick photos of the plans, then dropped the phone back into my purse and returned to our table.

"I'm calling it," I said loudly to Hannah. "These shoes are just sparkly torture devices, and if we don't leave soon, I'm going to eat everything on that dessert cart."

Hannah looked relieved, and I knew she was anxious to discuss both the rune and Whispering Seraph's Summoning Circle design. "Yes, I'm ready. Let's go." Hannah rose from the table and started looking around for her purse. She winced ever so slightly as Harold shouted behind her, "Get off that stage, Marigold! You can't sing worth a damn!"

While I waited for Hannah, I spotted Talia a table away, deep in an emotional exchange with Campbell. Her face was glazed with tears. My curiosity got the better of me; I skirted around the room's perimeter until I reached the bar, and positioned myself so that both Talia and Campbell's backs were turned to me. I snatched a glass of champagne and slowly backed myself away from the bar, shifting myself just a bit to the left so that one of the decorative pillars blocked me from their view.

"...just don't understand why he's not communicating," Talia was saying, with a sob in her voice. "You had no problem connecting with him before. I mean, what am I doing here if you can't—"

"Talia, my dear, calm down," Campbell said, placing a consoling hand upon her shoulder, which she immediately shrugged away. "You've got to have faith! There are a hundred reasons why Grayson may be staying quiet right now. We can't know for sure."

"Why? Why can't we know for sure? That's why I'm here—to know for sure! Why don't you just ask him? Or maybe he's not even here anymore and you just don't want to tell me?" Talia cried.

"Of course he's here with you!" Campbell said soothingly. "My angel can feel him here, still tied to you. But just like with living people, we can't always force spirits to speak up. He might be scared or nervous about what he needs to say. He might be worried how you'll respond."

"There was never anything he couldn't tell me," Talia snapped. "Never."

"I can't say why he's choosing to stay silent right now," Campbell replied, shaking his head sadly. "But I know he's here for a reason, Talia, and we will find out what that reason is."

Talia shook her head, looking disgusted. "And if I write you a nice big check for your new project? Do you think he'll start talking then?"

Campbell looked genuinely affronted. "Talia, you know that's not how it works!"

"I don't know anything anymore!" she cried. Overcome with tears, she got up and fled the dining room.

Campbell closed his eyes and ran his hand over his face. He looked really tired all of a sudden, like sleep had eluded him for the last few days and exhaustion was finally catching up with him. It was strange how quickly tiredness came over him, how the circles beneath his eyes just seemed to appear out of nowhere.

"Ready?"

I yelped. Hannah had come up behind me, and now looked impatient. Milo floated at her side.

"Yeah, let's go.

The second we were clear of the dining room, I pulled my phone out and texted the pictures to Finn. "*WE HAVE A PROBLEM. Found a rune too.*" I typed.

We half-ran back to our room without exchanging a single word, but we broke into frantic discussion the moment we closed our door safely behind us.

"It's a Summoning Circle! He's turning this place into a giant Summoning Circle!" Hannah cried. "And what about that rune you found?"

"The basement is Warded Hannah! The rune was tiny enough, and hidden, but definitely there. Under a padlock on the basement door."

"But why? What's down there?" Hannah asked.

"I have no idea. And I'm not convinced that Campbell does either."

"Wait, how could Campbell not know?" Milo asked. "He's got to be the one who put it there."

"Maybe, maybe not. I'm starting to wonder if Campbell's as much a pawn here as the rest of us," I said.

Hannah frowned. "What do you—"

"Think about it! This angel just shows up one day. It gives him the power to communicate with the spirits. It sends him visions that lead him to buy a former Durupinen property, and then instructs him on exactly how to turn his purchase into a Summoning Circle. It tells him just enough of what the spirits are saying to keep the money coming, but not enough to clue him in to how unhappy the spirits are. Whatever that angel thing is, it knows about the history of this place, and it knows a lot about the Durupinen, but I don't think Campbell does. The angel is using him!"

Milo gaped. Hannah let out a dry sob. They both knew I was right; I could see it in their horrified expressions.

"It's got to be the Necromancers. There's no other explanation, is there?" Hannah whispered.

"I just don't know!" I said. "There is definitely someone—or something—involved here using Durupinen knowledge for their own means."

"We have to get out of here!" Hannah cried. "What if we've stumbled right into the middle of a Necromancer plot?"

I could hear the absolute, desperate panic in Hannah's cry. Our experience with the Necromancers was harrowing for all of us, but no one was more affected than Hannah. The Necromancers' manipulations, which played masterfully on every fear she'd ever had, were probably more traumatic for her than the sum of her eighteen years as a "mentally ill" orphan.

"I'm with Hannah on this one," Milo said, looking uncharacteristically serious. "This shit makes the *Blair Witch Project* look like fun and games."

"Yeah, it does," I agreed. "But isn't this what we signed up for as Trackers? When Finn gets back, we'll get in touch with Catriona and tell her everything. Then we can get out of here and she can send in some expert-level Trackers to deal with whatever this is. But in the meantime," and here I paused, giving them both a warning look, "panicking is probably the worst thing we could do."

Hannah nodded and immediately took a long, slow breath. "You're right. We don't have to do anything. We'll just keep our cover, and leave as soon as we can. Okay, we can do that."

"Yes, we can," I said. "So, keeping our cool, let's discuss this rationally. Maybe if we put our heads together, we'll be able to figure some of this out."

"Okay. Right. Just brainstorming," Hannah said, still taking slow and measured breaths.

"Exactly. So, there used to be a *príosún* here. Catriona said the Trackers don't know where, precisely, it stood, but that it was somewhere on the property. Finding that rune on the basement door gave me an idea—what if the *príosún* was right under this house? What if that's why the basement is Warded?"

Milo's eyes widened. "You think the house is sitting on the jail?"

"I think it's possible," I said. "Especially if there was anything left of the *príosún* when this mansion was built. The people who purchased this land and built this house could've constructed it right on top of the old structure."

Milo frowned. "But why would they do that? Why would you build a house on top of rubble?"

"It was common enough," I said. "If the area was a good spot to build on once—access to fresh water, level ground, whatever—you'd build on it again. Plus, the *príosún* was probably underground, at

236

least partially. Many of them were, remember. Before power tools and backhoes, why waste time and money digging a whole new cellar? So there could've been stones, or debris, or even partial walls that got incorporated into this house when it was built. Who knows what kinds of residual Castings could be on the place?"

"Yeah, that's true!" Hannah said. "Or maybe they uncovered an artifact or something!"

"Exactly! So if the original builders of the house unwittingly incorporated Durupinen relics during construction, maybe Campbell found or disturbed something during the renovations," I said. "People find all kinds of weird stuff when they're renovating—in their walls, under the floorboards, in the foundations. In fact, lots of places aren't actively haunted at all until someone comes in and starts shaking things up, so to speak. Pierce used to tell me about it all the time."

Milo jumped in, sounding excited now. "Okay, brilliant theory time! Wait for it... Campbell's angel thing was trapped in the *príosún* here, and Campbell unleashed it when he started renovating the place!" Milo took a bow, clearly convinced he'd solved the mystery, but I was already shaking my head.

"The timeline doesn't fit," I said. "The angel found Campbell first, *then* led him to this plantation. If the angel had been trapped here, someone else let it out. The problem is, I don't think this property had been touched for a long time before that."

Milo drooped a little. "Okay, fine, theory busted."

I walked over to the window, on the lookout for Finn's car. He still hadn't replied to my text, and I was starting to get antsy—he never took this long to respond. "I just wish we knew what this angel thing is!" I exclaimed. "It's probably not a spirit—Hannah or I would recognize it if it were. It's too sentient to be a Wraith, I think. Maybe it's an Elemental, but Elementals are about fear and hunger, and I'm not sensing either of those things."

"Me neither," answered Hannah. "So it must be something we don't know about yet. But why does it know about the Durupinen? Why does it need a Summoning Circle?"

"Jess, have you tried drawing it yet?" Milo asked suddenly.

I turned away from the window and frowned at him. "No. It doesn't look like anything we've ever seen before. It's just a... cloud. Why would I draw it?"

"Well...you drew Grayson without his revealing himself to you.

You hadn't actually seen him, but you zeroed in on his energy and got a really detailed image. Maybe if you drew the angel, you'd be able to show us something that our eyes didn't see."

Hannah's face brightened. "Hey, yeah! That is a really good idea! Your Muse gifts might tell us something more. And if not, we'd at least have a drawing to send to Catriona. Maybe she'd notice a detail or a clue that we missed."

"Umm... okay, sure. Why not?" I said, leaving my window vigil and crossing the room to grab my sketchbook. I thought it was a waste of time, to be honest; I'd only ever been able to use my abilities as a Muse to draw spirits, and as far as any of us could tell, this angel wasn't a spirit. But Milo's suggestion had calmed Hannah's anxiety a bit, and she seemed eager for me to try. I knew at least part of her eagerness stemmed from this being a plan that we could execute in the relative safety of our room, so I decided to humor her.

I tossed my phone over to Hannah as I flipped open the sketchbook. "Just do me a favor and keep an eye out for a text from Finn, okay?" I said. "If he answers while I'm drawing, just tell him to come up."

"Sure," Hannah replied, placing the phone on the bed beside her.

I put my pencil to the paper, and searched through my connection to the spirit world, trying to find the moment when I'd first seen the angel.

"Here goes nothing," I muttered. And nothing was exactly what I expected to happen.

That was the last thing I remembered.

§

"Jess?"

Holy fuck, my head hurt. Someone had stuck it in a vice and was turning the crank, crushing it. I tried to answer, but all that escaped me was an agonized moan.

"She's responding!" said an excited voice. A familiar voice. Hannah's voice.

"Stay back, though. She might attack again," a second voice cautioned. It was Finn.

I tried to speak again. My mouth was so dry it felt as though it had been stuffed full of cotton balls. I gagged and tried to wet my lips. The pounding in my head intensified.

"Jess? Can you hear me?" Finn said slowly.

"Stop... loud..." I managed to choke out before I gagged again and dry-retched. As I rolled over, I realized I was on the floor.

"What is it? What did she say?" cried Milo. He sounded absolutely terrified. They all did.

"I said... stop... talking... so... loud!" I gasped. I felt warm salty tears sliding down my face and into my mouth, and that's when I realized I was crying. Sobbing, actually.

I tried to open my eyes, but the light in the room was like daggers straight to my eyeballs. "Why is it so bright in here?" I gasped. "I can't see anything!"

"Kill that light!" Finn commanded. "And the one on the table, too."

I saw the room darken perceptibly through my closed eyelids. Very slowly, I opened my eyes by tiny degrees, until I was just barely squinting at the room around me.

The first thing I saw was Finn, who had backed into the corner of the room between the door and the closet. He was kneeling on one knee, with his hand extended out in front of him as if he were about to fend off something dangerous. Hannah crouched behind him, with the top half of her face peeking out over his shoulder. Milo hovered in the corner above them near the ceiling; he looked ready to spring into action at any second.

As the pressure in my head slowly began to recede, fear flooded in. What was everyone so afraid of?

"What is it?" I asked hoarsely. "Is it behind me?"

"No, there's nothing behind you. It's... okay now, I think. How do you feel?" Finn replied, very cautiously.

"My head is killing me and I can hardly see," I said. "What's happening?"

"Nothing anymore. I think it's over," Finn said gingerly.

Hannah burst into tears. She attempted to scramble out from behind Finn and come toward me, but he held her back. "No. Let me go first, just in case."

Oh my God. They were afraid of me. My own sister, for whom I'd almost literally come back from the dead, was afraid of me.

My heart began to pound even more violently. The tears welled up again. "Finn, you're scaring me. What's going on?"

Finn walked slowly toward me with his hands up, as if I were pointing a loaded gun at him. "Can I come sit beside you, Jess?"

"Of course you can!" I cried. "Finn, you're really scaring me!"

"I'm sorry," he said. His voice, although uncharacteristically soothing, had a tremor in it. "I'm not trying to scare you. I'm only trying to keep everyone safe."

"Safe from what?" I sobbed. I was afraid to move, to open my eyes any further. What would I see? What had I done?

"You had a... when you started drawing the angel, you went into a sort of... state," Finn explained, although I could tell that *state* wasn't quite the word he'd been looking for. As he took the last few steps toward me, I noticed he was limping.

"What's wrong with you? Are you hurt?" I squeaked, and then—as the awful realization hit me—"Did *I* hurt you?"

"I'm fine. No need to concern yourself with me," he replied, using the same intentionally calm and even tone. Even as he said it, the pain in my head receded just enough that I was able to open my eyes a little wider. The very first sight my gaze fell upon was his right thigh: My pencil, the one that I had picked up to draw with, was protruding from Finn's bloodied leg.

"Finn, your leg! Did I... what the hell... did I *stab* you?" I shrieked.

"It's just a pencil. I'm fine," he intoned, but I was absolutely losing it now. Suddenly, I couldn't remember how to catch my breath, how to climb out from under the weight of this panic. This was far too much like my Prophecy mural experience at Fairhaven, when I'd awoken out of a Psychic Trance to find Celeste cowering beside me. Holy shit—what could be *worse* than the Prophecy?

"I don't remember anything, I can't—" I looked down at my own hands and my eyes fell on the wall beside me. It was covered in runes and Castings, scribbled everywhere in a wild hand. In horror, I sat upright and took in the rest of the room. Everywhere I looked, I'd scrawled more runes—on the walls, on the furniture, on the doors.

"I didn't... I don't... oh my God!" I yelped, before my throat itself started to close up on me. Clutching at my neck, I managed to gasp, "Finn... can't... breathe..."

Finn placed one hand on either side of my face, gently but firmly. "Look at me, Jess! Look at me." I found his eyes and locked onto them. "You are okay," he continued. "Everything is okay. Breathe. Proper breaths now. Just breathe, alright?"

240

I looked into Finn's face and breathed with him. In and out, in and out, in and out. As my throat relaxed itself, I lay my forehead against his and tried to rein in my sobbing, but I couldn't—at least not yet. Finn stroked my cheeks, brushing the tears away as they fell. He continued to direct my breathing, guiding my breaths over and over, reminding me how to breathe. And I did. I breathed in the smell of him and the closeness of him until I was all cried out. I felt my heart rate start to stabilize as the pain receded from my head and my vision cleared.

"There now," Finn said slowly. "I'm here with you. All calm?"

"Yes," I said, forcing my swollen eyes open. "Yes, I think I'm alright. Now can you tell me what happened?"

Finn pulled his hands away from my face and sat back on his heels, wincing slightly as he did so. I tried not to look at the wound in his leg, the sight of which made me queasy. "Hannah will have to start. I didn't arrive until you were already in the middle of... whatever that was."

Hannah stepped hesitantly away from the wall, twisting her hands nervously together, but before she could take another step, Milo shot down from the ceiling and placed himself between us.

"Milo, you really don't need to—" Hannah began.

Milo shook his head obstinately. "Sorry, sweetness, but I'm not taking any chances," he said.

Hannah gave me a weak, apologetic smile from behind Milo. "Sorry, Jess, it's just... you were—"

"Don't apologize!" I said impatiently. "Just tell me what happened."

Hannah wet her lips. "You sat down next to me on the bed and closed your eyes to draw the angel."

"Yeah, I remember that part," I said.

"But then, the moment you started drawing, you started... shouting."

"Shouting? I was shouting?" I asked, horrified.

"Well, it was loud," Hannah said, her voice cracking. "You started to draw a shape—I thought maybe it was the outline of a head—and then all of a sudden you were yelling in Gaelic and scribbling on your sketchpad. Thank goodness the floor was deserted... everyone else was still down at dinner. Look what you drew!"

She held my sketchbook up so I could see the image I'd created. It had the vague form of a human, but it was composed entirely of violently scribbled letters and runes, all jumbled together on top of each other.

"What was I saying in Gaelic? Could you tell?" I asked. My Gaelic skills were dicey at best; speaking it fluently was akin to a possessed person speaking in tongues.

Hannah shook her head. "No... you were speaking too fast, and I was in shock. I kept saying your name and trying to reach to you, but you wouldn't respond to me. Then Milo thought if we took the sketchbook away from you, you might stop. So I grabbed it, but—" Hannah gestured helplessly around at the room, now thoroughly graffitied. "And then Finn showed up."

Finn took over. "This was well beyond a Psychic Trance, Jess—I know how to break a Trance's hold. It was rather like a forced Habitation. You couldn't see or hear us—or you couldn't respond if you did. I thought if I could get the pencil away from you, we might break you out of its hold, but... well..." Finn glanced down at the pencil still sticking out of his leg.

"You tried to take my pencil, so I stabbed you in the leg." I said it blankly, because I couldn't quite believe it. "I stabbed you?" I said again, although this time it was a question.

"That's about the whole of it, yes," Finn said quietly.

I took another long, slow breath. "So what finally made me stop?"

"You flung yourself at me trying to get the pencil back, but I fought you off. You had nothing to draw with anymore, so you started scratching at the carpet, but you couldn't make any more markings. I was about to try to expel the creature from you, even though that would've been quite painful for you. But not being able to draw anymore was the key that freed you. Your hands started moving more slowly, and then finally, you sort of... drooped."

I ran a shaking hand through my hair, pushing it back from my face, which was slick with tears and sweat. "I'm sorry, Hannah. Finn, I'm so sorry. I don't know why or how that happened."

"Why did you try to draw the angel?" Finn asked. "What prompted you to attempt something so foolish?"

I bristled. "That's not fair! It wasn't foolish! Well, okay, *now* I can see that maybe it wasn't the best plan, but it seemed like a really good idea when Milo suggested it! If it had worked, it would've been by far the easiest way to get a visual on the angel. And if it didn't, we would've been no worse off. Don't pretend you could've predicted this."

Finn gave every indication that he was about to argue, but Milo stepped in.

"You're not the only one whose job it is to protect her," Milo said firmly. "It's my job too, and I gave her the idea. It was just a Muse drawing. She's done thousands. Even the ones that happen spontaneously or while she's sleeping have always been harmless enough. The room's Warded—there wasn't a single spirit in here who could've forced a Habitation or a Psychic Trance. Can you seriously tell me you would've objected if you'd been here?"

Finn let out a long sigh, and when he spoke he sounded almost weary. "No. I can't honestly say I'd have tried to stop you. I'm not trying to blame anyone. I was just... properly alarmed. I'm sorry. I shouldn't have called you foolish, Jess. That wasn't fair... or true."

I was almost too surprised to answer, but I managed to mutter, "That's okay."

"But we do need," Finn went on, "to make fewer assumptions collectively. We assumed, and quite rightly," and here he nodded at Milo, "that the Wards would protect you from Habitation, but obviously the angel has some immunity to Wards, or knows how to undo them. I realize our dealing with the spirits may feel quite old hat, but you're Trackers now. There'll be whole seas of unchartered waters for us to navigate." Finn paused and shot a serious, almost headmaster-ish, look at each of us. "But enough about that. We need to act quickly."

"He's right," said Hannah, who was now examining the runes under our windows. "These should have held against any spirit—you should've been protected. Oh Jess, this isn't good."

I turned to Hannah and gave her a calming look. "Then we'll just have to use stronger Wards, and a good protective Casting. It'll be ok." I turned back to Finn. "Act? What do you mean?" My head was still swimming, and I couldn't imagine doing anything right now except popping a handful of Tylenol and passing out.

Finn picked up my sketchbook from the bed and held it up. "You may not have captured the angel's image, Jess, but you've certainly captured something powerful. These aren't just random scribbles and doodles. All of these runes and Castings must mean something—and we're going to find out what. Or rather, Catriona is going to find out for us." At this, Finn slid his cell phone from his pocket, preparing to take pictures.

"Um, Finn?" I said tentatively.

"Don't be bothered, my mobile's been encrypted. Campbell's security can't detect it," he said, snapping picture after picture of the sketch I'd produced.

"No, Finn... it's not that. I mean... don't you think... wouldn't you like to remove the pencil from your leg before you do anything else?"

Finn looked up at me and then down at his leg in mild surprise, as though he'd entirely forgotten that there was a writing implement protruding from his thigh. "Oh, right. Yes, well spotted, that. Here Hannah, take the photos, would you?" He tossed Hannah his phone and then disappeared into the bathroom to bandage himself and possibly perform some light surgery.

Hannah came and sat beside me. "Jess... can I give you a hug?" she asked, still tearful.

"Yes, of course you can!" I cried, pulling her to me and squeezing her tightly. "I'm so sorry that I scared you. I don't know what it was, but it's gone now. I feel completely normal, except for this headache."

"That was some *Exorcist* level shit right there," Milo said with a delicate shiver. "Seriously, I was about to call a priest!"

"Aw, Milo, don't be jealous. You know you're the only spirit I willingly Habitate with," I said, trying to bat my eyelashes at him—but even that was painful.

"I'm so flattered," he said.

"I just wonder what all of this means," I said, gesturing around to all of the runes. "Hannah, do you recognize any of it? I only know a few of these runes."

"Sure," Hannah said, getting to her feet. "There's the rune for protection. The rune for darkness. The rune for concealment." As she explained, she snapped a picture of each rune with Finn's phone. "That's one of the runes used in a Binding. That over there looks like part of the casting for a Caging. And there's a bunch of familiar Gaelic words—'Mask,' 'follow,' 'haven,' 'shroud.' She paused, scanning the room for anything she might've missed, before asking, "Can I get some more pictures of your sketch?"

I held the sketch up for her, and noticed, for the first time, a dull ache in my right hand from the speed and intensity with which I had been drawing. Then Hannah handed the phone to me, asking which shot I thought was clearest. The sight of the image on the screen triggered my memory; my heart, which had finally settled into a normal rhythm, began pounding again.

"The pictures!" I cried. I called into the bathroom, "Finn, did you get the pictures I texted? The ones of Campbell's new plans for Whispering Seraph?"

Finn emerged from the bathroom, still limping slightly, with a thick gauze dressing wrapped around his pant leg. "I did, and Hannah informed me about the rune, too. That's why it's even more crucial that we act quickly! I'm certain now that this angel—with or without Campbell's cooperation—is trying to restore this place to a hub of Durupinen power. This sketch," and here Finn took the sketchpad from Hannah's hands and gazed at it intently, "is just further proof of that. The angel is hidden, Masked possibly, and this drawing is the only clue we have to exactly how it's shielding itself. If Catriona and the Trackers can figure out what this drawing means, we might be able to reveal this angel for what it is... and stop Campbell once and for all."

Finn took his phone back from Hannah and began emailing Catriona the pictures we'd taken, then followed up with a phone call. When she didn't answer, Finn looked about ready to punch his fist through the nearest wall, but he took a deep breath and left an urgent voicemail instead. "Right," he said, after hanging up.

Finn pulled the *Book of Téigh Anonn* from his suit jacket and began the protective Casting. He was finished in under a minute.

"Right then," he said. "That's sorted. I've got to go."

20

A MOMENT IN THE MOONLIGHT

"YOU'RE GOING? NOW?" I ASKED, A BIT DESPERATELY. I was still so spooked from the Muse incident that the thought of Finn's leaving made me feel vaguely panicky.

"I'm going out onto the grounds to investigate this new layout," he replied, before pausing and furrowing his eyebrows at me. "If that's alright with you. I could... that is... do you need me for something?"

I laughed inwardly. "Comfort?" I thought. "To keep me from utterly falling apart?" I thought. But what I actually said was, "Can I come with you?"

Finn looked taken aback. I nearly told him to forget the idea, but the words were only halfway to my lips when he said, "Alright, then. If you're up to it, let's go."

"I stabbed you in the leg," I reminded him. "If you're up for it, I'm up for it."

A small smile betrayed him. "Fair enough. Let's crack on then, before it gets too late and the security starts paying attention to who's outside."

I turned to Hannah just in time to see her and Milo exchanging a sly look.

"What?" I asked defensively.

"Nothing!" they both insisted at the very same time.

I narrowed my eyes at both of them, but let it go. This was no time to indulge their theories—whatever they were—about me and Finn. "I'll be right back," I said. "Will you be alright while I'm gone?"

Hannah rolled her eyes. "You were the one causing all the chaos," she said. "Get out of here before you get the urge to draw something else! We'll start cleaning this up." She gestured broadly, indicating my Muse-inspired mess.

Milo pointed silently but sternly toward the door, as if we were puppies who'd just messed on the rug. Feeling unaccountably nervous—maybe I was still just jumpy from the Muse episode—I followed Finn out into the hallway, which was deserted. Finn closed the door behind us, but not before instructing Hannah to lock it and not to open it for anyone.

"We don't want anyone seeing Jess' artwork before we have the chance to tidy it up," he said. "But before you start cleaning, re-do those Wards. Top-levels now, don't take any chances."

We practically tiptoed down the hallway, even though there was no reason to hide. Downstairs, a lively buzz of laughter and conversation bled out into the lobby from the dining room, where the after-dinner revelry was still in full and raucous swing. For a moment, I had a hard time reconciling their mirth with the solemn and often tearful people I'd shared the retreat with thus far, but after considering it for a moment, I realized I understood them well; it made me sad. I knew many of them would wake up tomorrow full of regret, despairing at their decision to drown their sorrows instead of facing them. My mother had been, unfortunately, the queen of that particular destructive pattern, and I had dealt with the fallout over and over again my entire childhood.

"They've been at it for quite a while in there," Finn said, cocking his thumb at the dining room as we walked onto the porch. The hot and humid night air greeted us like a wet blanket to the face.

"Yeah, and we're damn lucky they are, or our cover might've been blown tonight," I said.

Finn grunted in agreement. I followed him out across the expansive front lawn, then crunched with him down the wide gravel drive. At last, without warning, he stopped abruptly and turned back to face Whispering Seraph. I smacked right into him, then stumbled back so that he had to catch me by the arm to prevent me from falling to the ground. As per usual.

"Sorry," he said gruffly. "I should have given warning."

"That's okay," I said, tugging my arm from his grip and massaging it gently. "Where, exactly, are we going?"

"When you sent me that picture of Campbell's new plans, I was already on my way back with a few photos of my own," Finn said, pulling a manila envelope from his waistband. "Iggy's been hard at work. He's pulled together some very interesting satellite views of Whispering Seraph. The picture you sent confirmed what I was already beginning to suspect." Finn pulled a picture from the envelope and handed it to me. "Notice anything?"

I took the picture from his outstretched hand and examined it in the pool of light coming from one of the driveway's lampposts. It was an aerial view of the entire property. There was a gray, rectangular shape in the center, which, of course, was Whispering Seraph itself. There were several other shapes I recognized—the small pond, where I'd had my disastrous first encounter with Talia; the parking lot, where we'd parked our sedan yesterday; the barn, which was now being used to store golf carts. "Can you give me a hint? What am I supposed to be noticing?"

Finn indicated several highlighted spots on the map. "These are the blind spots Iggy told me about. If you're in any of these locations, you can't be seen by Campbell's cameras. It's not surprising that Whispering Seraph has these blind spots—it's nearly impossible to surveil a property this large without creating a few. But there's also something strategic about these blind spots."

I looked again, pinpointing the highlighted locations. There were four of them altogether. "They're so evenly spaced," I said, running a finger over each one in turn. "If you connected them, they'd make a perfect diamond shape."

"Or, if you looked at it another way," Finn said, and he traced the pattern with his finger, first top to bottom and then left to right, "the four points of the compass. Geographically, that's exactly how they line up: Due north, south, east, and west."

"Okay, but why's that significant?" I asked. My head, still pounding to the steady beat of my pulse after my Muse experience, felt sluggish.

"That picture you sent me shows the layout of Whispering Seraph as a massive Summoning Circle, but what if I told you that many of the basic components of the Circle were already in place?" Finn asked.

"Really? How so?" I asked.

"Well let's start with the spot where we met earlier today," Finn said, pointing down at one of the blind spots, which lined up perfectly with the place by the garage where we'd talked after Kyle's outburst. "You remember I selected it for that very reason, so we could properly chat."

"Yes, I remember," I said, a bit impatiently. It had only been a few hours ago, after all.

"Do you see what else is there?" Finn asked. But before I could play his guessing game, Finn pointed down the driveway to the giant fire pit a few yards from the garage. Someone had been using it; a rosy little fire burned merrily away. I could just make out a few wine glasses and some empty plates; a handful of guests had clearly broken off from the dinner party to enjoy the relative solitude.

"Yes, I see it, Finn. What's your point?" I asked.

"My point," Finn said, "is this. If Campbell is trying to turn this place into a Summoning Circle, he's going to need fire." He stood glaring at me, waiting for me to catch up.

Suddenly it clicked. "Candles! We always need candles to create a Summoning Circle! So, does that mean... does the fire pit operate like a giant candle?"

"Precisely!" Finn said. "And not just any candle. As you know, there needs to be a candle representing each element. Here we are on the west side of the property, and so this fire pit, when lit, will represent water. And of course, what's located just beyond it?"

"The pond!" I cried. I could see the moon, now high in the night sky, reflected on the water's surface.

"Top marks!" Finn cried. He turned back to the aerial shot, holding it out so I could examine it too. "I think each of these other areas on the map must have a fire pit as well, with each representing one of the four classical-element candles. I'll also wager that there's something at each location corresponding to the necessary element. Or there will be, by the time Campbell is finished. The fifth candle, the Spirit Candle, will probably be part of the house itself."

"I don't believe this," I said. "This is insane. What can Campbell even do with a giant Summoning Circle? It's completely useless without a Durupinen to control it!"

"I don't think Campbell rightly knows what's going on," Finn said. "If you ask me, I'd bet that angel creature is using Campbell every bit as much as it's using the guests."

I nodded grimly. "I think you're right."

We walked together down the long driveway toward the garage. Then we examined the fire pit closely, tensed all the while in case someone interrupted us; thankfully, whoever had been enjoying the fire had abandoned it. The fire pit was ringed in gray stone, with a number of large blue stones, like massive, polished marbles, inlaid among the masonry.

"This is incredible," I whispered, brushing my fingers over one of the blue stones. "Blue, just like the blue candle we use to Summon the element of water. Do you think the other fire pits are the same, only with different colors?"

"Only one way to find out," answered Finn. "Time to investigate."

We set out across the lawn, taking a leisurely pace so that we looked as if we were merely taking a casual stroll after the party.

Through the mansion's windows, we saw that the party was breaking up at last. Only a few people remained in the dining room, while a half-dozen or so others were milling around the lobby. Their loud, drunken voices spilled out onto the porch.

We skirted along the lawn's perimeter, staying to shadows whenever possible. We walked a full quarter of the way around the property. As we turned around an enormous oak tree, we found what we were looking for: A second fire pit was under construction.

We approached it cautiously, but the area was deserted. The fire pit was sectioned off with traffic cones and yellow "caution" tape. A sign hammered into the ground read: "Please pardon our appearance. Area under construction. Do not enter." We ignored this warning, ducked under the tape, and walked up to the partially completed fire pit.

"If we've read this map properly, and I'm quite sure we have, this location should correspond with the element of air—which means... yes, yellow stones. They've already set some of them," Finn said, smiling in grim satisfaction. We squatted down, side by side, to examine the yellow gems set into the fire pit's half-completed stonework.

"What do you think they are?" I asked. "Amber?"

"Most likely. Or topaz or citrine. It would be ideal if we could find a sample to send to the Trackers for testing. It might be an important detail."

"Let's have a look around," I said. "There could be pieces of it around here from the construction."

Finn immediately dropped to his knees, pulling his cell phone from his pocket to use as a flashlight. I followed his lead; we crawled around in silence for several minutes, carefully feeling around in the cracks and crevices of the masonry for a sample. Two-thirds of the way around the fire pit, I discovered a burlap sack tucked into a gap in the rocks. I tugged it out; it was unexpectedly heavy for its size.

"Finn! Come look at this!" I hissed.

He crawled over to me and we peered together into the bag. The light from Finn's cell phone threw golden glimmers off of a pile of smooth, perfectly round yellow stones; each one was about the size of my palm.

"Whoa," I said softly, picking up one of the stones and turning it over in my hands. "These are huge. Do you think they'll notice if one is missing?"

"Worth the risk, I think," Finn said, taking it from my hand. "We *are* in a blind spot after all. They'd have a job proving we were the ones who took it, even if they cared to investigate where it went."

A sudden cracking of twigs made us both freeze. Someone was walking—well, stumbling—in our direction from the other side of the fire pit. We waited, with our hearts in our throats, hoping that whoever it was would veer away, but with every passing second it became clear that they were headed straight for us. Any moment they would see the two of us crouched in the fire pit, with the open bag of gemstones conspicuously between us.

Finn looked up at me, and I saw my panic reflected in his eyes. Maybe it was just a valid reason to act on what so much of me longed for so badly, but I had a sudden, wild idea. I yanked the elastic from my hair, quickly slid the strap of my dress off of my shoulder, and pulled Finn on top of me.

"What are you—"

But I didn't let him finish his question. "Sorry about this," I said. Then I grabbed his face and kissed him full on the mouth.

He froze at first, but then I felt the moment when he realized what we were doing and why. He snaked his arm under my back and pulled me closer, pressing our bodies together, and began kissing me back. My pulse began to thunder in my ears, my breath to escape me in gasps. I very nearly forgot this was just a ruse. I threw myself hungrily into the kiss; Finn's lips seemed just as ravenous as my own.

"Oh, my! I'm so sorry, I—" Marigold cried as she rounded the corner.

Finn and I leapt apart. He jumped to his feet, then reached out a hand to help me to mine. Marigold swayed where she stood and squinted at me, trying to focus on my face.

"Jess? Is that you, sunshine?" she slurred.

"Uh, yeah... it's me. Hi, Marigold," I said, pulling the strap back onto my shoulder and hastening to smooth my hair.

Marigold was so drunk that she looked as though she were trying to get her bearings on a ship sailing through a squall. Even in the moonlight, I could see that her mascara had left wide black tracks down her face; her lipstick was smeared all over her teeth. I think she tried to wink at me, but couldn't get her eyelid to cooperate.

"Well, look at you, sugarplum! Having a little fun for yourself." She stumbled a bit before adding—in a loud, drunken whisper, no less—"And he's so handsome! What a catch! Where'd you find him hiding?"

I stepped over to Marigold and pulled her to me conspiratorially. "Yeah, he is handsome. He's also my bodyguard, and my parents would kill me if they knew we were dating. But I can't help it! We're in love!"

Marigold's bloodshot eyes filled with moisture. "You're in love?"

"Yes," I said solemnly. "So please, please don't tell anyone you saw us here together, okay?"

Marigold pressed her lips together as if she were trying to repress a sob, and then saluted me. I took this as a positive sign.

"I'd promise just about anything in the name of true love, and you'd better believe it!" She teetered for a moment before adding dreamily, "I'll just leave you two be, and let the moonlight work its magic." Then she set off toward the house, singing "People Will Say We're in Love" from *Oklahoma!* while conducting an imaginary orchestra with the high-heeled shoe she clutched in her hand.

I heaved a sigh of relief and turned back to Finn, who was watching Marigold weave up the path. "I'd be surprised if she even remembered she saw us, but if she does, hopefully she'll remember her promise, too," I said.

"Right," Finn said quietly, not quite meeting my eye. The fire that had roared through my body moments before fizzled out and died as swiftly as if he'd doused me in cold water.

§

Even as my heart sunk fully and completely, I resolved that there was no way I was going to show my disappointment to Finn. No way was I going to betray even a hint of the swirling bliss he'd

253

inspired in me, no way I was going to let him know how deeply and desperately I needed his kiss. I snapped my guard back up, determined to get out of this moment with my dignity intact.

"I'm sorry if that was... unpleasant for you." I mumbled.

Finn frowned at me. "Unpleasant?"

"Yeah. I'm sorry. I didn't ask you first—I just did it. And I know you don't have any interest in kissing me anymore. You've made that pretty clear. So, yeah. I'm sorry."

"Just stop," he snapped. "Stop apologizing. I don't think I can stand to hear you say the word *sorry* again!"

I looked up at him, taken aback by his sharpness. "Look, I was only trying to—"

"I know! I know what you were trying to do. I just... don't say you're sorry. I'm the only one who has anything to be sorry about."

"What are you talking about?" I asked, perplexed.

"It's my fault that it's all cocked up between us! It's my fault that you felt the need to apologize for kissing me. All of this is my fault, and I can't fix it!" He ran his hands through his hair, pulling much of it free from his ponytail. His face was contorted, twisted with pain.

"Are you going to explain what you're talking about or not?" I asked.

"It's not that I don't want to kiss you! It's never been that I don't want to kiss you!" he cried. He had closed his eyes and raised his head toward the sky, as if he couldn't stand looking at me while confessing this. It only made me feel worse.

"I don't understand you, Finn!" I replied. "Three years ago, I thought I knew what was happening between us. I was sure enough that I asked you to stay the night with me! I've never asked anyone to do that. Ever. But then you basically told me I'd imagined the whole thing. You made me feel like a delusional, lovesick school girl! I've never been so humiliated in my entire life. But now you're saying... what? That it was all a lie?"

"Of course it was a lie! I'm in love with you! Can you honestly say it hasn't been written on my face every time I've looked at you? I can feel it laid bare for the world to see! Seamus certainly saw it, and he made bloody well sure I'd never act on it again!"

My anger turned to ice in my veins. "What do you mean? What does Seamus have to do with anything?"

"He was waiting for me. That night, three years ago, after we kissed—after I'd promised you we'd be together soon. Seamus was there, waiting in my apartment. I have no idea how he knew what had happened between us—he never did do me the courtesy of explaining that bit. All he said was that I needed to end things between us immediately or risk being reassigned."

"He threatened you? Because we kissed?" I asked, with my voice hollow from the shock of it. "But that doesn't make any sense! The Prophecy was the only real reason they banned Durupinen-Caomhnóir relationships in the first place, and it's over! Why do they care anymore?"

"But the rule still stands, and they're still properly enforcing it. Seamus threatened to personally reassign me somewhere on the other side of the world. I told him he couldn't do that. I'm sworn to your Gateway—that's a lifetime vow. But he told me that entering into an illicit relationship with you was violating the terms of that oath—leaving the Caomhnóir free to nullify our contract. When I tried to argue, Seamus went a step further and threatened repercussions for you and Hannah as well."

"Repercussions? The Caomhnóir have no control over the Durupinen—you're strictly Guardians."

"That doesn't matter, does it? It's about who has the power, not who's in the right! Seamus told me that many on the Council wanted to find ways to control you and Hannah, to ensure that you didn't become too powerful. They didn't want you growing too independent of the Northern Clans. And Seamus could see to the Council's properly ruining the lives you were building! I couldn't let that happen—not after you'd both worked so hard for your independence."

"So you told me you didn't love me." My voice cracked from the emotion of the memory.

"I had to," Finn said sheepishly, casting his eyes to the ground. "I couldn't let my own selfishness impede your happiness," Finn said.

"But you *did* take it away, don't you get that? You were a huge part of that happiness! I'd never trusted anyone the way I trusted you, I'd never let anyone in like that. But then the moment I took the leap, you let me fall. Hard."

"I know. I *do* know that. So, you see? I'm the one who needs to say sorry. I owe you that word a hundred times over, yet it will never be enough!" Finn cried, beating his hands against his head as if he could knock the memory of that night onto the ground and stomp on it.

Something blazed in me. For one wild instant I thought I wanted to hit him, but one look into Finn's eyes transformed my anger into a different sort of heat. I rushed forward and seized both of his wrists, pulling his hands away from his head.

"You want to show me you're sorry? Then kiss me. Right now," I said. "Kiss me the way I've wanted you to for three years."

And damn it, for once in his life, Finn Carey listened to me.

A frantic and hungry energy pulsed through me, and his lips were the only thing that could stop that longing from consuming me. I wrapped my arms around Finn's neck, pulling him tightly to me. I wanted him to fill every aching, hollow place in me—every place that I never knew was empty until that moment—until the burning in me lit in him and we were consumed together into ash.

Finn's hands were suddenly everywhere at once—on my back, in my hair, around my shoulders—and all I knew was that I never wanted to experience another moment when he wasn't touching me. But then he plucked my hands from his shoulders and pulled away, gasping for breath.

"What? What is it?" I asked.

"We can't."

"Wow, you're shit at apologies, aren't you?" I panted.

"This doesn't change a bloody thing, don't you understand that?"

"No, Finn, I don't. I don't understand that. The only thing I understand is that I can't be without you anymore!"

"Jess... they could ruin us. Both of us."

"Stop it! Stop it!" I cried, pounding my fists against his chest. "I know what you're going to say, and I don't care, do you hear me? I don't care about the Durupinen and the Caomhnóir, or their rules, or their prophecies, or any of it! I. Don't. Care!"

"But I care!" he cried, but even as he said it, he pressed his forehead against mine, as though something magnetic and irresistible was keeping us locked tightly together. "Seamus was right! How can I protect you if I can't think rationally when I'm with you? I can't protect you like this, I can't!"

I took his face between my hands, forcing him to look me in the eyes. "But you did protect me! Your loving me is the only reason I'm still alive!"

Finn froze and gawked at me. "What do you—"

"That night when I went through the Gateway, I got lost on the other side. It was beautiful there, Finn. It was familiar and beautiful—like going home for the first time," I whispered. I took a deep breath, steeling myself for the confession I now had to make. I'd never told anyone what had happened when I'd gone through the Gateway—not even Hannah. "That world deep beyond the Gateway, it wants you to stay, do you understand? It draws you in until you forget that the living world even exists!"

Finn's eyes were beginning to glisten with emotion. I gently brushed the moisture away from them with my fingers.

"But then, out of someone else's mouth, came your words—your poem. The one you showed me the night we fled the Traveler's camp. And those words were so loud, so strong, that they broke the hold that place had on my soul—when that place should've held me more strongly than anything else in existence. It was your poem, Finn, that reminded me there was a living world... and why it was worth coming back. Hannah Called me, but it was your words that told me to come home. I couldn't have found my way back without you." I paused, taking another long deep breath. "You saved me. You protected me. Your love did that."

Finn was truly crying now. I pulled his face to mine and kissed him again; the tears on our cheeks mingled together.

Our lips were still touching, still in half a kiss, as I whispered it. "I love you."

Finn let out a moan that was half longing and half terrible pain. "You don't know how long I've waited to hear you say that."

"And you don't know how long I talked myself out of finding the courage to say it."

All the reasons not to be together still existed, yet everything had changed. As we looked at each other, we decided—together—that none of those reasons stood between us anymore. In that moment in the moonlight, the only word which existed between us was *yes*.

21

PSYCHIC HABITATION

WITH HIS TONE DRIPPING WITH DISBELIEF, Milo asked, "And that's everything that happened?"

"Yup. That's it."

"You're sure you're not leaving anything out?" he pressed.

"Nope. Hannah, pass the Windex please."

It was early the next morning, and Hannah and I, already dressed for the day, were scrubbing away the remaining graffiti from the night before, while Milo was giving me the third degree. After Finn and I had gone to inspect Whispering Seraph's expansion plans, Hannah had swiped some cleaning products and paper towels from the supply closet across the hall. She had fallen asleep by the time I'd crept back into the room, but sadly, nosy Spirit Guides never sleep... or mind their own damn business.

"I can't believe this. Fire pits that are giant element candles? How can Campbell possibly know the details of Durupinen Castings?" Hannah asked, scrubbing violently at a rune on the side of the bureau.

"I'm not convinced he does. But the angel certainly does, so that's where our focus should be right now. Campbell could very well be one of the angel's pawns, just like the rest of us."

"Where's Finn?" Milo asked pointedly.

I looked up to see him waggling his eyebrows suggestively at me. I looked quickly away and continued scrubbing the wall.

"How should I know? In his room, probably. Damn, I really need to start surrounding myself with washable art supplies."

Hannah chuckled, but warned, "We'd better hurry up and finish this. We're due at the next communication session in an hour or so, and I want to have breakfast first."

We'd awoken that morning to a new schedule slipped under our door. As he had promised, Campbell had broken the communication sessions into smaller groups. We were a part of Group A, which was meeting bright and early at 8:30 AM. Campbell may or may not have been conning these people, but he was undoubtedly a morning person; I held that, if nothing else, against him.

"Maybe we can just put the 'Do Not Disturb' sign on the door until we have more time to get the place cleaned up," Hannah said a bit desperately. "I think we might need to try something stronger to get this off the wallpaper. If the staff sees it, we might as well pack our bags now."

"That's a great idea," I said. "Based on the number of wine bottles that went around those tables last night, I bet there'll be quite a few 'Do Not Disturb' signs out this morning. I don't think housekeeping will even bat an eye."

Looking somewhat relieved, Hannah clambered up from her knees, grabbed the door placard from the bedside table, and opened the door a crack. Then she let out a squeak and leapt back as Finn came charging into the room.

At the sight of Finn, a warm light flared inside of me, tucked deep in the center of my chest. Against my will, the light tugged the corners of my mouth into an involuntary smile, and sent shivers of delight up my spine and across my scalp. I tried to compose myself, knowing Milo was waiting to pounce on the first sign that Finn and I had—as Milo so tenderly put it—"hooked up."

"Hi," I said, keeping my tone as neutral as possible.

Finn stopped short when he saw me. "Morning," he answered, trying to feign his typical gruffness. It didn't quite work; I desperately hoped Milo hadn't picked up on it.

Finn stood there, looking at me in silence until I finally said, "So... what's up? Why are you here so early?"

"I've got Catriona on the line. She wants to talk to all of us. Right now," replied Finn, holding up his cell phone. "She and some of the other Trackers sorted the pictures we sent last night. She has some important information and instructions for us."

We all froze as though Catriona had actually walked into the room. After exchanging a few nervous looks at each other, we gathered around Finn as he put us on speakerphone.

"Catriona? We're all here now. We can all hear you," Finn said.

"Well, well, well," came Catriona's lazy voice. "You Ballard girls certainly are overachievers, aren't you?"

Hannah and I frowned at each other. "I'm sorry, what?" I asked.

"I send you on what we all think is a simple open and shut case, and you stumble upon a massive Durupinen-centered conspiracy," she said, with a tinkling laugh in her voice.

"I'm so glad this is amusing you," I said, trying—but failing—to keep a steely note out of my own voice.

"What can you tell us about the pictures we sent?" Finn asked, jumping in before I could open hostilities too early. He gave me a look that clearly said "back off;" for once, I did my best to heed him.

"I can't tell you a bloody thing," Catriona said. "But Fiona can... and here she is."

We all heard a crackling noise as Catriona handed over the phone, then Fiona's sharp voice cut into the room like a dagger.

"Jess? Can you hear me?"

"Yes, Fiona. We all can. We're on speakerphone," I said.

"Alright, whatever," Fiona said. "Cat showed me those photos of your episode last night. How are you feeling today?"

"Fine, I guess. A bit of a lingering headache, and my hand is still sore, but otherwise I feel totally normal," I said.

"No fecking heroics, now," Fiona warned. "Are you sure you've recovered?"

"Yes," I replied, and I looked up at Finn to reassure him, too. "I swear, I'm absolutely okay."

"Good," Fiona said, sounding uncharacteristically relieved, "Now for heaven's sake, do *not* attempt to draw that thing again."

"Contrary to popular opinion here, I am not an idiot," I answered. "I have no intention of trying to connect with the angel again. But can someone over there tell me why that happened? Why did I lose control like that? And what do all the runes mean?"

"What happened was that you attempted to draw something that didn't want to be drawn. In fact, it doesn't want to be drawn, seen, felt, or heard! It was protected from detection by a Casting, and a right powerful one at that; that's why you drew all those runes. What's happened to you is called a Psychic Habitation—in this case, a defensive one. The angel used your Muse connection to grab onto your subconscious, taking control of you... likely in an effort to keep its own Casting intact. Psychic Habitations are rare, but far stronger than Psychic Trances. They're also bloody dangerous."

"Psychic Habitations?" I asked, feeling my mental defenses kick into gear. "If they're so dangerous, isn't this something you should've told me about?"

"Dogs!" cried Fiona. "Don't they teach Apprentices anything these days?"

"And what about Campbell?" I asked. "He can't be using a Casting, can he?"

"Don't worry about Campbell," Fiona snapped. "He's the least of your problems."

"But, if he's using—"

"Oi!" Fiona shouted, and I knew if we'd been in the same room, some object would now be hurtling toward my head. "If he's using Durupinen information, it's on the orders of that angel creature, or whatever's hidden on the other side of that Casting. That's what you need to concern yourself with."

Finn, in his best Caomhnóir voice, broke in. "Fiona, I want proper instructions on how to release her if it happens again. We were lucky this time, the angel released Jess with minimal interference. I won't chance that happening again."

"Yes. Carrick has experience with this. He's with Braxton putting together information for you as we speak," she replied.

"Quite right." declared Finn. I'd never heard "quite right" used as a command before, but somehow Finn managed it.

Fiona turned her attention back to me. "Jess, that angel has intimate knowledge of the Durupinen, and, more importantly, now—whatever that thing truly is—it knows how to get to you."

"Everyone keeps saying 'whatever it is,'" began Milo, "but is anyone going to offer some thoughts on what 'it' could be?" His voice, alarmed, was higher than usual. "Like, what are the options? Animal, vegetable, or mineral? Can we start with that?"

"We don't know what it is," Fiona admitted. "And we won't until we strip that Casting away and get a good look at it. Now untwist those knickers and listen to me. The angel, for want of a better word, is using a Casting called Masking. When a spirit is Masked, it's camouflaged so that it can hide in plain sight from both the living and the dead—just like what the Masking bracelets are doing for you, but for spirits."

"But it's not hidden, really," I said. "We can still see that it's there. It just looks like a cloud instead of its regular form. And for all of us who are Sensitives, it affects us with headaches and dizziness, too."

262

"Don't interrupt me, I'm getting to that!" Fiona snapped. "Either someone has done a poor job with the Casting, or the thing being Masked is not a normal spirit. Either way, the Masking is not functioning properly. But more alarming than that, is this: That angel shouldn't have been able to force a Psychic Habitation with you in a Warded room."

"So what are we supposed to do then?" Hannah asked.

"That's not my job—Cat will talk you through that," Fiona said dismissively. "But Jess, I've got special instructions for you, and you're to carry them out to the letter, you hear me?"

"Okay," I said, knowing it was always futile to push back even a little where Fiona was concerned. "What is it?"

"I'm sending all the details for a Casting to block your Muse abilities," Fiona replied, in a tone that sounded as though the words left a bad taste in her mouth. "It will only work temporarily, but it will help to keep you safe while you're still at that place."

I squirmed, hating the thought of messing with my gift. "Isn't it enough that I won't try to draw the angel again?"

"Not a chance we're taking!" Fiona snapped. "It shouldn't have got past those Wards in the first place, and now that you've connected with it once, you're more likely to be involuntarily drawn to it. Psychic Habitations don't just take over your consciousness like Psychic Trances do; they take over your subconscious—the very part of yourself you can't control. So either you muffle the Muse in you, or you risk a Psychic Habitation that you can't wake up from."

"That can happen?" I asked, horrified.

"If you come up against a powerful enough one, it could," Fiona replied. "A spirit once Psychically Habitated in me, and I spent three straight days creating a tapestry depicting her death in the Fairhaven *Príosún*. Someone found me in my studio and released me, and I consider myself fully lucky. No telling how long that spirit could've held me. Don't risk it, Jess. Follow the instructions I send you. You got that?"

Hannah, Finn, and Milo were all staring at me like I'd suddenly turned into a ticking time bomb. "Okay, okay. I will, I promise."

"Good. I'll hand you back over to Cat now. We'll talk about the artwork you left with me after you've finished your assignment there. There were two or three sketches that weren't complete rubbish, so, I guess, well done you."

I rolled my eyes. "Thank you. As usual, I appreciate the extravagant praise."

We heard a muffled curse as Fiona tried to hand the phone back to Catriona without dropping it. Then Catriona's voice began oozing from the speaker.

"Now, then. We've been over all of the pictures from last night, including the ones of the property, and the Council has decided that we can't allow Whispering Seraph to continue. The place must be nixed, and quickly. But before the Trackers can swoop in and shut things down, that angel needs to be Unmasked and contained. And you need to do it."

We all looked at each other; dismay and alarm were painted on each of our faces.

"Why do we need to do it?" Finn asked; I could tell he was trying his best to sound reasonable and levelheaded. "We haven't any experience with this sort of thing. Wouldn't it be better to let a Senior Tracker handle this?"

"You're hardly out of your skill set, Caomhnóir Carey," Catriona said, with a sly smile in her tone. "Honestly, if you can't oversee a simple Casting or two, perhaps you shouldn't be assigned to a Gateway."

Finn's complexion turned a dusky red and he dropped his eyes. I wondered why Catriona thought it was a good idea to mock the very Caomhnóir she was trusting to keep us safe during the Unmasking.

"He's just doing his job, Catriona," I said coldly. "Keeping us out of unnecessarily dangerous situations is his primary function here." Finn raised his head to look at me; he had the merest suggestion of a smile on his face. I returned it and went on, "You, on the other hand, seem to have no problem throwing your mentees straight into the fire, so I don't really think you should be talking about who's better at their job."

Catriona clicked her tongue. "Now now, I do believe I detect a note of sass from you, Jess. I'm not generally accustomed to taking attitude from anyone. But under the circumstances, I'm going to chalk it up to fear overriding your good judgment. I'll give you a pass this time."

Oh, she wanted sass, did she? I opened my mouth to let it fly, but Hannah reached out and clapped her hand over my mouth.

"Fine, Catriona, we're listening," Hannah said loudly. "Just tell us what we're supposed to do, and we'll do our best until the other

264

Trackers get here." I pulled my face angrily away from her hand, but the gesture had done its job; I kept my mouth shut and listened.

"Your assignment will hardly overstretch your abilities. Find a way to get the angel into a Circle. I don't care how you do it. Once it's in there, seal the Circle so it can't escape. Then follow the instructions I'm sending to you to Unmask it. Once the angel's been Unmasked, its true form will be revealed; Cage it, or seal the Circle, until the Trackers arrive. But remember, even with your Muse abilities blocked, the Wards might not properly affect this creature, so you can't count on them for protection. Other than that, it's really quite simple."

Again, Hannah, Finn, Milo, and I looked at each other. I could think of about a thousand ways Catriona's "simple" plan could go disastrously wrong. I knew Hannah, Milo, and Finn could each come up with a thousand more.

"Right, let's assume we manage to do all of that," I said slowly. "What are we supposed to do with Campbell until you get here? I doubt he's going to just stand aside and let us threaten his angel."

"Separate him from the angel, if you can, so he can't interfere," Catriona replied, her tone almost bored. "Distract him somehow."

"But we've never seen the angel without him before," Hannah pointed out. "We've only ever seen them together."

"But you've seen Campbell without the angel," Catriona said flatly.

Hannah frowned. "Well, yes, but—"

"Well, the angel must go somewhere when they separate. Someone follow it," Catriona instructed, as if this were the most obvious and mundane course of action in the world. "Must I walk you through every tiny detail? Haven't you any common sense?"

I very nearly grabbed the phone out of Finn's hand and hurled it at the wall. He must've known I was ready to boil over, because he broke away from our circle and swiped at the screen before bringing the phone up to his ear. "Yes. We'll do our best, and report back to you with our progress. Nonetheless, you should send the other Trackers as backup immediately. In the meantime, if the situation gets properly dangerous, if the risk is too great, I am pulling my Gateway out, mission be damned." And he hung up.

The silence that followed hung especially thick in the absence of Catriona's condescending tones. No one spoke because no one knew what to say. We'd been handed what felt like was an impossible task.

"Right, then," Finn finally said. "We've got our orders. Do we follow them or disregard?"

Hannah looked surprised. "Do we have a choice?"

"We always have a choice," Finn answered. "You aren't required to follow Catriona's orders when a mission becomes too risky. Not even the Council would fault you, if it came to that. We can walk away right now if you want to. Just say the word."

I looked at the fear Finn was trying so hard to keep out of his eyes, and I wanted to embrace him right then and there. Of course he wanted to give us this out... because of course he wanted us to take it. But weirdly enough, I didn't want to.

"Here's the thing," I began. Hannah turned eagerly toward me, clearly hoping that I would make the decision for both of us. "As much as I want to tell Catriona to take a flying leap, I don't think we can. We're in too deep already. No one else will ever be able to get the kind of access to Campbell and the angel that we already have." I picked up the schedule detailing the time of our session, which was now less than an hour away. "We've got an ideal chance to end this now, and I think we should take it."

"But now the angel knows how to get to you Jess, And we have no idea what we're doing!" Hannah cried.

"That's not entirely true," I said. "Take the fear out of it for a second. Logically, we've already faked our way through one communication session—we can fake our way through a second one. When it's over and the angel leaves, Milo can follow it at a distance." I turned to Milo, surprised that he hadn't objected to the plan already. "I know you can be stealthy when you need to be. You can keep an eye on the angel while staying out of sight, can't you? Just to see where it goes?"

Milo squirmed a little. "Yeah, I guess so."

"Good," I said, and turned back to Hannah. "So Milo finds out where the angel hides, and we all go after it. Once we get it alone, you and I are more than capable of creating a Circle, aren't we?"

Hannah bit her lip, but conceded with a nod.

"Finn knows how to control a Circle, it's Novitiate-level stuff. If the angel gets too feisty, he can expel it. Isn't that true, Finn?"

Finn nodded. "Yes. I can definitely handle that."

"And, if we succeed in Unmasking the angel, Finn already knows

266

how to seal that Circle to contain it. If a seal isn't strong enough to hold it, we can Cage it. Remember, we read all about Cagings—they're much simpler than Uncagings. And you and I are probably the only Durupinen on this continent who have experience with either one."

"I don't like Cagings," Hannah said warily.

"I don't like them either," I agreed. "And maybe we won't have to use one, but we do have that option as a last resort. So why don't we just end this, for everyone's sake? And yes, I'll be protected. Between Finn's instructions on how to break me out of a Psychic Habitation, plus the Casting to take away my Muse abilities, I'll be at least as safe as the rest of you. Then we can go home and let the other Trackers clean up the mess."

"Ugh, I hate it when you're right and I'm forced to agree with you," Milo groaned. "It takes all the fun out of my afterlife."

Finn sighed, but his face looked determined. "Right, then. Let's give it a go. But on one condition: If things get out of hand and I give the order to abort, everyone complies, no questions asked."

I bristled at *order* and *comply*, but it was a knee-jerk reaction. I knew Finn wasn't really trying to wield control, he was just trying to keep us safe; he was doing all he could to minimize what was a potentially a very real threat to our lives. I could get behind that. I trusted him, and I trusted his judgment. Now more than ever.

"No questions asked," I said quietly. Hannah and Milo both stared at me, but then hastily agreed as well.

"We haven't much time," Finn said. "Jess, I'm sure Fiona has already emailed the instructions for blocking your Muse abilities. Take care of that first, so we know you're safe. And then we'll start planning."

22

THE ESCAPE ARTIST

OUR COMMUNICATION SESSION WAS TO BE HELD, once again, in the drawing room, and I could only hope the staff had cleaned up the shards of glass from yesterday's explosion well. From the blurb on the schedule, it sounded as though there would be at least a few other guests sharing the session with us, although we had no idea who these guests would be.

Before going downstairs, we decided to send Milo on a search for Campbell. Milo reported back immediately: Campbell, sans angel, was on the porch, mingling with the guests at breakfast. Much to my stomach's dismay, we then all agreed to forego breakfast so that we could investigate the drawing room before the session for Group A began. Milo agreed to keep an eye on Campbell while we investigated.

Hannah, Finn, and I split up, each taking a different route to the drawing room. The hallways were deserted; those guests not at breakfast were sleeping in—and likely nursing their hangovers. We each arrived at the entrance to the drawing room without being seen or stopped by anyone. Finn tried the handles, but the French doors were locked.

Finn pressed his ear to the door and listened intently for a few moments. "Empty," he declared, as he began digging into his pocket. "How much time do we have?"

"Twenty minutes," I said, bouncing nervously on the balls of my feet. "But I guarantee people will be lining up at the door before that."

Finn grunted in agreement, then began picking the lock with the instruments he'd extracted from his pocket. I opened up my mouth in surprise, but closed it again as I remembered that Finn—always a prepared Caomhnóir—routinely carried a lock-picking kit. In a matter of seconds, a clicking sound came from the keyhole; Finn pushed the French doors open.

"Right," he said, turning swiftly to us. "I'll get the Circle set up. Get a seat on that settee right there, because that will put you within the Circle itself. If Campbell leaves, and the angel remains behind, we'll Unmask it right there. If it leaves before Campbell does, Milo will follow it to wherever it's hiding out; we'll set up a Circle there later."

My heart was thudding like a bass drum. "Got it. What about the other people in the room?"

"Try to get them to shove off as soon as possible. They won't know what's happening, but they might sense something if the angel gets spooked," Finn answered. "Right. I'm going in. Stall the guests for as long as you can. If anyone starts approaching these doors before I've re-joined you, you know what to do."

"Start calling out loudly for Milo!" Hannah said, as if she were answering a game show question.

"Precisely. Here we go, then," said Finn.

"Good luck..." I whispered, as he slipped through the door and closed it behind him.

Hannah and I immediately trained our eyes on the grandfather clock in the nearby corner, watching the seconds stretch agonizingly into minutes. Only seven of those minutes had actually managed to tick by when we heard footsteps behind us.

Marigold, donning a headscarf and an oversized pair of sunglasses as though in homage to Jackie O., was approaching us. As we watched her come closer, she stopped and put a hand out on either side as though to steady herself. Hers was a particularly vicious hangover—I knew the signs well, thanks to my mother's own drinking. I was surprised Marigold had even made it out of bed; perhaps she was more determined to communicate with Harold than I'd realized.

I also recognized the signs of imminent hyperventilation within myself. "Oh God, please," I thought. "Please tell me she was too smashed to remember seeing Finn and me last night!" The last thing I needed now was trouble from the Council, or Seamus, but it was Milo's guaranteed snickering that I dreaded the most.

"Good morning, sunshines," Marigold said as she arrived beside us, clutching a water bottle for dear life. "You're in the first session this morning?"

270

"Yes, we sure are!" Hannah said in an unnaturally loud voice, which had the dual effect of making Marigold wince and alerting Finn to Marigold's having joined us outside of the room.

"Whoa there sugar!" Marigold said, putting a hand to her head as though trying to keep it from tumbling off her neck. "Could I trouble you to kick it down a notch? Mama had just a bit too much to drink last night."

"A bit? A bit!" cried Harold, who had appeared at Marigold's side quite suddenly; it was all Hannah and I could do to keep from jumping back in surprise. He was very focused on his wife, though, and paid us no attention. "Woman, if you'd drunk any more, you could've bled into a whiskey barrel and sold it for profit! What in tarnation's the matter with you?"

"Sorry about that," said Hannah, with her voice lowered to just above a whisper.

"Not as sorry as I am," Marigold muttered. "I'm a gold mine of regret right now, I'll tell you that much."

"I've got some Tylenol in my bag here somewhere, if you want some," I offered.

Marigold shook her head and instantly regretted it. "Thank you kindly, but I've already had enough painkillers to take down a horse. I might add that so far they've done diddly-squat." She paused and squinted at me through her tinted lenses. "Didn't I see you last night?"

"Of course," I said, as offhandedly as I could. "At dinner. I'm pretty sure you sang a whole verse of 'Don't Rain on My Parade' to me."

Marigold made a sound halfway between a groan and a laugh. "Oh, good, Goldie came out to play. She's my lounge-singer persona. Haven't seen her in a while."

"Wish I could say the same!" Harold barked.

Marigold made a movement as though to reach toward the door. I stepped in front of her. "It's still locked, we just tried it." To stall her further, I asked, "Do you know if anyone else is going to be in this session?"

Marigold dropped her hand to her side again. "I've got no idea. *I* almost wasn't in this session. I don't know what he calls this ungodly hour, but I'm going to complain," she replied.

"Good! Complain! Get good and riled—then send yourself packing before you ruin everything I built for us!" Harold cried.

There was a genuine note of desperation in his voice now. I wanted so badly to put him at ease, to tell him that we were going to break the hold this place had on Marigold and end things once and for all. But that wasn't an option; I had to satisfy myself with the knowledge that Harold wouldn't have to suffer much longer.

Two more figures rounded the corner. Campbell and Talia walked side by side, deep in conversation. Campbell gesticulated supplicatingly, while Talia kept her arms folded tightly across her chest.

Two figures? No—make that three figures.

Several paces behind Talia was Grayson, whose eyes still blazed with anger. Thank goodness I was accustomed to hiding my reactions to spirits, or else my jaw surely would've hit the floor. I didn't think it was possible for Grayson to be any angrier than he was yesterday, but the fire in his eyes was even fiercer today.

I nudged Hannah subtly with my elbow. She followed my gaze and audibly gasped at the sight of Grayson, but luckily the sound of footsteps approaching from the other side had caught Marigold's attention; she had turned away from us and had noticed nothing.

Campbell spotted us; he instantly transformed his troubled face into a winning smile. Talia, despite being a celebrated actor, felt no such need to put on a show—she looked defensive and miserable as they came to a stop beside us.

"Good morning, ladies!" Campbell said, and although his tone and expression were bright, the bags under his eyes were more pronounced than ever. He had also apparently nicked himself shaving; a tiny round adhesive bandage was tucked discreetly at the corner of his jaw, just under his left ear.

"Good morning," we all said together.

"Are you feeling alright, Mr. Campbell? No offense, but you look like you barely got a wink of sleep," I said.

Campbell chuckled. "In my younger days I might've been insulted by that remark, but you just happen to be correct. I'm so over the moon about the new plans for Whispering Seraph that I was up most of the night working! But don't you trouble yourself about me. I'll take a nice long nap this afternoon, when the communication sessions are over for the day. And..." he waggled a finger at me, "I really must insist you call me Jeremiah."

"Right. Jeremiah," I replied.

"Are we waiting on anyone else, Jeremiah?" Marigold asked with an especially saccharine simper.

"No, this the entirety of our little gathering this morning. Aren't I a lucky man?" he said, oozing, as usual, with charm.

Harold muttered something; I didn't catch all of it, but the words "hunting rifle" were distinguishable. Then he shouted, "Just you try communicating with me now, you two-bit hustler!" and popped out.

Campbell, who—without the assistance of his angel—had heard none of this, was all gallantry as he unlocked the doors, which fortunately Finn had remembered to re-lock behind him. "Shall we go in ?"

"No!" Hannah cried loudly, making us all jump. Campbell stared at her in surprise. "I just, um... want to make sure that Milo is with us," she said sheepishly. Then she threw her head back and shouted, "Milo! Milo, are you there?" as though she were calling for a lost dog.

Campbell chuckled. "Ms. Taylor, I assure you there is no need to shout. Milo's presence was positively shining around you yesterday, I've no doubt he's ready for our little meeting."

"No harm in checking, though, right?" Hannah said, laughing as well—although her laugh was a bit hysterical.

"No, I don't suppose there is," Campbell said with a grin. He grabbed both of the French doors' handles and opened the doors widely.

For one heart-stopping moment, I was sure we'd see Finn cornered inside, with the makings of a Circle strewn around him; he'd barely had ten minutes to complete his task. The room, however, was completely empty—not a knickknack seemed out of place. Only the keenest of observers would've noticed that the settee had been pushed forward a few inches so that all four of its carved feet rested on the large Persian area rug; only a Durupinen might ever have suspected that there was now a Circle beneath that rug waiting to ensnare the angel.

As we followed Campbell into the room, a voice breathed in my ear, "I'm here. It's ready." I spun in shock to see Finn standing just behind me. He gave me a fleeting smile as he, very gently, brushed a finger along the inside of my wrist, melting away the better part of my anxiety.

"How did you get back here?" I whispered.

"Out the window and across the porch, then circled back behind you," he replied. "Now we need to see if the angel cooperates." I keenly felt the absence of Finn beside me as he broke away and took his place as my security guard against the wall by the door.

Hannah was trembling from head to foot as we sat ourselves on the settee. I grabbed her hand, willing her silently to keep a grip on herself. In the absence of the angel, I took a chance and reached out, as subtly as possible, to Milo though our connection. While it was true that we weren't supposed to communicate in this way when Campbell was around, I was also afraid one of the other spirits might somehow pick up on it; our Masking bracelets had a limited lifespan, and I didn't want to push it.

"Hurry up!" I thought-spoke to Milo. "I don't know if you can feel her nerves through this connection, but Hannah needs you here."

Milo popped between us almost instantly. "Ask and ye shall receive!" he trilled. At the mere sight of Milo, I felt a tiny part of Hannah relax.

"Good. Now keep your freaking cool, because Grayson is here." I warned, before snapping our connection shut.

"What! What?" Milo asked aloud, looking around wildly. He sucked in his cheeks to show his cheekbones to their best advantage while simultaneously smoothing out his hair.

Luckily, Grayson only had eyes for Talia, who had sunk into the chair closest to the fireplace and was twisting her fingers together apprehensively. There was such agony in both of their faces that I had a hard time looking directly at either of them—which I guess was fortunate in a way, since I was supposed to be pretending that I couldn't see Grayson in the first place.

"Well, my friends, I think this new format will ensure that we are all a bit more protected from the more unpredictable aspects of the spirits," Campbell said. For the first time, I saw just the smallest hint of strain behind his smile. Was he nervous about communicating with the spirits after yesterday's events? Or maybe he was starting to realize that all was not as it should be?

Campbell had clearly decided to forego the theatrics this morning; I counted that as a small blessing. "And so, without further ado, let's get started, shall we?" he began. "Everyone take a deep breath, center yourselves, and tune into the person you so long to speak with. Consider any lingering questions that you want

274

to ask, or any unresolved feelings you want to express. This is your time to find what you need. Open yourselves up."

A dry sob escaped Talia. Grayson reached a hand longingly toward her shoulder, but then closed it into a fist, which he then brought up to his temple as though he wanted to beat himself with it. With a roar of frustration, Grayson blinked out of view; he reappeared a moment later in the corner, as far from Talia as he could manage without actually leaving the room.

Why was Grayson following Talia everywhere, but then disengaging at the very moment Campbell offered to communicate? It didn't make any sense. Had the angel been singling him out in some way? Grayson was clearly angry, but was he also afraid?

Meanwhile, Campbell's own eyes were closed, and his arms were open wide as he readied himself to receive his angel. In his reverence, there was something almost desperate on his face; it was as disturbing to witness as Grayson's misery. For the first time, I felt something like pity for Jeremiah Campbell: We were fairly certain by now that he was as much of a victim as anyone else here.

I felt the angel before I saw it. A wave of dizziness swept over me, blurring my vision. Hannah tensed beside me, and I knew she felt it, too. Through squinted eyes, I looked around the room for the first signs of the angel's arrival, and spotted a fog seeping up from a crack in the floorboards near the fireplace.

Something in my head clicked. I whipped my head around, making myself even dizzier in the process, and looked at Finn. "The basement," I mouthed.

His eyes widened and he nodded. This had to be why the basement was Warded and padlocked. It wasn't a storage space, it was the angel's lair.

Foggy tentacles snaked across the floor, wrapping sinuously around each other until they formed a single, undulating mass. Now that I knew I was looking at a concealment Casting, I realized that the cloud form had several layers, one inside the other, with the outer layers serving to obscure the inner ones. I couldn't make out any more than that, though—each time I attempted to focus on any one part of the angel, a throb of pain shot through my head or stung my eyes.

I ignored the pain as best I could, and watched as the angel approached the center of the room. With my Muse abilities now blocked, the angel gave no sign of recognizing me after last night's Psychic Habitation. I was thankful for that, but my anticipation was mounting by the second. Any moment now, the angel would cross into the Circle Finn had chalked beneath the rug; once it was inside the Circle, we could hold it there.

"Come on, now, you creepy bastard, just a bit farther," I heard Milo murmur. Out of the corner of my eye, I could see Finn on red alert, practically coiled like a jungle cat about to pounce; he'd readied himself to expel the angel at the slightest provocation.

The upper part of the angel's cloud form morphed into a nearly human shape as it drifted toward Campbell, preparing, I assumed, to curl itself around Campbell's shoulders and whisper the words of the dead into his ear. But just as it reached him, the angel came level with the edge of the rug, resting one of its tentacles across the Persian design. There it stopped, perhaps sensing the Casting, but even one stray tentacle was enough: The angel was in the Circle.

§

A deafening, inhuman, agonized screeching assaulted our ears. Everyone, including Talia and Marigold, flung their hands up over their ears desperately. The angel, caterwauling wildly, contracted its pulsing black smoke violently, like an injured spider curling in on itself.

Campbell's eyes flew open and he gazed around wildly. "What? What is it? My angel, what's wrong?" His panic became instantly palpable.

The screams renewed, and within them, individual phrases became nearly intelligible. But even though I pulled my hands away from my ears, I couldn't distinguish a single word.

The angel's words were clear enough to Campbell, though; he shouted in reply, "Trap you? What do you mean? I would never trap you!"

The shrieking rose in a fevered crescendo. Trying to lift the area rug, the angel shot a tentacle of smoke outward, sending the coffee table toppling. Then the creature rolled itself up protectively, like a giant scroll.

Finn's chalked Circle, slightly smudged from the movement of the rug, lay exposed for all to see. When the coffee table had overturned, Marigold and Talia had scrambled into to a corner in desperation. Although neither woman knew it, Grayson was hovering in front Talia as if ready to fight the angel himself, and Harold—having popped into the room when the shrieking began—was now cradling Marigold as she cowered. Campbell himself was shaking his head wildly, lost somewhere between sheer panic and utter bewilderment.

"I swear to you, my angel," he cried, almost sobbing, "I don't know what's under that rug! I've never seen it before! Please, you must believe me!" He reached toward the angel with a supplicating gesture as he fell to his knees, genuinely begging.

The angel shook. It writhed. It thrashed. Its screams grew increasingly desperate. The temperature in the room plummeted, and Hannah and I could feel the tension mounting in the air's energy, like a sudden shift in barometric pressure. Milo felt it too; he threw his arms over his head as if signaling for us to duck. But before we could even begin to think about what to do next, the angel exploded outward, transforming into a violent shock wave of pure negative energy.

The room became a chaotic whirl. Talia, Marigold, and even Campbell himself screamed as books toppled from the shelves, furniture overturned, and the mirror above the mantle fell to the floor and cracked in its frame. Hannah and I toppled backward across the floor as the settee was blown out from beneath us.

I felt it happen as I slammed into the wall; the force of the blow knocked the Masking bracelet from my wrist, throwing it across the floor. Instantly, a familiar tingling began to flow through my veins, and I knew my Gateway was exposed. Harold looked up as if he'd sensed yet another change in the room's energy, but it was clear he hadn't recognized my Gateway; he curled himself even more tightly around Marigold, bracing for another explosion. Grayson however, like a predator scenting a kill, whirled around and stared straight at me. And I stared straight back at him.

"Finn, my bracelet! Expel him now!" I cried.

But Finn had seen what happened. He was already tossing the bracelet back to me, and mere seconds later, Grayson was propelled through the wall with incredible force.

I hastily jammed the bracelet onto my wrist and scrambled to a kneeling position just in time to see the last vestiges of the angel—reformed now into its usual cloud of smoke—squeeze itself through the floorboards and out of sight.

"Milo! Follow it!" Hannah cried through our connection.

"I'm on it!" Milo cried as he shook himself out of his own shock. Faster than I've ever seen him move, he slipped down through the fireplace.

Why hadn't our trap worked? How had the angel conjured enough energy to break the Circle's seal? And did it sense the Gateway, just as Grayson had? Was our cover now completely blown?

Meanwhile, Talia, Marigold, and Campbell were picking themselves up off of the floor. Thankfully, they remained oblivious to Grayson's detecting my Gateway, but there were still plenty of questions to be answered. And Hannah and I had to remember to play along.

"What in the world?" Campbell gasped, placing his hands over his ears again as though the cries of the angel were still echoing in his head. "My angel, are you alright? Where are you? What's happened?"

"I heard it! Actually heard it! Screaming—fit to be tied!" Marigold cried excitedly, as her eyes darted around the room. "Oh my word, did y'all hear that?" I think the shock of it all—and the accompanying adrenaline rush—had cured her hangover.

"Of course we heard it!" Talia replied in a shaking voice. "Everyone within a mile must've heard it!" As she said it, I realized I was surprised that Campbell's security hadn't come rushing into the room.

"That was the angel screaming, wasn't it?" Marigold asked Campbell. Now that the initial shock was over, she was back in her seat, alight with eager curiosity—as if everything we'd just experienced was an exciting, amusement-park attraction. "Is it still here? Jeremiah, can you still see it?"

"No, it's gone!" Campbell replied as he began searching the room, almost as though he might find the angel crouching behind a chair. "I don't understand! We were nearly fully connected—I could feel it. But then the screaming started, and... it vanished!" Campbell sounded close to tears.

That cinched it: Campbell was indeed a pawn. His shock, confusion, and desperation were real; not even the best of actors could fake the swirling, colliding emotions now reflected on his face.

Campbell walked toward the middle of the room, but stopped

several feet short of the Circle, clearly too nervous to approach it further. Every eye was now drawn to the Circle.

"What is it, Jeremiah?" Marigold asked in a whisper.

"I have no idea," Campbell said. "It looks like witchcraft or Devil worship!"

Judging by Campbell's horrified fascination as he stared at the Circle, it seemed as if he thought Satan had just materialized in our midst, complete with a pitchfork and cloven hooves. Even with my nerves stretched as taut as bowstrings, I was still able to register my annoyance at the quintessentially ignorant reaction that some people had to anything even remotely pagan.

Hannah, in an effort to cover our asses, chimed in. "Who do you think put it there, Mr. Campbell? Could one of the staff have done it?"

With his characteristic smoothness now decimated, Campbell opened and closed his mouth repeatedly, unable to answer. He had no reassuring smile for us, no flawlessly prepared speech to put us at ease. He was now a flustered, terrified man who'd finally come to realize that he was entrenched in something more complicated—and malevolent—than he'd ever suspected.

"I don't know, but I think... I think we'd better stay away from it, whatever it is," Campbell said at last. "No one go near it. I'm going to have the staff seal off this room until we know what these markings are and how they got here. I must find my angel. I'm canceling all further communication sessions until we get to the bottom of this."

Without another word to us, Campbell staggered from the room, giving the Circle a wide berth as he walked away. He barked instructions to a bewildered Maya, who had just appeared in the hallway with a walkie-talkie in her hand, ready to call security.

"Well, that was certainly an adventure wasn't it?" Marigold said enthusiastically, standing up. I gave her a cursory smile in return, but my real attention was on Talia, who—with her eyes full of tears—was now slipping out the door onto the porch. As she closed the door, Grayson appeared beside her. As I watched him hovering protectively, he turned and stared at me again.

Finn appeared beside me. "Let's go. We need to follow Campbell and see where he goes."

"You and Hannah will have to do it," I said. "I've got some damage control to do with Grayson and Talia."

"But that's not in the plan. We need—"

"Finn, I've got to do it now," I said, cutting him off. "Right away. If Grayson starts following me around or telling the other spirits about me, we're screwed."

"We're screwed already!" Finn hissed. "Perhaps you missed it, but the angel now knows the Durupinen are trying to trap it."

I scowled. "Don't be sarcastic with me. This is important, too."

Finn looked like he wanted to argue further, but he pressed his lips together and took a deep breath through his nose. "Fine. Hannah and I will follow Campbell. Just... be quick about it."

"I will." I squeezed his hand surreptitiously before following Talia outside. I didn't know what, exactly, I could do to help her, and I didn't know how I was going to calm a spirit as angry as Grayson, but I had to try. The angel would just have to wait; not everything in life was about the Durupinen.

23

FORBIDDEN MELDINGS

A S I WALKED ONTO THE PORCH, I knew who I would see before I even turned around. Grayson was standing just behind me, and I didn't need to be an Empath to keenly feel the pain radiating off of him like heat.

"You can see me," he said curtly, without preamble. There was a frustrated anger in his voice, but it wasn't directed at me.

"Yes," I whispered, giving him a conspiratorial nod. Grayson understood.

I leaned myself on the porch's railing and scanned the area. At this early hour all seemed deserted, but I wasn't taking any chances—I couldn't be seen talking to thin air. I walked over to the corner of the porch, which was out of direct sight for anyone in the house, and faced the lawn. Anyone who happened to catch a glimpse of me from behind would think I was just taking in the morning's beauty.

I subtly motioned for Grayson to follow. He came to rest directly in front of me, floating above the lawn. "That's why you rescued her from the pond. You heard me that night—heard everything I said, understood all of it."

"Yes. Every word," I answered, as reassuringly as I could.

"And you... there's something else. You can send me... home."

"Yes, I can. And I will... if that's what you want."

I could almost see Grayson's collision of conflicting emotions; for an instant this confusion threatened to tear him apart. But then he swallowed those feelings and set his face with determination. "You've got to help me first. Talia. I have to explain to her."

"I'll try to help you, but you need to promise not to give me away. I can't let the other spirits know what I am yet. It's not time."

Grayson didn't ask questions or argue. He simply nodded and said, "Whatever you need—just, please... please help me."

"We also need to be quick. Campbell's angel now knows my friends are here—we might not have a lot of time left to stop it. That has to be my priority, do you understand?"

Grayson nodded in assent. "I don't know what that thing is," he said, "but it's no angel."

"I know," I replied, as much to Grayson as myself.

"Will you come with me?" Grayson pleaded. "Talia is alone now."

We set off across the lawn, with Grayson leading the way. He led me right to Talia, who was sitting on a bench by the edge of the pond. Her agonized face was red and swollen from crying. She looked up and saw me standing there—apparently all alone—and laughed aloud.

"Wow. Why is it always you who finds me when I'm losing it? You must think I'm unhinged," Talia said, wiping more tears from her eyes; it was a futile effort, though—her eyes just kept filling right back up again. "Am I confirming all of your suspicions about how screwed up Hollywood people are?"

"No, of course not. I just came to see if you were alright," I said quietly.

She gestured to her face with a wry half-smile. "I'm most definitely not alright, and I'm tired of pretending that I am. Have you ever had one of those days when... when it's like every painful emotion you've ever had is pressing itself right up against you from the inside? Where it's so bad that if someone brushes against you or looks at you the wrong way, you'll just go to absolute pieces?" She paused, trying, once again, to dry her eyes. "God, you probably have no idea what I'm talking about."

"Actually I know exactly what you're talking about," I said, very truthfully. You see this tattoo?" I asked, pulling my short-sleeve blouse all the way up to my shoulder. "It represents a whole year of my life filled with nothing but days like that. We all have them. It's called being human—and it's allowed, you know."

As if Talia had been waiting for someone to give her permission to be "human," something in her eyes softened gratefully in relief. "I never really used to be this emotional," she began, "which you might think is weird for an actor. We're supposed to have all that raw emotion right in our back pockets, ready to exploit when the cameras start rolling."

"Yeah, I've always heard that the best actors are pretty screwed up in real life," I said.

She laughed again. "I was always remarkably unscrewed up for an actor. Until recently."

Grayson let out a soft moan of agony. I shot him a look which I hoped conveyed both "I'm sorry" and "be quiet" at the same time.

"If it makes you feel any better, I was remarkably screwed up from the beginning. Maybe I missed my calling," I offered.

"We could... trade," Talia said. "You can do the acting thing and I'll... sorry, I have no idea what you do."

I smiled grimly. "Stick to acting. Trust me."

Talia wiped at her eyes again. "I never should've come here."

"Is it okay if I sit down?" I asked.

She nodded and scooted over on the bench to give me room. The morning sunlight sparkled cheerfully off the water. It was much easier to look at the pond's glimmering beauty than at each other, even though the water's very brightness seemed to be mocking us.

"Why did you come here?" I blurted out suddenly. "Sorry... that came out wrong. We're all here for the same reason. What I meant was, how did you find out about Campbell?"

Talia hesitated a moment, then began, "He was at a party I attended. It was the first time I'd been out since... in a while. I didn't even want to be there, but my friend dragged me. She swore I'd start feeling more like a human if I started doing human things again, which was a goddamned lie. Instead, I got wasted off two glasses of champagne because I hadn't really eaten in days. And then I accidentally locked myself out on a balcony."

I grimaced. "So, as first outings go, not very successful." My grimace was real; a pang of guilt had shot through me. Building intimacy on the basis of my lies was no way to start a relationship. I could only hope that she'd forgive me.

"Couldn't really have gone worse," said Talia. "I was just about to start banging on the window and shouting for help when Jeremiah came out. He opened the door and said, 'I'm terribly sorry, do you two want to be alone?'"

I faked a shiver. I didn't know how else to respond—all I could manage to say was a vague, "Oh?"

"Yeah," she said, shaking her head. "I was creeped out too. I remember looking around and asking, 'What are you talking about? It's just me out here.' Then Jeremiah got all flustered and started apologizing. Looking back on it, I wonder if it was all an act—if he was setting me up. At the time, though, I was too desperate for... too desperate to consider that possibility. I guess that's how Campbell reels people in."

"He certainly finds people at their most vulnerable moments, that's for sure. I don't think he's trying to hurt us, though, if that's any consolation."

"I don't know. Maybe he is, maybe he isn't," she said, shrugging. "He's either a far better actor than I am, or he really believes in what he's doing." She took a deep breath and stared the at the pond for a moment. "Anyway, Jeremiah told me that... that Grayson was here with me." Talia's voice caught on Grayson's name, and I wondered if it was the first time she'd spoken it out loud since he'd died—other than to the paparazzi, of course. "He told me Grayson was sending me a message—that he was so sorry for leaving me, and that he wanted me to keep the ring. It's a family heirloom, the ring he gave me. The family wanted me to give it back, but Campbell told me Grayson wanted me to keep it." She ran a finger along the chain around her neck; I knew the ring lay concealed in the folds of her shirt. "Campbell left then, but I was too overwhelmed to follow him. But when I sobered up, I was desperate to talk with Grayson. I had so much I needed to say."

Grayson made another sound, like he wanted to speak. I made the tiniest of gestures by my side, instructing him to wait.

"Jess!" Milo's voice, along with a tidal wave of nervous energy, broke through our connection. "I could only follow as far as the fireplace down here, the rest of the basement is Warded—I need one of you with me to go any further." Milo groaned in frustration; he hated being held back by Wards. "But listen, when Finn and Hannah followed Campbell, he headed straight for the door Kyle showed you—then locked it behind him! And from what I can see down here, there's no sign of the angel. But I did see Campbell go into a room. He's holed himself up in there!"

"Okay, just give me a few minutes here," I thought-spoke back to him, attempting at the same time to send a calming energy to him. "And try to center yourself, you'll give me an aneurysm bursting through the connection like that."

"Girl, you are *not* telling me to calm down right now!" Milo cried. "I'm telling you the angel is missing and Campbell is locked in that base—"

"And I'm telling you I will be right there!" I replied firmly, and pushed him out of my head. I tried to refocus on Talia.

"...had my agent track Campbell down, and I came here. I was sure closure with Grayson would help me move on, but he's not communicating with me anymore. Jeremiah insists that he's here, that he's listening, but Grayson won't speak to me. I just don't understand why he'd..." Talia couldn't finish; she dissolved into tears again.

"Because that man is using us!" Grayson shouted, unable to contain himself any longer. "I let him and that black angel speak for me because I wanted to say good-bye—but I didn't think Talia would remember it in the morning, because she was so drunk. So I decided to stay, to try again. But now—"

I turned to Grayson and muttered as quietly as I could, "Wait. Please."

But I hadn't been quiet enough. Talia looked at me, confused. "Who are you talking to?"

I took a deep breath. Apparently, I was shit at undercover work; I'd already revealed myself to Kyle and Grayson, and now I had to tell Talia the truth, too. That she deserved to know the truth was only a small comfort.

"Talia, I don't have a lot of time here, so I'm just going to come right out with it. I'm not here at Whispering Seraph because I lost someone I love. I'm here because I can see and speak with the spirits."

"You... what?" Talia asked; her face went perfectly blank, as if I'd suddenly started speaking another language.

"My sister and I... we can both see ghosts. In fact, we help them to Cross over when they're stuck here."

Talia frowned at me, her mouth pulling itself into a tight knot of anger. "If this is a joke, it's a terrible one."

"I'm not joking," I said. "Believe me, I frequently wish it wasn't true. But the fact is, my sister and I are here to take Campbell down. When we heard about the Sanctuary at Whispering Seraph, we thought Campbell was probably a scam artist preying on people." I paused for a moment, wanting to tell her more but knowing I couldn't. "There's... more to it than that, but basically, that's why we're here."

I'm not sure why she believed me, but I saw my truth light up in Talia's eyes. I went on before she could ask me the hundreds of questions she was surely formulating.

"As you can probably tell from that session, things are falling apart here—I may not have another chance to do this with you. Grayson is here with us, right now, and he can hear you."

Talia shook her head at me. "No, he isn't."

"Yes, he is. He came here with you. He's the one who told me you needed help in the pond—that's why I went in after you. He's been following you, keeping an eye on you, but he's been staying hidden during the communication sessions."

"Why? Why would he hide when he knows how desperately I want to talk to him?" Talia whispered. She was scanning the empty air around us, aching for a glimpse of Grayson.

"He was afraid Campbell was taking advantage of you—and using him to do it," I told her. "Is that right?" I added over my shoulder to Grayson. Talia stared wildly at what appeared to her to be nothing but air.

Now that he was finally getting a chance to speak to Talia directly, Grayson seemed almost unable to form the words. "Yes!" he finally gasped. "It's not that I didn't want to talk to her! God no! It's Campbell! The way he manipulates what we say, leaving people wanting more. He practically traps his clients—and their wallets—here!"

I relayed this to Talia, who dropped her face into her hands. "I should've known better than to come here. I *did* know better. But I was so desperate!"

"And I never should've let him say good-bye for me on that balcony," said Grayson. "Because Campbell doesn't let people say good-bye."

I told Talia this, and she heaved a huge, shuddering sigh. "And that's why people stay! They never really want to say good-bye, and Campbell makes sure they never do."

"Jess!" Milo called again, breaking through my mental block. "I am not messing around here, you've got to get inside! The staff is coming around, ordering everyone into their rooms. The place is going into lockdown!"

"Okay, okay!" I said to Milo, and then turned back to Talia. "Look, I'm not supposed to do this, but I need to get back to my sister. I don't know how well this will work, or for how long—maybe only a few minutes. But it should be enough to say good-bye. Grayson, come over here."

Looking puzzled, Grayson floated over so that he stood just over my shoulder. I extracted a pen from my purse and grabbed Talia's wrist.

"What are you doing?" she whispered, with an expression on her face that was at once bewilderment, concern, and hope.

I muttered the words to the Melding as quickly and quietly as I could, while drawing the necessary runes onto Talia's hand. I felt a gentle dissipating, a lifting of the limits of human sight. Then I heard Talia gasp, and I knew the Melding had worked.

"Is... is that him? I think that's him!" Talia said. She was squinting at the place where Grayson stood.

"Yes! It's me! You can see me!" Grayson cried, floating closer so that he was kneeling before her, a supplicant on his knees.

"I can hear him!" Talia sobbed. "It's so faint. He sounds so far away."

"That's because he *is* far away," I said gently. "You belong in two different worlds now. I could forge a clearer connection if I knew you both better. But I know something about good-byes and losing someone you love, and that was just enough for me to connect you, I guess."

"Oh God, thank you!" Talia whispered. "Thank you so much!"

"I'll leave you two alone. Don't waste this time. Say what you need to say before the connection fades, and let each other go—or you'll never be able to move on, either of you."

I didn't know what Talia and Grayson needed to say to each other—and I didn't want to know, either. The moment was only for the two of them, and I respected that. I knew too well that some moments in life are almost unbearably intimate, and, for Talia and Grayson, this was one of them. I walked—and then ran—away before the sheer humanity of it all could overwhelm me.

§

A state of hysteria awaited me in the lobby. Angry and frightened guests were grouped around staff members, loudly demanding to be told what was happening.

"I refuse to be sent to my room without being told exactly what's going on!" Tom Owens shouted. "We're paying good money to be here—and I won't be kept in the dark."

"Sir, please try to keep calm," a security guard replied. "We are simply dealing with a situation. It would make our job easier if—"

"You think I give a good goddamn about what makes your job easier? I demand—"

Marigold's voice overtook Tom's. "Where's Jeremiah? Y'all get him out here right now. He won't stand for this! Imagine being treated in such a manner!" The flustered young waitress Marigold was shouting at turned even paler as another voice rose above the commotion.

"Is there an intruder? I heard someone say there was an intruder!" a frightened voice called.

"Sir, there is no intru—"

"We were guaranteed a communication session today!" shrieked another woman. "You can't cancel it! I need to speak to my sister!"

"Have our things sent down! I'm calling my lawyer right now!" a man barked at Maya, who looked close to tears as she tried to manage the chaos.

In the commotion, no one noticed me quietly skirting along the lobby's perimeter. I slipped down the corridor behind the staircase, then ran the entire length of the deserted hall. I flew around the corner, where I found Finn, Hannah, and Milo huddled around the basement door.

"I'm here, I'm here!" I panted. "What's going on?"

"Finn picked the lock, and now Hannah's undoing the Wards before we go down. We want her to be able to Call reinforcements if we need them," Milo said.

"Any word from Catriona?" I asked Finn.

Finn shook his head grimly. "I reported the incident. She said the Trackers are on their way, but they're at least an hour out—and we can't wait that long to Unmask that angel. The angel could be gone by then, and we can't leave Campbell alone down there with it—assuming that the angel *is* down there. None of us have seen it since it got away from Milo." Finn turned to the door, examining Hannah's work, then asked me, "Everything go okay out there?"

"Yeah," I said. "I let them say good-bye. Grayson gave me his word that he won't blow our cover. Not that it matters at this point. If we're not totally exposed already, I think we're about to blow it wide open ourselves."

"We bloody well are," Finn said, with a whisper of a smile on his lips.

"Okay, I did it, I think," Hannah said, stepping away from the cellar door. "The Wards should be lifted now."

"That's it then," Finn said. "Let's go."

"Let's go?" Hannah cried, with a note of hysteria in her voice. "We're just going to go charging down there? Don't we need a plan?"

"Under ideal circumstances, yes," Finn replied. "But we have no idea what we'll find down there. We'll just have to wing it."

"Winging it is my favorite kind of plan. I'd wing everything if I could," Milo said with a somewhat tense smile, injecting levity for Hannah's sake. She didn't seem to notice.

As I chuckled at Milo, something caught my eye. A tall cylindrical object, rolled up like an oversized scroll, was propped up against the wall beside Finn.

"What's that?" I asked Finn, pointing to it. "Is it yours?"

"It's a Circle," Finn replied, with a note of pride in his voice.

Genuinely baffled, and increasingly eager to go after the angel, my mouth refused any attempts at eloquence. "Huh?"

"It's a Circle. I got the idea when the angel pulled back the rug in the drawing room. When the rug was curled back, I noticed that the chalk had rubbed off on its underside, creating a second Circle. That rug was too big to take with me, so I nicked one of the yoga mats from the studio and Cast a Circle on it. This mat is a proper, portable Circle, and—"

"—and if we can get the angel cornered somewhere, we can slide the mat under it and boom! We'll seal it in the Circle!" I finished for him. "Finn... that's one of the most brilliant ideas I've ever heard."

Finn smiled at me. "Thank you. Don't be bothered, I won't let this go to my head."

"Well, grab that Circle and let's get this over with," I said. And, with much more confidence than I felt, I flung open the basement door.

24

WHISPERS OF THE WALKER

A SHARP, BESTIAL GRUNTING. A dull, muffled scraping. A clatter and a thud.

These sounds began drifting up the stairs before we'd even started our descent. Then came the words—words that, as we reached the bottom of the steps, I knew were definitely not in English.

Someone had jammed a single torch into a bracket on the wall at the base of the staircase. It was by this wavering light that we crept, single-file, down a long, dirt-floored passageway.

"Is that someone talking?" whispered Hannah, as we approached the gaping, black-mouthed doorway at the end of the passage.

"Yes," Finn answered. "It sounds like Campbell, doesn't it?"

We all stopped and listened. The voice did indeed have the same tone and timbre as Campbell's, but there was something different about it, too. It had none of Campbell's smooth and sultry Southernness; it sounded harsh.

"Is that... Russian?" I asked, as Campbell's voice floated toward us again.

Finn nodded. "Or something like it. Definitely Eastern European. Come on."

With Finn in the lead, we slid along the wall single-file until we reached the doorway; it opened into a perfectly round stone chamber covered in runes. By the light of several more torches, we found Campbell—his bare torso dripping with sweat and grime—hoisting large stones onto a dais at the very center of the room. He stacked the stones into piles, carefully troweling mortar in between each layer, working to create two tall pillars. As he stacked the stones, a steady stream of grunting and cursing in rapid Russian came from his lips. There was no sign of the angel anywhere, but suddenly the deep bags under Campbell's eyes made perfect sense.

"Where's the angel?" I whispered.

"I can't be wholly sure, but possibly it's... that is, perhaps it's..." Finn began. He cut himself off mid-sentence, changing course. "Do you think it likely someone of Campbell's background speaks Russian? Fluent, proper, Russian?"

"A real estate guy from North Carolina? Not likely, no," I replied. Suddenly, my brain put the pieces together. "The angel! It's the one speaking Russian. It's Habitating in him right now, isn't it?" A small whimper of dread escaped Hannah as I spoke.

Finn nodded. "I think it must be. It's using him to do... whatever it is he's doing in there."

"Yeah, and on that topic, what the hell *is* he doing?" Milo asked.

"I don't know," I replied in the merest whisper. "Building something, it looks like."

"Or rebuilding something," Finn said. "Those stones look quite old."

Hannah clapped a hand over her mouth in horror as she realized what Campbell was building. Then she pulled her hand away from her mouth and hissed, "It's a Geatgrima!"

We all turned back to Campbell. Now that Hannah had figured out what he was building, I couldn't believe we hadn't recognized it immediately.

Finn motioned for us to retreat further back into the passage. Not until we reached the foot of the stairs did Hannah ask, "But how? How can there be a Geatgrima here?"

The only Geatgrima I'd ever seen was in Fairhaven's central courtyard. It was there that I had Walked into the world beyond the Gateway when we were fighting the Necromancers.

The words that next came from my mouth possibly constituted the understatement of the year. "This is bad, isn't it?"

"Yes, it's bad," Finn replied.

"But it's just a structure!" said Milo. "Campbell can't control it, can he?"

"*Geatgrimas* aren't just structures," Finn murmured. "Their locations are carefully chosen. There's always a link to inherent spirit activity—to places where the spirits congregate naturally. *Geatgrimas* are built to shore up and concentrate that energy, to attract the Fifth Element nearer to our realm. It's the closeness to the Aether itself that causes the immense pull and power coming from a *Geatgrima*."

My heart began racing again. "So that Geatgrima was here, hidden in the basement all this time?"

"It must've been, yes," Finn said. "I can't understand why the Trackers didn't know it was here! This is a Gateway incarnate; the Durupinen are the Gatekeepers. They're supposed to know the location of every single Geatgrima."

"They knew this plantation was an abandoned Durupinen stronghold," Hannah said. "They just didn't know why."

"But why didn't we sense it? We can feel the pull of the Fairhaven Geatgrima a mile away!" I said, as my panic mounted.

Finn gestured back down the passage. "Castings. You saw the runes in there. The Geatgrima has been hidden—just like the angel has been hiding behind its Masking. Hidden in plain sight, the pair of them."

And it's possible," began Hannah, thinking out loud, "that our Masking bracelets dampened our sensitivity to the Geatgrima, too. Maybe they Mask our Gateway from the Aether?"

"It's possible," I replied, as I began unclasping my bracelet.

"Don't Jess—not yet! Not until we've got a solid plan," cried Finn. Hannah shot me a look warning me not to argue.

I was about to object, but Milo cut in. "But it looks like that Geatgrima has been a pile of rubble until now. Maybe it was destroyed?" he asked, almost hopefully.

Finn shook his head. "You can destroy the structure, but its pull and power remain. And if the being who's controlling Campbell is rebuilding with the Geatgrima's original stones, there's a chance the Geatgrima will be fully active when he finishes putting it back together."

We all stared at each other for a moment, letting the horror of that possibility sink in. An unguarded Geatgrima, if it were active, could disrupt the entire Gateway system. And if someone or something were actively manipulating that Geatgrima for their own dark purposes, the consequences could be even more dire.

"So this has got to be the angel's endgame. It wants control of this Geatgrima."

Finn nodded. "I think so, yes."

"But what can the angel possibly do with it?" I asked. It can't control the Geatgrima... can it?"

Finn ran a jittery hand through his hair. "I have no bloody idea."

"No. Not again," said Hannah, with a fierce determination in her voice. "The last time we lost control of a Geatgrima, it was my fault. I'm not letting that happen again!"

Three years. Three years and my sister was still torturing herself. "We've been over this Hannah. It wasn't your fault. It was the Necroman—"

A resounding crash came echoing through the passage; Campbell's angry stream of rapid Russian followed immediately.

"Yes, we *will* put an end to this," Finn assured her. "But Hannah, I want you to stay here."

"What? No! I'm coming with you!" she hissed. "I'm not letting this happen again. I can help!"

"I know you can! That's exactly what I'm asking you to do." Finn explained. He put his hands on Hannah's shoulders and bent down; he looked straight into her eyes. "Stay right here and listen to what's happening. If we need help, you Call every spirit you can reach and get them in there. That room is under heavy Castings; we can't be sure you'll be able to Call if you get trapped in there with us."

Hannah swallowed. "Yeah. Okay, that makes sense."

"I'll stay here with you, sweetness," Milo told her, and then looked back at Finn. "That way no one is left unprotected. And Jess and I will leave our connection open."

Finn nodded. "Yes. Right then. Good plan. Jess, when we get in there, you distract the angel. I'll prepare to expel it from Campbell's body."

I squirmed. "Give me a chance to convince the angel to come out on its own first. Expelling that spirit would be painful for Campbell, and I don't want to hurt him if we can help it. The guy's already been through enough."

"Fair enough," Finn answered. "But if the angel won't cooperate, and quickly, then I'm going to expel it. Agreed?"

"Agreed."

"Good. Once the angel's left Campbell's body, we'll try to Unmask it. We won't know what our next step is until we know what that bloody thing actually is. You ready?"

I smiled broadly. "Absolutely not."

He smiled back before declaring, "Here we go. Once more unto the breach!"

I slipped into the chamber, keeping my back to the wall. Finn followed me, but crept along the wall in the other direction. He dropped to his knees behind a pile of rocks. He looked up, found my eyes, and gave one determined nod.

Campbell, bent low over a huge block of stone, had his back to me. "Hey, Mr. Campbell, this looks like fun. Can I help?" I asked. My voice was louder than I'd meant it to be; it filled the chamber with a barrage of echoes.

Campbell spun around and locked onto me. When he spoke, it was in his usual polite Southern drawl. "Ah, Ms. Taylor. I'm afraid I'm occupied at the moment with a little project. Perhaps you could come back another time?" He attempted a smile, but what surfaced on his face was far closer to a manic grin.

I shook my head. "Look, I'm not buying it. I don't know who I'm talking to, but I know it's not Jeremiah Campbell. I also know that you're no angel. Let Campbell go and show yourself!"

Campbell's face smiled at me again, but it was like no smile those features had ever worn before. It was a leering, wicked thing that made Campbell look less like himself than ever. The voice that next came from his mouth, however, left no room for doubt: I was not talking with Jeremiah Campbell. The angel was speaking now.

"I see. So you've found us out," said the being I was now speaking to. Its voice was bitter and full of pain, carrying vengeance in its very tone. "I can only assume you're the one who left the Circle for me beneath the rug?"

"Yes, that's right. Who are you?"

The being cocked Campbell's head back and let loose a self-satisfied cackle. "Do you honestly not know? I thought that was what brought you here in the first place. Surely fate hasn't thrown us together again by chance?"

I frowned. "Do we know each other?"

"I certainly didn't know *you* at first. This Mask makes me virtually invisible, but it also clouds my own perceptions. It's become hard to see the physical details of the living. And it's been so long—so, so long—since I've been in my own body. It wasn't until you revealed your Gateway that I realized who you were."

My mind was racing, trying to understand. With the countless amounts of weird shit I'd encountered since becoming a

Durupinen, I could barely fathom who, exactly, this could be. But if the angel knew me, I was going to use that to my advantage.

Out of the corner of my eye, I could see Finn twitching with anticipation. I made a subtle gesture at my side, signaling for him to wait. I just needed another moment more; the being would reveal its true self if I kept it talking—I was sure of that much.

"If we know each other, why the disguise? You've got nothing to hide anymore. We've found you. It's over. Reveal yourself and talk to me face-to-face."

"You've found me, good for you. But stopping me? No! You can't, not now." And here the being made Campbell heave another stone onto the *Geatgrima*. "But very well. I'll show myself. I confess I'm disappointed—I thought you'd recognize another like yourself."

My heart began to race even faster; my thoughts became a dervish. "Like me" how? A Durupinen? A twin? A Muse? What did this creature think we had in common? And why did it know me?

My mind came up blank. Finding my voice, I finally asked, "Another what?"

"Another Walker, Northern Girl."

The pit of my stomach jolted in shock. But before I could say another word, Campbell's body dropped to its knees and began to convulse. Then he threw his head forward and began to scream; from the gaping hole of his mouth, the smoky form of the angel poured like blood from a wound. It pooled on the floor and then rose, shedding its smoky screen, to reveal a form and a face that I knew well—although hadn't seen in more than three years.

"Hello, Irina." I managed to whisper. Watching Irina manifest left me so bewildered that I was surprised my mouth could form any words at all.

Irina smiled at me. "Hello, Northern Girl."

At the sight of her, my shock gave way to a profound sadness. "Irina, what are you still doing here... here, in the world of the living? When I saw you in the woods after the Necromancers attacked, you were free and happy. I thought your body died—I assumed you Crossed years ago."

Irina's face twitched, and her smile slid off. "That... didn't work out," she said vaguely.

"What do you mean?" I pressed. "That's not really an answer, Irina. Surely we know each other better than that."

"Alright Northern Girl, I will tell you. Like so many others, my body was wounded in the attack, yes, but my clan refused to let that body die. I kept waiting for the moment when I'd feel the connection let go, but they treated me, healed my body. I remain connected to that body—that cage—like a weight I must drag around with me!"

Trying to make sense of what I was hearing, I replied, "But I thought you were happy when you were Walking? When I first met you, all you wanted in the world was freedom from your body. Aren't you content to remain in this form, Walking?"

"There was a time when that was true, Northern Girl. But the Durupinen have destroyed even that joy for me. After the attack, my body was hovering so close to death that I felt it anew: The call, the pull of the Gateway. Far stronger than ever before. It was so powerful, you cannot possibly imagine."

The smallest of sardonic smiles tugged at one corner of my mouth. "Actually, I think I have a pretty good idea about that." No part of me would ever forget Walking in the world beyond the Gateway.

Irina went on as though she didn't hear me. "I waited for my body to die, but the Travelers preserved that device of torture, hoping one day to be able to force me to return to it. I can't be content here in the living world now that I've felt the true call of the Gateway! They've stolen my last refuge... Walking, ruined forever!" Irina paused, as if she were fighting tears. Then, with her voice slipping into a growl, she added, "But before I Cross, I will forge a path for others to do the same without the Durupinen lording over them."

I still couldn't make sense of it. "But why are you here, so far from home?"

"I came for this," she answered, gesturing to the partially rebuilt Geatgrima. Campbell, semi-conscious and moaning, now lay crumpled beside it.

"Yes, I figured that part out," I said. "But what possible use can it be to you?"

"I've been wandering... wandering for so long... so far, for so long," Irina began, almost as if she were singing sadly to herself, but her tone quickly turned harsh again. "But if the Travelers will not free me, I will free myself. With this!" She ran a spectral hand along the rough surface of the nearest Geatgrima stone. "This once-beautiful Geatgrima, like so much that's been entrusted to the care of the Durupinen, was neglected and forgotten—they let it rot in their very hands! But now I will use it to free myself! "

"Free yourself? Your body is back in England, Irina, but you are always free to Cross. The Durupinen don't hold spirits—or Walkers—here against their will. In fact, Hannah and I have dropped everything many times to complete an emergency Crossing!"

"No!" spat Irina. "I will free myself apart from *all* Durupinen, without their opening the Gateway for me. They will not control how I leave this world! And as soon as this Geatgrima is finished, they will no longer control when others are allowed to Cross, either."

"But how did you find this place?" I asked. Again I saw Finn twitching behind the stones, ready to spring into action. I took a deep breath to cover my gesture to him, bidding him to wait. If I were going to assuage Irina, I needed to truly understand everything she needed to say.

Irina took no notice of my signal, or of Finn himself. "The spirits whispered to me as I Walked—that's how I came here. They told me there were forgotten places unguarded by the Durupinen. I knew if I could find one, I could Cross in peace, alone. And then I heard this place." She nodded her head solemnly. "It's true. I heard it calling to me, singing to me. The song of the Gateway led me here, to this very room."

"But you couldn't Cross through?"

"No. This Geatgrima was destroyed long ago, but I knew I could rebuild it, if I could only find a living body to Habitate."

"And so you forced Habitation on Campbell," I said, looking back down at him. He was still prone, too weak to do more than stir weakly. "But why him? How did you find him?"

"He was here in this house, walking through its empty rooms, all alone," Irina replied, looking down at Campbell fondly—as if he were a pet she doted upon. "He looked lost in the place, and lost in himself. So I gave him a purpose—my purpose—that we could fulfill together."

"But why would Campbell be—Ah, I see, he was touring the place." I realized the answer to my own question before I had even finished asking it. Campbell had been in real estate; the plantation had been for sale. He was probably looking for an investment. His touring the property at the time of Irina's arrival must've been pure chance—the poor bastard had merely been in the wrong place at the wrong time.

"I began to whisper to him," Irina continued. "Softly at first, and then louder and more persuasively. He was fearful at the beginning, but then he learned to trust me. He thought I was an angel, and I allowed him to believe it; that was how I gained every last bit of his faith and trust. Once I had that, I began bending him to my will."

"You hijacked his life!" I cried, as my anger started to surface; it mingled with my intense pity for Irina.

"I borrowed him," Irina said with a shrug. "I would've returned him, once we'd completed our task."

"Jess!" Milo's voice broke through our connection, making me jump. "The spirits have figured out the Wards are gone. They're starting to drift down here—they can feel the pull of the Geatgrima now!"

"Have Hannah Call them and order them to stay out!" I thought-spoke frantically. "If we get interrupted now, Irina might panic and flee!"

"Irina?" asked Milo. "Irina from the Travelers? The Walker?"

"Yes! No time to explain. Just keep the spirits out of here!"

"Okay, we're on it," said Milo. He withdrew from the connection, freeing the space in my head for Irina's next words, which she offered without any prompting.

"It wasn't easy. For weeks—months—I had to coax Campbell into believing he was destined to rebuild this place. We traveled, finding those who were both truly haunted and had the means to fund the restoration. We built relationships with them, gaining their trust. And when we could be sure of their loyalty, we opened Whispering Seraph and brought them here—like one big happy family." Irina smiled, but it only made her look more unhinged.

"Wouldn't it have been easier to Habitate in Campbell when you first met him?" I asked her. "You could have just marched him down to the basement, used him to rebuild the Geatgrima, and then let him go."

"I nearly did, but that would've been very, very naughty of me," Irina replied, waggling her finger playfully. "That would have helped me certainly, but what of the others?"

"What others?"

"All of the others forced to wait their turn! All of the spirits left to the mercy of the Durupinen! The Durupinen, who dictate when spirits are allowed to Cross! Why should they have this power over us? I will create a Gate liberated from the tyranny of Gatekeepers! Have you ever heard of anything so beautiful?"

I bit back my argument. I wanted to again tell Irina that the Durupinen weren't monsters who trapped spirits on earth. I wanted to say that we committed our lives, and sometimes sacrificed them, to ensure that spirits could Cross to the other side. Hannah and I performed lunar Crossings each month, and had performed Crossings by necessity more times than I could count.

But what could these words possibly mean to someone like Irina? Here she was, trapped against her will, held in this state by the Durupinen. This, after years of being denied the freedom to Walk, of being tethered to her body by Traveler Bonds. Any arguments I could make in defense of the Durupinen were directly contradicted by her own experiences—and in truth, the Durupinen were less than black-and-white as far as I was concerned. The more I thought about it, the more I couldn't blame her at all. Nevertheless, I had to stop her.

I tried a different tactic. "I understand why you feel this way, Irina," I said, in as calm and soothing a voice as I could. "No one will ever fully understand what you've been through. I don't blame you in the least for wanting to create a place where spirits can Cross on their own."

Irina narrowed her eyes at me, as though sure this were some kind of trick. "You're humoring me. You say what you think I want to hear."

I shook my head vigorously. "I'm not, I swear to you. The Durupinen have destroyed your life and now they've even stolen the joy of Walking. You *should* hate them."

Irina continued to glare at me through narrowed eyes, but she listened without interrupting me.

"But there's a big problem in your well-deserved plan for revenge, Irina. When this Geatgrima is rebuilt, you'll have no control over it. The Aether may become more present here than almost anywhere else on Earth, but the barrier between worlds will still exist. Without the Durupinen to open and close the Gateway properly, you can't know what will happen to the spirits who try to Cross through it. You could risk their getting trapped in the Aether. Is that really what you want—to risk other souls just to satisfy your vengeance? Or worse, to leave an unguarded Geatgrima exposed?

The Necromancers will surely regroup someday, and who knows what other threats may be out there?"

A spasm rippled over Irina's expression. For a moment, she looked tortured and torn before her features settled into a grimace. But when she spoke, her voice was calm and unruffled.

"That's a chance that I'm willing to take."

I felt my body tense again. I had heard Irina out, listened to all she had to say. But with the deliberate calmness so evident in her last words, I now knew that Irina would carry out her plan no matter how much talking we did. "I'm sorry, Irina. I pity you, truly I do, but that's not a chance *I'm* willing to take."

"And what exactly to you plan to do about it, Northern G—"

"NOW FINN!" I shouted.

Finn leapt out from behind the pile of stones, flinging the yoga mat out in front of him and shouting the Casting that would seal the Circle as he sailed through the air. As he landed, he curled into an army roll and pulled me to the ground just as the mat slid to a stop right underneath Irina.

For a fraction of an instant, Irina stared down at the mat, perplexed. Then her eyes widened and she looked up at Finn, just as the final word of the Casting fell from his lips. A ripple of energy shot through the air, and I knew the Circle had worked—Irina was trapped within. Almost instantaneously, the realization of her imprisonment hit Irina with the force of a bomb.

She threw her head back and let loose an insane, keening scream of fury. The loose piles of Geatgrima stones—and some from the unfinished Geatgrima itself—tumbled to the floor in a spirit-fueled avalanche. Irina hurled herself again and again at the invisible barriers of the Circle now holding her, but it was no use. She was trapped—as trapped as she'd been when I'd first seen her chained up in the Traveler's wagon.

At the sound of Irina's screams, Hannah and Milo came flying into the room, charging blindly into battle. The spirits that Hannah had Called drifted in behind her, ready to be of service, but there was nothing for them to do. They simply hovered, like so many strangely shaped balloons, around the room's edges.

"What the hell?" Milo muttered. "It was Irina! It was Irina this whole time?"

I didn't answer him. All I could do was watch Irina struggle, confined in what I knew to be her worst nightmare. As my adrenaline began to wear off, I felt tears welling in my eyes.

Hannah, who had never met Irina, hurried over to Campbell. She kneeled beside him as he stirred. "Mr. Campbell? Are you okay? Can you sit up?"

Campbell struggled into a sitting position with Hannah's assistance and then gazed around the room, blinking. "What... what happened?" he murmured. "Ms. Taylor? Where am I?"

Campbell's gaze came to rest on the space above the yoga mat, where Irina hovered. He couldn't actually see her, but I knew he could sense her presence in some way; Irina's rage was so powerful that it was radiating through the chamber in dark, despairing waves.

"Can you feel that?" he cried. "It's so... terribly angry...so very... sad! Is that... is my angel still here?"

"Yes, but she's no angel, that's for damn sure," I said, much more to myself than to Campbell. Under my breath, I added, "And she doesn't deserve this."

25

THE TRACKER DIVISION

A S THOUGH I COULD SHAKE THE SIGHT OF IRINA from my eyes, I shook my head hard. Irina's screams had ebbed to pained, desperate growls before fading to quiet, but tortured, sobbing whimpers. Having exhausted herself from struggling, Irina's form had faded into a flickering shadow of her true self, a candle about to burn out.

I turned wildly to Finn. "We can't do this. We can't do this to her!" I hissed.

Finn looked startled. "What do you mean, we can't do this to her? She's captured, Jess. It's over. The threat is contained."

"Look at her, Finn! Look at her! She's fading, miserable, frightened! We did that to her! And the Durupinen will do far worse if we turn her over to the Trackers."

Humoring me, Finn cast a cursory glance at Irina, who was now moaning pitifully as she tapped feebly against the Circle's barrier. "I see her, Jess. I realize she's upset, but the Circle isn't harming her one bit. It's merely containing her. And you're a proper Tracker now, you have protocols to follow."

"No, you don't understand. You didn't see her at the Traveler camp, Finn. It was horrific! It was torture for her, being trapped there all those years. And when the other Trackers get here, she's going to be imprisoned all over again! Permanently!"

Finn's confused expression softened into a pitying one, but his pity was all for me. "Jess, I know it's difficult for you to see her like this, but we haven't a choice, you know that. We can't release her; she's too dangerous."

"I know," I said, with a barely contained sob. "But there must be something—anything—we can do!" I looked desperately around the room, as though I would find a solution scrawled among the runes on the walls. My eyes fell on Hannah, who was still tending to a disoriented Campbell; the patience and tenderness she offered to him inspired the answer I was looking for.

"We can Cross her," I said, with a note of real hope in my voice. Our goal as Trackers was to shut down Whispering Seraph, and the key to that was stopping Irina. Having her Cross would accomplish the mission while keeping her from yet another Durupinen prison—if she agreed to it.

"Sorry?" Finn replied.

I spun back to him. "We can Cross Irina. Right now. Hannah and I can open the Gateway. If it's between Crossing and imprisonment, I bet she'll choose to go. Voluntarily."

Finn's eyes widened as though I were suggesting something crazy.

"Why are you looking at me like that?" I asked.

Finn struggled to answer. "I think... it's admirable, wanting to help her, but..."

"But what? Spit it out, Finn!" I cried.

"It's not our decision what happens to her, is it? We've contained her, but it's up to the Senior Trackers and the Traveler Council to decide her fate," Finn answered.

"Screw the Senior Trackers!" I shouted, with a fervor that surprised even me. Finn's mouth fell open; Hannah's head jerked up. "They're the ones who threw us in here on our first-ever case and told us to 'handle it.' And screw the Travelers and their Council, too. They're the ones who used Irina like a lab rat, then imprisoned her when she exercised her free will! If we Cross Irina now, all of her bitterness—all of her thirst for revenge—will Cross with her. We will still have done our job. Please, Finn. Hannah. I can't hand her back over to them. I just can't do it."

Finn opened his mouth, but no words came out. I knew the battle raging inside him; the deepest parts of him were struggling between his desire to do what I wanted, and his almost pathological need to follow procedure. I'd seen that look on his face many times before.

Hannah, clearly caught in a similar struggle, bit her lip. "We might get in trouble, Jess. Shouldn't Irina have to answer for what she did? She hurt a lot of people."

"You wouldn't be asking that question if you'd seen her in the Traveler camp, sweetness," Milo said, floating forward and inserting himself into the conversation. "They had her caged there like an animal. In chains. Filthy, too. And half-insane from it all! Jess is right. Irina's a victim, too. I'm not saying what she did here at Whispering Seraph was right, but she's served her sentence a hundred times over. She won't be a threat after she Crosses. You will have still accomplished your mission—you caught her and stopped her plan. But isn't it time for it to be over now?"

I looked at Milo, and shot a beam of silent, thankful energy to him through our connection; he returned it tenfold. That energy mingled with my sadness, bolstering me against it.

Hannah carefully extricated her hand from Campbell's grip and stood up. She pressed her mouth into a determined line before declaring, "You're right, Jess. I'll help you." With that, she slipped her Masking bracelet from her wrist; I did the same.

Finn's expression softened, and I knew the battle within him was over—at least for today. He pulled a Casting bag from his pocket and tossed it to Hannah. "We need to work quickly. This needs to be done before Catriona and the others arrive. And we need to get Campbell out of here. He's seen and heard too much already."

Hannah scurried over to the Circle on the yoga mat and began converting the existing Circle into a Summoning Circle. Finn picked his way across the rubble and pulled Campbell gently to his feet. I watched as he guided the weak-kneed Campbell along the outside of the room, then out into the corridor.

With the coast clear, I approached Irina. As gently as I could, I said, "Listen to me, Irina. There isn't a lot of time. Do you want to Cross?"

Irina's form became still, even limper. "Cross?"

"Yes. My sister and I want to open the Gateway and Cross you over now, if you're ready."

Irina moaned like a wounded animal. "What trap is this, Northern Girl? What trick do you play? Why do you try to ensnare me further?"

I shook my head. "This is no trick. I know you have no reason to believe me—"

"No reason at all. Your words are empty, Northern Girl, as are all words that fall from Durupinen lips. Hollow, empty lies."

I tried to keep my tone measured, although I was frustrated enough to reach through the Circle and shake her. "Irina, haven't you just told me how badly you want to answer the call of the Gateway? This is your one chance—the Council will not give you another once they have you in custody. And the Trackers are coming for you now."

She didn't answer, but let out another pathetic, whimpering howl.

A sudden rush of energy flooded me. I looked down; Hannah had all four element candles lit. She clutched the fifth one, the slender white Spirit Candle, in her hand.

Irina lifted her head like a dog picking up a scent. She had felt it too, the nearness of her escape, the path home at last. She turned wild eyes on me.

"We're ready for you," I told her.

Irina's face twisted and twitched, transforming itself into a battleground for her warring desires. "If I go, nothing will change. The Durupinen will still hold all the power! All those spirits—all trapped here in this wretched mansion. What of them, Northern Girl? What will become of them?"

"No one here is trapped," I said as soothingly as I could, although my heart was pounding in my throat. "All the spirits here will have the choice to Cross whenever they're ready. In fact, some of the spirits who are here with us now may even choose to Cross with you."

"So many," she moaned. "So many others. They must have free passage!"

"Irina, it's not like that. If you think back far enough, you'll remember your Apprentice training. You'll remember what you were taught about the Durupinen role in the spirit world. We don't judge who stays and who goes; that's not part of our job. Those spirits who are still here have chosen to stay behind. But when they're ready to go, they're always free to make the choice to Cross. And I promise you, any spirit who needs to will always be able to Cross through *my* Gateway."

"I was never free," Irina spat.

"You were never a spirit, Irina. In fact, you still aren't a spirit now. You're a Walker, like me. Being a Walker is a strange and powerful thing. I know that too well Irina, but your clan didn't. And since they couldn't understand you and they couldn't control you, they began to fear you instead. They let that fear cloud their judgment and demolish their empathy. But I see you, Irina. I see you."

"You don't see me. I don't exist," Irina whispered. "I'm gone. I am only my pain now."

Never before had so few words caused such a wave of disparate emotions in me. I struggled to master my own face as pity and anger, fear and empathy, sorrow and frustration all collided within me. "Then let's end the pain," I said, with my voice shaking madly. "Let go of the Durupinen. Leave them behind you. It's time to go home."

Irina stared into my eyes. I stared back, refusing to blink, despite the tears blurring my view.

"Come on Irina. Believe me. Choose to let go. I owe you so much, you taught me to Walk. You gave me that freedom. Choose to let me free you now."

The words resounding so sincerely through me also reached deeply within Irina; the anger and indecision fled from her face. The rage behind her eyes melted away, and without that anger to blind her, she could finally see.

Irina's next words were soft, but firm. "Yes. If you will remember your promise, Northern Girl. Open passage for all spirits through your Gateway, always. If you vow to honor your words, I will go home. I want to go home."

"I give you my word." I gasped, as a fresh stream of tears fell from my eyes.

I wiped the moisture from my cheeks, and turned to find Finn, who had quietly reentered the room, watching me with a tender smile on his face. "Well done," he said.

I nodded my thanks and then turned to Hannah. She was smiling as well. "Ready?" she asked me.

"Ready."

She closed her eyes and released her hold on the other spirits in the room. As though waking from a long slumber, they each blinked bemusedly, wondering where they were and how they had gotten there. Then, one by one, each of their faces registered the same understanding—the same knowledge that the Gateway was near, waiting for them. A few, backing away, looked wary, but others drifted toward the center of the room, drawn to the beauty of the Gateway.

I crossed the boundary of the Circle, and felt the strange rippling of energy that told me I was now within the confines of the Circle's seal. I looked up at Finn, but he answered the question before I could even ask it.

"Once the Gateway has been properly opened, I'll lift the seal," he said. "The other spirits will be able to enter the Circle then, and Irina will be free to Cross."

I smiled at him. "Thanks."

"Of course."

I looked around at the waiting spirits. Grayson was nowhere to be seen.

"Grayson's not here," I told Hannah.

"I didn't Call him with the others. I wanted to make sure he and Talia had all the time they needed."

I smiled gratefully at her, then turned to the waiting spirits, who were watching us expectantly. Each face was awash with a mixture of curiosity, fear, awe, and anticipation. I'd seen those expressions many times now; they always made me anxious, and filled me with an uncomfortable awareness of the awesome responsibility we carried. I always had to repress an urge to turn and run from it all.

With her trademark dignity and gentleness, Hannah addressed the waiting spirits. "Whispering Seraph is closing. The angel who heard your words was a being much like you, but she hid herself from you. Your loved ones will not be taken advantage of anymore. We are here to Cross you over now, if you desire to go. It's your choice, but we encourage you to take it. This world isn't for you anymore."

A movement in the periphery of my vision made me turn. Kyle was drifting backward slowly, shaking his head. He shivered out of sight.

I turned to Milo. "Would you? Now?" I asked him.

"Say no more. The Spirit Guide is off to deliver some guidance," Milo said with a little bow, before he too popped out. I sent my heartfelt thanks thrumming to him through our connection. I knew talking with Kyle would dredge up painful memories of Milo's own parental issues, and I didn't take that lightly.

Every other spirit was still watching us intently, entranced, but it was Irina's eyes I sought when I asked, "Are you ready?"

"Yes." The word escaped on a sob. "Yes, I am ready."

I choked back a sob of my own as I leaned in and whispered, "This is the right choice Irina. You will forget this world—the world beyond the Gateway will heal you. It will give you back the freedom stolen from you in this life. I promise."

I turned my head as Hannah struck a match against the floor, then held it to the wick of the Spirit Candle. Every eye was fixed on the candle as the wick caught, as the tiny flame began to dance.

I took Hannah's hand in mine. With each pulse of the now-familiar energy humming through us, every spirit in the room drew in closer, eager for the moment the Gateway would open, when its current would catch them and carry them to the distant shores that they so ached for.

We closed our eyes and repeated the words of the Crossing, words we had said so many times together that our voices seemed to melt into one.

> *"We call upon the powers endowed to us of old.*
> *We call upon the connection that binds us together.*
> *With the joining of hands and the joining of blood,*
> *The Gateway we open, the spirits we Summon."*

I felt the Gateway begin to open between us. Hannah and I began to chant, *"Téigh Anonn..."*

§

"Téigh Anonn. Téigh Anonn. Téigh Ano—"

"What the bloody hell are you doing!" A voice screamed.

Hannah yanked her hand from mine in alarm, causing the half-opened Gateway to snap shut tightly. We turned as Catriona barreled into the room. With one swift kick, she sent the Spirit Candle spinning across the floor. It hit the wall and snapped in half; the flame extinguished in a little puff of smoke.

"Catriona, what—"

But before I could even finish my question, Catriona had begun throwing handfuls of salt and sage dust into the air while shouting a Casting I had never before uttered. Yet I knew what this Casting would do, for I had prepared it only hours before.

A Caging.

"Catriona, no! Stop!" I shouted, but it was too late. The force of the Casting blew through the room like a shock wave. I pulled Hannah to the ground as the wave surged over our heads and collided with Irina, who, still trapped in the Circle, could do nothing to dodge it. The other spirits in the room, so eager a moment ago, all disappeared instantly, retreating into the relative safety of their realm.

Irina's body jerked violently. Her arms flung wide open as she threw her head back, releasing a scream that no one—neither human nor spirit—would ever be able to hear. Then she crumpled into a heap on the floor and lay utterly still, fading to little more than a shadow.

Catriona, her face set in a grim smile of satisfaction, stared down at Irina for a moment. Then her satisfaction turned to fury as she set her gaze upon us.

"What the bloody hell are you playing at?" she demanded.

"We were performing a Crossing," I cried. "Until you destroyed it!"

"Yeah, I can see that, I'm not blind!" Catriona shouted. "But why? I told you to contain the angel. Contain it! Not Cross it!"

"You told us to Unmask it, which we did!" I cried, crawling over to Irina's form and crouching beside her. "Take this off of her!"

"I bloody well will not!" Catriona said. "She could've escaped the moment you opened that seal!"

"She didn't want to escape! She wanted to Cross!" I shouted back.

Finn stepped forward, clearing his throat. "Catriona, we had things properly under control. There was no longer any threat here."

"Not from where I'm standing! From where I'm standing it looks like you were about to let the culprit Cross without facing proper justice!" Catriona spat at Finn. She turned back to Hannah and me. "Now explain. Who is this Unmasked spirit and what the hell is happening here?"

I opened my mouth, but Hannah cut me off—which was probably for the best. The tirade I was poised to let loose wasn't going to do us any favors.

"She's not a spirit, Catriona. She's a Walker."

Shock wiped all trace of anger from Catriona's face. "A Walker?" she asked incredulously.

"Yes. I'm sure you've heard of her," began Hannah. "Jess told the Council about her during our testimony. This is Irina, the Walker in the Traveler camp who taught Jess how to Walk. Without Irina, my sister never would've been able to close the Gateway and save us all from the Isherwood Prophecy."

Catriona's eyes widened even further. She stepped forward and began examining Irina with great interest. "Blimey. I've never seen a Durupinen in this form before. She's been missing since the Necromancer attack on the Traveler camp, hasn't she?"

"Yes," I said. Hannah looked at me warningly, but I held up a hand to assure her that I was in control of my emotions, at least for the moment. "Her body was injured in the attack, but then the Travelers nursed her body back to health. But Irina's spirit—with good reason—will never return to that body, and so she's trapped in Walker form."

Catriona seemed to forget her initial anger as curiosity set in. "Fascinating," she said. "She looks almost like a spirit. How in the world did she end up here?"

As succinctly as I could, I related the entirety of Irina's story, detailing first her harrowing existence among the Travelers, then explaining how she met Campbell, and lastly recounting her plans for creating free passage at Whispering Seraph. Catriona walked around the room as she listened, examining the runes on the walls and running her hands repeatedly over the pile of stones that had very nearly become a rebuilt Geatgrima.

"A Geatgrima here?" she said, more to herself than to us. "Had she managed to open it, it could've had devastating consequences. And what's this about free passage?"

"She wanted free and unguarded passage," I replied. "She wanted to take the Gateways back from the Durupinen."

Turning back to us, with her expression stern once again, Catriona barked, "In that case, I'm even more staggered! How could you consider Crossing her without consulting us!"

Finn stepped forward, braced for a fight, but remained silent. Perhaps he thought Catriona, in her ire, might just attempt to smack me across the face. Not that I wouldn't have smacked her right back.

"But Catriona, didn't you hear what I said—she was imprisoned by the Travelers for years! Decades of torture! She only wanted to prevent others from being trapped here."

Beside me, Hannah was nodding her head vehemently in agreement. A tiny "Breathe, Jess. Don't lose it now," came from her lips.

"Oh, I see, so Irina's in the right, then? She's allowed to wreak havoc and then be on her merry way, is she?" Catriona asked, with her arms folded across her chest. "I thought you had more sense than this! You've allowed a suspect to play on your sympathies and manipulate you into aiding her escape."

"She's not manipulating anyone!" I replied. "Well, not anymore anyway. But don't you see, it was the Durupinen who drove her to desperation in the first place!"

"Her past experiences are pitiable, but pity doesn't excuse her from facing repercussions for what she's done," Catriona said, in a tone that couldn't have been more dismissive or more devoid of sympathy. "I realize you didn't answer to anyone when you were chasing down scam artists on your own, but the Trackers have a system in place—a system you agreed to properly adhere to when you joined us. We have procedures. Irina must be tried and formally sentenced for her actions, and she must be made to carry out whatever sentence the Council finds to be fit."

"Come on, Catriona," I pled. "Hasn't she been punished enough?"

"That's not our decision," Catriona said firmly. "And now you are coming dangerously close to facing disciplinary action yourselves. It would be a right shame if you were booted from the Trackers on your very first case, wouldn't it?"

"It's starting to look like a good option, actually," I said through gritted teeth.

"Are you forgetting the alternative?" Catriona asked. "Sod it all, then, if you like. But make no mistake, if you throw away your position with the Trackers, you'll be sent back to Salem with a team of Caomhnóir watching your every move."

I opened my mouth and closed it again. What else could I say? There were no arguments left. I looked to Finn, but his expression was mirroring my own hopelessness. I turned from him, searching fruitlessly for an ally in Hannah's face. Their eyes both held the same, sad truth. There was nothing we could do: Irina had to be turned over to the Trackers. She had to face the consequences of what she'd done, little though she deserved them.

Catriona watched me come to this conclusion with a satisfied smile on her face that made my blood boil. "That's a good girl," she said. "We'll squash that rebellious streak yet. Now, I've got work to do, but your part is done. With the exception of your poor judgment there at the end, you've all done well."

"She obviously knows nothing about your so-called rebellious streak," muttered Milo quietly, as he materialized beside me.

Catriona ignored Milo. She walked up to me and placed a hand on my shoulder. "The longer you do this, the stronger you'll get. Their pain and sadness won't affect you so much. Then it gets easier to do the right thing."

I shrugged her hand away. "I'm not sure you and I agree on what the right thing is," I replied.

Catriona raised an eyebrow. "Perhaps not." She turned and headed for the door, calling out instructions to the Caomhnóir in the doorway as she did so. She didn't spare another glance for Irina, who was still huddled in the Circle. "Come along, then. Your work here is done," Catriona said to us, before disappearing into the passageway.

Finn and Hannah followed her. Only Milo remained by my side. Only he saw as I knelt down, closing the distance between Irina and myself. Only he watched as I moved forward, finding Irina's gaze, until our faces were less than a breath apart. Only he listened as I leaned in and whispered to Irina.

"I promise you. I promise you, Irina, I will not leave you like this. I will set you free. We are the Walkers, you and me. Whatever they say to you, and whatever they do, know that I am coming. I will find a way to set you free."

I didn't expect her to answer—the Caging should have made communication impossible. But Irina was a Walker, not merely a spirit; we were traversing areas that few Durupinen had ever encountered, and none could predict. Perhaps my being the only other living Walker—the only one who'd existed in the same extra-spirit state—meant that Irina and I couldn't be fully Caged from each other. When she opened her mouth to answer, her words, although I couldn't physically hear them, reached inside of me, echoing and singing their meaning.

"I will wait for you, Northern Girl." Within me, I knew Irina's words carried the faintest trace of true hope.

I tore my eyes from Irina and stood up. I looked at Milo and saw my promise blazing in his eyes, too. His approval hummed through our connection, strengthening my resolve.

Just over his shoulder, Catriona's two Caomhnóir, stony-faced yet somehow impatient, waited for us to follow them.

And I had no choice but to turn my back on Irina and walk out the door.

EPILOGUE

THE NEXT DAY, I WALKED OUT OF WHISPERING SERAPH for the last time. But as we were preparing to leave, I left I felt none of the ebullience that had filled me after we'd debunked Freeman and his *Ghost Oracle*. True, we had completed our first mission as Trackers. We had dismantled the Whispering Seraph scheme, and we had captured the "angel" at the heart of it all. We had even prevented Irina from taking control of a *Geatgrima* and potentially spreading chaos across the entire Gateway system. And just last night, Hannah and I had opened our Gateway uninterrupted; every last one of the spirits at Whispering Seraph had Crossed. I should've been elated by our triumph, eager for our next case. Instead, the only thing I was eager for was a nap.

"I know what you mean," Hannah said when I confided this to her. "I'm feeling sort of downhearted, too."

"Really?" I asked.

"Of course," she replied, with her own quiet wisdom apparent in her tone. "We did a lot of good, but there was sadness and injustice here that we couldn't fix. Poor Jeremiah was really a victim, wasn't he? He wasn't knowingly doing anything wrong—and I really do think his intentions, at least at the start, were good. But now his dreams of helping people are over. And so many of the people here are going home just as sad and empty as when they arrived, which is a shame. But you were right, Jess. Crossing Irina would've been the kindest way to end this, all things considered. I'm sad about that. I mean, she did take advantage of these people, but she also gave them a kind of hope. It wasn't even false hope either—not totally."

The walk through the lobby did nothing to make me feel any better. Kyle's parents were standing at the front desk, tearfully demanding resources about other mediums they could contact, while a bewildered-looking Maya explained that she simply didn't have that kind of information.

Marigold sat on a window seat as she waited for her car. She was on her cell phone, talking to someone. "I'm not really sure, sugar. There's nothing else I can do. I'll just come home, I guess... Yes, honey, I know—maybe I should get myself a dog?" Her laugh ended in a barely concealed sob.

She looked up and we caught each other's eye. Marigold smiled sadly at me; I smiled back.

Neither Marigold, nor the Owenses, nor any of the other guests was haunted any longer. Harold, relieved to see the Whispering Seraph scam destroyed, had been more than ready to Cross. Kyle, after a long, tough-love talk with Milo, had forgiven his parents before Crossing; I knew he had left the last of his anger behind in the Aether, where it couldn't poison him anymore.

When we'd finally be able to open the Gateway, not a single spirit had refused to Cross. All the spirits lingering behind at Whispering Seraph were strong; I could be fairly certain that each had passed successfully through the Aether and into the world beyond. These spirits would be okay; I could only hope the same for the people they left behind.

"Did you forget something?" Hannah asked, as I stopped in my tracks at the bottom at the bottom of the porch steps.

"No. I'll meet you at the car in a minute," I said. I had just spotted Talia, who was waving me down from beside her town car. "Tell Finn I'm coming."

Hannah followed my gaze. When she saw Talia walking toward us, she nodded her head in understanding and trudged off toward the parking lot, with her suitcase bumping along behind her.

"I was hoping I'd catch you before you left," Talia said. Her face was drawn, and there were bags under her eyes, but she was smiling. It was a different smile than the few I'd seen her plaster on her face previously; there was something peaceful in it now. So very sad, but peaceful.

"I'm glad you did," I said. "How are you?"

She shrugged. "I'm okay. Or I will be."

I smiled at her. "Yes, you will."

"I honestly couldn't have said that before and meant it," she admitted. She reached up and tucked a rogue tendril of hair behind her ear, but it floated back out again on the sultry Louisiana breeze. I could see that the runes from yesterday had almost completely faded from her hand. "And I have you to thank for that. Deeply thank you."

"You're welcome. It takes time to heal, but now that you've had closure, you'll get there," I said. "Sorry if that sounds like a psychiatrist's sound bite, but it's true... I promise."

Talia sighed as she shrugged in agreement. Then she nodded in the direction of Catriona's car, where a Caomhnóir was sitting behind the wheel, ready to escort Campbell to the Lafayette Boarding House. Campbell was sitting in the backseat, looking like someone had clubbed him over the head. His expression was bewildered, like a child who'd looked up in a crowd and found his mother gone.

"What about Jeremiah? Will he be alright?" Talia asked.

"I think so," I replied. I knew that he had many hours of Tracker interrogation to look forward to, followed by a long and messy cover-up—and I had no idea how the Durupinen were going to explain any of this to Campbell without divulging their secrets. But luckily, none of that was my problem; I'd leave the Trackers, and their blind adherence to the Council, to take care of all that. But speaking of cover-ups...

"Hey, so I realize that I didn't have you sign a fancy non-disclosure agreement, but—"

Talia laughed—actually laughed a true laugh. "I'm not going to tell anyone. Besides, who in the world would believe me if I did?" Her smile faded. "I can never thank you enough for what you did for me. I know you weren't supposed to connect Grayson and me like that, and I... well, the least I can do is keep your secret."

"Good. Well, I guess I'll see you around," I said, and turned to go.

"One last thing, actually," Talia replied hesitantly. "Can you tell me... I mean, I think I already know—I think I felt it, but I just wanted to be sure..."

Her emotion rose up and cut her off, but I didn't need to hear the end of her question. I knew what Talia was asking, and I was relieved to be able to tell her the whole truth. "He's gone, Talia. Last night. It was peaceful."

She sniffed and nodded slowly. "Okay. Thank you."

I leaned forward and hugged her, because really what else could I do in a moment like that? Sometimes even the most heartfelt of words are inadequate.

§

I found Hannah, Milo, and Finn waiting for me by the car. "Are we all ready to go?" I asked.

Milo looked like he might start crying himself. "You're by yourself. Does this mean Talia isn't coming to live with us?"

I laughed. "No, you adorable stalker, I let her get back to her own life. But if she ever invites me anywhere with a red carpet, I promise you can be my date... *and* you can dress me."

Milo went starry-eyed and turned to Hannah. "Sweetness, we've had a nice run, but Jess is my favorite twin now."

Hannah laughed. "You can't break up with me that easily. We're Bound, remember?"

"Hey, wait. Are Iggy and the team still at the Boarding House?" I asked to no one in particular. "That will complicate things, won't it?"

"Catriona sent them home when she arrived yesterday," answered Finn. "They left on a flight late last night. Proper first class tickets, from what I was told. We're meeting with them in Salem the day after tomorrow."

"Good," I replied. "And I'm dying to see Tia too. Poor thing, she probably thinks I abandoned her! But then again, maybe she hardly noticed—she might be in her happy place, under a pile of anatomy textbooks."

Finn cleared his throat. "We should get moving. Catriona expects us back at the Lafayette Boarding House for debriefing," he said, as he opened the car door for us. Hannah and Milo climbed into the backseat.

I shuddered. I was not looking forward to seeing Catriona and the Durupinen-Tracker protocols she stood for. I knew it would take every ounce of my civility not to start hissing in her face again. Whatever Catriona's reasoning, her refusal to Cross Irina was the true crime here, as far as I was concerned. Okay, so Irina was—both literally and figuratively—no angel, but after decades of abuse, who wouldn't lose her way?

"Hey Jess-Jess, would you care to join us?" Milo quipped from the car, breaking me out of my thoughts.

I looked up to see Finn still holding the car door open. "Ugh. Okay, but I am not sleeping in that nightmare factory again. After our meeting, I'm booking myself into the nearest hotel."

"I might just join you," Finn said under his breath, as I walked by him to get into the car.

"You'd better," I replied just as softly.

It was nice to imagine, but we both knew it wouldn't be that easy. We knew we'd made a decision that would undoubtedly have serious consequences down the line. But we also knew we couldn't go back on it. Not now. Not ever. And the Durupinen would have to deal with that.

Our car pulled away, leaving Whispering Seraph behind in a dust cloud that only an unpaved Southern country road could create.

"I'm not sorry to leave that place!" Milo said.

"Me neither," I replied. "Although the food was great. And that bed too."

"We never even got to try the spa," Hannah said a little wistfully.

"I can turn the car around, you know," Finn said jokingly, although not without a touch of his usual impatience. His aggravatingly endearing impatience.

I pretended to think about it. "No, we're good."

The property may have been behind us, but much still weighed on me from Whispering Seraph. Most keenly, I felt the weight of my promise to Irina. Soon the day would come when I would have to make good on that promise. I had no idea how I would manage to keep my word, or what the fallout might be. My life as a Durupinen carried with it a long and complicated legacy, a legacy full of dedicated service to the spirits, but also a history riddled with mistakes, willful errors, and a multitude of egregious sins. Perhaps I'd never be able to reconcile the two. I knew I would never be a Council sycophant or a Tracker who could blindly follow orders, but there was one thing I was determined to be, for my own sake as much as for Irina's: I would always be a Durupinen who kept her promises.

Acknowledgments

I can't begin acknowledgments without first expressing my boundless gratitude for my readers, who have taken this journey with me and embraced the World of the Gateway with the same enthusiasm that I put into writing it. From the bottom of my heart, thank you all for turning those pages.

To my husband Joseph, whose encouragement coaxed these books out of my head and onto the page, thank you so much for always believing in me, and for all of your hard work in getting these books out into the world. I can never thank you enough for helping me to realize this dream, which is now our dream. You are the very best partner I could hope for.

Many thanks to my cover designer James T. Egan at Bookfly Designs. Although we hope people will not judge a book solely by its cover, the fact remains that your amazing work tempts reader after reader to pick my books up and give them a closer look, and for this I am very grateful.

Ever writer needs a wonderful editor, and I have found one in Erika DeSimone. Erika, thank you for being that organized, detail-oriented left side of my brain I've always wanted. Your insight, commitment, and humor have been invaluable to me. Thank you for giving so much of your time, energy, and talent to this series.

Many thanks to my family and friends, for their constant support and encouragement, and especially to my two littlest loves, Lily and Myles, for interrupting my writing time in the best ways possible. I wouldn't trade my days with you for anything in the world. Thank you for being my two most beautiful reasons to keep writing.

About the Author

E.E. Holmes is a writer, teacher, and actor living in central Massachusetts with her husband, two children, and a small, but surprisingly loud dog. When not writing, she enjoys performing, watching unhealthy amounts of British television, and reading with her children. Please visit eeholmes.com to learn more.

CPSIA information can be obtained
at www.ICGtesting.com
Printed in the USA
FSHW010154120821
83932FS